Praise for *BloodAngel*

"[An] unusually compelling story of the supernatural . . . hopefully the harbinger of a major new talent."
—*Chronicle*

"Keeps you turning the pages up to the end."
—SFRevu

"A great new writer on the horror scene [who] will appeal to fans of Karen Koehler and Poppy Z. Brite . . . it is hoped that there will be future books featuring the Summoners." —The Best Reviews

"Gripping . . . Musk has created an array of fascinating characters and an intricate plot which is vaguely reminiscent of early Anne Rice . . . should appeal to readers who prefer their fantasy to be unsentimental."
—*Romantic Times*

Also by Justine Musk

BloodAngel

Lord of Bones

Justine Musk

A ROC BOOK

ROC
Published by New American Library, a division of
Penguin Group (USA) Inc., 375 Hudson Street,
New York, New York 10014, USA
Penguin Group (Canada), 90 Eglinton Avenue East, Suite 700, Toronto,
Ontario M4P 2Y3, Canada (a division of Pearson Penguin Canada Inc.)
Penguin Books Ltd., 80 Strand, London WC2R 0RL, England
Penguin Ireland, 25 St. Stephen's Green, Dublin 2,
Ireland (a division of Penguin Books Ltd.)
Penguin Group (Australia), 250 Camberwell Road, Camberwell, Victoria 3124,
Australia (a division of Pearson Australia Group Pty. Ltd.)
Penguin Books India Pvt. Ltd., 11 Community Centre, Panchsheel Park,
New Delhi - 110 017, India
Penguin Group (NZ), 67 Apollo Drive, Rosedale, North Shore 0632,
New Zealand (a division of Pearson New Zealand Ltd.)
Penguin Books (South Africa) (Pty.) Ltd., 24 Sturdee Avenue,
Rosebank, Johannesburg 2196, South Africa

Penguin Books Ltd., Registered Offices:
80 Strand, London WC2R 0RL, England

First published by Roc, an imprint of New American Library,
a division of Penguin Group (USA) Inc.

First Printing, July 2008
10   9   8   7   6   5   4   3   2   1

For Jacques
1990–2006

You deserved more.

I

Suffer For It

. . . but the thing about Maddox? Making music came so easy to him. Scary easy. He knew how to work hard, sure, but it was almost like he didn't respect his own talent 'cause it was so fu—it was so frikkin' easy. He thought he needed to struggle and suffer for it, you know? Live on the dark side and shit. Like me. That was the weird thing. He wanted to be like me, but I always wanted to be a real natural, like him, you know, have that whole gift-from-the-gods thing. Guy was a natural if ever I saw one."
 —excerpt from an interview with ex-Slippage bandmate
      Jared Hollander, *Rolling Stone*, July 1997

. . . Won't give up my head on a plate
'cause he likes the way you dance
This ain't a diddy on masters, slaves
Or a cry for the fucking blood I gave
I don't think on you at all
Don't dream on you at all
This is not a
This is not a
This is not a goddamn love song
  —from the notebooks of Lucas Maddox

Chapter One

Ramsey

The woman and the youth had been on the road for eight months, although it seemed longer. In the beginning there was a man who traveled with them: very tall, broad-shouldered, with cropped dark hair and vivid, changing eyes.

But then he would leave, and they were alone.

The youth's name was Ramsey. He had just turned seventeen. He was thinner and smaller than he'd like to be, yet he had no problem in bars. Sometimes, like tonight, the bartender would hitch in a breath to ask for ID and Ramsey would tilt his head and look at him. Just look at him. The bartender would stand there and stare, and a moment would pass in which neither said anything. It wasn't like Ramsey possessed any real supernatural power—not like some people he knew—but there was something about his eyes, Ramsey had learned, his eyes and his scars, that made people like this bartender always step back and say, "Okay. So, what'll it be?"

"Scotch," Ramsey always said. "Neat."

He rarely drank it. He just liked to order it.

They had come south through the Canadian/American border and tonight they found themselves in wine country. Ramsey had spent the afternoon kicking around the town, enjoying the sweeping vistas and clear, lemon-colored sunlight after all those days of northwest rain. Maybe when this business of theirs was finished and the world was set right again—at least, set back to what it was before Asha's demons found their way into it—they could move here, live here, the three of them, Jess and Kai and Ramsey. Be like an actual family. Have a horse ranch or something. Ramsey knew nothing about either horses or ranches, but he liked the idea. A lot.

The town seemed a mix of stylish yuppies who drove up from the Bay Area for the weekends and aging long-haired hippie types in sandals and tie-dyed T-shirts.

The girl at the bar didn't seem to be either.

She was brown-haired, brown-eyed, and she caught Ramsey's eye for several reasons. One was because she reminded him of someone he had known not so very long ago—his first love, you could say, if you were inclined to say it. He still had trouble believing she was actually, and most unfairly, dead.

The other reasons were things that clawed his spine.

The girl noticed him—people did, although never in the ways that Ramsey preferred—but her gaze went flat with disinterest. She was talking to a couple at the bar. The man and woman were both tall and fair-colored, looked like siblings, although earlier they'd been engaging in some serious public affection involving tongue. Ramsey had to hope that brother-sister wasn't the case.

The brown-haired girl tossed her head back, displaying a pale sweep of throat. The man and woman exchanged glances and the man gestured for the bartender to serve the girl another drink.

Beyond the windows, the sun finished setting. Darkness gathered deep and close and silent, that darkness of the country that still unnerved him.

The couple was getting up from the bar. The dark-haired girl spun round on her black leather stool, stumbled as she got off it, and laughed. The couple was quick to close in on her. She clutched both their arms for support, muttered, "It's these frigging heels," and laughed again.

They left the bar, the girl's heels tripping across the polished hardwood. Then they were heading out the double doors and down the wide porch steps, and Ramsey touched the knives, strapped flat and cool along his forearms beneath the sleeves of his sheepskin-lined denim jacket, felt the presence of the Rugers that had been spell modified just for him: the .45 auto holstered at his hip, the 9mm at his ankle. There was a small bone amulet on a black leather cord around his neck. He touched it for luck. Jess would be furious, he knew, but there was no other option.

You saw what you saw and couldn't unsee it.

You had to do the right thing.

He left money on the bar and followed them, the couple and the girl.

The motel was a crumbling Spanish-style affair that had once been charming and romantic. That was a long time ago.

The air held the scents of jasmine and citrus; the shadows were layered and lush. The couple, the girl sandwiched firmly between them, was passing through an archway draped with dead ivy and into the overgrown courtyard when the tall, fair-haired man lifted his head and took notice of Ramsey. Behind him, water pooled in a broken stone fountain. The only light came from the stars overhead.

"Hey," the guy said. "Kid. You following us?"

"The girl," Ramsey said. "Get away from her."

The woman looked across the girl's head to her partner. "Taylor, who *is* this freak?"

Taylor said, "And there's some reason you think I should know this?"

The girl looked through the shadows to Ramsey. "Maybe you should go home," she said quietly.

She shook herself free of the arms around her shoulders and came forward, one step, two steps, her face and body edging into enough starlight for Ramsey to see the way her eyes widened. "You," she breathed. "Hey. I *know* you. From the *desert*."

The woman said, "You know this freak?"

"I tasted him," the girl said, and grinned. "We talk about you. There are lots of rumors. But you're ordinary now, aren't you? You're like any other stupid kid."

Ramsey clicked off the safety and aimed the .45 at her face. "Get away from her," he told the couple. "She's not what she seems."

"Hey," the man said. "Hey. Wait a sec. You don't have to do this—"

"Get away from her."

"You want money? We'll give you money—"

"She's not what she seems."

"I'm not," the girl agreed.

Her mouth opened wide, and then wider, and her tongue snapped like a whip across the fifteen feet that separated her from Ramsey. The end of the tongue lashed round the barrel of the pistol and he had a moment to see the wet pulsing texture, the wine red color laced with black, before the gun was ripped from his hand and flew across the courtyard. The woman was screaming, while the man's face went loose with shock. "Get—" Ramsey yelled, which was the only thing he had time to say before the girl was coming at him, her face twisted, her hands up in the air and curled into claws. She had not Altered but he could glimpse the demon in her anyway, as if her human skin had turned transparent and her demon face was there for the whole world to see—and wouldn't that be a traffic-stopping sight on Main Street.

He punched her in the throat. It was a good, well-aimed blow, the way Kai had taught him, and the force

was enough to put her on pause, stagger her back a few
steps. They locked eyes for a moment; then she grinned
and darted into shadow. A bullet slipped past his cheek,
the crack of it wild in his ear. He threw himself behind
the stone fountain, the smell of wet, rotting plants in his
nostrils. Shadowy figures were moving along the second-
floor walkways. One of the doors slammed open, then
shut again. Then came the sound of a deep, throaty chittering. They were *talking* to each other. How many of
them were there? The blond woman was running out
through the archway, into the parking lot. The man was
right behind her but, as he stepped beneath the arch,
shadows moved in from either side and swallowed him
from view; there was a wet, terrible crunching sound,
and then the screaming turned high-pitched and liquid . . .
and ceased.

A bullet buried itself in the stone fountain. Chips flew
against his face. Ramsey ducked and moved round. His
palms were slick with sweat and he wiped them quickly
on his jeans before grabbing the second pistol from the
ankle holster and switching off the safety. The gun
warmed quickly in his hand, not just because of his touch
but also the spellcasting Kai had worked over it just
before he'd left them. Ramsey took aim at one of the
shadows on the walkway and fired. He could see the
glints the bullet made in the air as it shimmered apart
into stronger, faster versions of itself. One of the chittering shadows crumpled against the wall; another slumped
over the railing. Ramsey waited for—wanted—it to fall,
craved the sound of impact, but it remained there like
a busted toy.

Usually the hybrids didn't bother with guns, barely
knew how to use them. They wanted to bite and claw
and rip. They craved the intimacy. The taste.

The chittering grew more frantic, filled the air; there
was laughter, shouts of "Boyo, boyo!" and someone
made a crack about fresh, tender boy-meat. Ramsey was
in overdrive now, firing at the shadows, at the faces that

came looming out at him. And then there was nothing left in the gun and he tossed it aside, slipped out a knife, and hurled it at the thing that was coming at him from his left, a kid near his own age with a pockmarked face and eyes that weren't eyes but sockets filled with blood. The knife went deep into his chest and the kid who wasn't really a kid hit the ground and went into convulsions. Then the kid pulled the knife from his chest and laughed, and started chopping off his own fingers. *Crazy,* Ramsey thought, not for the first time and not the last. *God, they're so fucking crazy.*

And a thought behind that, even as he slipped the other knife from its sheath: *I am outnumbered.* Doors were opening, shadows coming out into the courtyard, onto the walkways. Nobody was firing anything at him anymore. They weren't running toward him, either; they were taking their time, watching him, enjoying this. "Hey," one whispered. "Hey, chick-chick. You're a tough little chick-chick."

"A cute little chick-chick," said a female voice from the other side of him.

"Cute on the inside too, I bet," said someone else. "Let's find out."

And there was a new shadow in the doorway.

A woman. Tall, slender, with long dark hair hanging down her back, dressed in jeans and a black hooded cardigan. She looked younger than her twenty-nine years, until you got close-up and saw her eyes; then she looked older. "Ramsey," she yelled, "take cover."

Ramsey felt the pulse in the air as unseen power swept the courtyard. The doors to the motel rooms all slammed shut. The hybrids were trapped in the open.

Take cover. She didn't mean it in the usual sense. What she meant was for him to grab the amulet around his neck and fold himself into as small a ball as possible. The amulet burned against his palm, which hurt, but he knew better than to let go. He felt a strange shivery sensation as the spell encoded in the amulet kicked into life and sent threads of what looked blue and electric weaving round him, knitting into his own personal force field.

The air was raining fire.

He did his best to shut down his senses to what was happening round him: the shrieks like acid that ate the air, the stench of peeling, burning, roasting flesh. He went away to a good place in his mind. He thought of Lauren kissing him in the little attic bedroom in his foster parents' house in what now seemed a very long-ago time.

And then, when it was done, when the last of the screaming had curled itself into nothing, when there was nothing left but the stench of hair and skin and clothes and something else, a bilious blood-rot kind of smell— if cancer had a smell, Ramsey thought, it would be this, of dead and dying demon-things—the nature of the flames began to change, the color taking on a faint bluish hue; death triggered something deep inside the hybrid body that made it burn from within, consume itself until it was nothing but amber-colored ash.

"Jess," he said. Except he had no voice. He cleared his throat and spoke again, louder, stronger. "Jess."

A female voice hissed in his ear, "So that's her name?"

An arm around his chest, so tight he couldn't breathe; a claw in his hair, yanking his head back.

The brown-haired girl from the bar.

"Summoner," she called out. "Summoner . . . Where are you? Come out, come out and play . . ."

The corpses burned, casting light and shadow across broken tile, the moss-covered stone of the fountain.

"I'm here," Jess said.

She stood in front of them, the light carving out her features. Dark hair fell across one eye; the other had a blue, calm, hollow cast.

"Good!" crowed the girl. "I wanted you to watch!"

Hot breath on Ramsey's throat and, just as he felt his

skin start to break beneath jagged teeth, he was free again, the hold against his chest turning spasm-tight and letting go. He got to his feet and turned in time to see the girl in Jess's arms. Jess was whispering in her ear. They might have been lovers, except for the look in Jess's eyes, flat and cold like a shark's. The girl-thing was grinning, her teeth smudged with blood. Her body arched and she made a long, rattling sound; and then she was gone.

Jess knelt and ran her hand across the girl's eyes, closing them.

The false Jess, the magic-summoned illusion that Jess used as a decoy, remained standing in front of Ramsey, the calm, hollow eye still on him. It gave him the creeps. He said, "How much longer will that thing last?"

"Not long."

The false Jess flickered and went out.

"Illuminate," Jess muttered, and for a moment Ramsey thought she was talking to him. But sometimes she talked to herself when she was casting, particularly when she was tired or distracted; spoken words helped her focus. Light shimmered up from her right hand, and she knelt in front of Ramsey. He found her gaze unsettling and was unable to hold it for long.

"I'm okay," he said. "Just . . . a bit, you know, shaken."

The light danced along his vision.

"You can't take these kinds of risks," she said. "If nothing else, think of me. How I would feel if I lost you. Okay?"

He wanted to say something—*I would never do that to you,* maybe, or *I would rather die than cause you pain,* which seemed not just mushy but stupid, since she was warning him not to die in the first place—but all he could do was nod.

She hugged him fiercely, both of them on their knees,

the cold feel of her cheek against his. She let go just as hard, pushing him away.

The demon-things were burning less brightly now. Ramsey heard a shifting, crumpling sound as the body nearest him collapsed into ash. "I only thought there was one of them. You know? Or maybe just a few, at the most. At the very most. I figured I could handle it. They've never—they've never hung out in these kinds of numbers before. They took over the entire freaking motel."

Jess was so still and silent it was hard to distinguish her from the shadows. "Yeah. This looks like it was some kind of . . . *gathering*."

Before this, they'd found hybrids in singles or pairs, roaming, hunting. The largest group they'd encountered had been the hybrids who'd hijacked a Greyhound bus in a desolate stretch of Montana. They had been playing games with the corpses, the bones. There had been five of them.

Ramsey cleared his throat. "How did you find me?"

"How do you think? I was on the Dreamlines." She cast him a sidelong glance. "Lucky."

The Dreamlines. She was talking about the in-between place, the borderland, the place that bridged different worlds, or realities, or states of being. *Think of it as a kind of Twilight Zone if you wish,* someone had once told Ramsey. The Summoners were made and defined by their relationship to it. The Dream Children, Ramsey had heard them called once, although he couldn't remember by whom. The Dreamlines were their source of power and knowledge. Summoners spent a staggering amount of their lives in deep meditation, leaving their bodies behind as they mindshifted into the Lines; Ramsey compared it to plugging in your cell phone for recharging. The longer, deeper, harder you knew how to travel on the Dreamlines, the more powerful you were and could become. If you didn't die first. Or go crazy.

When they were on the Dreamlines, the Summoners could track one another along what Ramsey imagined as psychic pathways. Every living entity belonged to a Dreamline, Jess had told him, and Ramsey knew that Jess could home in on his own Line like a dog could track steak on the barbecue. On the one hand it made him feel like he had a hovering older sister whom he was powerless to avoid; on the other it was infinitely reassuring, given what his life had become. And it was why, he realized now, he'd felt confident enough to try some demon-killing on his own. *Lucky.* Jess meant she could have been doing something else; they were supposed to be on downtime, after all. Except that was the thing. Jess wasn't exactly someone who kicked back and watched reruns of *Battlestar Galactica.* Ramsey wasn't even sure if she slept anymore, or what the sleeping requirements were for someone like her, who had laid down her humanity for the dream- and blood-magic to hammer into something new. Something that had a hell of a lot more in common with their absent companion Kai Youngblood, who was more than seven centuries old, than Ramsey did himself.

"The hunting." He was feeling the need to defend himself. "It's never been like this before. I mean, it's gotten so—"

"Easy."

"I thought I had gotten pretty good at it. I mean, I *am* good at it. Right?"

"Up until now has been the beginning." Her voice was detached and mild; the kind of voice you might expect from a sociopath, Ramsey couldn't help thinking, although Jess was hardly that. "Warm-up stuff," Jess said. "For them. For us. It's going to get harder."

"Harder?"

This was not the narrative Ramsey had worked out in his mind. After all, it had been a finite number of demon-things that had escaped into the world, and they were being tracked and hunted down by a number of other Summoners who were at least as capable as Jess, and much more experienced. And it wasn't like these things could go off and reproduce. So Ramsey had just figured that they'd keep getting killed, one by one and two by two, until there were no more left to die. And people like him could get on with their lives.

Find that horse ranch, maybe.

"Come with me," Jess said. "Stay close."

Many of the rooms had been trashed—curtains and cushions clawed apart, wallpaper splashed with stains about which Ramsey felt no desire to speculate. One room buzzed with flies. There was a dead woman propped in the armchair, her stiffened arms around a child's teddy bear. The toy had been decapitated, the head placed atop the television, so that toy and dead woman stared at each other with the same dull gaze. This was the kind of thing hybrids did for fun. As Ramsey recoiled from both the sight and the stench, Jess's voice was detached, sociopathic again. "I wonder how long she's been missing."

It was in the last room that they found something interesting.

The toilet had been uprooted from the bathroom and placed on the second bed. Ramsey glimpsed something in the toilet bowl—something that looked like a head with dark hair—but this room didn't have that *eau de rotting corpse* scent. It smelled of Taco Bell and urine. Maybe the thing in the toilet bowl was just part of a doll that had suffered the same fate as the teddy bear. Doll parts, human parts. Demon humor. *Ha, ha,* Ramsey thought, and wanted to throw up.

"Look at this," Jess said, tapping a cheap DVD machine. "They were watching something."

The chairs in the room were angled toward the television, including chairs that must have been dragged in from other rooms. The TV was on, although the screen showed nothing except a smooth blankness. Jess pressed play. Ramsey flashed on the room as it must have been

just a few hours ago: filled with hybrids, their own multiple presences making them jittery, musky stench rising
off those unwashed bodies. All of them turning to watch
what he and Jess were watching now.

A man stood in a bare, featureless room and talked
at the camera.

"That's demon language?" Ramsey said.

The man's voice rose and fell in odd rhythms; the
words, if they were truly words, seemed to slither and
hack at the air.

"One of their languages," Jess muttered. "Kai says
there are thirteen. That they know of."

The man was medium height, medium build, dressed
in a brown suit too big in the shoulders. He looked like
the kind of salesman you might buy something from only
because you felt sorry for him. He looked like a loser.
Except as his little speech went on Ramsey felt himself
getting caught up in it, the strange slashing rhythms of
it, and the man's eyes were intense and hard.

"Lucas Maddox," he said.

Ramsey's body jerked with surprise.

"What—" he said, but Jess had already bolted to the
DVD player, stabbing at STOP and REWIND. The speech
played again—the stream of gibberish, then the name,
clear and distinct: "Lucas Maddox."

The name came again near the end, and then the man
walked toward the camera and his hands came toward
the lens—his nails were long, pointed, and tipped with
scarlet—and the screen went dark.

Ramsey noticed, then, the way Jess's body turned
rigid. The way she had turned away from him, as if she
didn't want him to see her face. She was pushing buttons
on the DVD machine. It rattled and hummed, then gave
up the disc.

Ramsey said, still watching her, "Haven't heard that
name in a while."

"You thought he died back in the desert?"

"I don't know." He was thinking about how they'd never really talked about Maddox. During all the time they'd spent together, on the road, in motels, during the stakeouts and the brief celebratory periods after, relying on conversation and humor—when Jess was in a light enough mood to even have a sense of humor—to relieve some of the grim awareness of what they were doing and what was at stake, they had touched on pretty much every topic you could think of.

Except one, Ramsey realized now.

Except him.

"Maybe I was hoping," he said finally. "And you? Did you think he was dead?" Hell, maybe he was. Just because a hybrid was talking about him on DVD doesn't mean he's still—

"No," she said, and lifted her head and looked at him. "He's out there. I've always known that."

Kai was waiting for them.

Their motel was set back along the road that ramped up onto the freeway. He was standing half in and half out of the glow of a streetlamp. He knew Jess would have been aware of him first, but she gave him the joy of discovery. "Dude!" he shouted, tumbling out of their Land Rover and running across the parking lot. He must have seemed like a little kid, but he didn't care. "Hey, you! Youngblood!"

Kai Youngblood, Ramsey had learned, possessed the reserve of a man from another place and time, but that did not mean he was cold, or that he couldn't laugh in pleasure and delight as Ramsey hurled himself at him with youthful affection. Ramsey slapped him on the back, becoming envious all over again of the size and strength of the man. Most of the Summoners had height, but Kai had the broad, muscled build of an ex-jock who kept himself in shape through the years. You met him for the first time, you wanted to ask, "You played professionally, right? What position?" But the man couldn't or wouldn't follow a football game if his life depended on it.

His hair was longer, his clothes more casual than when Ramsey first met him, and he suspected this was Jess's influence. Even a seven-century-old Summoner, it seemed, was not immune to a little style modification thanks to his much-younger girlfriend. "How are you?" he said to Ramsey, and managed to give him his full attention as Ramsey stammered out an answer, before his eyes slipped to Jess.

Ramsey recognized his cue to step back.

They moved into each other as if this had all been choreographed a long time before and they were only following the steps. At five nine, Jess was hardly a small woman, yet crushed against Kai like this she seemed a child. Ramsey wanted to give them their privacy, yet felt the need to see this for his own sake. It countered the coldness in Jess's eyes and detachment in her voice as she—who had once been a bartender and rising young artist in New York, struggling with boyfriend and apartment issues—surveyed the carnage that had become her life's work.

Jess stepped back—possibly, Ramsey thought with amusement, so she could breathe again, Kai's grip being what it was. She was very pale. Kai whispered in her ear and Jess nodded and smiled and glanced sidelong at Ramsey. Ramsey had the feeling that information had somehow been exchanged between them—about what had happened that night, and the role he had played. But Kai's expression held no judgment.

"She needs to eat," Ramsey said. "She needs serious protein. She needs, like, the whole cow."

Jess rolled her eyes. Ramsey had appointed himself her dietary watchdog ever since he'd noticed the physical toll the magic exacted on her.

"I could eat as well," Kai said. "It's been a while."

Been a while could mean anything from five hours to

five days. Summoner appetites did not run along regular lines. When Ramsey sat down at a table with Kai, he never knew if the Summoner was going to have a bowl of soup, and leave it unfinished, or put away four massive steaks while Ramsey worked through a hamburger and fries.

Ramsey said happily, "There's a Sizzler across the road."

Kai winced. "Someplace with a semblance of a wine list. *Please.*"

Kai had left them abruptly about three weeks ago, following a vision he'd picked up on the Dreamlines about a bizarre series of murders happening in New York. There had turned out to be a half dozen of *them,* Kai said, holed up in a warehouse in Brooklyn . . . and a few human helpers as well.

As the waitress displayed the bottle and poured the wine, questions lined up in Ramsey's mind: *But demons don't exactly mingle. Their bloodlust makes them too crazy. How could they tolerate humans hanging around them without tearing them to pieces?*

And what were they doing in a city in the first place, particularly a metropolis like New York? In Ramsey's experience—although it was beginning to occur to him that his "experience" wasn't so considerable as he'd started to allow himself to think—the demons gravitated *away* from urban areas. Possibly because they'd been born into this world in the desert, amid miles and miles of stark, vast nothing; possibly because cities, crammed with noise and buildings and technology and humanity, were just too strange and overwhelming after whatever kind of realm had been *home* to them before this one.

The waitress moved away.

Kai said, "They were styling themselves as vampires," and Ramsey nearly choked on his crab cake.

"Vampires?" he said.

He remembered the girl from the motel, her breath on his neck.

Kai speared an heirloom tomato. "They had the clothes—velvet, lace, that kind of thing. They had borrowed what they thought of as aristocratic mannerisms, I suppose; it was weird and kind of darkly amusing. They were savaging their victims by ripping out their throats and drinking their blood."

"I guess they saw a few movies," Ramsey said.

"I think they might have been making some kind of statement, or even issuing a challenge. To us, I mean. The Summoners."

"I don't get it . . . Oh." Ramsey realized he was touching the scar on his own throat. "Because when you guys—I mean, not you specifically, but the Summoners who came long before you—were traveling the world and spreading knowledge and healing and stuff, people started to turn on you. They got suspicious and started inventing all those vampire stories—"

"Tell us about New York," Jess said quietly.

"They had attracted some people—I guess you could call them vampire groupies—to them, getting them to run errands, help with food and shelter and money, teach them about the modern world in general and the city in particular. As a reward, these people—these followers—were promised eternal life. So you can imagine the disillusionment when they found out"—Kai took a moment to drain his glass—"when they found out eternal life wasn't exactly in the offing. But by then—"

Ramsey nodded. *But by then it was too late.* He said, "So you killed them all?"

"I watched them for as long as I felt I could afford to. They were—different. They were amusing themselves with theatrics—playing games—but beyond that, there was a certain amount of . . . They could have just rampaged through the city, but they were holding back. They were watching, learning. As if preparing for something. Waiting."

"For what?"

"I'm not sure."

From the way he exchanged looks with Jess, though, Ramsey knew it was a lie. Kai and Jess sometimes withheld information from him, like he was just a kid who couldn't handle the truth.

"But you killed them," Ramsey said. "So it doesn't matter what they were doing, or learning, or organizing. They were like this . . . freak advanced species of demon, but you wiped them out. And then came back to us."

Kai looked at him.

"You came straight back to us," Ramsey said.

"I came straight back to you."

Kai's gaze was calm and steady. It always was. Even now, when Ramsey sensed—with the uncanny intuition that the war-angel had left him, picking up on the tiniest shifts in expression, minute clues and signs that hardly anyone else could catch—that Kai wasn't telling the truth.

Jess had not said anything yet—Ramsey noticed she was already halfway through her butter-drenched lobster. But now she and Kai swapped looks, and Ramsey could feel the communication pass between them: a charge in the air, as if the space over this pleasant candlelit table was about to crack with thunder.

Ramsey said, "So they're, like, evolving?"

This has been the warm-up stuff. It's going to get harder.

Jess said, "They're beginning to access their human side—the memory and personality of the person whose body they took. Which means they're more capable of self-control, patience, planning."

"Some of them, anyway," Kai said.

Jess caught Ramsey's eye and gave a small nod. Trying to keep it as simple and short as he could, Ramsey told Kai about the DVD they'd watched, the hybrid who starred in it, like a motivational speaker from the seventh circle of hell.

"Maddox," Kai muttered. He abruptly reached for the wine bottle and drank directly from it. "He should do us a favor and just get himself killed."

"You think he's becoming one of their leaders or something?" Ramsey said.

"No."

Jess's answer was so definitive that Ramsey felt a little startled.

"That's not his style," Jess said.

"But he's a bad guy," Ramsey said. "I mean, he's on their side—"

"He's on his own side. At least for now."

"When did you become such an expert on him?"

"Ramsey, honey, these are just basic observations."

"I think she's right," Kai said. His gaze lingered on Jess, who was staring into her wineglass. "Given what we know about Lucas Maddox—"

Ramsey interrupted. "What do we know about Lucas? That he was some rock star turned washed-up junkie? That a demoness found him and made him her bitch? That he tried to bring on the end of the world?"

"Asha is gone. Maddox isn't much on his own." Kai was still looking at Jess.

The waitress stopped by their table to ask if everything was all right. Ramsey's gaze moved around the restaurant. So civilized. Amber sconces throwing soft light along the California landscapes, people talking in low voices as they dined on steak and seafood. He had never thought much about civilization one way or the other, but now he pictured all that delicate glassware smashed, tables overturning, men and women leaping at each other's throats, candles spilling flame onto tablecloths and curtains. Maybe that was closer to the natural order of things. How many people in the world, after all, ever got to sit down in a restaurant like this? Civilization suddenly struck him as a frail and expensive achievement: a stained-glass surface beneath which dark shapes circled and waited.

Ramsey stepped out of the shower. He rubbed the steam off the mirror and stared.

His scars.

The ritual was always the same: count the scars on his left arm first, and then his right, and then his throat and chest, and then along his thighs. All the scars were the same: thin raised lines of flesh, pale against his lightly tanned skin. The legacy from his time in the desert. What Lucas Maddox had helped do to him.

Lucas and Bakal Ashika.

Asha.

It went back to the days of the Labyrinth City, deep within the African desert, the home of the Sajae, the race of men and women descended from angels who could channel Dreamline energy down through their bodies and express it as magic. As a small child, Asha had been banished from the Labyrinth with her mother. Years later, she reentered the city as a slave, her unusual coloring allowing her to pass as one of the barbarians, the outworlders. But she was of the same powerful bloodline as the crown prince himself, and came into the forbidden forms of magic that had long gone underground. She mastered them and gathered six disciples trained in the deepest demon magic.

They opened themselves up to the demons.

They became the first human-demon hybrids that Ramsey knew about, but they were unlike any of the hybrids he and Jess were hunting today. They were so powerful that they had turned the Labyrinth to sand, scattered the surviving Sajae race across the medieval world, and then hunted them down over centuries. They had a special interest in the Summoners: talented Sajae, like Kai, who had trained in and graduated from the Rites of Deep Magic—also known as the Trials—and who had always held an exalted place in Sajae society even as they sacrificed many of its comforts.

Kai and his own Pact of Summoners had eventually overcome Asha and her six, with the help of a war-angel whom Kai's great mentor Shemayan had summoned into this world for that purpose. Now—still unable to kill them—the Summoners guarded the seven demons in magic-bound prisons around the world.

Or had, until Asha escaped last year.

And the wounded war-angel, still trapped in this realm so alien to it, had sought refuge inside Ramsey's body. Ramsey had been carrying the presence ever since his near-death experience at five years old, growing up in a series of foster homes, noticing that even though people liked him, they didn't seem comfortable around him for long. He remained without real friends, real family.

Until Jess.

She had discovered him through dreams, through the powers of her own latent Sajae blood that Kai Youngblood had quickened into life. Kai had believed that Asha was after Ramsey, and the war-angel he carried, for revenge; but Asha had wanted Ramsey for a different reason. For a rare and arcane ceremony, held out in the Mojave Desert, which would have created a multitude of new followers to help her reshape this world; a ceremony that would unite demon soul with human flesh through offering up Ramsey, and the being he carried, as the Bloodangel, the entity meant for sacrifice.

But all that was over.

What Asha had made was now being unmade.

The war-angel had left him.

Asha was gone.

You're just another stupid kid.

He fished some change from his pocket and stepped outside to get a Diet Coke from the vending machine.

A figure stood at the end of the walkway.

"Hey," Jess called out as she turned. "Can't sleep?"

He shook his head. And as he walked toward Jess, he couldn't help thinking of the double she'd summoned in the courtyard to act as a decoy, its eyes a soulless void. Then, and now on the walkway, in that half moment before Jess had turned around, he hadn't recognized her at all. He had seen a total stranger.

Chapter Two

Jess

She followed him into the motel room and kicked shut the door. Kai turned to her and said, "The other Summoners have—"

"No talking," Jess said.

They stood looking at each other in the center of a motel room that smelled of astringent, air freshener, stale cigarette smoke. Jess was accustomed to the smell but knew that Kai—whose senses were much more heightened than her own—could tolerate it only out of love for her.

"Wise woman," Kai said, stepping closer. So close now. His eyes darkened with a desire that made her breath catch. He slipped the sweater coat off her. Then the T-shirt, up and over her head; she felt the soft fall of hair along skin. "You're a waif," Kai said, disapproving. "Look at this." He ran his fingers along her collarbone, sending a quick shiver through her. He touched the outline of a rib.

"Magic seems to burn about ten thousand calories a day," Jess said. "Maybe I should write a book. *The Summoner Diet: How to Eat All You Want and Still—*"

"Your body is still adapting." Kai frowned. "But you need to get better control, or—"

"What did I say about talking?" She pressed her fingers against his mouth. Felt him smile.

He smelled as he always did: elegant, well groomed, yet beneath the layers of soap and cologne and the faint lemony starch of his shirt was something else, a hint of sulfur that was him, Jess knew, uniquely him, as if beneath his civilized appearance he was burning. Always burning.

She craved him in a way that unnerved her. It wasn't just his way of bringing her to orgasm, the trembling that began at the molten center and ran out along her body until she felt herself break, over and over, no longer caring if Ramsey could hear them through the wall. It was also what happened in those moments, the alien wave of images that tumbled through her, as if all boundaries of skin and bone had disappeared and part of his soul moved inside her, so old and strange and powerful it couldn't help but obliterate her own. If just for a moment.

But this was Kai, Kai, *her* Kai, and if having him meant she had to drown herself like this, then fine. *Not healthy,* some inner, postfeminist voice told her primly, no matter how much she told that voice to shut up and screw off. *This is not how it should be, and it cannot continue. You know this.* But if this was what made the rest of her life possible, was it so bad? The hunting and the carnage and the terror; the death-spell she had whispered in the female hybrid's ear; the evidence Ramsey wore on his skin, in his eyes, of what Asha had done to him, evidence that confronted Jess all over again every time she saw him. She had given up everything—everything—to come on the road and be this kick-ass demon-slayer, this ultimate tough chick who wasn't one thing or another but caught in between. She was not a true Summoner, but she wasn't the woman she had been. She was fine with the sacrifice, she wasn't resentful . . . she truly wasn't . . . so would it really kill her—or the world—if she took refuge in this man whom she loved? His hands, his voice, his body, the deep luxurious sensuality of him; had she not earned these pleasures, over and over?

And if sex with him felt, at times, a little bit like self-immolation—taking her so deep into a white-hot space that felt a little bit like death—it was only for a moment. The moment always ended.

When they moved apart, and she slowly, painfully, came back to herself, to the dimly lit interior of the motel room, she let the last of the foreign images move through her. Images that belonged to Kai, not her, released from his memory and now braiding themselves into hers. She saw the inside of a pub, stone walls and dirt floor and wood smoke, a young man with artfully windblown hair and a linen shirt and velvet waistcoat taking a drink from his cup and chuckling, *"So, you're like me, then. Mad, bad, and dangerous to know!"*

Jess had never been to college—had earned her GED as a talented runaway scraping out a life in New York City—but had the scattered erratic knowledge of a lonely adolescent who used books as an escape. Jess said, "You never told me you knew Byron."

"What?"

"Lord Byron."

Kai tilted his head, remembering. Jess had learned that Summoner memory could be a spotty thing; parts of Kai's long existence would be clearly available to him one day, then slide into obscurity the next, as different parts shifted into view. Kai had developed his own theory on this. It was a survival mechanism. *A perfect memory,* he told her once, *would be relentless. Would drive us insane.*

Which happened, from time to time. Summoners did go insane.

Salik, for example, the jax-dealing Summoner who had turned against his own kind, betraying Ramsey to Asha in order to curry favor with her and secure a place for himself in her future. He was now believed to be the one who had helped Asha escape from her prison in the first place. The prison in which Kai and his Pact had bound her over five centuries ago.

"He was a friend," Kai allowed, and for a moment Jess thought he meant Salik, who *had* been a friend of his, once, a long time ago in the days of the Labyrinth. He meant Byron. "I liked his writing. Not all of it, but some of the poems. He had some strange ideas about wanting to be a warrior. Eventually he took off for Greece, fought for a cause he didn't really understand."

"He was a romantic," Jess said.

"I never understood romantics."

"And yet you're such a romantic figure," Jess said, and grinned. "You should have seen yourself in the parking lot when Ramsey and I drove up—I knew you by your shadowy brooding. No one does it half so well."

He laughed. "I was thinking how I'd have to spend the night in this *pit.* Jess, you have access to money. A lot of money—"

"Your money."

"So? Take advantage."

"Places like this *have* some advantage. You know that. We could go through the lobby dragging three-headed aliens, and nobody would care. Or even notice."

"I think they'd notice *that.*"

She shrugged.

"You need some beauty," Kai said, "some elegance, or you will burn out. Become more and more like the thing you're hunting."

"That's a dramatic statement."

"Trust me on this. Take your beauty where you can, Jess."

"I do," she said. "With you."

He touched her face. Then he took her right hand and placed her palm along the side of his neck. It was a Sajae gesture, she knew, something you did only with the closest of intimates, signaling your trust and love and vulnerability. She was so focused on the feel of his pulse against her skin, the current of emotion twisting through her, that she had to force her mind to what he was saying.

". . . what I might do for you," he was saying. "That worries me. The choices I might be capable of. I think it makes me dangerous."

Mad, bad, and dangerous to know.

Jess grinned. His seriousness always lightened her a little, as if she had transferred onto him some of the burden of her own thoughts. "Dangerous to what?"

He got off the bed, light and shadow sliding across him. He looked at her, seemed about to answer, then picked up a pillow and tossed it at her instead. "Forget it. I'm done stroking your ego. For now, anyway."

"Come here," she said. She furled her arms around his shoulders, pulled him as close as she could. She buried her face in the hollow between his neck and shoulder. His skin felt cool and warm at the same time: like a smooth marbled surface, with heat pressing up just beneath. "I love you," she whispered. "I love you to death."

He picked up her hand, stroking her fingers. "You could leave off that last part," he said. " 'I love you' works fine."

"Okay."

He folded her fingers in his, brushed them against his mouth.

"Try not to go away again," Jess said.

"It might be you leaving me next time."

"I doubt that."

He looked down at their hands, readjusting his hold to lace his fingers through hers. She saw the metallic silver of his nails, a sign of the magic that marked him. Her own nails had just started to take on that hue. "We do what we have to," he said. "Don't we? We have no choice."

She pulled away from him and backed up against the

headboard, hugging her legs to her chest. "Okay," she said. "Let's do this. Let's talk about my Trials."

The Trials of Deep Magic: it was what took a Sajae-born and transformed them into a Summoner, someone who worked in the deep magic free-forms of the Dream-lines. The Rites were elaborately designed by a Summoner specifically trained for the task and the whole thing was done, as far as Jess could tell, with great pomp and ceremony, which is how Kai's peer group seemed to like to do things. Jess was the *krikkia,* the Sajae word for Summoner-candidate. Kai would attend as one of the *sajaks*: official witnesses.

"There's a date and location."

She stared. "You're kidding. Where? When?"

"Vegas."

"The desert," she muttered. "It had to be the desert." Then: "Vegas? You mean somewhere outside of Vegas, right?"

"Actually, no. It'll be in a new hotel on the Strip. The Eden. You might have heard—"

"I've heard of that place," she said suddenly. "That's the famous hotel guy—what's his name? Donnelly?"

"Daughtry."

"That's his huge new luxury palace—"

"Daughtry is a Summoner," Kai said simply.

She stared at him.

"He's also the Designer." He added, needlessly, "Of your Trials. He's eager to meet you. He hasn't had the chance to design Trials for a very long time."

"So, when?"

"Next week."

"What?"

"Next week. Summoners and Sajae-blood are gathering out there even now. It should be quite the event."

"A Summoner conference," she muttered, and Kai laughed. Then she said, "Wait a minute. No. That's too soon. That's—"

"Jess."

"—too fucking soon."

"Jess." He spoke with a calmness that suddenly infuriated her; she wanted to smash through it, to whatever emotion lay beneath. Sometimes his self-control seemed too much like a machine. "You're gifted enough to handle everything they'll throw at you."

"It took you years to prepare for the Rites."

"Your own Rites will be modified according to the circumstances at hand—"

"Modified," she said. "Modified. That's lovely. So they'll always be able to say, she's an air quotes Summoner—"

"An air quotes—" He looked amused.

"A 'Summoner'" she said again, this time demonstrating the air quotes for him, "only because they modified the Rites *according to the circumstances*—"

"The Rites are individualized for everyone, Jess. That's how they work. That's how the *magic* works—"

"It's different for me. Don't pretend it isn't."

She stared at him, challenging him to contradict her. He did not. He stroked her leg instead. She felt herself delighting in the feel of him, as she always did, as she couldn't help but do, even as his long fingers slipped round her ankle, grasped it, like a shackle.

She said, "I'll never be one of them. One of you." Her emphasis on the last word was slight, but she thought she saw him wince all the same.

The Summoners. She knew how they saw her—an outsider, an interloper, and still so very, deeply human, and although Kai refused to discuss it Jess could sense their prejudice. The Sajae themselves were a hybrid race, descended from humans as well as angels, but it seemed the less human you were, or seemed to be, or could pretend to be . . . the better. In the old, long-gone city of the Labyrinth, Jess had learned, the bloodlines regarded as the most angelic had formed the aristocracy from which the rulers and priests and teachers and Summoners were drawn, and the most prominent artists as well. The most impure—which meant the most human—

families became relegated over time to life along the
outer edges of the Labyrinth, including the warrenlike
slums near the marketplaces and even the no-man's-land
beyond the final gates.

If the other Summoners didn't trust her—if she wasn't
qualified enough to fulfil their delusions of angelic
grandeur—well then, screw it. She refused to give a
damn. The only reason she was going along with this at
all was because of Kai.

"Jess. Jessie. You'll prove your worth. They'll recognize you for what you are."

"You really think so," she said, marveling. "You
really think this."

"They'll recognize you. They'll have no choice."

"Does he know?" Lucas Maddox was asking her.

They were on an abandoned rooftop, the wraparound
grid of Los Angeles smoldering beneath them, the moon
bloodred overhead.

The dreams had been set in different places, but
lately they were all in LA. Always, Lucas was obscured
by shadow so she could never get a good look at him.
They watched each other from a distance. Yet his voice
stirred right in her ear:

"Does he know?"

She flashed her irritation. "I don't keep things from
him."

"That's not true," Lucas said mildly, "and you know
it. I've got a song for you. Want to hear it?"

"Hell no."

He laughed.

A yellow paper scuttled against the toe of her boot.
She picked it up. She expected a flyer advertising a rock
band, but all she saw was a number printed in stark,
jagged lines. She knew it was important, but the more
she tried to make it out, the more the wind blew grit in
her eyes until she couldn't see anything at all.

"That's the age when you die," Lucas was telling her,

in that voice, that honeyed, rock-star voice. "You die young, you know. You always die young."

She awoke with a crushing sensation inside her head. Her breathing was high and rapid. She got out of bed and then doubled over, pressing both hands to her temples. Moments passed, and she started to feel normal again.

Kai was sleeping: the deep, restorative sleep of a Summoner who had trust in his surroundings. She didn't want to wake him, wasn't even sure if she could.

The room was closing in on her. The shadows were long and narrow like coffins. She pulled on jeans and a T-shirt and stepped outside, realizing she was barefoot, realizing she didn't care. The air was cool and laced with exhaust.

You always die young.

She paced the walkway, feet padding off the grit of the cement. The jagged feeling inside her was only getting worse. Then she became aware of the presence behind her, the warm earthy sense of it: Ramsey.

And it was like something slipped into place in her mind. She closed her eyes for a moment, letting that Ramsey-sense wash through her. No way he could know, she thought, and not for the first time, what his presence did for her, or how much she was starting to depend on it.

She turned. Pretended to notice him for the first time.

"You look a little spooked," she said. Although from the way he walked toward her, it was as if she was the spooked thing, some wild creature he was carefully attempting to corner.

He took in breath to speak, then paused.

Then said, "I wanted to ask you . . ."

"Ask me what?"

"Lucas," he said. "Lucas Maddox."

And the name just hung there, like smoke that wouldn't dissipate.

"Ah," she said. She did not feel surprised. He was like this; he had a talent for seeing straight through her in ways that even Kai didn't seem to. Or want to.

In the fluorescent lighting, Ramsey's face looked pale, the scars on his throat standing out vividly. "We've never talked about him," Ramsey said, and she realized how much he did not want to be having this conversation, was doggedly forcing himself through it.

She could deny this, spurn him, be scornful. "What's to talk about?"

"Something. There's something. You're not being honest with me. Are you?"

He looked at her with that open, level gaze, and she felt a crumbling inside her.

"I dream about him," she admitted.

She watched him take this in; it had a sharper edge for him than for anyone else in her life.

"You mean like you used to dream about me?"

"No." She waved a hand. What she would give for a cigarette, or even a line of cocaine. Her old vices, given up just before Kai came into her life, as if on some level she'd sensed his coming and that she needed to steel herself, throw away her crutches, her methods of self-sabotage. Which didn't mean she couldn't find new ones.

She said, "That was different. You were . . . elusive, you were like this phantom I had to chase down, or die trying. You were a stranger in my dreams. I only got to *know* you in real life."

"Which means he isn't a stranger, and you're getting to know him?"

"No. That's not it. That's not at all what I mean."

"What I can't figure out," the kid said slowly, "is if you're lying to me, or to yourself."

Ice rumbled in the nearby vending machine. Someone down the block was smoking; her senses picked up the scent, kicked up her own craving another notch. Unfair.

Ramsey was waiting. He could wait forever, she knew,

if he had to, although that didn't necessarily mean he would.

She said, "We talk. Him and me. In the dreams."

"Just talk?"

"Pretty much."

"Does he say anything useful? About the hybrids, or what he's been doing, or—"

"No." She paused, and then said, "He hasn't been involved with them. Any of them. He wants to get away from all that, wants to reinvent himself. He's been on the road."

"Does he regret what he did?"

She pushed her hands through her long hair, swept it over her shoulder. "No. They're just dreams."

"Right. Just like they were with me."

"I told you, those were—"

"Different. Yeah, I know. Did you tell Kai?"

"They're only dreams," she said again. "I'm not sure there's anything to tell."

"Then why don't you find out?"

That look in his eyes—*lying to me or to yourself*—made her want to lash out. As if sensing this, Ramsey took a step back, and in that moment she hated herself.

"Take care," he said. "Just take care, okay?"

She nodded.

"Good night," he said.

As he was walking away from her, she called his name.

"Yeah?" He half turned, looking back at her over his shoulder.

"I hope you know," she said. The words weren't coming easily; she had to force them. "I hope you know. You should never feel afraid of me."

"Of course not."

But his response didn't satisfy her and she didn't think it satisfied him, either. She watched him fade down the walkway.

Take care.

She could hear the swish of late-night traffic on the freeway, the grind of big rigs downshifting. Take care of yourself. He was always trying to get her to do this, convinced she wasn't eating properly, pacing herself properly, his frowning look of concern so often aimed at her.

Maybe you should find out.

You could only put things off for so long, she reflected. Wasn't this always the grim truth of it? Because sooner or later those things came for you anyway. They started to eat you alive.

Chapter Three

Lucas

There was a space of time, after the events in the desert and before the madness caught up with him, when it was just him, the dog, and the road.

It was all good.

He bought the guitar in a shop outside of Dallas. It was only a few hours after that when he came across the roadhouse. A sudden drift of memory put him back in the early days with his band, Slippage, when they were touring for the first two albums, not getting play on the radio, not getting much attention from their own record label, playing just for the hell of it, in roadhouses just like this one.

Next thing he knew, he was stepping into the beery, shadowy interior: peanut shells crunching beneath his boots, click of billiard balls and canned laughter on the television, and a bored, pretty bartender. When he asked to speak to the manager she said, "At the moment, that would be me." She was sucking on a candy. Chipped black polish on her nails. When he made his request, she eyed him dubiously, but then there was a shifting in her face that might have been recognition.

"What's your name?" she said.

"Max."

"Right." She sucked on the candy another moment, then shrugged. "Do what you want. Can't hurt none, now can it?"

He nodded.

He hoisted himself onto the edge of the bar and drew his guitar across his body.

The strings bit into his fingers and his fingers bit back, hunting down the notes and setting them loose again. Something slithered deep inside him, moved through his gut and up along his spine. *You have in you the music of angels,* Asha told him once, *dark angels,* which is why she had chosen him. Or had he put himself in her line of sight to be chosen? He was no longer sure. Not that it mattered, as the ashes of Asha moved through his blood. He was playing hard and fierce. Just like in the old days, when Kelley Minghella—their lead singer who would not live past thirty—cavorted all around the stage and did backflips off the edge, and Lucas wouldn't consider it a good night unless he left blood on the strings.

He kept playing, not knowing what he was going to play until he heard it himself. At some point he became aware that all conversation in the roadhouse had ceased, the TV turned off. People were looking at him and more people were drifting in through the doorway to listen. Then he fell into the music again—and then right through it—falling into a memory of being a kid in Montreal and asking his sad, brown-eyed mother, *What's a prodigy?* because he'd overheard bits of a strangely hushed conversation between his mother and his music teacher. *Someone who has to practice very hard,* had been her response, and she refused to discuss the matter any further. But he practiced piano, and later guitar, because he wanted to, because nothing else felt as good, doing all the classical stuff his parents wanted from him until he discovered funk and punk and rock, and became more and more obsessed. No Juilliard for Lucas; screw the scholarship. He drifted south. By then his father was out of the picture and his mother had looked at him with a new, hard wisdom in her eyes and said, *You do what you want and need to do. You hear me? Fuck the rest of it.* He drifted west. He ended up in Seattle because that's where the interesting music turned out to be, and that's where Paula was. Then one day he decided that the interesting parts of his life were all done, the band was over, Kelley was dead, Paula was dead. He drifted between Mexico and LA and tended to the project of slowly killing himself.

All of these memories he played out through his music, and when it was done—when the music and memories were through with him, at least for the moment—he looked up, blinking like a newborn cub, and even though it was past three in the morning and the kitchen and bar had shut down long ago, no one had left. There were more people grouped at the tables and standing around the door than when he'd come in. There was silence. They looked at him and he looked at them and shrugged and said, "So I guess that's it."

People started to slip on their jackets and gather their bags and move out into the night. They had dazed expressions. There was no applause. The only person who even spoke to him was the bartender, and this time he saw the recognition so deep and clear in her kohl-lined eyes that he knew she must have been a Slippage fan. Maybe she'd even been a fan of Trans, the band he had built around Asha. Or maybe he was reading too much into her attractive but unremarkable features. She tilted her head and popped her gum—she'd exchanged the candy for gum; he wondered if she was trying to quit smoking—and said, "Why Max? I mean, why call yourself that?"

"Why not?"

"Just wonderin' if there was a reason. Maybe sentimental."

"I like the name. Good name."

"Sure it is. Just not yours."

"Tonight it is. Tomorrow, too, probably."

His dog, a black mutt with silky fringed ears he'd named Ronin, was waiting for him in the dirt driveway outside.

And then they were back on the road.

He dreamed about her. He went into his dreams seeking her. He knew her full name—Jessamy Shepard—but thought of her, simply, as the painter. Even in the dreams she kept her distance. *Where are you now in real life, not the dream life?* he wanted to stop the music enough to ask. *Who are you with and what are you up to?* From the mocking curve of her lips he imagined that she could hear those questions anyway. Maybe they reached her along with the music. *What exactly do you think we are?* that smile seemed to say. *Friends? Drinking buddies? Potential lovers?*

He wanted to tell her, *I'm not an evil man.*

Just not a good one, that smile seemed to say. *So where does that leave us?*

And he would wake up, and address the pale light of another anonymous motel room, Ronin stretched out on the twin bed opposite. Sometimes there was a woman . . . The demon-knowledge moved within his body: Asha's gift to him. Asha's mark on him. *Painter,* he said, *you don't even begin to know.*

So he wandered, and went nowhere, and drifted through bars and steakhouses and cafés and small clubs, any place that seemed like a good place to set up for a night. No manager or owner ever turned him down.

In fact, they seemed glad to see him.

Like maybe they were expecting him.

And the crowds were growing.

He began to feel uneasy, as if what he thought he was doing—being spontaneous and freewheeling and unpredictable—wasn't quite true. Especially when he started seeing the same faces in crowd after crowd, as if word was racing ahead of him; as if this bearded, long-haired, guitar-playing dude who called himself Max was cultivating the kind of fan base that could predict where he'd be before he even knew himself.

Especially when he saw the twins.

He noticed them the first time because they were hard to miss. Tall, angular, with smooth milk white skin and cropped white hair. In the dim light of the café, as he straddled the stool in the corner and let the music take him where it would, they drifted along the back wall, silent and faintly gleaming, like ghosts.

They showed up again two nights later, at a club called the Speckled Armadillo with hardly anyone on the large, gleaming dance floor. But as he played, cars began pulling up onto the dirt lot outside, people slipping through the door as if hearing themselves called, as if prepared to follow. Then he lost himself in the playing for a while, and when he looked up again several hours had passed and the twins were there, by the bar, one of them standing, one seated. The standing one raised a glass to him, its—he couldn't tell if it was a man or a woman, either of them—eyes flashing from the neon light of the beer signs in the windows.

And in that moment of eye contact, something odd happened. It was as if the twin's face opened into a dark void—surely a trick of the light, but unsettling all the same—and a noise came echoing down through that void, traveling a vast and ancient distance. The sound of footsteps, of something massive and unspeakable, slowly but surely slouching toward him.

Footsteps matching their rhythm to the rhythm of his music.

No, he thought.

His hands stilled on the strings. His performance that night was over.

He looked for the twins the next night, and then the next, but they were not there, the crowd empty of their milk white faces, their staring eyes, and he was relieved.

* * *

All he wanted to do was get into that zone where the rest of the world fell away and the music was him and he was the music. A paradox: even as the music took him through his past, his fingers tripping his memories out along the strings, the past itself ceased to matter. It was as if all that shit—the good and the bad—had happened to someone else, and inside the music he was pure and untouched. He was Max, the dude who had walked out of the desert all shiny and new.

This is what he tried to explain to the painter, those nights when she visited his dreams, when she refused to come anywhere near close enough and he struggled to make himself heard through the smoke and shadows and crowds and whatever else got between them. *That guy you met in the desert?* he said to her. *Okay, yeah, kind of an asshole. Didn't treat you the way you should have been treated. But that was someone else, someone else, someone else. Not me.*

In one dream they were facing each other on opposite ends of a hallway. There was a dark shifting shape between them: not shadow or smoke, but . . . something else. He didn't want to look too close.

Oh, I get it, she relayed to him. *You were under Asha's influence, not responsible for your actions. Sure.*

Things are different now.

No. The kid had it right. You're Asha's bitch, always have been.

Which is when a smooth, blind face pulled itself out of the dark shifting mass, the pit of its mouth opening to speak to him, say his name, as if it already knew him—

And he opened his eyes to another motel room. For a moment he thought he saw the painter—blue-eyed, dark-haired—watching from the corner. He searched himself for a response to her last comment—Asha's bitch—and came up with nothing. No anger or shame or regret. What broken thing had he been when Asha found him? *You have in you the music of angels. Dark angels.* She had shown him who he was. Who he could be. How could he regret what Asha had done for him— *done to him*— no matter the cost, to himself or to others or the whole damn world?

Then one night he was calling Ronin to him, coming down the steps, guitar case slung across his back, feeling purged and restored from the night's playing, when the dog planted his feet and growled at something in the shadows. "Ronin," he said quietly, and the growl turned to a whimper. The dog trotted to his side, pushed his head against the back of his leg. Lucas gave him some love, rubbing his neck, behind his ears, when the dog started to tremble.

The twins were waiting by his car.

"Hello," they said, their voices in perfect unison.

One of them came toward him. This close, he could make out subtle differences that marked one as a man, the one behind him a woman.

The man said, "Lucas Maddox," as if his name was some grand pronouncement. "It's time."

He bit. Couldn't help it; he was curious despite himself. "Time for what?"

"To come with us," said the woman twin, stepping up behind her brother, placing one long-fingered hand on his shoulder. Her brother smiled.

Lucas said, "So what've you guys been smoking?"

"We know what you are," the man said, "what you're meant for. It's been shown to us. Some of it, anyway. You are an *accident*, you realize, but that makes it all the more glorious. In my humble opinion." He grinned, flashing teeth even whiter than his skin.

"There's no such thing as accidents," the woman murmured. "There's a design behind it all."

"And everything happens for a reason," Lucas said. "Right. Please get out of my way. I'm asking very nicely."

"So you're not a believer?" the woman said, and the man said, his voice picking up at the end of hers so smoothly, with the same inflection, that it could have been the same person talking. "How interesting. We didn't expect that."

He heard the crunch of footsteps in gravel. From behind him, then all around him: many footsteps, many figures drifting from the shadows. In one sweeping glance he took in his audience, people who'd been in the roadhouse not so long ago listening to him so rapturously: mostly normal, mostly overweight men and women in their jeans and denim jackets, some of them studded with rhinestones that gleamed and flashed like faraway stars. None of them spoke. And it was the silence that finally got to him, putting his gut on ice. The anticipation, the expectation, of a crowd waiting anxiously for a performance that he knew right then, right there, he did not want to give.

He looked into the face of the twin and heard, again, the echo of footfalls—louder now, closer now, as something pulled itself out of the void, toward him.

"The music of angels," the woman said, and he started, his head jerking toward her, and his expression made her smile. "Dark angels," she said.

"It is a gift," the man said, "and it was not even meant for you. The blood of you. Coming down through the ages."

"It was meant for a prince," the woman said, "who paid a very high price for it. Black market magic—"

"Underground magic," said the man.

"It makes a good story," said the woman.

"Your story," said the man. "Come with us," and we'll show it to you. As it was shown to us."

"We'll show you many things."

"And you will play."

"You will finish what you started."

"You will open the doors," said the man, "and he will come. He will unmake and remake the world—"

"—Yes, he will remake it—"

"—and give it to us. His faithful."

"His visionaries. His children."

And Lucas said, "Asha."

The woman shook her head. "No. The one that made her."

And those ice fingers reached up through his gut and wrapped themselves around his chest and started to squeeze.

"We're your friends," the man said. "We want to be your *good* friends. Come with us now, and we'll help you—"

"—help you take your rightful place," said the woman.

The man came toward him, his hands held out by his sides, palms up.

Lucas punched him.

Lucas observed his fist flying at the man's face, the hard smacking sound of contact, pain shooting back through Lucas's hand, the man spinning back with the impact, falling to his knees in the dirt as his sister cried out and dropped beside him, peering anxiously at his face. The man shook her away, one hand coming up to gingerly probe his jaw. He turned his head and spat blood, with the gleam of what might have been a tooth.

Lucas pushed his way through them, the dog at his heels. Then he was slinging his guitar into the passenger seat and slipping behind the wheel, the dog jumping into his accustomed place in the back, to his blanket and chew toys.

He thought maybe they'd try to stop him, but as he gunned the motor and moved forward the shapes in the darkness, his silent, watchful audience, parted to let him through. When he glanced in the rearview mirror though he saw them falling in together, a crowd of roughly two dozen, watching his taillights slip off into darkness. Awe in their faces.

*   *   *

When he reached LA he moved back into his house in the Hollywood Hills, and as night fell the noise and music of Sunset Plaza drifted up to him and made him restless. He stood on his windy terrace and looked out over the city, lights burning below like the fires of an army camped on the plain.

The city felt like home to him, its lights beckoning him down and onward; it was the house that felt empty and alien. He had been at this point too many times to count. When a voice in his head would say, *Let's get high!* And his body would respond, *Well yes, sir, sounds like a fine, fine idea!* Then he'd be whipping down the freeway into the dark twisting streets of downtown LA, going to this alley for heroin, that corner for coke, or better yet through a certain strip club to a special little room where you could get everything: one-stop shopping at its finest.

He could go right back to that. Fall inside that groove again.

Nothing, no one stopping him.

Get the stuff, find a sleazy motel room or luxury hotel room, didn't matter, or bring it all back to the house—if he could even make it that far before giving in and shooting up—and disappear for a while.

But that was then. This was now.

He called Jared Hollander the next day, as if they hadn't been out of touch for the past four years, as if he didn't doubt this was still Jared's number.

A woman answered. "Who is this?" Guarded.

Before he could answer, there was a rustle of movement, and a familiar voice came on the line: "Hello?"

"Jared. It's—" *Max,* he thought, but said instead, "Lucas."

"Lucas? No shit?"

"I thought you could come over and we could, you know, just jam for a while. Like the old days."

"Yeah, dude. You at the same place?"

"I am."

"Right over."

The man who showed up at the door was not the same man Lucas remembered. For a long while he and Jared had been running partners, scoring drugs and partying intensely, before Jared's family and friends staged an intervention and Lucas took it upon himself to drive up the coast, where he fell in with a trust-fund shit who was hardly worthy of being Jared's replacement, but beggars—and dope fiends—couldn't be such choosy choosers. Jared turned thin like a concentration camp victim. He'd lost teeth. He had the most fucked-up arms Lucas had ever seen because the guy refused to learn to shoot up properly, would just jab with the needle and hope for the best.

But the Jared in his house now was muscled up and healthy, sucking on a fruit smoothie, lifting his guitar. The sweetness in his eyes, though, hadn't changed; there had always been something soft and open and too vulnerable about them. Lucas built a fire in the massive stone fireplace and they sat in the front room amid the sparse furniture and the painting of an incubus that ran the length of one wall. "Forgot about that," Jared said with amusement, eyeing the purple breasts. One taloned hand clutched the hair of the latest male conquest, leathery wings sweeping the night.

"Don't remember why the hell I bought that," Lucas said. It had seemed a good idea at the time: lugging it out of the gallery and down the street to his car, flying so high on coke and heroin he thought he and the incubus might take off together. "Think I liked her wings."

"Her wings," Jared said, and laughed.

Jared had never been the type to talk much, even when he was wasted, which was a quality Lucas appreciated. They slipped back into playing together as if they'd never left off, as if this musical conversation between them ever since they first met had never been so rudely interrupted. For a while Lucas had the happy feeling that if he looked over his shoulder he'd see Kelley Min-

ghella nearby, shuffling and snapping and popping to the
music, jotting words and phrases in a notebook, telling
them to stop, play that over again, play that last bit over.
This was how a lot of their songs evolved: this messy
collaborative process, fueled by caffeine and whiskey
and bad pizza at all hours. Their other songs—including
"Black Box," the strangely for them elegiac single that
took them from the margins and dropped them, to the
shock of one and all, into the thick of mainstream
culture—Lucas composed on his own, alone and removed, as if conducting a clandestine affair.

They played on, just screwing around, playing for no
purpose other than playing, and time disappeared and
Lucas felt himself slipping away, as if the music kept
opening trapdoor after trapdoor and he had no choice
but to fall through every one of them, ever deeper into
the hole of himself. His friend Jared was with him,
though, and that made it especially fine. He was getting
tired of being alone. So together they played through
the history of their band, Slippage, the rise and fall of
it, so bittersweet. The drugs had always been there.
When the label gave them money for their second album
they assigned a healthy portion of it to drugs, for what
Kelley termed "inspirational purposes." By that point
Ken, their drummer, had termed himself a straight-
edger, wouldn't touch a beer, took what the rest of them
could only regard as a deeply perverse pride in self-
denial. Lucas was the next to kick, when his on-again,
off-again relationship with Paula turned on again and
she gave him the ultimatum. Rehab, AA, twelve steps,
work the program, the sharp and heady delight of sobri-
ety, his woman in his arms, his band's great music. For
a while it had all been so good. Too good to be true, he
murmured into Paula's hair at night, too good to last.
Except he didn't truly believe that. The universe was
rich and abundant. Until Kelley Minghella crashed his
motorcycle one slick and rainy night and died in the
ambulance; until the ache in Paula's hip turned out to

be an astonishingly vicious bone cancer. *I call the shots, I say when and where, and I'm getting off at the top.* They spent her last days in Puerto Vallarta. And she was gone down the pathway with the gun in her hand. *Don't you dare follow me. I love you. I'll always love you. Don't you dare.* And Lucas had not, because in that moment he was filled with awe and love for her, because he believed he understood her, and realized too late he would never forgive himself.

The drugs were always there, though.

Let's go get high, said the voice in his head, and the voice in his body said, *Yes, sir,* and he was floating off the cliff, drifting dreamily to the bottom, where it turned out his buddy Jared was already waiting for him, beloved stick man with the weeping arms.

They played their way through the sad, violent energy of the drug years. Jared was right with him in the music, through every chord and riff. Their stories were different yet the same. He didn't need Jared to tell him about his stints in various rehabs: the relapses, the justifications and rationalizations, the way it got worse every time, the addiction biting deeper, the poison more potent. Lucas saw it all in the music and felt the echoes in his own life. Asha had found him, saved him. Now he found himself playing all this out, not for himself but for Jared, wanting someone to understand him.

He didn't shy away from the carnage in the desert. He showed Jared all of it, ripping at the strings, slamming down the riffs. And Jared didn't hesitate. Jared was right there with him.

And then the music changed.

The music opened other, deeper doors inside of him, and Lucas followed it down, down, down . . .

He plays onstage to a crowd of screaming fans. The painter is in the front row. He holds her gaze, that calm intelligent gaze, but then her eyes shift to a point beyond him and she steps back and shakes her head in sorrow.

He turns.

Nothing behind him but mirrors, reflecting himself and the crowd, doubling the room's population. Except as he watches, the faces grow long and distorted, lips wrinkling back from jagged rows of teeth. The glass itself seems to melt . . . and then disappear . . . so that he is looking into real space, other-space. He could step right through if he wanted to, into that surging crowd—

He whips around. His eyes search for the painter.

She is gone.

And then arms rocket out from behind him, through the mirror that isn't a mirror, cold dark arms, and so many of them, although he knows instinctively they belong to the same individual who traveled so far through coldness and blackness to get here, to this prized destination, and as the arms pin him in place, holding him tight, tighter, until his bones begin to break, to crush, the crowd screams and moves as one with a rippling, liquid grace up on the stage. They come at him with claws and teeth. They are going to rip him apart, as they are meant to, as the stories foretold long ago.

Lucas's hands stilled on the strings.

He stopped. Jared played on and didn't seem to notice. Lucas set the guitar on the floor, and stood and went over to the window. It was daylight. He saw past the tumbling hills—studded with the balconies and pools and Spanish-tiled roofs of multimillion-dollar homes—to the streets and buildings of the city below, the city that waited to swallow him, as it had so many times before.

"You can't quit now," Jared said, startling him. "You have to play on."

He turned.

Jared was wired. His eyes were blazing, his jaw clenched, his shirt soaked through with sweat despite the frigid air-conditioning. He looked as if he'd dropped several pounds. Lucas had to steady himself against the wall. How long had they been playing? He caught a glimpse of his reflection in the mirror. He looked fine, refreshed even, as if he'd woken up from a long healing sleep.

"The stranger," Jared said again, and came right up to Lucas. His breath had the foul odor of someone who hadn't eaten in a very long time. "He's coming for you, and the other one. He needs you to play."

"What are you talking about?"

"He needs you to play. I saw it all in the music. The music opened the doors and I looked through them and I saw. I saw. The stranger, the traveler, the one who breaks souls and slays angels. He needs you to play. He needs—"

"You have to get out of here," Lucas said. "You have to stay the fuck away from me. I shouldn't have invited—I shouldn't have brought you into this."

"They will rip you apart in the end," Jared said calmly. "You know this. You saw it."

But then Lucas was grabbing the smaller man by the shoulders and half lifting him, half dragging him out through the sliding doors onto the terrace. Wind whistled past their faces, colder than Lucas expected. "Hey," Jared said, "What the fuck? You can't do this to me— hey, dude—" Lucas dragged him over to the stairs, kissed him on the forehead, and hurled him down them. Jared stumbled, grabbed at the railing, stumbled again. He looked up at Lucas with those open-wound eyes, and Lucas turned away rather than look in them again.

"Go," Lucas said. He could taste salt from Jared's skin on his lips. He went back inside his house and locked the door.

He needs you.

He needs you to play.

So what. It didn't matter. Because Lucas didn't need anything. He sure as hell didn't need to play for some freak.

Asha had given him back to himself, and damned if he was going to give that away ever again. He was his own man now.

The next morning the telephone rang.

A woman said, "What the hell did you do to him?"

Still groggy, Lucas rolled over in the bed, rubbed his forehead. "Who is this?"

"Jared was at your house and what did you do to him?"

He swung his legs over the side and looked up to find his shaggy, bearded figure in the mirror. Since when did this house have so many fucking mirrors? "What happened to Jared?"

"He's dead. You hear me? He's dead. He was clean for two years and then he goes to your place and next thing you know he's OD'd in some dive in North Hollywood. You hear me? You hear me? So I need to know. *What did you do to him?*"

He didn't answer.

He sat on the edge of the bed in this strange empty house and listened to a woman he'd never met holler and wail. When the phone slipped from his hand to the floor, he barely noticed. He was thinking of the first time he and Jared ever played together, how it had seemed so close to magic.

He went down through the house to his guitar and picked it up and smashed it against the edge of the stone fireplace. Smashed it again and again, until he was sweating and breathing hard and staring at the mess of splintered wood in his hands.

He'd been chained to heroin, chained to Asha, but that had all just been part of the recovery of himself. He had come out of the desert a new man, a free man. So fuck anybody or anything that wanted to claim him again, no matter where the hell—or which hell—it came from.

Chapter Four

A Stranger Comes
to Town

In truth, the surfer had noticed something earlier that morning, although he put it out of his mind right after.

There had been one wave. One perfect wave. He saw it on the horizon and thought it must be some kind of heavenly gift, because this was one of those times when the sea wasn't up to anything much. Surfers saw him getting out of his truck with his board over his shoulder and greeted him with the dreaded, *Hey, mate, should have been here yesterday*. He agreed with them—he should have been here yesterday, *meant* to be here yesterday, except his girlfriend's mother arrived early and threw his plans to hell.

But then this wave came out of nowhere, and he eyed and measured the moments and paddled out for it, and man met wave in perfect salt-spray communion. He was flowing out of the water with the board beneath his feet. The sea swept him high. He crouched and carved through this world of blue-green streaming wonder, salt on his lips and in his eyes, and his heart roared along with the ocean.

Someone else was in the wave with him.

He registered it in pieces. The shadow rising inside the

wall of water. The slithering touch across his shoulders, a
thick wet whisper in his ear. The sense of *presence* which
had nothing to do with the sea, slipping through the
spray and light. Riding the sea. Riding him.

Then it was gone.

So that was the first thing. Perhaps it was a warning.
It might have helped him, saved him, if he had heeded
it as such: a sign that the world was not quite right today.
Better to get off the water, detach himself from his
board, spend the day on the sand with his girlfriend in
her fetching white bikini, her skin smelling of coconut oil,
the icebox packed with beer and roast beef sandwiches
and ice cream, part of her strategy to lure him away from
the waves for at least a little bit, so she could spend quality
time with him instead of her Peter Carey novel.

But he was a water baby grown into an ocean prince.
The sea was his home. This presence he had sensed had
nothing to do with the ocean. It came from somewhere
else entirely. So he dismissed it as some odd, fleeting
phenomenon, a trick of the light and the mind. Believing
in it would be like believing in a ghost, and, despite what
many in his family considered to be his highly flaky, New
Age kind of nature, he was too practical for that.

So he straddled his board, and floated, and meditated
on the beauty of the day.

He was thirty-seven, lean and leathered from a lifetime spent outdoors. His long, straight hair had turned
gray by the time he was twenty-five, silver ten years
later. Around his neck he wore a tiger's-eye for luck and
guidance, a shark's tooth for power and virility.

Sunlight on his shoulders, sunwarmed water sweeping
round his dangling legs. In the near distance, Bondi
Beach curved like a thick golden smile into the sea.
Music and voices floated over to him—British and German tourists. It was quieter here, on the south side,
where rip currents made life more hazardous. But he
was a strong swimmer, always had been. He and the
sea understood one another. He had survived a near-

drowning experience as a child, an encounter with a tiger shark as a teen. Twice the sea could have killed him, but it chose to let him go. He loved it for that.

So when the shadow came up beneath him, he noticed it first with a sense of detachment. He thought, *Shark?* and drew his legs onto the board, but it didn't really move like a shark—rising and expanding, a blooming darkness in the water—and that was when he felt coldness along his spine and in his belly, because of the wrongness, because there was nothing in the ocean that should look or move like that.

And then the thing turned over.

Turned over slowly, slowly enough for him to realize there was a shape, a body to it, and he realized he was going to see its face as the water swelled and streamed beneath him and the board rose up, and a whimper escaped him and too late he thought to close his eyes because of the face, the deep lipless pit of the mouth and rows on rows of teeth, the small ashy glints of countless eyes and they were all gazing straight at him, and he saw the intelligence in them, and he saw the black streaming limbs floating up toward him, leisurely, as if this thing had all the time in the world, and the surfboard flipped over with that same insolent laziness, and he was in the water, thrashing, cold smooth blackness folding over him, what felt like thick-fingered hands skating his body and latching on his calves, and he thrashed at the surface of the water and spat out water and screamed, not even screaming words, his mind had gone beyond words, and then he was screaming down through the water, watching the river of bubbles of his life force from his wide-frozen mouth as he felt himself pulled down, down, to where the sunlight filtered out completely and all warmth vanished and there was nothing but the cold and the dark.

Absorbed in her novel, Hilary looked up because she thought she heard something: the kind of cry that should have nothing to do with a sunny Sydney day at the beach.

Johnny? she thought. Except that couldn't have been him.

And her mind circled back to a recurring nightmare: a great white somehow getting past the shark net and homing straight on Johnny. It was a fear that Johnny himself liked to laugh at. "That's 'cause you're from Canada," he would tell her. "You know how people here will think Canadians get attacked by, like, bears and shit? It's the same thing."

"Canadians do get attacked by bears," she said defensively. "I mean, every once in a while."

"Every once in a while."

"It does happen."

"You know someone personally who's been attacked by a bear? You know even a friend of a friend who got eaten by a bear?"

"There are shark attacks in the news. I read about them."

"They're in the news," he said reasonably, "because they are news. If there was anything ordinary about them, they wouldn't exactly be news, now would they?"

And he gave her that grin, that broad white grin flashing against his tanned face, deep lines radiating out from his eyes. *All that man is, is a child grown older,* Hilary's mother had sniffed, but then Johnny turned that same smile on her, called her ma'am and held open doors and asked what kind of wine she liked so he could go buy a bottle before putting the chicken and corn on the grill. *A child grown older,* Hilary's mother had repeated, before relenting a little. *But he's got nice manners, that one. And he seems to treat you well. You seem happy.*

Hilary stood up in the sand, scanning the water, twisting the small diamond ring along her finger.

She saw surfers in the distance, bobbing in the bright blue as they waited for waves that didn't seem to be coming. They were too far away to tell if Johnny was among them. The cry lingered in her mind, uneasily, like a dream you couldn't remember enough to figure out why it disturbed you.

And then, in the stretch of water directly in front of her, she saw his silver head break the surface.

See, she told herself, *you were just being silly* . . . But there was no denying the weakness in her knees, the long sigh escaping her.

Still.

Something odd about the way his face and torso were . . . rising from the surface like that. Something odd, too, about the way the little kids acted. Busy with their pails and shovels and castle building, they saw him coming and broke, scattering up the sand, one of them yelling "Mama! Mama!"

Water streamed off his body, that silver hair he was so proud of slicked along his head and shoulders. She saw he was naked. He had gone into the water in blue and white boardshorts and was coming out smoothly nude, just the tiger's-eye necklace circling his throat, and the black leather cord with the shark's tooth falling between his nipples, as unconcerned about his genitals swinging freely between carved-out thighs as if emerging from the shower with only herself to witness.

Then his eyes locked on hers, and he came toward her in a way that seemed much too fluid, and he gave her a grin, white jagged teeth inside that tanned skin, and it was not the grin, the teeth, she remembered.

And Hilary felt, in that moment, the first unhinging of her sanity.

He was right in front of her and he smelled of seaweed and something else, something that made her remember her father's gleaming coffin beneath its weight of roses, and he took her wrist in his hand. His grip was too tight and too hot. He brought her gently to the ground and knelt in front of her, the two of them on her oversized red towel, and he said, "What's my name?"

"What—"

"What's my name?"

"Johnny."

He cocked his head. "Maybe we can think of something else. Where do I go?"

She stared at him.

His eyes were like sun-scorched discs of violet. No man had eyes like that. Those were not Johnny's eyes. Johnny's eyes were blue, like faded denim. This man's pupils were like small black pits she could see all the way down into, to where things slithered at the bottom. The hot grip on her wrist, the dripping nakedness, were repulsive to her, and she tried to squirm away but he pulled her closer.

"Where do I go?" he said. "Where is the heart?"

"The heart?"

"The heart of things. The center. I have people waiting and I mustn't be late." Again, the grin. "It's rude."

"I don't know," she whispered. It was very hard to get the words out. She said, "What happened to Johnny? My Johnny?"

"Oh." Casual flick of his head. "That one's gone." He lowered his face to hers, breathed in deeply, his nostrils quivering. She was aware of her own long body, exposed in the white bikini. She felt very cold. The sun seemed to have gone away. Maybe that's why she was trembling?

"Ahhhh," he said, and smacked his lips. She caught again the sharp white teeth. Cannibal teeth, she thought. Didn't cannibals file their teeth like that? And this person, this thing, who was not Johnny even though he was in Johnny's body, rocked back his head and rolled it along his shoulders and said, "It's good to be back. It is." Then the scorched-out eyes leveled with hers and she tried to look away, but he grasped her jaw and guided her face back to his. Once again she was spiraling into the black void of those pinprick pupils, pinpricks that widened and deepened as if to take her in and swallow her down. For a moment she thought he would kiss her and she felt, again, that odd freewheeling sense of a mind coming loose, the first bricks tumbling out of a wall. "Look at you, little puss," said the Johnny-thing. "I guess we could have some fun," and he was tugging her to her feet, and she wanted to scream but her voice was snuffed out and she wanted to run yet felt herself padding after him, as he hummed and sang, as the beach stretched away on either side and surfers waited for waves and sunbathing tourists went about their day. As if it were any other.

Chapter Five

Lucas

In the dream, the painter asked him, *What's your name? What's your game?* She was almost singing it, like she was onstage and he was, for once, the audience. Then she straddled him on the chair and brought her lips to his throat.

He swept hair away from her cheek and smiled at her. That was when her skin began to darken, and her eyes rolled back, showing only the gleaming whites, which then dissolved into blood, spilling down her face, and he saw that her mouth was stitching itself shut and yet still she could speak, the voice an ancient thing from the underside of the world. *Ashes to ashes,* it said, and *dust to dust,* and it said, *Asha,* and it said again, *Asha,* and he realized this face was actually his face, that he was trapped behind it, blind and mute, the name beating in his skull like someone pounding on a door—

And he woke.

He woke with the image of a pretty young woman clutching a human heart in her hand, he woke with his hands flying to his chest, but it was intact, his own heart secure inside its bones.

*   *   *

He didn't like the silence, the way it filled his house. He grabbed up the remote and turned on music through the rooms. The sun was just starting to rise.

In the shower he let the hot water stream over him, let John Coltrane fill the space around him. Steam and water and "Naima." He leaned his forehead against the smoked-glass shower door and closed his eyes.

. . . and he could feel her out there, in the city, moving toward him . . .

Coltrane. Focus on Coltrane. He turned off the water.

. . . and he could feel her, she was turning off Sunset, walking up Griffin Road, past the pretty pretty houses of the rich, loose stones scattering out beneath her boots, hillside falling away to her left, gaps in the trees affording glimpses of the plaza beneath, the city beyond . . .

"Ashes, ashes," he heard himself muttering. "We all fall down."

Except Asha was gone.

He toweled off his hair and wrapped another towel around his waist. He needed to smoke. Trailing footprints of wet along the floorboards, he padded down the hall to his bedroom, checked for cigarettes, couldn't find them.

. . . she was coming up his driveway, up to the stainless-steel gate, she was leaping up onto the gray brick wall and down the other side, she was drifting past his black Mercedes SUV, his small collection of motorcycles, she was at the front door . . .

He checked the living room, where he found the coat he'd thrown across one of the sofas. He patted down the pockets, but his smokes weren't in them.

In the kitchen, he chugged down half a beer and pressed the cold can against his forehead. The dog slept on the floor, unconcerned.

John Coltrane went away.

The music snapped off like a bone cleanly breaking.

He listened to the sound of his front door open and close.

Footsteps in the hall.

. . . *she was moving down the hallway and through the front rooms now* . . .

Sound of the terrace doors, sliding open.

He took a moment to finish off the beer, then tossed the can in the recycling bin—*You might bring on the end of the world as you know it,* a voice said inside him, *but at least you recycle*—and walked through the ground floor to the terrace.

The scent of cigarette smoke was the first thing he noticed. He scanned the terrace: the bar at one end, the deck furniture, the elevator and stairway. Nothing, no one. Although, as he turned, he caught a flash of movement at the very edge of his vision.

"Painter," he said quietly.

He noted again the shifting, multilayered shadows by the bar.

"Come," he whispered, his eyes on that patch of dark. Something was moving inside it. "Come play."

But when he finally heard the footsteps, they came from behind him.

A large crow fluttered up from behind the bar, perched briefly on the railing, and took off.

Feeling that gaze on him, the cool, steady weight he thought he'd know anywhere, Lucas turned.

She stood some feet away from him. Keeping that same careful distance as in the dreams. She wore a thin leather jacket over a tank top and black silk pants, flat-heeled boots: clothes you could move in. Her dark hair was longer than when they'd met in the desert, sweeping back from a dramatic widow's peak and dropping in a straight, heavy curtain down her body, but he knew that from the dreams. What he hadn't expected—what hadn't registered in the dreamlife—was the loss of weight. As if something had taken her lean, athletic frame and stripped it to its barest essentials. It made her look almost unbearably fragile, which he knew she wasn't, and both older and younger at the same time. She stepped into an oblong of light thrown off the glass doors and he saw those blue eyes, which looked oldest of all.

"Good to see you." He heard how soft his voice was, as if she were a deer he might scare away. No, not a deer: something that itself could be vicious and predatory: bobcat, perhaps. Her hands were by her sides, his eyes dropping to the cigarette between her fingers. "I thought you quit."

"Yeah," she said, sighing out the word, and flicked the cigarette over the railing. He saw the pack—the same pack he'd been looking for—on the deck table behind her, along with his own silver Zippo. He was sure he hadn't left them there. He was sure that just minutes before they had been deep in the house.

"So how is everyone?" Lucas said. "The kid, the not-so-significant other? How are things at the office?"

She smiled at the last, which he hadn't expected. "Work sucks."

"You mean you don't love what you do?"

She held herself still for a moment—she now possessed, Lucas noticed, an incredible stillness, another quality he hadn't picked up on in the dreams, and moved her head ever so slightly from side to side.

He felt a strange sensation in his chest, as though a bird's wings brushed against the organ there. Lucas said, "So is that why you've finally come to me?"

"I haven't 'come to you.'"

"And yet you're here."

"I need to know about the dreams."

She was studying him carefully.

"The dreams," he said blankly.

He saw her bite down on the inside of her cheek. She said, "If they're truly shared between us."

He snorted. She had traveled all the way here from wherever the hell she'd been for such an obvious answer? "You mean you seriously—you doubt this?" He examined her face inside the frame of light. She was a Summoner, he knew, or at least the next best thing—

but the Summoners he'd seen in the desert, including
that arrogant prick of a so-called "boyfriend," who should
have died and burned on that fucking rock—yet he recalled their eyes as light and heat, changing hues according to some internal register of magic or emotion or
both. But the shade of the painter's eyes never changed.
And they always seemed cold.

"You doubt this?" he said again, and she stepped
sideways into shadow, and out of his scrutiny. But not
before he thought he'd glimpsed something in her
expression—that cold-sky gaze—that intrigued him. Even
though he stayed where he was, he could feel himself
pulled toward her. Just as in the dreams. "I never
doubted," he said. "I always knew."

She was melding into the shadows in some weird, unnatural way, but his eyes had adjusted to the near dark
and he'd figured out what to look for. If he wasn't able
to follow her as she moved around the terrace, as silent
as smoke, he could angle himself, his words, in the vague
direction of where she was. He didn't consider himself a
particularly talkative man, but now he seemed positively
chatty, as if the weight of his speech would keep her anchored here a while longer. He wished she would step
into the light again. He wanted to see her. He wanted to
touch her.

"I know everything about you, painter," he said.
Then, "Well, maybe not everything. But I know where
you were born. How old you were when your parents
died in that plane crash. I know that's when you first
encountered . . ." The prince. The boyfriend. Lucas
knew his name, but couldn't bring himself to say it. "I
know the man, the uncle, you went to live with after
that and what he did to you. Tried to do to you. I know
you ran away. I know you depended on the kindness
of friends and maybe some strangers while you made a
life for yourself in New York. I know how desperately
you wanted to become a painter, a good one, a great

one. And you did okay. You had some success. But you're not painting much anymore, are you? Why is that?"

Damn. Maybe she was getting better or he wasn't as good at detecting her presence as he'd thought, because she'd slipped away from him. He thought she was at the edge of the terrace—the woman-sized shadow there—but he wasn't sure. He knew she had not left. He still felt that cool, steady gaze, like balm on a sunburn.

"I know this," he went on, "because of all those conversations we had. In the dreams. In various places in the dreams. And you know so much about me now, don't you? More than you'd like, probably. You know what I've been doing, where I've been playing, who I got to be for a while . . ."

"Max." The name floated from the dark, and he could hear her amusement in it. He'd been right, she was at the corner of the terrace, and now drifting along the edge of the roof.

"Does he know?" Lucas said. "The little prince?"

She didn't answer.

"You're sinking, painter. Beneath the weight of it all. I can see it. Why can't he?" He was thinking of what he'd glimpsed in her eyes, and how she'd recognized his recognition, ducking into shadow. She did not answer him. "Does he know," Lucas continued, "just how lost you're getting, all alone inside yourself, inside all that magic?" He wasn't saying it to manipulate her; he genuinely wanted to know.

No answer. Nothing.

The sound of sirens spiraled up from the grid of the city below.

He scanned the terrace for her, looking for that shadow that wasn't quite a shadow, but found only silence and different shades of dark. Had he blown it? He thought he knew how to challenge her, provoke her, in the way she liked, or maybe needed, to be challenged and provoked. He'd been looking forward to her response. He hadn't expected this . . . absence.

Movement flashed through his peripheral vision.

She was sitting on the railing, fully illuminated in the mingling of city light, moonlight, and house light. She was looking at the pack of cigarettes in her hand. When she knew he was watching, she flung it into the empty space beyond her. "You should really quit."

"Jesus, woman, give me a break. I can only get rid of so many vices."

"They're looking for you."

They.

"The hybrids," she said. "Asha's leftovers. They want something from you."

"The music," he said.

"Why?"

"I don't think I know."

"You don't think . . . ?"

"I don't think they know either. They're not what you'd call thinking creatures."

She pressed her lips together, looking out at the city. He wondered if she was thinking of the hybrids still out there, maybe lurking and living right in Los Angeles, although he doubted it. They gravitated away from dense urban areas. Maybe that kind of packed population aroused a bloodlust even they couldn't handle. *Nice place to visit . . .*

Jess said, "Maybe all we're doing is culling. What if some of them are smarter than we ever thought? Have some kind of plan, have had it all along? Maybe we're working for them and don't even know it."

"Culling the weak ones from the herd," he said slowly. He held the idea in his mind, turning it this way and that: he found it interesting.

"The sick ones. The crazy ones."

"They're all crazy."

"Maybe," she said. Then: "I should probably kill you."

"You could try." At that she laughed, and he took note of the arrogance in the sound. *Careful, painter. You don't know the kind of songs I have in me.* "If you could truly pull it off," he said, "maybe that's how it's meant to be."

"I didn't know you were so fatalistic."

"If I were to die by someone's hand," he said, liking the old-fashioned nature of *by someone's hand,* "I'd want it to be yours."

She lifted her head, her eyes widening.

He grinned. "It's a compliment."

She was attempting to bite back a smile. "I bet that's the nicest thing you'll ever say to me."

"Hope not."

She looked at him sidelong—rather warily, he thought. The moment felt awkward. To get them past it, he said, "But that's not why you came here."

"The . . . music. Will you give it to them?"

And in that moment, he went past the decision he'd already made, into a whole new kind of resolve. "I'd rather die."

"Really."

Her eyes flashed, and he could feel the hairs stir on his arms, the back of his neck, as a thin electric sensation skated the surface of him. He felt himself probed, gauged, and measured. He lifted his hands a little, showing empty palms. "I'd rather you kill me right here and now. I don't want what they want, don't trust it. The kind of world they want. And there's nothing they can give me—"

"Power."

"I don't care about power."

"There's power in your music. You care about that."

"I have enough," he said. "I don't need to sell my soul. What's left of it."

"You nearly sold the world."

He shrugged. "What's done is done. We've moved on."

"There's been so much death. And you don't regret any of it. I should kill you just for that—"

"But you won't," he said. "You want to know why?"

"Enlighten me."

"Because we're linked," he said. "I'm all tangled up in your soul, and vice versa, and not even your royal highness of a boy toy can say that. I'm closer to you than anyone. Anyone. And it murders your insides to know this, but if I go down, you go with me. That's right, isn't it? You can't kill me without sacrificing yourself."

"It won't always be like this."

"You think you can change us? The nature of us?"

"Good night, Lucas. It's been real. It's been very real."

She brushed past him, deliberately, bumping him out of her way so he could feel close-up the strength in her. And the anger. He reached for her and caught her arm. She didn't break from his grasp and he didn't expect her to. She looked at the hand on her biceps, the large palm and long, strong fingers of a born guitarist crushing her sleeve. Beneath the leather she was muscle and bone. There was no softness.

"Whatever happens," he said, "I won't hurt you unless I have to. I would kind of like to protect you."

"From what? Bad dreams?"

"I'm not an evil man," he said, and deep down he believed this. "I'm just not a good one." It was a decent parting line, he felt, a good moment for them to break off from each other, but she continued to stand there, and the moment slipped into the next moment and she was still with him, and it was better than the dreams. It could never be like this in the dreams. "Why did you come here?" he said. "Why did you really come here?" Maybe he pulled her into him or maybe she stepped into the space of him, he didn't know. Maybe it was both.

When Jared's voice arrowed up from his memory: *He's coming for you and the other one.*

But the memory chose not to end there, Jared's voice

slipping on through the folds of his brain: *Of course she's the other, how could it be any other way, because you're tangled up in each other and you don't know why. But he does. You can bet money on that, my friend. And your life and your soul while you're at it.*

"Jess," he murmured, "Jessamy," and he lowered his face toward hers, and saw her flinch, but he wasn't trying to kiss her. He touched foreheads, and they continued to stand there, breathing each other in, and somehow the gesture comforted both of them. *He's coming for you too, painter.* He needed to explain this to her, if she didn't know this already, but not now. He could save it for the dreams. For now he could savor the flesh-and-blood feel of her, and know she was savoring him in return. No matter how much she denied it. *It murders your insides.* If he was a different kind of man, he thought, something like that would hurt his feelings.

His hands glided up to her shoulders and her face, her skin smooth and cool beneath the backs of his fingers. It was enough—at least for now—to touch her like this.

"Be careful," he said.

She pulled away from him, and he let her. She walked toward the edge of the terrace, where it jutted out over empty space. "Damn men," she called over her shoulder. He laughed out loud.

In one smooth, fluid move—it was lovely to watch—she grabbed the railing and vaulted over it, body streaming into the long drop.

He got to the railing in time to see her land on her feet, knees bending deep and hands touching road. Then she was rising, moving with that long-legged stride toward the motorcycle parked on the shoulder. *Turn,* he thought. *Look.* And she did, gazing up across the distance at him, swinging her leg over the bike. She didn't bother with a helmet. "So when did you learn to ride one of those?" he muttered, and realized that the bike she was now peeling away on was his own Ducati.

Hell, she could have it. He had others.

*   *   *

He was whistling as he walked back into the house.

The twin stood in front of the fireplace, cocking his head at the oil painting on the wall of the woman-thing with her leathery wings, her flesh-and-blood prize clutched in her talons. He stood so motionless that for a moment Lucas could believe that he himself was an object of art, chosen specifically for this room, this corner: a tall, angular figure in white shirt and slacks, lock of white-blond hair artfully grazing the tip of one high cheekbone. His body tossed a long shadow across the wall and the shadow, too, seemed to belong there as if designed to be there, part of a study in contrasts. All this whistled through Lucas's mind in the moments it took for him to fully register what he was seeing, as the statue came to sudden life, swiveling around, leveling a beatific smile in Lucas's direction.

Lucas said, "How the fuck did you get in here?"

Which is when he heard the slightest of footfalls behind him, the gentle give of a floorboard, and he turned to see the fire poker coming at his head.

He fell into a darkness too thick for dreams. A pulse rose up through the dark, found him, and closed round him and then moved inside him, throbbing to the rhythms of some unseen monstrous heart, until the pain in his head slammed along to the heart and words rose from the sliver of space in between: *Coming for you. Finish what you started. Coming for you. Finish what you started. . . .*

He woke up in chains.

Chapter Six

He thought: *This can't be right.*

Stone floor.

Cold.

Motherfucker of a headache.

Steel at wrists and ankles.

And—every time he moved—the rattling snake song of chains.

Also, he seemed to be naked.

Groaning, feeling the cold air in every nook and cranny, he forced himself to open his eyes. Black concrete pressed his face. He lifted his head, a fresh wave of pain breaking through it, to squint at the figure across the room: Some other guy, also naked, tattooed, and chained up, lifting his head to stare dazedly back at him. It took a full minute for the realization to work itself through his sorry brain that the other dude was in fact himself; he was staring at a wall of reflective glass.

He brought his arms up in front of him, chains clinking, and rolled over onto his elbows. It took a moment to brace himself before he dared to lift his head again, the pain sliding around his skull, thrusting fingers of nausea in his gut. *This can't be right. 'Cause if it is—*

"You," he croaked.

The man in white stood in the corner, his reflection looming in the mirrored wall behind him. His pale hair was slicked back from his high-boned face as if he'd just stepped out of the shower. He looked, Lucas thought, positively dewy. Lifting a cut-crystal glass to his lips, fingers splayed against the shimmer of wine, he regarded Lucas with narrowing eyes.

"My name is Stefan," he announced. As if this should mean something. He took a sip of wine, closed his eyes, and held it in his mouth a long moment before swallowing. Lucas thought, *Pretentious fuck.* "Maybe when this situation is resolved you'll share a bottle of this with my sister and me. We could get to know each other."

He's a psycho, Lucas thought, and forced down a rising sense of panic. *He's going to torture the shit out of me and peel off my skin and hang it on his bedroom wall or something. This can't be right. This can't—*

He shut down hard on that line of thinking; it wouldn't help him. The freak watched him, smirking and sipping wine, as if expecting a response, but Lucas would be damned if he'd say anything before he had some idea of how to play this. Instead he rocked back into a sitting position, the concrete damn cold beneath his naked ass, and took in the situation. His wrists were cuffed with a slight play of chain between them, another chain extending to hook through a steel pole. Like a dog chained in a front yard, Lucas thought, the kind of dog you passed and saw and felt sorry for. His ankles were also shackled. The room itself was small, bare, and gleaming. White walls, track lighting overhead, poured-concrete floor. It was like an art gallery. And he was the sole installation. He looked at the glass wall doubling the size of the space and wondered who was behind it, gazing out, perhaps right through his own reflection. The sister? Others? How many?

They're looking for you.

The painter had told him this. And he had already

known. Why hadn't he taken it more seriously? Had he considered himself so invincible, the hybrids and freak twins so inconsequential?

Well, yes, actually. He had.

"I feel wretched about this," Stefan said, in a tone that suggested otherwise. "But we do what we have to." His English was clipped, carefully pronounced, a rich-kid transatlantic English picked up in some jet-setter academy somewhere. "Because it's kind of an honor to have you with us. I mean, really. I hope you know that." Lucas felt another rising bubble of panic. *Fuck off, panic. You are not helpful.* "But it's easy enough for you to set things right," Stefan said. "And then we can show you to a room that's a lot more luxurious. You can get the VIP treatment you deserve."

He waited for a response. Lucas reached up to brush the hair out of his eyes. The pain in his head was receding. At least that was something. His fingers grazed the still-crusting ridge along his temple, the surrounding skin gone stiff with dried blood. Stefan lifted one shoulder in what might have been a shrug—C'est la vie—and said, in that milquetoast tone of his: "All you have to do is play."

He lifted his hand, angling his fingers toward a spot behind Lucas. Lucas saw a guitar leaning prettily against the wall. It was well within the reach of his chains.

And now he chose to speak, dredging up his voice from a throat gone thick and bone-dry. "So that's it? I play, and the devil comes to town?"

"Kind of dramatic to call him the devil."

"Whatever promise he made you, you really think he's gonna keep it, once you're done running these errands for him?"

"You were Asha's little errand boy. It worked out well for you. You went from complete loser to . . ."

". . . a naked dude in chains. Good point. But that was different."

"*Is* there a difference? *I* don't see the difference. I

know this is hard for you." Stefan cradled the glass in both hands. His voice curdled with a sympathy that set Lucas more on edge than he already was. "It's not easy to be so gifted. It might even be a kind of burden. The responsibility of fulfilling your own potential, the moral obligation of sharing that gift with the world."

"The *world* needs a cure for global warming. It couldn't give a shit about somebody's artistic *gifts*."

"You underestimate yourself, my son."

Son? They were about the same age.

"I've been there, Lucas. You and I are of the same kind. I spent some years, some very dark years, wrestling with my own gifts. Did you know I died once?" Again, that bizarre assumption that Lucas should know anything about him at all. "When I was a child. I was struck by lightning, can you believe that? The odds of that? My heart stopped. I was dead for twenty seconds. When I came back—to the blubbering gratitude of my parents, as you can imagine—I had a new vision. A new understanding of the world. He gave that to me."

"He," Lucas said.

"The eternal stranger. The Soulbreaker. The Lord of Bones. He goes by many names, of course—he'll choose a new one once he gets here. He speaks to me, Lucas. Even from such a vast distance. Ever since I was a boy."

Oh, God. Lucas buried his head in his arms. He said, his voice muffled, "There are medications for that kind of thing."

"His voice doesn't come to me in words. It can't be contained in the tiny boxes of language. His voice is like a bright light that flares up inside me. It scalds my blood, scorches the insides of my body. I feel like I'm dying all over again. But then, in that flash of light—some new piece of knowledge is placed inside me. That's what guided me here, Lucas, to this country, this city, this very spot on this very street. That's what led me to design this *very special* house"—Stefan held out his arms, as if not just to gesture at whatever extended beyond this room but to embrace it—"and oversee its construction. Because everything had to be just right. The angles. The calculations. Even the timing. And that's what guided me to you. Because no one else can hear his voice, embody his mission, surrender body and soul to his imperatives. I was chosen. He chose me. There is greatness in surrender, Lucas. You would do well to learn. In order to become the true master, you must learn to be the slave."

"Usually the slave stays a slave. He tries to rise up, the master flogs the shit out of him."

"Your vision is too limited, Lucas. But that's okay. I'm here to help you." Stefan smiled, then, still smiling, hurled his goblet against the wall above Lucas's head, the smash a cloud that rained jagged glass. As Lucas ducked, Stefan came forward with neat, dancer's steps and kicked him in the spine. The pain was like fire. Lucas hit the ground, unbalanced by the pain as much as the kick. Then Stefan was crouching beside him, grabbing his hair, pressing something sharp against the underside of his jaw. "How dare you," Stefan hissed, his breath smelling of overripe berries. "You are not worthy of what you carry. You really are a *mistake*. A freak accident." He dragged something sharp along Lucas's throat, then shoved his head away and stood. He held a thin silver dagger in his hand. He licked Lucas's blood off the blade with the same expression of pleasure he'd had with the wine. "But it's not too late to step up. The way you did with Asha."

"I loved Asha," Lucas said. He could still feel the dagger at his neck. "I don't think I love you."

Stefan smiled down at him. "Just give it some time."

They gave him over to the howl of his own body: for food, for water, for sleep, all of which they denied him. Noise invaded the room at all hours, blasting through the speakers set high in the corners: sirens blaring and dogs barking and people screaming, Japanese pop music

played at high speed, canned laughter from television
sitcoms, commercial jingles, the same Barry Manilow
song played over and over for hours. They kept him in
total darkness, then blazing light, then hours of strobe
light. At intervals too uneven to predict they turned the
sprinkler system on and drenched him with ice water.
Even as he curled up like a shivering animal on the
concrete, he opened his mouth wide for the water.

Every so often the door opened. Stefan stood inside
the frame holding the guitar with the awkwardness of a
man who had never learned a single chord. "Will you
play for us?" he would inquire politely. Lucas's response
was not so polite. Stefan would sigh, shake his head,
step back, kick the door shut, and the room filled again
with overlapping voices of people shouting—at that
point Lucas could believe the voices had bodies right
there in the room with him, shouting at him in German.

And then the noise stopped, they allowed him to be
dry and warm again, and Stefan brought him a bowl of
soup, setting the tray on the floor and pushing it to just
within reach of the chains. He knew he probably shouldn't
eat it. He thought of all the different things they could
have put in it. He wolfed it down, tipping the bowl to
get at every creamy, meaty, salty drop. Only when he
was convinced that he'd consumed every speck did he
toss the bowl into the corner and stretch out on the floor
and fall asleep, wondering if he'd wake up, how he'd
wake up, but in that moment not caring.

Pain again.

Dark blooms of pain through his kidneys. His lower
back. He opened his eyes to the inside of a blindfold.
He was strung up, his weight dragging at his wrists, his
bare toes just touching cold floor. His throat felt like a
creature trapped beneath a magnifying glass beneath the
blazing sun. The soup, he thought. Salt in the soup. Another blow to his right hip. Someone using him for kick-

ing practice. He could hear the person breathing. Whoever
he was, he sounded heavy on his feet, clumsy. Which
didn't stop the kicks from being any less painful. There
was a pause, and he had just started to hope it was
over—this part of it, anyway—when the next kick connected with the back of his head and knocked him
into blackness.

"That's enough," a woman's voice was saying as he
came to. "You're done. You can leave now."

The footsteps, the heavy breathing, retreated.

A door opened and shut.

Then someone else was stepping up close to him.
"Poor little rock star." The touch of fingertips on his
face, soft and smooth, gliding the length of his jawline.
The press of something cold against his mouth. Oh god.
Water. Thank god. Water. Drops of it spilling into his
mouth, his withered throat, his whole body jutting out
for it as she held it just beyond his reach, so that he
could sense it, smell it, his need so gripping and intense
he could practically see it through the blindfold.

Then he sensed her moving away from him, taking the
water away from him, and he might have cried out. He
heard a gentle clink as she set the glass on the floor.
Then she was behind him, her fingers moving up through
his tangled, matted hair as she tugged off the blindfold.
He closed his eyes against the sudden glare.

When he opened them again she was sitting cross-
legged on the floor, studying him, her head tilted to the
same angle her brother's had been. A manila envelope
lay in front of her.

"My name is Ingrid," she said.

"I don't care."

"You're a lonely man."

Fixating on the glass of water beside her—he could
feel the beads of moisture as if they were slipping down
his own forehead—he barely heard her.

"Because this is the part where we threaten your

loved ones," the woman said. "Except there aren't any
loved ones to threaten, are there? Your mother. Your
sisters. When was the last time you saw them? Or cared?"

He wished she would shut up. All he wanted was that
fucking water.

"Do you even know where they are? We can tell you.
People like them are so easy to hunt." She slipped photographs out of the envelope and fanned them out across
the floor. "The younger one grew up to look like you,
don't you think? We can give you their addresses, phone
numbers, e-mail, if you'd like to get back in touch. Our
colleagues are keeping a very close eye on them. And
speaking of our colleagues." She withdrew a second
group of photographs and spread them out above the
first. "This is some of their work," she said. "This is
what they specialize in."

His gaze swept over the images, the demon-torn, partially eaten female bodies. Whatever.

The *water*.

"You know what they believe, our hybrid friends?"
the woman said. "That by eating us they will somehow
absorb the secrets, the essence, of humanity."

"I think they're just really, really hungry."

"What do you think they'd like to do to your pretty
sisters, your mother?"

"What about my dad? Let them go after him."

"Generous of you, Lucas, but he's already dead."

Lucas shrugged.

"Play for us, Lucas. What do you say? Play, and the
rest of your family can die a little more pleasantly."

"Dead is dead. Doesn't matter."

"Oh . . . I think it matters a lot." She rose, leaving
the photographs scattered below him. "You're a hard
man. It seems your heart is very cold. So why resist, and
put yourself through such discomfort, if you care for
nothing, no one?"

Lucas hung from the chain and searched himself for

strength to speak, to endure words dragged through his tortured throat. "Do you believe what your brother believes, or are you just along for the ride?"

"My brother is a great man."

"Your brother has no idea what the fuck he's getting into. And if he cared at all about you, he would have stashed you somewhere safe. If that place even exists. Look. I've seen this shit up close. You don't want any part of it. No matter what's been promised you. Because all you are," Lucas said, and paused to find more strength, endure more dragging, "is a slave, and this guy—this Lord of Bones—isn't the type to keep a promise to a slave."

"You don't know what you're talking about."

"I see stuff in the music," Lucas said. "And the music's why you're going to all this *effort* for me. So I'd listen to me, if I were you. Cut me loose. Go back to Sweden, or wherever the fuck you're from. Find a career, get married, have kids—have kids with your brother if you want—just forget all this. It's not too late. This is our moment to step . . . back. From the edge. *Your* moment."

"You play mind games with me."

"No. Your brother does that."

"My brother is my life."

And he saw, then, there was no getting through to her. It wasn't just that she was stupid and stubborn and proud, although she seemed all these things. Or that she was damaged, in a way different from her brother but that ran just as deep. He had the sense that there was no *there* there. He had no hope of reaching her. There was nothing to reach.

"My brother is my life," she said again.

"Christ. I'd rather be tortured than listen to this crap."

"We can do that."

She picked up the glass of water and left the room with it, door slamming shut behind her. Lucas hung there and listened to the pain in his body and watched himself in the reflective glass. At least it was something to do.

Stefan returned with a silver jar in his palm. He tipped it toward Lucas to show off its contents. Lucas saw a pale violet glimmer, breathed in a nightflower scent. "Pretty," he said. "What the fuck?"

"You should really tone down the profanity," Stefan said. "You know what jax is, don't you?"

The word *jax* got his attention. It was a paranormal drug absorbed through the skin. Users painted themselves and others with it, and heavy users compulsively scored the same designs over and over in their flesh until the jax-marks became permanent scars.

It took you on a hell of a trip. It took you into another state of being, another reality, granting you the supernatural power of mind travel you didn't have on your own. Ultimately it broke down your mind, destroyed it utterly, but it was a lot of fun getting there. Lucas, who had never touched a drug except caffeine and nicotine after Asha weeded him off his own addiction to heroin, hadn't tried it and didn't want to. But he had watched what it did to others. Kept them dreamy and passive. He had watched what it did to Ramsey Doe, the Bloodangel. Kept him disoriented and helpless and contained, their prisoner in the desert.

But that jax had been blue. Not purple.

"That must be the new stuff," Lucas muttered.

"You're going to go on a little trip, Lucas. You won't enjoy it. It's not a nice place. But I want you to remember something." And he lifted his other hand, showing Lucas a syringe filled with clear liquid. "Think of this as your ticket home. Which makes me the ticket master. You can come back anytime you want. All you have to do is pay me, and I think we know how, yes?"

"Go fuck your sister," Lucas said.

Stefan grinned and tossed the powder in his face.

Lucas rocked his head back, expecting some kind of impact, but for a moment nothing happened. Then the air around and above his head took on a violet shimmer, and Lucas felt some kind of energy charge the air, felt the pressure of it all along his body, squeezing his chest, his stomach, his bowels. The violet light began to . . . harden, then just as quickly to dissolve, into a fine rain sifting over his head, clinging to his skin, slipping in through his mouth and nostrils, the edges of his eyes. At first he felt nothing. Then his skin began to burn. He shrieked, pulling at the chains, looking down at himself, expecting to find flames licking out from his own body, swarming merrily toward his face . . . but all he saw was that film of powder disappearing through his skin.

Something strange was happening with Stefan's face. It was unhinging, the flaps of it peeling away, revealing nothingness behind it. Lucas knew what he saw. The abyss. And the wind came whistling out and right into his face. So cold, so cold, and as it swept over Lucas he felt himself turn into nothingness too, caught on that wind and hurled through Stefan's face into the pit beyond.

For a long time there was darkness and cold.

Slowly, his vision cleared.

He felt ground beneath his feet again.

He was in a hell-land.

A road of black, broken stone swept up to the horizon, lined with telephone poles that were doing double duty, Lucas saw, as crucifixes. Bodies were nailed to each and every one, as far along as he could see, and the air carried the cries and moans of those still alive enough to make them. Beyond them rose buildings and skyscrapers: some were intact, while others lay in ruins, rubble shifting and spilling as creatures dragged themselves through it.

The creatures. Judging from their soiled and tattered

clothing, they had once been human, but now there was no name for what they were. They pulled themselves forward on their bellies, dragging misshapen legs, their faces melted and twisted beyond hope of recognition. Shards of blood-stained mirror jutted from the places where their eyes had probably been. The one nearest Lucas lifted its head, and the skin around the jagged holes puckered and quivered; with a moan, it lurched itself toward him with new speed. Lucas realized it was smelling him. Its brethren joined in with moans of their own. Black shapes fluttered overhead, settling on the telephone wires: birds, Lucas saw. They looked like crows, except for the strange little almost-human faces peering down from the oily nests of feathers. They squawked at Lucas—a sharp syllable of a sound, put on endless repeat, *jag-jag-jag-jag-jag*—and Lucas began to run, although he didn't know what purpose it would serve or where he could possibly go. He ran until the buildings thinned out and there was nothing but waste-land sprawling out to either side, and the birds swooping overhead, their *jag-jag-jags* mingling with the whimpers and cries of the dying.

He kept his eyes averted from the crucified—*so many of them,* a voice kept repeating in his head, *so many so many so many, why wouldn't they just* die *already?*— until a bird swooped low over his head—*jag-jag-JAG!*— and Lucas felt a hard peck at the back of his head, the crawl of warm wet blood on his neck. He grabbed a rock and hurled it at the bird. And missed. The bird shrieked again. And Lucas saw that the men and women had been nailed up in the same position: with one arm stretching out toward the same horizon, as if pointing the way.

As he crested a hill, Lucas shielded his eyes with one hand. Beyond and below, he saw a dark cluster of build-ings, smoke twisting up into the sky.

"Lucas . . ."

Lucas looked up. Saw wound-eyes peering from a wrenched, collapsing face.

"That's where you need to go," whispered the twisted, gaunt, dying thing, as blood poured down his wrists and forearms. *"That's where he waits for you."*

A hand wrapped his ankle, held tight.

One of the belly-slithering creatures, the dark nostrils sniffing and trembling. Lucas yelled and stumbled backward, trying to shake the goddamn thing off, even as it unfolded a different section of what appeared to be its face and Lucas saw the rows of teeth, snapping toward his ankle—

The ground gave way, crumbling, and Lucas felt himself crumbling with it, sliding down into earth. Below waited more of the creatures, an endless pile of them, shifting and churning over one another, their moans like bats spiraling up to meet him. He scrambled for purchase but found none, only the collapse of the earth sliding down, down into the place where those things waited for him with their long-fingered arms and useless legs, the melted faces, multiple mouths opening to show the gleam of teeth—

He scrambled at the dirt, knees slipping. A creature reared from the mud and set its teeth into his ankle. He felt himself being dragged, earth trailing through his clutching hands, the creature taking him down to share him with its kindred. And in the seconds that followed Lucas came to understand how he would be eaten alive, in small bites, and how long it would take him to die.

"I'll play, I'll play, goddammit I'll play—" He screamed the words without registering their meaning. Anything to make it stop.

He opened his eyes, and he was back in the gallery, its sole installation. *Variations on Man Hanging from Chain.* Different parts of his lower body either blazed or itched or crawled; he looked at himself and saw cuts and welts forming a pattern of what looked like bite marks. He felt the throbbing at the back of his skull where the bird had pecked him.

Stefan studied his face, the slack hang of his body.

"I hope you're not too broken for our purposes," he said mildly.

He snapped his fingers in front of Lucas's eyes. He sighed.

Lucas was vaguely aware of two hulking hybrids closing in on either side, the pungent animal smell of them. One freed his wrists from the hook, lugged him none too gently to the chair, and threw him down. Stefan approached with the guitar. "You'll enjoy this, Lucas," he said. "After all, this is what you *do*."

Lucas accepted the guitar, attempted to tune the strings, but couldn't seem to get his hands working. The guitar slid to the ground. "Sorry," Lucas mumbled through his hair, "sorry," and Stefan sighed again. Closing his hands around the neck of the instrument, Lucas counted to himself—

One—

Two—

And on *three* he rose, swinging the guitar at the hybrid behind him. When he heard the happy smash of impact he let go and lunged at Stefan, and looped chain around Stefan's neck, jerking tight. "Get back or I snap his neck," Lucas barked at the hybrids. "I swear to the Lord of Bones himself I'll snap his fucking neck. And you need him, right? He's like your prophet, right?"

"Not him," one hybrid said. "You are."

Neither of them made any movement toward him; they stayed where they were, with something in their eyes that looked like—awe. *You have the mark of Asha on you.*

Lucas looked toward the reflective glass wall and yelled, "Ingrid!"

She appeared in the doorway, a can of Diet Coke in her hand, her jaw slack.

"You're going to give me a gun," Lucas said, "or else you're going to have to start living for somebody else."

"I can't give you a gun," Ingrid said calmly.

Lucas yanked on the chain so hard that Stefan arched backward against him. Stefan coughed and gasped and said hoarsely, "Do what he says, sister."

"But—"

"Are you a fucking retard? Do whatever he says!"

She set the soda on the floor. She drew a 9mm from the waistband of her jeans and held it out to Lucas. Her arm was shaking. "Closer," Lucas said. He didn't dare take any steps himself, afraid he might trip in the shackles and end the game right there. When she was close enough he lifted his hands from Stefan's throat and shoved him to the ground, then grabbed the gun and remembered to turn off the safety. He pointed the gun at Stefan. On his hands and knees, hanging his head and coughing, the other man barely noticed. "Free me," he ordered, and when Ingrid hesitated he shot Stefan in the kneecap. Stefan screamed and dropped to the ground. The hybrids continued to watch Lucas with that same transfixed expression. Looking on the verge of tears, Ingrid approached Lucas and fumbled the key into the lock at his wrists. A loud snap, and Lucas was free, the chain clattering around his feet. He stepped carefully out of it. He was pointing the gun at the middle of Stefan's chest. It would be easy to pull the trigger. Very easy, and very nice. He could still hear the moaning of those things, those no-longer-human things, see bits and pieces of his own wretched expression in their mirror-shard eyes. He could still feel their teeth in his body.

"You said you wouldn't kill him," Ingrid shrieked. "You said."

And later, when he saw what they had become, Lucas would think that of course he should have killed him. He should have killed them both. Instead, he sighed and shot Stefan in the other kneecap. To his deep irritation, the man's screaming increased in pitch and volume.

Casting glances at the two hybrids, who remained exactly
where they were, Lucas looped the chain around Ingrid's
body and pulled it snug, trapping her arms to her sides,
then snapped the lock and pushed her back on her ass.
"Stay," he told her.

He grabbed the can off the floor and gulped down
the soda.

He turned his attention to the two hybrid goonies.
They were between him and the door, and as he took a
step forward they took a step back. And in that moment
Lucas understood what he was to them: some kind of
prize or treasure they wouldn't risk harming and didn't
feel equipped to handle on their own. *You have the mark
of Asha on you.* The taste of blood and ashes filled his
mouth. An idea came to him then and he turned to the
hybrid closest to his own size. He felt Asha in his eyes
and his voice, and from the hybrid's expression Lucas
knew he sensed her too. Lucas said, "Give me your
clothes."

Then he was out of the room and running down a
hallway. It opened up just ahead into something shadowed, cavernous—

He jolted to a stop.

Wind swept his face. The tiled floor beneath his feet
had given way to hard-packed earth. He stepped forward, one step, two steps. He saw gradations of shadow,
a curve of rocky wall.

The hall simply ended in a cave. In the near distance
he could hear the trickle of water. And as the moment
stretched on a new sense overtook him: of some strange
vastness opening in front of him and stretching to either
side, as if the walls and ground he knew to be there
could be easily peeled away, as insubstantial as window
dressing, and the truth that waited behind it was the
kind that would swallow him whole.

He turned and ran in the direction he'd come from,

palms sweating, so that he had to readjust his grip on the gun. He turned left and was in another hallway; and as more turns turned into more hallways he could feel a dark thunderhead of panic threatening to take him apart—

The knowledge he put inside me.

What led me to this place. What led me to design this house.

It wasn't a house. It was some kind of paranormal monstrosity and he was a rat in a maze. Somewhere there was probably a lever for him to press, and they might give him cheese.

He was on the verge of screaming when the monotony of the hall gave way to a staircase. The steps were long and flat, a pale, gleaming marble, and he took them three at a time.

Another hallway.

But this was different from the others. The walls were not smooth and featureless. They were marked by a staggered succession of doors, each one outlined by a radiance that cast eerie shadow patterns across the marble floor. Between the doors hung tall gilded mirrors.

Something familiar about this place.

He felt as if he'd been here before.

In dreams.

Not necessarily his *own* dreams.

He switched the gun from hand to hand, running his palms down the sides of the too-big black jeans he'd taken off the hybrid. Nowhere to go but forward. He wasn't sure why he had such a creeping, crawling feeling; they were only mirrors, after all, and one of these doors would be the way out.

The silence broken solely by his own breathing, he moved from door to door, trying each handle. Locked. And locked. And locked. His reflection ghosted along both sides, pausing at the edge of each frame and rejoining him on the other side of the next (locked) door.

The mirrors opposite each other threw reflections into
reflections, so that his image echoed away from him and
down to the vanishing point.

Something else was in there with it.

A speck. Down at the bottom of the nested reflections.
The only reason he noticed it at all was because of the
sense that it should not be there. It was wrong. As he
moved past mirror after mirror the speck grew larger;
turned into a shadow; lengthened, took on edges; became the dark shape of a man. A walking man. Coming
toward him from the other side of the looking glass.

And that dark cloud inside him came apart, and his
breath hitched in his throat and he aimed the gun at the
mirror to the right of him and fired, and to the left of
him and fired again. The sound of shattered, raining
glass was so satisfying that he shot out the next mirror
he came to, and the next, and kept on pulling the trigger
until there were no more bullets left.

And in that moment he came to the end.

He had run out of hallway.

There was nothing more, just a wall. The final wall.
His breath left his lungs. This couldn't be right. He had
come so far. He had made such an awesome escape.
There had to be something more here, something he just
wasn't seeing.

There was a soft scraping and rustling behind him.

He turned.

The broken glass littering the floor rose in unison,
throwing off scattered gleams of light, becoming an undulating wave that hung, suspended, within the reach of
hall. For almost a full minute, nothing more happened.
The glass seemed to shiver in the air. Lucas stared, his
mind in free fall. He couldn't seem to catch his breath.
Then the bits and studs and pieces of mirror began to
move, drawn toward the same single point at the end of
the hall, slowly at first and then faster and faster, as if
into a vortex. Lucas saw how the glass was assembling
into a shape. The shape of a man, tall and slender, his

mirrored skin turning bright, brighter, until it was such
a dazzling white that Lucas had to turn away or go blind.
Then all the light streaked back into the mirror-man the
same way the glass had done, and the shape consumed
it all—

And fleshed into something human.

"You," said the man born from the mirror-thing, and
began to walk to him. He held out his arms and those
arms seemed to lengthen even as Lucas watched, so that
the man could trail fingers along both walls. And the
smell of him came wafting down the hallway until Lucas
was breathing it in: a scent like jasmine, appealing, until
you detected another note behind it, something fishy and
briny, with wet green things just starting to rot. "You
made things difficult for me, my friend," the man said,
and the shadows lifted away from him and Lucas saw
his face.

It was one of those faces lined and beaten by the sun
so that its true age was impossible to tell: it could have
been a youthful old man or a prematurely aging young
one. He had a lean body, the sleeves of his rumpled
white linen suit pushed up on tanned, corded forearms,
and he moved with a rippling motion that started at the
base of his throat and flowed downward as each foot
came forward, as if something were snaking through his
body into the ground with every step. Smooth silver hair
brushed his shoulders; tiger's-eye and shark tooth neck-
laces looped his throat. His eyes weren't eyes at all, but
sockets filled with smoke; but then he closed them, and
opened eyes that were normal, if an unusually vivid
blue-green. The color of a summer sea.

Lucas's hand was shaking badly, but he managed to
lift the gun. Except he had no bullets left. It hardly mattered. The mirror-man rolled his eyes. "Oh, Lucas," he
said as the gun twisted out from Lucas's hand, and then
the man was holding it, looking at it. The gun became
a thin black snake that wove through the man's wrists
and disappeared inside the white jacket.

Something pressed the back of Lucas's legs. He glanced down over his shoulder and saw nothing, even as the pressure turned painful and forced him to his knees. Lucas saw a hand coming at him, large palm and skinny fingers tipped with daggerlike nails, and Lucas thought of a preacher, some crazy demon preacher about to bless him by driving those nails through his eyeballs. He flinched, but the mirror-man only smiled, a gentle benevolent smile, and said, "You made things difficult for me, but I forgive you. Yes?" Fingers twined in his hair, pulling his head back, so that the man-thing's face hovered above him, flat and large and vivid-eyed, distorted in a way that was not from the angle alone. "Call her," he said, "the child of Shemayan," and a pressure began to build inside Lucas's head, pushing at the inside of his skull. The man said, "Tell her it's time to come together," and Lucas could hear someone screaming, and realized that of course it was him.

Chapter Seven

Jess

The question seemed to come from very far away, and for a moment she thought she was dreaming.

"Are you scared?" Ramsey looked at her across the backseat of the town car.

The driver, a slim man in a black suit, had met them at the Las Vegas airport, amid the *ding-ding-ding* of slot machines and smells of coffee and fast food. He took their luggage—they didn't have much—and ushered them into the hot, dry air, the sun hammering down in that way she remembered.

"Now," she said, "I'm trying not to think about it." Except he deserved a more honest answer. "Yes."

"You'll do just fine," the kid said loyally. "You'll blow them all away."

She had to bite back a smile. He made it sound like she was going in for a job interview.

How odd that the Trials—her Trials—should happen here. Ever since, months ago, Kai had brought up the possibility, Jess had just assumed that such an event would happen somewhere remote, isolated. Instead she found herself gazing out at the newest, biggest hotel to tower over the Strip: the Eden.

Butter-colored walls rose into blue sky, rows of arched windows forming a honeycomb of stone and light. There were no sharp edges or corners to this place; the lines were soft and curved, so that the whole place seemed to undulate, soaking up the sun. They passed between elaborate wrought-iron gates and followed a sweep of road lined with lush, tropical foliage, elaborate fountains, animal statuary, an aviary filled with bright darting specks of birds. Then doors were opening, valets in spotless white inviting them out of the car and through gilded doors, taking her duffel bag out of her hands before Jess could form a protest. "This way, please," said the man with their luggage, leading them through the vast marbled lobby, past the gleaming reception area, where people stood in line to check in, their carry-ons beside them like pets. From somewhere beyond came the ever-present sound of slot machines, the echoing conversations of the massive, shifting crowd. Past an indoor garden and into a small, hushed room with leather-paneled walls. Coffee, tea, and plates of cakes and biscuits ranged prettily across a sideboard. After the clamor they'd passed through to get here, the quiet seemed eerie.

"Is this, like, a VIP room or something?" Ramsey said, looking around him. "Who—"

"Ms. Shepard. My name is Nathan Kinross."

The man facing them was slight of build, nattily dressed, with an olive complexion and dark, gleaming eyes, heavily lashed in a way some women would kill for. "I'm the manager of this hotel. The owner, Jack Daughtry, wanted to greet you himself, but he's been detained. Come with me." Nathan inclined his head toward a door nestled discreetly in the leather panels. Then they were stepping into a brown and gold space flanked by elevators. "This was built for them," Nathan said. "The Summoners. Although never in my wildest dreams did it ever occur to us that there would be—that someone like you . . ." He gazed at her, his mouth opening a little, until Jess felt her face go warm. She looked away. An elevator finally slid open and Nathan beckoned her inside, remembering at the last moment to include the kid as well.

"Call me Jess." She looked at the small man. "So you've had dealings with them. You know about them."

"The Summoners," Nathan said, the word sliding off his tongue with such ease. It gave Jess another jolt; never before had she discussed them with anyone other than Ramsey or the Summoners themselves. "I'm from one of the friend-families—they call us *harigkkinon,* which is also a Sajae word to describe a type of bridge. Or so I've been told. We pass down our relationships with the Summoners from generation to generation. Like heirlooms."

"I've never heard of that," Jess said. "Of—*harigkkinon.*" At least she could get the word out. Kai had given up trying to teach her the Sajae language. She had no ear for it, or for any language. She was waiting for the day she'd find some kind of spell-form that would do the learning for her.

Nathan nodded, as if her ignorance did not surprise him. "Just another sign of a broken, disintegrating culture. Their culture, I mean, not ours. Perhaps that's about to change. Think of what you represent, Ms. Shepard—"

"Jess."

"—fresh life, fresh blood, fresh magic. You are what they need to lead them into the future. Whether or not they want to realize it. Which many of them don't. Arrogant bastards. But you did not hear me say that." He slipped his keycard into a set of double doors and pushed. The suite could have doubled as someone's lavish apartment, Jess thought, as Nathan showed them through the rooms. "You'll be dining with the Summoners tonight," he told them. "Someone will fetch you at eight. In the meantime, relax and enjoy." And he was gone.

"Look at this place," Ramsey said. "It's so . . . I don't know. What's the word?"

"Organic?"

She meant the curving, swooping lines, the way the place didn't seem constructed so much as sculpted, molded. The warm golden tones of the walls and furniture seemed to bend their shimmer around her. She touched the gleaming bronze swirl of a floor lamp, ran her eyes over richly textured rugs. Things seemed familiar yet strange, as if these items she could put the most mundane of names to—table, bed, window—were being viewed through some alien prism, created by a consciousness worlds removed from the other parts of the hotel, where tourists shopped and ate and lost money and had no idea what was going on up here, beyond these walls, these secret elevators. This suite had nothing to do with Vegas—or any place that Jess had come from, or known, before now.

This was built for them.

She turned, saw herself reflected in the gilded full-length mirror.

"Jess!" Ramsey was in the next room. "Check this out!"

She caught a blur of movement at vision's edge. In the mirror. Behind her. She looked over her shoulder, but the room was empty. No one here, only her. No one's image in the mirror, other than hers. She formed a quick mindcast and sent it through the suite, probing for any signs of presence other than Ramsey's. Nothing.

"Jess! Are you coming or what?"

The suite's massive central room was divided into a study and a sitting area. Ramsey was kneeling beside the low, heavy table carved from gleaming burlwood; an elaborate architectural model took up the whole surface. Except as Jess drew closer she saw it wasn't a building that had been so carefully rendered in miniature, but some kind of city.

A labyrinthine city.

And she saw in the model the same arabesque lines, undulating walls, and sun-baked desert tones reflected in the suite, as if the one had inspired the other. Her eyes traced—attempted to trace—the model's network of passageways, rising and falling to a rhythm of shifting walls. She saw the gates, the tiny courtyards, the series of gardens and pools, the rambling markets, the crowded warrenlike housing that lined the outer edges, the elegant towers that rose up from deep inside the Labyrinth center.

"A mistake, to make that thing," a familiar voice said from the doorway. "Although I appreciate Daughtry's intentions."

"It's beautiful," Jess said. "So this is it? The Labyrinth? This is the place you call home?"

Kai shrugged. "This is a vague attempt at a rough guess at a crude sketch of it." He was walking around the model, judging it from different angles, his shadow slanting across it. "What it can't get across, what you have to understand about the nature of the place, the essence of it, is that it was a living, changing thing. It had a life all its own. Its own heart and soul. No one built the Labyrinth. All we could do was keep trying to map it as it built itself.

"Parts of it—the central area, here, and these areas spiraling out—were stable. Safe. But these outer edges, these stretches here, and over here, were constantly changing. They were dangerous. The ground could literally disappear beneath your feet; a new wall could suddenly form through your own body." Kai brushed the arch of a gate. "This is supposed to be the Westgate," he mused. "The Westgate marked off the farthest edge of the known world of the Labyrinth. Beyond it was . . ." Jess could see him searching for a phrase. ". . . toxic country. Toxic magic."

"Toxic magic," Jess said.

She was familiar with the phrase. Magic that got away

from you. Went perverse. Contaminated areas . . . and sometimes people . . . and made them dangerous, sometimes in the weirdest of ways.

Kai glanced at Ramsey. "The kind of magic that bends and changes things, according to its own unknowable logic. You didn't go anywhere near there if you valued your body, or mind, the way it already was." And he seemed to turn inside himself, as if searching through some private landscape. "But every now and then someone would plunge through those gates. Into all that wild, brutal magic. Would choose to do that. Many people considered it a form of suicide, but I think it was something very different. I think the place called them. Lured them. We called them Westgaters. We never saw them again. Or maybe we did, and we just didn't know it. There was no way to know them anymore." His eyes took on a soft, gold-flecked gleam. "That was a way of calling someone crazy. *You stupid Westgater.* You could also use it as a verb. *Go Westgate yourself.*"

"Go Westgate yourself," Ramsey murmured. He grinned.

Kai's gaze rested on Jess, his eye color turning a deep, warm hue that made it impossible for her to look away. She felt an inner stirring in response: heat rising through her, currents of a different kind of magic. *You.* Her mind formed the word. She felt the touch of his own mind in response.

You're sinking, painter.

And that other voice—that honeyed, crafty voice— broke through her memory. Broke the moment. And now she had to look away.

He doesn't know you like I do.

I'm all tangled up in your soul.

You can't kill me without sacrificing yourself.

She resisted the urge to press her hands to her temples. She kept her face averted from Kai, as if just the thought of Lucas had stamped a mark on her forehead—

or invoked a mark already there, just hidden. Something sick and cold was spreading through her gut.

Ramsey, she noticed, had disappeared from the room. Taking his cue like he always did.

"Hey," Kai murmured.

Rather than look up, she stepped into him, engulfing herself in the planes of his body, the strength and warmth.

"I wanted to see you before I step into my official role," Kai said.

She nodded into his shoulder. "You have to be professional."

"*Try* to be professional."

"But you're good at that. Detaching yourself."

"That's all you need to do, Jess. I know how scared you are—"

"I wouldn't say I'm *scared* —"

"—just step out of all that emotion, and into stillness, calmness. That point of communion with the Dream-lines. Work from there. And you'll see your way clear. You'll feel the flow-forms of the magic, how best to shape them. You'll be wonderful. I can't wait to watch you."

"You'll be watching," Jess said.

"You won't be able to see me. But I'll be there, through every step of the process."

Jess grinned. "Kind of like a stalker."

He gave a smile that meant he was acknowledging her humor without fully understanding it. "I love you. I love you to the point of pain."

"You could leave off that last part. 'I love you' works fine."

He laughed. "I should probably get over myself."

"I love you too," she said. Then, as her grin faded: "To the point of pain. Beyond."

He watched her. Said: "Good."

She rocked up on her toes to press her mouth to his.

His thin soft lips, the warmth of his tongue, the way his arms swept round her, nearly crushed her, lifting her right off her feet.

As he was leaving, her question stopped him in the doorway. It had been simmering in her mind all along, but it was only now that she found the courage to give it voice. "People have died during their Trials . . ."

The back of his shoulders went absolutely still.

"Haven't they?"

When he didn't answer, she said, "It's possible this whole process could kill me. Right?"

"Jess . . ." He did a slow turn toward her.

"I just need to know. That's all. I have a right . . ."

She saw how his eyes had gone all the way to ink black. He stood there on the threshold and she saw through the Kai she knew and craved and loved to another dimension of his character containing a ferocity that had never been turned on her.

"There are things I won't let happen," Kai said. He angled slightly away from her, as if concealing a mark of his own. He seemed on the verge of saying something more. But instead he slipped from view.

Chapter Eight

Jess

She spent the next two hours attempting the Dreamlines.

She took her position of meditation in the smaller of the two bedrooms, locking the door, tucking herself in the window seat, drawing the blinds. She sought out that mental zone of stillness and detachment that would allow her to drop deep into herself and mindshift to the Dreamlines.

Except it wasn't happening. Too many thoughts crowding in. Too much anxiety kicking through her bloodstream. Usually she could achieve the Dreamlines within minutes, and sometimes, on a very good day, in seconds. Yet now, just hours away from the series of tests that would make or break her, she might as well have been a novice all over again. She got close enough to feel that void and coldness, catch a flicker of light, hear the high song of the winds. Then she landed hard, back inside the flesh and bone vessel of her body.

Well, hell, if she was a novice again, she would rely on novice tricks. She closed her eyes and called up her training image: an intense visualization that served as a metaphor for what her mind needed to do. Kai's training

image, he once told her, had been a crisscrossing series
of paths leading to different points of a vast, wild garden.
Her own was of a subterranean corridor lined with
doors, all tilted at strange angles, each outlined by a thin
band of colored light. By focusing on what she needed
from the Dreamlines, she could stand at the end of that
corridor and see which door opened for her. Which spill
of light called her. Stepping across the threshold and
into that light became the mindshift.

It happened so easily and quickly she wondered why
she hadn't tried this an hour ago. Simple pride, she supposed. She entered the Dreamlines this way with a sense
of nostalgia: as if she were back in that chateau hidden
deep within the Pyrenees, in one of those rare sacred
places where different realities bled into each other and
the nature of time became altered; as if her body were
keeping itself still in that small, bare, candlelit room of
her training while Kai stood to the side and looked
on . . . and a demon hummed, slept, and dreamed in his
prison deep below. *Del,* she thought, and felt a rush of
what could have been affection, if it wasn't spiked with
something else, very cold, that made her draw herself
up and away.

When she returned to herself—that jolt into her body,
which she always thought would feel better over time
but didn't yet—she checked her sense of how much time
had passed. She had been on the Dreamlines for too
short a time to bring back the kind of power she wanted,
that would make her feel blazing, invincible. But she
could feel her heart racing in the way she'd come to
crave: beating against her chest as if trying to lift
through it.

And then came the surge of golden, living warmth,
sweeping through her blood, breaking over bones, and
she lifted her hands and looked at her palms. Wiped
smooth of all lines, the skin was blank and glowing, her
fingertips edged with nails that gleamed molten silver.

She felt the warmth rise behind her eyes. She turned to the mirror so she could watch her gaze fill with liquid light. She had learned to wait it out before leaving the room. She still remembered the expression on Ramsey's face that one time she came out too quickly, carelessly, while he was standing watch by her closed door, guarding her vulnerable, mindshifting body.

You should never feel afraid of me.

Of course not, he had said in response, but that could have been a lie.

When the light was soft enough to conceal, she slipped on tinted glasses. Another memory came reaching. Kai had been wearing sunglasses for the same purpose the first time she met him in the flesh, when she was still a child, in the sunlit library of a handsome Cape Town hotel. Somewhere in the ocean beyond the long windows, people searched the floating wreckage of a plane crash, soon to find the bodies of her parents. The tall man filled the chair in a way her child self found fascinating; his presence seemed a tangible thing, shimmering like summer heat coming up off the sidewalks. Everything around her ceased to matter, receding behind this eclipse of a man who beckoned her to him, then took off his glasses so she could see his eyes. So she could recognize him from her dreams.

Three, she thought now. There were three people she had met first in dreams, and then in real life. Kai, Ramsey, Lucas. One boy, two men. But Kai had been the first, keeping watch over her as she rose up through childhood the same way he had watched over those who came before her along the same bloodline—Shemayan's bloodline. He had cast complicated spells of dream magic—which she had still to master—to cross the vast distance between them, as she grew up in Boston and then Georgetown and he lived out a life in Barcelona. Nearly seven centuries old, he was, when they encountered each other in Cape Town.

She was six.

He was beautiful, of course: that strange Sajae beauty handed down from the fallen-angel ancestors. The height, the light bronze tone of his skin, the vivid, ever-shifting color of his eyes. His muscularity, she had learned, was an inheritance from his human side. In purist Sajae circles it had been considered a drawback rather than a virtue, so against the sleek, angular lines they prized Kai's build could mesmerize because they found it so grotesque. He had never minded so much, he told her, at least not when he discovered the *sakkarina* neighborhoods edging the southern and eastern quarters of the Labyrinth. Populated by those whose bloodlines were human-dominated, whose bodies reflected such blatant inferiority—the hair, sweat, and smell, the skin that bore such a staggering variety of blemishes, not to mention the diseases, the pitiful life span, the feeble connections to the Dreamlines that resulted in little more than trick magic, street magic. He described what a revelation it had been, discovering the chaos and colors of life in the *sakkarina*—the Sajae equivalent for the word "slums," which in the Labyrinth referred to those places where the inhabitants lived more and more according to the mundane laws of labor and less and less on flow-forms of magic. He liked these people. He found many of them attractive. He enjoyed what many of his peers held in disdain as their rough-edged, tumbling ways. All those parts of himself he had always felt to be lacking, growing up behind the rows of inner gates, he found there. In the bars and cafés and gaming halls, the markets and alleys and theaters and brothels, the young Sajae prince began to piece himself together. They were the last days of his youth and freedom before his family gave him to the Academy.

So much of him, Jess thought now, was still so alien to her. Things she had learned in high school history class—when she went to class—were things that he had personally experienced. They formed parts of his own living memory. He remembered Paris through the French

Revolution. She knew guillotines from pictures, movies, museums; he knew what it was like to see them in use, heads falling into baskets, lips and eyelids still twitching. The slaughter of a revolution gone so hideously wrong was one of those things that still haunted him, and another lesson—not the first, not the last—that humans didn't need demons in order to think up their own horrors. Kai had once mused on the absurdity of the word "inhumane," as if cruelty and violence were somehow unnatural to the human experience.

He had lived in Paris again during the days of the Second Empire, when the artists Jess had always loved were arguing in cafés and being rejected by the Salon, or being accepted by the Salon only to be jeered at by an uncomprehending public. She first came across Manet's *Olympia* in an art book when she was fifteen, would rework or reference the image in her own art too many times to count, had skipped school and hitchhiked to New York to see the painting when it was on display at the Met. Kai saw it, and the shock of it, when it was introduced to the world at the Salon in 1865, men in black frock coats whacking the canvas with their canes, people driven to such outrage that the gallery hired two policemen to flank the painting.

The man bore seven hundred years of history, Jess thought. All that accumulated damage, all that loss and war and pain and death: what must it do to you, even to a Summoner? He had watched countries born and broken and reborn, or at least redrawn on a map. He had watched friends grow old and die, had watched the world change, and once he'd learned and adjusted, watched it change again.

So what was she, her own little self, next to him and the depth and vastness held inside him? There were times when she could forget what he was. Could argue with him and tease him like they were almost normal people, living an almost normal life. He used to make her feel safe.

There were other times, though—and they seemed to be happening more often—when the strangeness of him seemed to lunge over her, and she felt its engulfing shadow. She looked at him in those moments and saw the odd-colored eyes, the too-sleek skin that lacked visible pores and body hair, the palms of his hands that always lacked markings, always, not just when he came off the Dreamlines. The more time she spent on the Dreamlines, the more deeply she realized just how far and long he had traveled on them: farther than any other Summoner who had lived, or stayed sane enough to tell the tale.

He believed in her, always had, yet she couldn't quite believe in his belief. How could someone like him look at her, so small and young, untested and unformed, and take her seriously? The other Summoners didn't. She knew this, even if Kai denied it, even if some of them made the pretense. She didn't think she could blame them. What had she ever done—saved Ramsey from his fate as the Bloodangel, killed a few demons?

He thought he knew her.

And yet she had been dreaming of the enemy, fraternizing with the enemy. She had gone to see Lucas in Los Angeles on some vague impulse of a reason. She should have killed him.

She had not. Could not. Instead she had stood inside his arms and wanted him.

Kai was the best and strongest of them all, the one who had sacrificed himself to the Dreamlines in order to restore the lost Summoner power; if there was to be a true hero in this, it would be him. There were Summoners who resented him. He stood up to them, cut against their opinion with a reckless confidence that bordered on arrogance; she herself was a walking example. He bore that resentment and distrust the same way he bore everything else. It wasn't crushing him. But it was maybe crushing her.

She closed her eyes. She needed inner stillness. Detachment. Emotion only distracted and disturbed her; she needed to get better at forcing it all underground—

"But isn't that the problem?"

The words were spoken in a child's voice, and seemed to be coming from somewhere in front of her. But the only thing there was the mirror. She saw a dark blur of motion deep inside the glass, in the space behind her reflection.

She didn't bother to look behind her. She knew there was nothing there.

Lifting a hand toward the mirror, Jess stepped forward, brushed her fingers across the glass. She sent a quick mindcast rippling through it to probe the space beyond. Only wall. Just an ordinary mirror on an ordinary wall.

Except . . .

She held herself still, heightened her senses. For a moment she thought she felt something odd—a cool breeze rising out from the glass, smelling of brine and seaweed. It touched her face, slipped inside her mouth, tasting of salt. She gagged and recoiled. She turned her face away and felt the breeze wind itself around her throat, then slip down inside the collar of her shirt, running across her breasts and belly.

She doubled over so violently she had to shove herself away from the counter in order to protect her head from the edge. She got to the sink just in time, retching. Good thing her stomach was empty. She spat again, and again, and then drank from the tap to rinse her mouth.

When she lifted her head and looked into the mirror, the reflection of a little girl hovered just behind her own.

"You're not made like they are," said the girl, and the words rose up through the mirror, rounded and distinct. "You can't keep yourself underground."

The girl was maybe ten years old, with a fair, heart-shaped face edged with straight brown hair. Her eyes were the blue-green of a calmed, sunlit sea, gazing steadily at Jess from beneath a thick fringe. She wore a white

T-shirt, a beaded tiger's-eye necklace at her throat, a shark's tooth on a leather cord. Odd jewelry for a child.

"What works for the others is damaging to you," the girl said. "Your master never realized. But you must learn to use emotion. You must learn to use the distractions inside and around you."

Jess felt her lips shaping a word—it might have been "use"— but her voice was a croak of a thing. She wanted the girl to continue.

"You must learn to use all of yourself to reach the deepest level of concentration. When you do that, nothing can shake you. Nothing can rattle you. Because emotion and distraction will only make you stronger. More whole. Don't you want to be whole, Jessamy?"

Jess stepped back from the mirror, lifting her hands as if in defense. "What are you?" she said. Tried to say. Was this part of the Trials? Kai had warned her that they would start unexpectedly, try to catch her off guard—

The girl touched the tiger's-eye at her throat. "You're not made like they are," she said again, and then was gone.

Jess realized she was touching her own throat, as if in imitation of the young girl, or as if she had become the reflection. She pushed both hands through her hair and let out a slow, deep breath. Was she trembling? Maybe she was. Maybe just a little. She checked inside herself for how she felt—and realized she wasn't even sure. As if that place of detachment she'd worked so hard to arrive at now refused to let her leave. She was supposed to think of it as calm. But it felt more like a state of . . . numbness, as if every time she did this she renounced her life, her self, just a bit more, floating higher up to look down from the Dreamlines. But that was good, right? That was what she had been taught to do . . .

You're not made like they are.

Does he know how lost you're getting, inside all that magic? . . . I can see it, why can't he?

Lucas had said that to her. But Lucas was operating

from some agenda of his own that she would be insane to trust. This thing with the kid in the mirror might be related. It could be some kind of trick. A trap.

She would love to know the spellcraft behind this. She'd love to be able to do it herself. It was like a variation on a golem, except instead of material matter it was somehow composed from mirror images like the double of herself she sometimes used as a distraction or decoy— except instead of extracting the image from the mirror, you were somehow inserting—

Loud thumps on the door.

"Jess!"

She started. She'd completely forgotten that Ramsey had even come to Vegas with her, let alone shared the hotel suite.

He was in an outfit that, for him, qualified as "dressed up": new, clean jeans that weren't holey, patched, or frayed, a button-down that he appeared to have actually ironed, and sneakers. He was freshly showered, his damp hair brushed back.

"You," she said. Again she felt startled but wasn't sure why.

Ramsey lifted his eyebrows. "Me."

"You look . . ."

"Like the urban sophisticate you knew me to be?"

"No." She considered him a moment: the fine angles of his face, the fuzz along his jawline. When had his features gotten so defined? When had his expression gotten that ironic? "Older," she said.

"Older than, like, a couple of hours ago?"

"Just older." A thought bloomed inside her. The fact that it seemed so obvious didn't make it feel any less a revelation. "You should be in college."

"You only need your GED to fight demons," Ramsey said, and grinned. "So I think I'm okay."

"A kid like you, with your kind of mind. You're smart as shit. You would get so much out of college. It's a crime if you never get there."

"You never went. And you were still successful—"

"I would have been a better artist with more education," Jess said. "An artist needs the ideas. Needs to have something to say."

"You managed to find something to say."

"Mostly about you," Jess said. "It's not the same thing."

"You flatter me."

"What I mean," Jess amended, "is that I was lucky. Those visions of you. Those dreams. I was lucky."

"And gifted."

"When—this—is all over, you're going to college."

"I'll go if you go."

She paused. "Okay."

They kept looking at each other, as if seeing some vision of some other life. She saw him as a college student, lean and scruffy, knapsack hanging off his shoulder as he strode through a tree-lined quad, limestone buildings rising around him. Saw him in a shabby low-rent bar, sharing a pitcher when he knew he should be working on a paper. Saw him churning out that paper three hours before it was due and knowing he'd still make an A. Saw the girls circling round him, drawn by that lost-orphan quality he played up so well, smarter ones sensing the fire and steel underneath. Saw him in cafés, libraries, his first downtown studio apartment, writing smart, shattering stories edged with humor and satire. Ramsey inclined his head a little, as if he could see it too. The life he was never to lead.

Jess heard herself say, as if from far away, her voice echoing strangely in her own ears: "I love you, you know. I should have told you this before, many times. I don't know why I didn't."

"It's a hard thing for tough chicks to say." Ramsey took in a breath. "For what it's worth—I mean, I think you should know—"

A high, sustained note chimed through the suite, surprising both of them.

Whatever Ramsey had been about to say, Jess saw his readiness to say it fading from his eyes.

"I guess that's the doorbell," he said instead.

Jess tipped a nod. "So I guess it begins."

"You seem ready. Calm."

"Calm," Jess echoed.

She suddenly wondered if she was wearing the right thing. She hadn't thought she cared. Since the Trials, whatever form they were to take, could begin anytime, she had kept to her usual uniform. Now, though, as she reached for the door, the conviction flashed through her that her outfit would prove just as wrong as the rest of her—

Her first impression of the person in the doorway was that it wasn't a person at all, but some creature dropped in through the Dreamlines.

Slender, androgynous, naked except for pieces of hammered gold strung strategically along golden wires that wound arms and legs and torso, throwing off sparks of light with every movement. White-blond silky hair was pulled back into a high ponytail. Delicate blue arabesques were drawn along the face and hands. The person looked at Jess with glowing violet eyes. She made out the thin ridge of the contact pressing against the eye; saw how the silver of the nails was only polish. Las Vegas theatricality, brought right to her door. For what purpose, though, she wasn't sure.

The androgyne—either a boyish young woman or a feminine youth—smiled and curled both hands in a beckoning motion, fingernails glinting.

And at some point as they traveled down the hallway they crossed into a different place, as if through an invisible border: the hallway suddenly arching high overhead and closing in on the sides, carpet giving way to gold-flaked stone. A scent of sandalwood hung in the air. The hallway widened and then ended in a set of double doors, engraved with a network of lines, shapes swooping through each other and swirling apart. They didn't seem strictly decorative, Jess thought, her gaze tracing the patterns. They seemed like part of a written language.

Two towering figures detached from the shadows flanking the doors: one man, one woman, both dressed in black, with thin golden masks concealing their faces and long braided hair dropping over a shoulder. One of them nodded at the androgyne. The doors seemed to open of their own accord.

Jess stood on the threshold and felt that numbness again, sweeping through and around her, as if sealing her off in a bubble of space. She was looking into a long, gold-toned room filled with people. Too many people. They sat in the alcoves, flowed through the doors set into each wall, drifted through the room, and stood in small clusters.

Summoners.

Not all of them, of course, but they were the figures her gaze sought out. There was an intensity and luster to their presence that marked them for what they were. They had surrendered themselves to a magic that carved new rivers within them every time they brought it down from the Dreamlines and gave it shape and release.

The magic changes you, Kai had told her.

She had learned this on her own as well as from him.

She was still learning.

She counted twenty-four Summoners, including the surviving members of Kai's Pact, the group he had crossed into deep magic with and was forever bound to by the Rites in a way that she, who would be crossing alone, would never be bound to anyone. Salik, who had betrayed them, was the notable exception, the one missing presence, but he was believed to be dead.

The others were Summoners she had never seen before. She didn't know whether they were also part of a Pact or if they were rogue, like she was to be. She had never seen so many come together like this, mingling among those who were not of deep magic, yet clearly

Sajae-blood. She had learned to look for some combination of the signs—the height and long, fluid lines of their bodies; the supple way of moving so that some of them almost seemed boneless; the subtle glow not just in their eyes but rising through their very skin—the latter was the Sajae equivalent of human sweat, which was not sweat at all. Their bodies converted the excess of energy into light that glimmered up through poreless skin.

As she became more attuned to the currents in the room, she sensed more Summoners: those who were here in shade form only. Rather than enduring the hassle of physical travel—or for reasons that made it impossible—they had left their physical selves in whatever corner of the globe they had come from, held within deep meditative limbo as they traced a way here through the Dreamlines. Jess heightened her vision and saw the shadows and flickers of them moving through the room like any other guests. There were even fainter traces of the presences who drifted along the walls or rode the currents of Dreamline energy up into the corners of the ceiling, assuming a bird's-eye view of what was to happen below.

People were turning in her direction, touching or gesturing to others so that they would look as well.

Silence moved through the crowd, took possession of the room.

Then the movement started. The crowd divided, falling away on both sides of Jess. She sensed the psychic network of Summoner communication in the air, vibrating through the crowd. Then it faded, the hum of many voices thinning out to one:

Welcome.

At the far end of the room, the last Sajae stepped aside.

It was as if they had cleared a road that led directly from Jess to the man, the Summoner, who waited on the other side. As tall as he was, the presence he cast off was even larger, so that Jess could feel it falling over her—the warm dark spice of it—despite the room between them.

Please come to me. Let me properly introduce you.

She forced herself to lift her head and meet the eyes of those she passed. She saw more sleek, androgynous figures wrapped in intricate patterns of gold. They were circulating through the room carrying arrangements of fruit—papaya, sapote, tamarind, prickly pear, kiwi, durian, dragonfruit, Chinese dates, lychees—on bronzed platters. She also saw, standing back in the crowd, several individuals she recognized from movies and magazines: Sajae-blood who had put their charisma and striking looks to use in Hollywood or New York.

And Kai.

She felt his mindcast—it came with no words, just that signature warmth that swept her mind and made her smile—before she saw him. He inclined his head toward her and she remembered that, outwardly, he was here only as mentor and witness to her trials.

"Not you."

She turned, thinking that those words were for her.

But the man was addressing Ramsey. He had stepped out from the crowd to block Ramsey's passage, pointing toward the doors through which they'd entered. "There is no Sajae blood in this one," he said. "He doesn't belong here."

"He stays," Jess said.

"He is not Sajae-blood!"

"He was the Bloodangel himself," Jess snapped. "So I think you can make an exception."

The man stared at her with an implacable expression. She felt the heat of her anger trigger some of the Dreamline energy inside her. The man stepped back into the crowd.

"Yeah," Ramsey muttered, and Jess had to smile.

Jack Daughtry lifted his arms.

"Jessamy." His voice was like melting Belgian chocolate: soothing in a way his appearance was not. He was one of the rare fair-skinned Summoners, his eyes a shade of blue—at least for the moment—that reminded Jess of her own. The two of them might have looked vaguely related, if not for the white-blond hair that curled and tumbled past his shoulders. A wig. Jess noticed further artifice: the deeply stained red of his lips, the powder that lightened his skin. She could sense the striking looks beneath, and knew he was a worker of deep magic. Yet he seemed to be pretending to be a normal human pretending to be a Summoner.

He drew her to his side. They faced the crowd. "My friends," he said, and made a dramatic gesture, and the slender gold-clad servants began circulating the room with something new: trays filled with goblets spun from smoked glass. Daughtry went on: "Welcome to my hotel . . . inside a hotel." Chuckling swept the room. "Much like we, for over a millennium now, have formed our own world within a world." His voice sobered. "Even as we became exiles scattered *across* the world."

One of the servers came up to them, smiling, and Daughtry picked up a drink in each hand. "I haven't seen many of you in many a decade. And for others of you, it's been longer than that. We have come together and this is a special thing. So tonight I bring you something special. This is *rajika.*"

Many of the Sajae-blood looked at him blankly, but Jess saw how the Summoners' expressions changed, eyebrows lifting, some of them breaking into grins and shaking their heads. One of them lifted a glass to Daughtry in open awe. "I've made my life's fortune—my latest life's fortune—" There was another ripple of chuckling. Jess knew he was referring to the Summoner ritual of self-reinvention, killing off their old lives by renaming themselves, relocating, choosing new ones to seduce or to love and be loved by, if they were lucky enough to know how.

Her eyes sought out Kai.

Unlike those around him, there was no smile on his

face. His gaze held hers, and conveyed such intensity that she found herself looking away. She reached again for that state of calm that felt so much like anesthesia. She wanted the numbness. She didn't want the emotions so effectively driven behind, beneath it.

"—through the art of spectacle, illusion, imitation. But this *rajika* is the real thing, salvaged from the storehouses of the southeastern ridge even as the Labyrinth rained fire. I have preserved it all this time, waiting for a suitable occasion. My friends. The occasion is now."

He turned to Jess and handed her a drink. She accepted, staring at the thin lid set just inside the rim. A delicate spoon rested across it, some kind of cube nestling in the hollow.

"I built this hotel as homage to our great, lost Labyrinth," Daughtry said. "And because life has a sense of irony, it was while I mourned our lost past that I learned we *do* have a future. May I present Jessamy Shepard, *krikkia* of the one currently known as Kai Youngblood, first *krikkia* for the Trials in over two hundred years."

Jess jerked a glance at Kai, but he turned aside, murmuring to the Sajae-blood next to him. Two hundred years? So there *had* been Trials since the destruction of the Labyrinth, the flight of the surviving Sajae, the hunting of the Summoners, the demon wars? Why hadn't Kai told her?

Because something went wrong. The krikkia *died.* Jess stared down at the cube of silver powder, resting in the hollow of the spoon.

"And I realized," continued Daughtry, "that with this hotel—this feeble imitation, this mere suggestion, this faintest evocation of the Labyrinth—I had been building a memorial to everything I had come to believe was lost.

"Not just our old home, my friends.

"But us.

"I believed we had come to our end. Our link with the Dreamlines weakened more every day. Our powers dimmed, our spellcrafts faded. Sajae blood might flow on, however diluted—"

Someone snorted.

"—but the Summoners were becoming extinct, and our knowledge would die with the last of us.

"When we pass into deep magic, we surrender our right to have children. The magic takes those unborn from us. Summoner legacy is not to replicate ourselves, the power we carry, through biological copies. Copies of copies of copies turn corrupt. They would only destroy the balance of Nature and the Great Dreaming, the blood of the Worlds and the soul of the Dreamlines.

"But we failed to honor that balance another way.

"We failed to teach. Summoners do not bear their children; Summoners seek them out—in the ones who become their students, who carry the talent for the Dreamlines, and the ability to quicken it.

"The world changed.

"And it changes again.

"But because we had lost our own world, we refused to change with it. We did not want such new, strange materials to work with. We did not want to bring into our society those who did not already belong.

"My friends.

"Asha was our wake-up call.

"Jess might be our salvation."

She could feel the creep of a flush along her throat. But she didn't have to look at Daughtry to sense that he was grinning.

"Our salvation," he went on merrily, "because she will save us from the crisis of ourselves. We lost the vision of what we were meant to be. Our ancestors came down to this world to be part of it, mingle among it; but at the first signs of hurt and rejection we crumbled like children and closed ourselves off.

"We sought refuge in the Labyrinth.

"And as we lost our connection to the world, we lost

our connections among ourselves. The whole of a Summoner Pact is always more powerful than any single member. This has always been so. But we chose to forget this, to lose the old rituals, and to mourn them, when we should have been inventing new ones.

"So I propose a new beginning.

"We will return to the past—our true past—and bring it up into the future. We will become what we were meant to be: the healers and teachers and warriors of the Dreamlines, who fight to keep the worlds in flow, the Blood and the Dreaming aligned.

"We will seek out our children, nurture them, and see them into power.

"We will cultivate new bloodlines.

"We will merge ourselves with the world.

"For as the world we live in spins toward its own destruction, a new one rises on the horizon. I say we be the ones to take and shape it. I say we gather all the powers within ourselves, of darkness and light, of blood and dream, of all and one, and commit to the creation of a world we were always meant to live in. What the Labyrinth itself was meant to be.

"Except we will never hide ourselves again.

"This time, there will be no world within a world. Our world will be their world. We will be in them, and they will be in us.

"This begins now, tonight, as Jessamy Shepard, blood of Shemayan, the *senzanen*, the dream-child, of our last surviving prince, moves into deep magic and takes her place among us as a Summoner.

"My friends, look on her closely.

"For she is us."

He held up the little silver cube and slipped it in his drink. With a hiss, the glass flared brightly, and Daughtry drank. The other Summoners were doing the same. Jess followed suit, dropping in the cube. Green flame shot up through the liquid. She jerked her head back, but the flame was receding, liquid bubbling as the light spread evenly through it.

The taste was a bit like licorice, although richer and deeper, with a sweetly fading aftertaste, so that the following sip layered the first rich note over the last, and then again, in what had to be the most complicated drink she'd ever had. "A bit like absinthe," she muttered, and Daughtry laughed.

"Absinthe," he snorted. "Talk about a feeble imitation."

"Thank you," she said. "For the speech."

"I haven't designed a Trial since . . . Well. Since the last one. So this is incredibly exciting for me."

"The last one. Two hundred years ago."

He nodded. She was aware of people pressing in on them, wanting to talk to either her or Daughtry or both. "What happened to the last candidate?"

"He died. About halfway through his trials. It happens."

"Was there a candidate before that?"

"In 1742. Too hastily chosen, that one. There was another in the early sixteen hundreds but—"

"What happened?"

"The one from China died early on—literally burned himself out. And the other . . . well. He *did* pass. So that was cause for celebration. Until he woke up the next morning and proceeded to kill himself. But don't."

"Don't what?"

"Don't compare yourself to them. They were not— they were not like you, Jess. The fault was not with them. It was with us. They weren't failures so much as victims. You, Jessamy, are not a victim. Anyone who knows your recent history can see that."

"Maybe not a victim," Jess said. "But I could prove a failure."

He stepped closer, lowering his voice. "You could *prove* yourself to be a total idiot. Do you understand

how the prince has risked himself for you? His reputa-
tion, his credibility, his legacy—"

Daughtry broke off, but Jess could sense the unspo-
ken. Could remember Kai's voice in the dark the night
they turned lovers. *You are forbidden.*

*Summoners do not bear children; Summoners seek
them out, in the ones who become their students.* Once a
Sajae became a Summoner, his or her legacy was to be
the magic cultivated in others. It didn't matter if those
others were bloodkin. It was, Jess had learned, the
Dreaming's way of ensuring an ever-evolving diversity
of magic, and also to prevent a kind of brutal, biological
monopoly that could threaten the Dreamlines themselves. It was also why some Sajae—such as her own
ancestor Shemayan—made sure to have children first,
before entering deep magic. Those children inherited a
link to the Dreamlines—the potential of a quickening—
but not the manifestation, the flow-forms, of the magic
itself.

Shemayan, however, had taken the unprecedented
step of hiding his youngest child, sending her into the
world beyond the Labyrinth. Only that child had survived, her relatives hunted and slaughtered by those who
did not want to risk the rise of another Shemayan.

Which, Jess realized now, with a chill sinking through
her, was what she was somehow supposed to be. So
while she wasn't truly one of them; she was supposed to
be one of their greatest. No wonder she felt so light-
headed.

And there was something else.

A relationship such as hers and Kai's was regarded as
incest. She was his student of the Dreamlines, his dream-
child. It was outlawed and made taboo because of the
offspring it might produce. Not biological, but magic—
the magic he trained and cultivated in her. Incestuous
magic could turn corrupt.

Toxic.

She didn't know how well-known her relationship with

Kai had become. She knew Kai favored discretion, but that was his general nature. Neither of them had felt like they had something to hide. She had just assumed that taboo to be an outdated artifact from a time and place no longer relevant. She had never really thought that her magic could suffer because of it. Kai would never do that to her.

. . . *what I might do for you. The choices I might prove capable of. I think it maybe makes me dangerous.*

She had asked him, *Dangerous to what?* Her voice so teasing, so flippant.

She had never thought that perhaps he meant dangerous to *her.*

Others were pressing around her, asking questions, giving advice, reminiscing about their own Trials, or the Trials of someone they knew: Summoners she recognized from Kai's Pact and Summoners who were still strangers to her. There were also several Sajae-blood, who possessed, perhaps, mild to moderate psychic abilities: an uncanny flair for sleight of hand, an ability to communicate with ghosts or influence the minds of certain animals. Jess could see how some of them looked on her with envy, or even bewilderment. Wondering why it was someone like her who had a chance at this kind of power . . . instead of someone like them.

She couldn't focus on anything anyone was saying. Maybe it was happening to someone else and she was just the dream that other person was dreaming, if that made any sense. It *didn't* make any sense. Jess downed the last of her drink and frowned at the glass. Where was Kai? Or Ramsey? Shouldn't they be here with her, offering moral support?

She was saved from having to make conversation when Daughtry brought on the entertainment. The end of the room had been screened off, and now the lights went on and the screen lifted into the ceiling. An artful minimum of scenery suggested a desert. As the dancers moved onstage, their bodies weaving through one another in explosive, angular, lyrical choreography, Jess realized just what story they were telling.

The Bloodangel.

And then the dancers—wearing the kinds of colorful, bizarre, provocative costumes people had worn to the Bloodangel Festival, the rock concert in the desert where hell had literally broken out—moved reverently to the sides of the stage. A stark sandstone throne moved forward out of the shadows. Jess didn't remember a throne at the actual event itself, but it made for good visuals. On it sat a slight, striking woman with cropped white-blond hair. In her arms lay the motionless figure of an adolescent boy, naked, his body covered with the pale blue glittering lines of the paranormal drug that had rendered him paralyzed and helpless and nearly insane.

Jess tasted acid at the back of her throat. She knew what came next. She didn't want to watch but couldn't look away. The woman who played Asha arched her back and flung out her arms—more good visuals—and the naked youth rose into the air. He hung there, suspended, as one by one the dancers approached him. As they pressed their mouths to his skin. Stylized red marks appeared along the boy's body, intersecting with the blue, forming a complicated language of jax and blood. As the dancers continued to drink from the boy and then dramatically transform—their movements changing and costumes altering to suggest the first wave of the hybrids—Jess felt again the falsity of it. The blood-drink had required time to alter the chemistry of the human body, making it susceptible to the demonic energies waiting to claim it.

And then another figure stepped onto the stage: a tall, slender woman with blue eyes, fair skin, and long dark hair, wearing a black baseball cap that had ANGEL spelled out along the visor in cheesy rhinestones. She remembered that cap. She remembered how she'd gotten it off another woman with her first-ever use of a charisma spell. And as this other dancer Jess moved toward the other dancer Asha for their weirdly balletic showdown, the real Jess felt cramps seize her gut. She doubled over.

Something happened to her head. It felt very light. Then she was on the floor. She heard herself saying things. Things that didn't seem to make sense, but filled her with alarm and urgency. She wanted Kai. Where was Kai? She couldn't control her own gaze, it went jittering from person to person. What was this thing flopping against the floor? Was that her own body?

"What is happening to her? What are you doing? Stop it!"

Ramsey had broken through the crowd, surging toward her, but then arms slipped round his shoulders, pulled him back, kept him in place.

Kai.

Kai was holding him, whispering in his ear, and Jess saw, through the dimming, lengthening telescope her vision had become, Ramsey's face turn pale.

Those were her men. Kai, Ramsey. Yet they were too far away from her, and it was Daughtry's face looming in her vision, Daughtry bending beside her. There were others, too, but Jess didn't care. Her eyes were on Kai. He had brought her here. He was responsible for this. And he wasn't even letting Ramsey come to her as her hands and feet drummed the floor and she couldn't make them stop. Darkness moved over her, and she gave herself up to it. Glad. Preferring the darkness to this lost, strange thing that she had been calling her life.

Chapter Nine

Ramsey

The first time Ramsey saw the crazy skyline of Las Vegas, he imagined some mammoth beast striding the globe, plucking up the monuments that caught his eye—the Eiffel Tower, the Statue of Liberty, the Sphinx—and dropping them in a jumble in the middle of the desert.

So when he first walked into their suite in the Eden, he got it—that globe-striding beast had plucked *this* room not from some mythical paradise but from somewhere in the Labyrinth, which, he supposed, formed the Sajae equivalent of that mythical homeland they longed to get back to. The curving, organic lines, sandstone colors, sculpted furniture that seemed born of the room itself, bright jewel tones of rugs and vases and mosaics and silks. But it was the architectural model of the Labyrinth that riveted him. His gaze kept returning to the towers at the center, to what looked like doorways cut below the rooftops but with no stairways spiraling beneath them, no connecting bridges, nothing that could access them whatsoever.

When he had a chance, right after the speech the tall, theatrical Summoner gave to the room, and everybody set fire to a drink that Ramsey immediately decided to avoid, he made his way to Kai and asked him about it. "Those doors at the tops of the towers—what were they meant for? Who were they meant for?"

"The visitors," Kai said. He didn't miss a beat or seem surprised by the timing of the question. "The winged ones. Those doorways, those rooms, were meant for them. It was meant as a form of reverence."

"Winged ones? You mean . . . angels? You actually saw them?"

"No. By the time my generation came along—they were long gone."

"Where did they go?"

"Maybe the Dreaming called them home." Kai sipped at that weird, flame-bright liquid. "Or maybe they died out. No one knows."

"How could they die out? Aren't they supposed to be immortal or something?"

Kai laughed. "Immortality," he said. "Now *there's* a myth for the ages."

Ramsey could not look at Kai without thinking of what had happened that night at the motel. Tired, but still pumped with adrenaline from his run-in with the hybrids at that crumbling Spanish-style motel, he had gone wandering. He spoke with a clearly shaken Jess at the end of the walkway. *You don't have to be afraid of me,* she had told him. Except that wasn't quite it. He wasn't sure what he feared.

If it wasn't her, exactly, it was something that involved her.

Something that seemed to be changing her.

And it was that half-named fear, as well as the gauntness of her face and the shadow in her eyes that made him go to a room not his own.

He knocked, and when no one answered, he front-kicked the door in the way Kai had taught him. The door bounced off the wall and would have slammed shut all over again if Ramsey hadn't blocked it with his body.

Sprawled across the bed, naked, white sheets tangled along his bronze-skinned, hairless body, Kai had an arm slung over his face and seemed lost to the world. His nails in this light looked more smoky than silver. Ramsey flashed on images of Kai and Jess together, the kind of things they must do to each other. It was weird. It was kind of like when he was younger and friends told him how freaky it felt when they could hear or see evidence that their parents had sex. Except Ramsey had been orphaned at five, so he couldn't really relate. Besides, Jess was too young to be his mother. And Kai was sure as hell not his father.

"I want to talk to you," Ramsey said.

No answer from Kai. Ramsey waited. He had the feeling—he didn't know why—that Kai was all too aware of him behind those closed eyes.

"I'm not going anywhere until we talk," Ramsey said.

The arm slid away from the face. Kai turned his head toward Ramsey and opened one eye. After a moment he opened the other. They were brown, at least for the moment. Ramsey was surprised to see them look so normal. You could almost pretend that Kai was just some ordinary dude, relaxing in the happy aftermath of being with his woman.

Ramsey said, "Do you have any idea what's going on with Jess?"

The color of Kai's eyes did not change. "Is that a question," he said calmly, "or an accusation?"

"You tell me."

Kai rolled onto his side. Propped himself up on an elbow. "Jess told me you did well at the motel, in the firefight. You were stupid to put yourself in that situation, of course, but once there you handled it well."

"I was stupid, like you said. Jess totally saved my ass."

"You're good with the weapons you have. But I think maybe you could use something else. I've been keeping something for you, for when I felt you were ready.

You'll like it. You'll wonder why I never gave it to you before."

"What is it?"

"No." Kai grinned. "You have to see it."

Ramsey could feel himself getting drawn in, getting charmed. He wanted to ask about the "something" that he was now "ready" for. Instead he hardened his voice. "Why do you leave us like you do? Just go off. Disappear. And then come back and lie about it?"

Kai's grin went away.

He swung his legs over the edge of the bed, the sheet tangled over his thighs. Ramsey felt a jab of envy—he'd have to take steroids to have muscles like that, and he still wouldn't look that good, just freakish—before deciding that Kai was showing off, doing some kind of alpha-male bullshit thing, which annoyed him. Then he realized that if Kai, who was not particularly vain—at least not in that way—ever felt threatened or challenged enough to pull rank like that, it wouldn't be over someone like Ramsey. Which annoyed him all the more.

"So maybe you don't lie," Ramsey said. "But you don't tell us the whole truth, either. I don't know why Jess doesn't see it—"

Kai yawned. "She sees it."

"Maybe, but she's also kind of blinded by . . . the other stuff she feels for you. She doesn't see it like I do. Or else she'd be a lot more pissed off. No matter how good you are at . . . at . . . distracting her." He paused, then added, feeling a bit daring, "I see things about you two that you don't see about each other."

To his surprise, Kai said, "That's probably true." His voice had taken on that flat, edgy calm that warned Ramsey he was in unwelcome territory. "I'd be very careful about jumping to conclusions."

"Where do you go? Why do you keep leaving us?"

"It's not just one simple reason, Ramsey."

"So don't give me all the reasons. Try one."

Kai regarded him for a moment, his hands resting on the mattress to either side of him. "Okay," he said softly. "How's this. There's some business I need to keep an eye on. Which doesn't include you. Not yet, anyway." As Ramsey was thinking how to answer this, Kai said, "Don't worry. Eventually you'll know everything. Or almost everything. And then you'll wish you enjoyed your ignorance while you had it."

"I think you leave because you're not good for Jess," Ramsey blurted. "*Why* you're not, I don't really know, and maybe she doesn't either, but—but *you* know. Right? So what's up with that?"

"When you cross a certain line," Kai said quietly, and his voice had leveled into that flat, eerie calm again, "it's not like you can cross back. Even if you want to."

"Uh-huh. You're saying you want to."

"I'm saying it's a moot point."

"So maybe you should go away and never come back."

"Is that what you think she wants?"

"I think Jess wants what she can't have. Or what's bad for her. Just like most people." Ramsey paused. "Like you."

Kai averted his gaze, seemed to be looking inward, gathering something inside himself. His irises went as black as the pupils, a shadow spreading out through the whites of his eyes. Ramsey stepped back. When Kai spoke again, it was in a voice so low that Ramsey didn't understand how he could even hear him. Yet he could. Perfectly. "You think someone like you could know the *wants* of someone like me?"

"I—" He felt like a little kid again, an old, familiar ache lodging itself in his chest. "It's not what I want," he said finally. "I don't like it when you leave us."

Kai's eyes slowly lightened. Ramsey didn't realize he'd been holding his breath until he felt it issue out of him. The hurt in his chest left along with it.

"Come here," Kai said.

He reached out for Ramsey, settled a cool, large hand on either side of Ramsey's head. Ramsey felt an enveloping pressure . . . and then waves of warmth and light flowed through his brain. He felt himself swept high into white bliss. When it was over, he opened his eyes.

Kai was smiling a little. "Feel better?"

Ramsey nodded.

Then he said, "You know so many things you're not telling us. It drives me kind of crazy. It's not . . . it's not fair."

"Look." The Summoner's voice turned wry. "When you're as old as I am, you'll know just as much. And you'll have to pick and choose what to tell your loved ones. What's actually useful for them to know."

"You have the right to decide what others might find . . . useful?"

"Someone has to."

"Okay. So then what's *useful* to know about Lucas Maddox?"

Kai's eyes went black. He turned his face aside, but Ramsey saw. It had happened too quickly for him not to.

"Maddox."

Kai touched Ramsey again, but this time it was to push him out of the way as he stood up and moved, naked, to the far side of the room. He drew on the cotton drawstring pants Jess had bought for him. Ramsey waited. He had spent enough time observing Kai over the past months to know when he was stalling.

He felt an odd, slow thrill inside him, and as he spoke he realized he felt a bit of power over Kai. It had never happened before. "There seems to be some kind of connection between them. Dreams."

Kai's glance was sharp. "She told you this?"

"Yeah. I don't think she thought I'd turn around and—"

"—and tell me."

"Maddox is one of the bad guys. If he has some kind of hold over Jess, it needs to be broken. Now."

"Jess needs to focus on her Trials. Nothing's going to happen before then."

"You weren't there," Ramsey went on, "when his name got mentioned on that thing the hybrids were watching, that DVD. The way she looked. The way she tried to hide her reaction from me, the way you're hiding yours right now."

A beat of silence. Kai switched on the lamp.

"I met him once. Lucas. I noticed something about him." Kai was quiet, as if needing a moment to uncover this. "When you're with someone, even a hybrid, you can get that sense of their presence, that feel of who they are. Their essence, I suppose. It's a kind of signature you can use to identify them. It can linger behind them, like a perfume.

"With Lucas, though, there was nothing.

"At first I thought he was just . . . closed off to me. I was kind of impressed. I remember wondering how he'd managed to learn how to do that. Because I knew there was something—there—something I didn't know, and couldn't get at . . ." Another moment of quiet. "I remember wondering if it involved Jess. But I could not get in that guy's head. For all of my abilities, for all that the man was there in the damn car with me, it was like he didn't exist. Blank space.

"I also thought maybe I wasn't perceiving things correctly. Because circumstances at the time were rather stressed. For me."

Ramsey nodded.

They had both done some suffering in the desert.

"I don't know what Asha did to him," Kai said.

"Maybe he was already like that. Maybe it was part of what drew Asha to him in the first place."

"But she's really dreaming about him? The way she was dreaming about you, before she even knew you existed . . . ?"

"It's different. She said that herself. I think they're actually meeting each other, talking, you know, like in

a café or a bar. Except instead of a bar it's this—this
kind of—"

"Dreamspace."

"Isn't that a kind of magic? That's, like, dream
magic . . . ?" He had a vague understanding of the dis-
tinctions. There was the natural world and the Great
Dreaming. Blood magic had to do with manipulating
things in the physical world, using materials like blood
itself. Dream magic seemed to involve manipulating
states of being, whether it was the realm of the psyche
or the realm of the dead, or even those realms that lay
beyond the Dreamlines.

"Sometimes it's magic," Kai said. "Sometimes it's
something else."

"Like what? Some cosmic accident?" When Kai didn't
answer, he said, "Can't she stop it? Why doesn't she
stop it?"

Kai pushed a hand across his face. His physical appearance could range from thirty to forty-five years of
age, depending on how tired he was, or when he'd last
been on the Dreamlines. Now, though, in the play of
light and shadow, in the mood cast by these things they
were saying, he seemed beyond age altogether. He
moved among them, Ramsey thought, but he was not
one of them. He was alien.

"You know when people die," Kai said suddenly,
"their soul goes onto the Dreamlines—sometimes you
can catch it there—and passes through into whatever
realm is waiting for them. For us. But some souls are
marked to return to this world. To keep returning. Until
some kind of riddle or problem is finally played out."

"Jess," Ramsey said quietly.

Kai nodded.

And somehow this made sense to Ramsey, explained
so much about Jess, in ways he couldn't find language
for but felt in his gut to be true.

And looking at Kai now, he realized something else.
"And you. You've known her before. In those past lives—"

"No." The word seemed a little too sharp. "I never interfered, except for the most casual, distant kind of encounters. My charge was to track Shemayan's bloodline down through the centuries. And it was only after several generations that I began to see . . . a pattern. A man or woman who always died . . ." He paused. "Who always died too soon. And who always felt . . ." He paused. "Familiar."

"Their signature," Ramsey said. "Their essence."

"Think about it. What helps make you who you are? Genetics, experience, your time and place and culture. Those tangible, physical things, which vary from life to life. Those things are different, so you would be different. A different person each time.

"But then there's that signature sense of presence. It doesn't seem to change from life to life. It feels just as physical as blood or skin or hair—maybe not to you, but to me, to any Summoner—but it seems to be of the Dreaming. Who knows. Maybe it's the soul itself."

"So you've seen Jess go through one life after another."

Kai was silent. Then: "Yes."

"So what is this problem or riddle that needs to play out? Could it involve Lucas Maddox? Is that why she keeps dreaming him?"

"There are always—" Kai paused. Rubbed a hand across his face. His voice took on a note of anger that did not seem directed at Ramsey. "There is always the chance that—" He broke off.

Jess was in the doorway.

"The chance that what?" she said.

Kai went to her, touched her shoulder, then brought his hand up through her hair and swept it back from her face. They stared at each other like that, his large hand cradling the back of her skull. "No talking," he said.

And that, Ramsey figured, was his cue to leave.

*   *   *

It was clear he didn't belong here. He didn't need the
man with the long, sallow face who had pointed him
toward the doors to tell him that.

But Ramsey was used to being in places where he
didn't belong. He was the outsider who watched and
listened rather than participated. Now, as Jess got engulfed by the Summoners and Sajae crowding round her
and Daughtry, he drifted through the room, taking mental notes of what he saw. He would write it all down
later.

"Daughtry is such a ham," one of the Summoners was
saying. "And please. It's not like we crumbled at 'the
first signs of hurt and rejection,' like we just tucked tail
and ran crying from human society. They would have
burned us at the stake if they could. We gave them
everything—everything—and offered them even more,
and what did they do to us?"

"That vampire thing," his companion agreed.

"That whole goddamn vampire thing. That's what
we're supposed to be? Bite people in the neck, drink
their blood, prowl the night, wear velvet and leather
and lace?"

"You *do* have a fondness for velvet and leather—"

"You know what I mean."

"They pay their own price, the humans. It's happening now."

"It shouldn't be happening at all," the Summoner
grumbled. "And you realize that as they so stupidly skip
toward their own extinction, they'll kill off everything
else. Including us."

"The Dreaming won't allow it. Daughtry was right on
that count."

The Summoner sighed. "For a new world to be born,
the old one must die. It won't be a natural death. These
things never are."

"They had their chance. No one can say otherwise."

"It's just so ugly." The Summoner drank off his glass, then looked into it, as if hoping somehow there'd be more. "I never could stand the ugliness."

"And that one?" The Sajae pointed a finger toward Jess. "Do you think the prince is right about her?"

"Youngblood can be a spoiled, arrogant son of a bitch," the Summoner said. "But what makes him especially annoying—"

The Sajae smiled, in a way that suggested he held a different opinion of the prince. "—is that he tends to be right."

"One of these days he'll be wrong."

"About her, do you think? He *has* violated that relationship, has he not? I've heard—"

"It's the kind of thing he would do, is it not? Fall in love desperately with the one person he can't be allowed to have?"

"So why isn't he being penalized for it? The risks—"

"—Are not worth the loss of something else."

"Ah. Hope. The hope of a new beginning, a rebirth, a restoration, whatever you want to call it—"

"I'm curious to see if she turns out to be worth it." The Summoner started humming beneath his breath. The melody was familiar, and after a moment Ramsey recognized the song: it was John Lennon's "Come Together."

He thought the whole dance thing was pretty cool. It was so stylized that it didn't seem like it had anything to do with the very events it was attempting to describe.

Of all the living things in this world, the human body was the least equipped to serve as vessel for a demon soul: if the body didn't break apart on impact, the mind inevitably did, rendering the body gibbering and useless. But a Bloodangel Rite—the sacrifice of an angelic being, embodied in a flesh-and-bone package like Ramsey's—changed this, as if the Bloodangel's blood contained needed information it could then pass on to whoever drank it.

The least equipped, Ramsey thought again, eyeing the dancers as they spun and leaped and pirouetted, and yet the most desired. It was the human package, the human experience, the demons wanted. You didn't see them coming into this world seeking to inhabit dogs or cows.

He spotted Jess on the other side of the room, watching the production with her arms folded. She didn't approve. He was making his way toward her when he saw her step back, falter, and clasp her head.

Then she collapsed.

And as the tall figures closed in around her, Ramsey started to run—or would have run, if not for the people he had to plow through. He caught glimpses of Jess through the ring of Summoners and Sajae-blood. He saw her feet and hands beating against the floor, her head twitching. And she was saying things. He could hear her voice lifting from a murmur to a shout. He heard the words "bones" and "slave" and "love" but then her voice fell and the rest was inaudible.

A sudden barrier brought him up short. He felt himself pulled back, away from Jess. His mind was dimly registering that barrier as a pair of arms, the voice in his ear as belonging to Kai. "What is happening to her?" he yelled, not sure if the question was meant for Kai or anyone in the room who might have an answer. Kai was whispering something but he couldn't make it out. He was twisting against the Summoner's hold on him, so useless that he could have been a puppy in the big man's arms. Daughtry was kneeling beside Jess, doing something to her face that made Ramsey think of a priest giving benediction. Except Daughtry was no priest. "Stop it!" Ramsey yelled, but Daughtry was picking her up, now, the other Summoners who had been encircling her—Ramsey counted half a dozen—falling in behind him, two by two, as they moved toward the back doors,

Daughtry in front, Jess crumpled in his arms, dark hair falling across her face and shoulders.

And Ramsey finally clued in to what Kai was saying: ". . . all right. She's fine. This is how it's meant to go . . ."

The procession of Summoners—and that's what it was, Ramsey realized, a procession, complete with that air of formality and ritual—left the grand hall, the doors swinging closed behind them.

And Ramsey felt himself freed. He knocked Kai's arm away, spinning round on him, hissing, "That's just how it goes? She was having a fucking seizure—"

"Not a seizure."

"He drugged her! Didn't he? Daughtry drugged her—"

"Yes. He did."

It was a calm, blankly stated admission that shut Ramsey up in a way no denial could have.

Kai was eyeing him as if he might have to restrain him again. When moments passed and it didn't look necessary, he said, "It's part of Daughtry's job, what he needs to do. He will use what he learns from Jess to finish designing her Trials."

"How can he learn anything from her if she—"

"This isn't the stuff of normal conversation."

When you channeled energy from the Dreamlines, Ramsey knew, you were opening yourself up to the magic and letting it move through you—your mind as well as your body. The magic, Jess had told him, operated in general forms that were understood by everyone—and could be taught as such—but used symbols within those forms that changed from person to person, as if inside a public language shared by everyone there developed a private language meant for that person alone. Ramsey could only figure that in this case Daughtry was extracting something from Jess, some kind of private language that he could use in shaping his own magic.

He imagined someone doing that to him and recoiled.

"So did Jess know this was on the agenda? She agreed

to this?" When Kai didn't answer, he said, "Did you at least give her some kind of heads-up?" And when Kai didn't answer, Ramsey said, "Of course not. Why would I even bother to ask? It's not *useful* for her to know—"

"That is between Jess and me," Kai hissed, "and yes, we will deal with it. But it's what had to be done. You understand?"

"I want to go with her."

"You can't."

"But you can. So why can't I—?"

"Ramsey."

There is no Sajae blood in you.

Ramsey snapped, "Can't I be, like, your token human or something? Don't you need to be politically correct?"

"Look." Kai blew out air. Ramsey had the feeling he was managing to annoy the hell out of him. Good. So he could do that, at least. "Jess is where she needs to be. And I need to be with her. That's her job, that's my job, and you—"

"—so why can't I have a job? I've got—"

"—need to leave now so you can—"

"—I've got abilities, and talents, and so—"

"Ramsey—"

"—you shouldn't just dismiss me, like I'm some kind of kid—"

"Ramsey—"

"—or something, because only an idiot would just ignore what's standing right in front of him, you know, a resource, an opportunity, and I think—"

"Would you just shut the hell up?" Kai's outburst seemed to surprise himself as much as Ramsey. "Please," he added.

"But I just think you should know—"

"You have a job. Okay? There is something I need for you to go and get. Right now. Okay?"

Ramsey nodded.

"So then you—"

"I feel a little better now," Ramsey informed him. "I mean, about everything."

"I'm so glad."

Wait, that was sarcasm? Kai was being sarcastic? Despite himself, the whole situation, Ramsey found himself grinning. The grin seemed to do something to Kai, loosen a knot inside him, so that he turned aside and looked into the distance a moment and gave his head the slightest of shakes. When he focused on Ramsey again, the dark of his eyes—they had been dark a lot lately, Ramsey realized—had warmed into an unexpected amber. Ramsey felt caught by the glow of them, their richness and depth, and in that moment saw why Jess would stake her soul for him.

It didn't seem fair, for the power in their little triangle of relationships to be so weighted in favor of Kai. What was anyone, even Jess Shepard, against the force and charisma of an experienced Summoner, a Sajae prince? *Never trust what charms you.* Jess had told him that once. But even as he thought that, he felt so charmed by Kai that he knew he would do anything. The prince only had to ask. And Ramsey realized he resented Kai for it. He thought of those stories of vampires, how they could hypnotize you just with their eyes.

"Go downstairs," Kai said. "Someone is looking for you. They know what you look like. You just need to let yourself be found."

"And then?"

"Ask to be taken to Zazou."

"What's a zazoo?"

"Tell Zazou you're there to pick up the package."

"What's in the package?"

"Something you'll find very useful."

"And then I come back here?"

"No. Don't."

"So where do I go?"

"Los Angeles, I suspect. When the time comes, you'll know."

You'll wish you'd enjoyed your ignorance while you had it.

The memory of Kai's words from the motel room superimposed over the words he'd just spoken. Ramsey felt a scrambling in his stomach. He was beginning to realize what this was. Beginning to realize why Kai was looking at him that way, as if he were losing something or someone. Like maybe Ramsey himself.

"So wait." Ramsey cleared his throat. "So when do I meet up with you guys again?"

Kai regarded him steadily. "You were right, Ramsey. You see things other people don't. Trust your gut, what it tells you. Even when everything around you is telling you something else."

"But I am going to meet up with you guys? I mean— it's not like—" He paused. Took a moment to properly form the question. "I am going to see you again, right? And Jess?"

"I think so."

"You think so?" He thought he was going to say more, but he suddenly found that he couldn't say anything. He just kept staring at Kai, this man who knew so much more than he let on, standing there in the black, loosely cut suit that had been tailor-made to his proportions. The man spent a small fortune on clothes. It was one of the things that Ramsey had kind of held against him, but now he found he didn't mind so much.

"Go, Ramsey," Kai said. His eyes flared a deep blue-green. It was not a color Ramsey saw often, and he didn't know quite what it meant. "Time is short. We're already running out of it."

"So I guess I'll see you when I see you," Ramsey said, with an indifference they both knew to be fake.

Kai nodded and turned away, his jacket swinging with the motion. He was walking in the direction of the doors, of Jess, when he spun on his heel and came striding at Ramsey. It happened so suddenly that Ramsey barely registered it: how Kai reached out, clasped the back of his head in a way that was not gentle, in a way that felt like ownership, and pressed a hard kiss against his forehead. Kai let him go with a force that sent him stumbling. And then he really was moving away through the crowd; he was at the doors now, then was gone.

He still felt the electric shock of the kiss, the serotonin flush or whatever it was that Kai did sending waves of deep pleasure through his brain. It wasn't enough. He knew what he was now. He was alone.

Chapter Ten

Ramsey

When he stepped into the VIP reception area—with its club chairs and leather-paneled walls and smooth expensive silence—he saw the hotel manager who had introduced himself as Nathan Kinross. Nathan was talking to a tall man with black hair tucked inside the collar of his linen jacket. Ramsey caught only a quick glimpse of his profile, but the skin looked scarred, burned. As the man turned away from Nathan, Ramsey saw that he was holding a walking cane.

He thought: *Salik?*

But Salik was supposed to be dead, burned to death. Ramsey had seen him aflame, insane and grinning, applauding the entertainment of it all.

Even if he'd somehow gotten out of there with his life, he wouldn't be crazy enough to show up here, at a gathering of Summoners who now regarded him as corrupt, a traitor—who would gladly set fire to him themselves in order to finish off the job. Kai could barely spit out the man's name, this Sajae who had grown up with Kai in the long-ago days of the Labyrinth, gone into deep magic with him, been part of his Pact, fought the demon wars alongside him. Ramsey couldn't guess what

Salik had been like then. He only knew the man that he himself had met, who ran a gallery of obscene, violent art in San Francisco and made jax on the side. Who had kidnapped Ramsey and delivered him into the hands of Asha, using Lucas Maddox as the middleman.

"Ramsey. What can I do for you?"

Nathan Kinross was standing in front of him. Ramsey had regarded him as a mild-mannered dandy, pleasant and forgettable. Now he noticed how flat and opaque the man's eyes were, framed inside those dark lashes. Noticed the lizardlike way his tongue flickered over his lip.

That man. Is he a Summoner? Does he call himself Salik?

But it seemed smarter just to say, "I'm good," and walk away.

Entering the main lobby of the hotel, joining the flow of Midwestern tourists en route to their rooms, the gambling tables, the restaurants, and the shows, was like stepping back into a world he hadn't meant to leave. He felt the relief of the familiar loosen his shoulders a little. There was a man up ahead, taller than everyone around him, moving toward the gilded revolving front doors. Ramsey quickened his pace. The man had a black ponytail dropping down his back, and he had a cane. *If that's him,* an inner voice spoke up, *you probably don't want him to know you're here,* except he was no longer the Bloodangel, just some kid. What could Salik want with him now?

You're just an ordinary, stupid kid.

He had to know.

He broke into a run. He jostled through the crowd. An overweight blond woman shrieked, "Well, excuse me," in a tone Ramsey thought unnecessary. The tall black-haired man paused and turned around.

He looked a bit like Salik, but Salik would never wear a turquoise bolo tie or a shirt quite that . . . plaid. The man had a jacket folded over his arm and no burn scars anywhere. "Dear boy," he said in surprise, as Ramsey's eyes lingered on the details of his person, "would you like to come with me? I could buy you a very nice dinner."

Ramsey said nothing, backpedaling. Was this the dude he'd glimpsed in the VIP reception? He didn't think so . . . but then he'd been just as certain, at least for a moment, that this aged high roller in the dumb bolo tie would turn out to be the outcast Summoner. Maybe he was just projecting.

"This hotel has an excellent steakhouse," the high roller was saying. "May I buy you a thick, juicy steak? I wouldn't expect anything in re—"

Ramsey turned away, readjusting his hold on the strap of his duffel bag.

And someone crashed into him, sending him stumbling. He breathed in the faint tang of gin, as coarse, curly hair swept his cheek, and a well-toned body pressed against his for the briefest and sweetest of moments. Then the girl was backing away, giggling, wobbling a bit in her high-heeled boots, seeming not to notice when her right ankle turned over. A guy hovered behind her and rolled his eyes. "Samantha," he said warningly. Then, to Ramsey: "Sorry. She's a klutz."

"Not a problem," Ramsey said. He was looking at the girl. Woman. Mocha skin, scattering of freckles across a snub nose. Lively green eyes.

And he saw the intelligence and clarity of her gaze, out of place in a person so giggling and tipsy. The guy took her by the elbow and steered her past Ramsey, making sure that she got close enough to whisper, "Zazou says hello," and thrust a balled-up paper in his jacket.

Chapter Eleven

Outside, in the dry desert heat, as the valets drove away cars and summoned cabs and people flowed through the doors, Ramsey smoothed out the crumpled paper. It seemed like any other flyer for a concert or a club, except for the text:

> *Did you survive the Trans desert massacre??????*
> *You are not alone! And you're probably not as fucked up as you think!*
> *(Or maybe you are!)*
> *Come preserve your mental health*
> *Tonite—10 pm til whenever—20 bucks donation at the door*
> *Wear Pink. Just for the hell of it.*

He memorized the address, trashed the flyer, and joined the line at the taxi stand.

It was the kind of hotel that had seen better days.
A line of clubkids curled round the back of the building. The line was steadily moving forward—this wasn't

one of those elite velvet-rope places; as long as you could pay the entrance fee you were in. Yet a doorman walked down the line, pointing at people and beckoning them forward, sending them inside the club. "They don't have to pay," the purple-haired girl behind him told her friend. "Otherwise it's twenty bucks, you know? Pick me, pick me . . ." They seemed to be chosen at random, Ramsey thought. They weren't particularly cute or stylish or outrageous or any other thing likely to win special club privileges.

He saw a man in a suit talking on a cell walk up to the doorman. The man put away the cell and the two conferred for a moment. They scanned the line, and the doorman's gaze came to rest on Ramsey. "You," he barked.

"Unfair," whined the purple-haired girl behind him.

And then he was passing through a little vestibule, where a woman at a card table was taking money in and out of a lockbox. She waved him through. He felt that the fair thing was to pay, but on the other hand he wasn't going to complain about getting to save twenty bucks.

He moved into a crowded hallway where a long line of women waited for the bathroom, and stepped into a hangarlike space. People were milling around, or sitting at the little tables and chairs beneath sculpted iron mobiles, or taking turns on the giant swing set that filled the center space, or gathering near the stage, where strobe lights flashed and a half-decent DJ tripped through a set of hardcore dance music.

He listened for a while. He wasn't sure what he should be doing or who he should be looking for, but Kai's directions seemed simple enough: let yourself be found. Putting on his best come-and-find-me air, Ramsey bought a Diet Coke at the bar at the back and wandered through a doorway and down another hall that ended in a room of pink light. Pink shag carpeting on the floor. People sprawled on beanbag chairs or slouchy couches, or sat with their backs to the wall. Their voices rose and fell against the music thumping through the building.

It was the wall that drew his attention.

Covered with photographs, artwork, notes.

Photographs from the Bloodangel Festival in the desert. The first rows of them had been taken on calm, clear days, showing sun-scorched sky and a dense tangle of campers, tents, RVs, and cars, white canvas domes rising in the near distance where people had set up makeshift bars and clubs. Photographs of firedancers swinging flame against the twilight. Photographs of the Maze, sculpted and raised from the desert itself, and the stage that hovered just over the roof: an architectural and engineering feat that no one would ever be able to replicate, not without serious mojo to help them. Maybe he should be horrified, he thought; maybe he should be feeling some signs of post-traumatic stress disorder. Instead, a small bubble of pride rose up inside him. The Maze. He had made that thing. Not voluntarily, it was true, but he couldn't look on it now in these pictures without feeling a thin thrill of ownership.

And then the smile faded, because the next rows of photographs documented—or tried to document—the carnage. These images were hazy, obscured: by the fires, the blood-rain, the herky-jerky motion as people fled for their lives . . . or pressed in to lose them.

A banner below the photographs read:

YOU CAN'T TELL US THIS DIDN'T HAPPEN

Except, looking at those photographs, it was impossible to tell *what* had happened: only that there had been chaos and destruction and death.

He scanned some of the notes, many of which were tacked beside photographs of smiling young people:

DESERT SURVIVOR SUPPORT GROUP

I am a specialist in post-traumatic stress disorder and if you were at this event, please contact me. I am interested in putting together a support group whose sole goal

**would be to share information and make
sense of what happened that night . . .**

*MISSING: ALLEGRA CHESSMAN, age 27,
brown hair blue eyes, last seen near the Maze
before the hell started, wearing a bright yellow
jacket, called herself Crazykitten, if you had any
contact with her or know anything about what
happened to her please contact . . .*

. . . HAVE YOU SEEN THIS COUPLE: Julie
Hobbs and Ben Miller, driving a Ford Bronco
with the front fender seriously dented, last
time I saw them they were heading out to
the Trans concert in the desert and they
never came home

I AM DOING A DOCUMENTARY about the Trans
desert massacre and looking for people who were
there to interview on camera, if you were there
please call Kit at . . .

**ROOMMATE WANTED—someone who
was at the Trans concert because I AM
TIRED OF LIVING WITH PEOPLE WHO
THINK I'M CRAZY AND WANT ME TO
SHUT UP ABOUT WHAT I SAW THAT
NIGHT—really cute 2-bedroom Spanish
bungalow not far from Beverly Center . . .**

MISSING: Jamie Ishiguro, 23, black hair black
eyes, I KNOW SHE'S PROBABLY DEAD BUT IF YOU
TALKED TO HER THAT NIGHT AND KNOW ANY-
THING AT ALL PLEASE PLEASE PLEASE CALL . . .

GIRL MISSING, ONLY TWELVE YEARS
OLD—ran away from home, I think specifi-

cally to go to this concert—please if anyone knows anything contact ASAP . . .

HAVE YOU SEEN THIS MAN . . .

HAVE YOU SEEN THIS WOMAN . . .

FOR SALE FOR LIMITED TIME ONLY!!!! Sand taken from the Maze and pieces of wood from the Stage on which half the Trans band got Burned Alive! These items have Magical Properties! If Interested call Rudy at . . .

I am a PSYCHIC who specializes in LO-CATING MISSING LOVED ONES and can sometimes COMMUNICATE WITH THE DEAD, if there's anything I can do FOR YOU at reasonable rates call me at . . .

THE STRUGGLE IS COMING. BE BRAVE. BE PART OF THE SOLUTION.
For more information contact . . .

"Crazy, isn't it?"

Samantha, the young woman who had stumbled into him and slipped him the message, fell in beside him. She had a pink feather boa slung across her shoulders and was offering up a very pretty smile. She said, "So where's your pink?"

"What?"

"Supposed to wear pink, remember? I'm assuming you read *all* of the flyer?"

"Why? I mean, why pink?"

"It's the color of healing." She frowned. "Or something."

"So we're all here to heal?"

"We're here to party with a higher purpose." She tilted her head toward the notes and photographs on the wall. "The struggle is coming," she quoted, and snorted. "Idiot. It's already here."

"I need to see Zazou. You know that, right?"

"Zazzie? He will be here in"—Samantha checked her wrist, but realized she wasn't actually wearing a watch—"soon. Let's dance."

"I don't. Do that, I mean."

"Then I'll dance, and you can shuffle from side to side."

She grabbed his hand and pulled him down the hallway. He let himself be grabbed and pulled. She was starting to seem familiar. He was starting to think that they had met somewhere before. He rummaged through his memory and came up with nothing. Yet he couldn't shake the feeling that there was something about her that he should have realized by now, that he was missing completely.

And then she was flinging herself against him, and they seemed to be moving to the beat. He couldn't focus on the music, couldn't concentrate on anything other than the nearness of her, the scent like cardamom coming off her skin and hair, the boa tickling his neck as she twined herself around him and spoke right in his ear:

"So how is Kai?"

"Kai? He's, uh . . . he's fine. He's—you know him?" How stupid. Obviously she knew him. "I mean, how do you know him?"

"New York," she said. "We did a bit of work together. And the *girlfriend* of his. Jasmine or Jennifer or—" A hard note entered her voice. She knew damn well what the name was, he realized.

He answered with a hardness of his own. "Jessamy."

"So, what's she up to?"

"She's—" How much was he supposed to say? Who the hell was she, anyway?

"She's pretty busy with, uh, with work and stuff."

"Work." She was smirking. "You ever get the feeling she might be considering a change of employment?"

"What the hell is that supposed to mean?"

She laughed and pressed herself tighter against him. He felt his own body stirring in response and pushed her back a little. "What is this? Where is Zazou?"

"This is good music," she said.

That was debatable, but he let it slide.

She said, "So what's your favorite band?"

"My last favorite band"—he heard the acid in his voice— "was Trans."

"I thought they were so overrated."

"I guess you were smarter than the rest of us."

She cocked her head at him, and he had the sudden urge to slap her.

And now he was the one leaning in close. "Can we quit playing now?" She lifted her eyebrows. He saw again the intelligence in her eyes, its hard clear nature that cut against the pink boa, the silly grin, the way she had stumbled into him, wrapped herself around him, pressed her breasts against his chest.

He pushed aside her hair and whispered right in her ear: "I know you're Zazou."

She stepped back. Looked at him. Laughed.

"And I want my damn package," he added.

She laughed again. She pulled the boa off her shoulders and tossed it at his chest. He didn't try to catch it, letting it fall in a pink, fluffy puddle at his feet. And as she looked at him, something moved just inside her face, beneath the skin; she ducked her head and her eyes flashed a liquid red, as if suddenly filled with blood. Then she backed away from him, still looking at him, grinning, lifting a finger to her lips. *Shhhh.*

She was a demon-human hybrid.

She had felt familiar to him because all the hybrids were familiar to him; they had sipped his blood in the desert, stood close to him, touched him; some of them had caressed him, as the jax on his skin kept him prisoner, locked inside his body. He was bonded to them. It was not something he thought about in the day, but through the late-night hours when he couldn't sleep and fought the urge to stare in the mirror at his naked self so he could count the scars, he knew it to be true. He had helped make them, and now he was helping to kill them.

Now this one was talking to two guys at the end of the bar: the tall, fit-looking twentysomething dude with cutting-edge cheekbones and lustrous blue-black skin who had been with her at Daughtry's hotel, and a smaller, slighter, younger guy with floppy black hair and piercings in lip and eyebrows, who had put himself together in such a stylish, complicated outfit Ramsey wondered how he'd had time to do anything else.

They moved toward a door so nondescript that Ramsey hadn't noticed it until now, and only because the girl— Samantha? Zazou? the *hybrid,* he reminded himself, his inner voice rising up sharp and fiery, *she's a fucking hybrid, don't forget this, you can't forget this, and what are you doing here anyway?*—was opening it and standing aside, searching out Ramsey in the crowd and holding his gaze as if daring him to look away, which he absolutely refused to do. The two men disappeared inside. Zazou lifted her hand and made a beckoning motion to Ramsey, still with that wide, I-dare-you grin on her face. Then she, too, slipped inside. The door stayed wide open for several seconds, the bartender casting it a disinterested glance, and then began to inch shut.

Ramsey lunged through the loose crowd of dancers reaching the door just in time to slip his hands around the edge before it could lock inside the frame. If Kai had sent him here—to Zazou—there had to be a reason. He didn't understand how she could turn out to be a hybrid, but— well, hell, chalk that up as yet another thing he couldn't wrap his mind around—as if that ever mattered . . .

He was standing in darkness. Then a light clicked on below, and he saw a steel grate floor beneath his sneakers, and a railing slanting down beside steps.

He descended into a multileveled, stone and steel underground bunker.

At the other end of the rectangle of a room, steps led up to an area where Zazou stood and waited beside a long table. "Ramsey," she greeted him, her voice trailing down the length of the room. "Welcome to your life. So glad you could make it." Her voice was deeper now, shaded and nuanced with some kind of accent. This, Ramsey realized, was her real voice. He replayed her words in his mind just to pick that voice apart: he guessed her to be French, her English a second language picked up with that British tinge, no doubt at some posh international academy. This made him wary of her all over again.

"I have something for you," she said. "You want to come and get it?"

She laid her hand on a black velvet bundle on the table.

As he walked toward her, footsteps echoing off the stone, lights switched on to either side of him. Watching from the alcoves were some of the same people he'd seen upstairs, on the dance floor or in the pink room. They ranged in age from fifteen to forty, some of them nestled together on the benches, arms looped loosely around each other. Others stood with their legs braced, hands in pockets or dangling from belt loops, eyeing Ramsey with the same distrust he felt for them.

Several people were cleaning rifles, and several more were unloading wooden crates filled with weapons and checking them off against a list: Ramsey glimpsed AK-47s and M-16s and others he couldn't see well enough to identify or didn't know enough to identify, also grenades and some handguns. He walked past walls lined with more deadly, sleek shapes, past stacked crates that must hold more. He felt as if he'd strolled into some bizarre video game.

"Holy shit," he breathed. He came to the base of the steps, looked up at Zazou. He was conscious of all the eyes on him, even as he heard rustlings of movement, low muttered conversations, as some lost interest in him and became involved again in what they'd already been doing. "What is all this?"

"What does it look like?" Zazou beckoned him up the steps, and he felt annoyed that he'd been waiting for permission. He leaped them two at a time, stood in front of her with his hands in his back pockets. She wasn't very tall, yet she radiated such a sense of presence that her lack of height meant nothing. He stared at her face, as if at any moment he'd see through the human skin to the real face beneath, but hybrids only Altered when adrenaline flooded their systems, and Zazou looked calm. She was even smiling a little. "Preparation," she said, answering the question he'd forgotten he'd asked.

"For what, exactly?"

That calm expression, that trace of a smile, didn't change. "War."

"Against the demons." *Your own kind,* he thought, but did not say.

She nodded. "The Lord of Bones."

"The Lord of—"

And his mind flashed back to Jess in the grand hall, writhing and convulsing on the floor, yelling out words he could only partly make out. Bones. She had yelled it not once, but several times. Ramsey had heard slave and love but mostly, and most loudly, bones.

"He's on his way," Zazou said, her gaze slipping beyond Ramsey to survey the room beyond, the people that ranged the walls, some of them not much more than kids. Ramsey grasped the incredible fact that this—this ragtag group of . . . of . . . clubgoers—was supposed to be some kind of army.

"It's how we disguise our gatherings," Zazou said, as if glimpsing his thoughts. "It's how we come together to"— she grinned—"party with a higher purpose. Otherwise the wrong people might get suspicious." Ramsey thought of the people being plucked from the line.

"Who is the Bones dude?"

Zazou blew out air as if just the thought of grappling with the question was enough to exhaust her. "He is one of the original evils," she said slowly, and Ramsey felt an icicle dripping down his spine. "He can't live in a world without sucking it dry, ravaging it until even he can't live there anymore. So then he has to find a new one. That's why one of his names—he has a lot of names—is the Traveler. His own nature forces him to keep on the move." She paused. "And he's wanted this world for a long, long time."

"So how come he hasn't taken it already?"

"He tried. Once. A long time ago. The Summoners stopped him. They thought they had . . . neutralized him. But he had already passed something of himself into Asha, helped her become what she became. She was his legacy. In some ways she was also his revenge."

"Against the Summoners, the Sajae," Ramsey said. "Against the Labyrinth."

"Everything she destroyed. She was very willing. She had her own reasons. But she was also . . . twisted. Raging. Insane."

Ramsey said quietly, "Did you know her?"

Zazou stared at him. Her smile faded; the green eyes turned opaque. "Yes," she said, and her voice deepened even more, turned hoarse and thick, and Ramsey saw again the demon face shifting beneath the human one. "I was watching. Like so many of my kind, I had my face pressed against the skin of your world.

"You humans have always had a pull for us. A fascination. Just like with the angels in the ancient days who came down to walk among you, take you as mates and playthings. We want you from the inside out. That is why we crave you. Why we love to eat you." And it was a different smile this time, jagged, flickering across her lower face. "It's a compliment."

"You say shit like this, and I'm supposed to trust you?"

"Youngblood does. Do you trust him?" She gestured at the rest of the room. "He pays the bills. There are places like this all over the country. Mostly in the west, of course, but the movement's been spreading eastward for months now."

"How come I never heard of any of this?"

Zazou shrugged, as if to say that she was beyond caring.

"And you," Ramsey said. "Why—I mean, given what you are, why are you—"

"Hanging out with you guys?" Zazou rubbed her nose. She was staring at the black bundle on the table, which Ramsey knew was intended for him, but at the moment, at least, he was more curious about Zazou. "I have no love for the Lord of Bones," she said flatly.

Love. Ramsey remembered another thing Jess had said to him once, what she herself had learned from Kai: *Demons find human love grotesquely fascinating. They're kind of mesmerized by it. They find it so strange and exotic.* Interesting that a hybrid person like Zazou would even use a phrase like that; he wondered what it could even mean to her. But he could ask her about that later, assuming there *would* be a later; right now it was more important to suss out her motivations.

Ramsey said, "So 'The enemy of my enemy is my friend'?"

"I am not your enemy."

"You're a hybrid."

"I realize this."

"Demon soul in human flesh."

"That's a crude and simplistic viewpoint. But it works for you, doesn't it? Makes it easy for someone like you to kill someone like me. Assuming," Zazou said, that trace of a smile surfacing again, "that you even could."

Ramsey let that go. That was more dialogue for later, although he could already feel how her words and taunting voice had taken a piece of his mind, were twisting it inside out.

Ramsey said, "So all this—there's some kind of overall plan? Or is it just about a bunch of people collecting weapons and feeling cool and shit?" He regretted his sarcasm as soon as he spoke. Sarcasm was a refuge for weakness, he'd always thought, and he could tell from the flash of disdain in Zazou's eyes that she thought the same.

"I know what he does. I've seen this before. The Soulbreaker will need to make a few things," Zazou said. "That gives us a window—a narrow one—to figure out where he is." She shrugged. "We get this information to Kai and his Summoners. And then we storm the place."

"That's the plan? That's it?"

"We choose not to get locked into particulars."

"That's the plan?"

She regarded him with eyes like green flint. "Are you of any use to us or am I just wasting my time?"

"What do you want from me?"

"Your skills. Everything that Kai taught you. Everything you've learned from experience. We need you to teach *them*." She gestured at the room behind him. Ramsey did not turn to look, but could feel the gazes on him. The air seemed to have taken on weight, pressing down on his shoulders.

He was quiet for a moment, then said, "One thing."

Zazou lifted an eyebrow.

"Something else should be part of the plan. Like, high priority."

She rocked back on her heels. "Really."

"Yeah. Killing—" His throat went dry. "Killing Lucas Maddox."

"Him." The eyes narrowed. "He's already done his brand of damage. He isn't anything now, just a washed-up—"

"No. I don't think that's true."

"Then why haven't we heard from him in all this time? He fell off the radar. He's holed up somewhere picking his nose, watching porn, whatever. Doesn't sound like a Big Bad to me."

Ramsey had no good response for this. Instead he said, "Gut feeling."

Zazou shook her head so violently that strands of hair escaped her purple headscarf. "You don't get it, do you? That ritual he and Asha began in the desert—with you, with your blood—it *never ended*. Those tunnels they opened that let the demons come down through the Dreamlines—into *this* world—never closed. You and Jess and Kai and the other Summoners—what you did— you didn't *win*. You just slowed everything down."

"Demons still can't manifest here unless they find a human vessel," Ramsey said. "And vessels have to be prepared. And for that, they need blood of the Bloodangel. Last I checked, there wasn't any. The Bloodangel doesn't exist anymore."

"God, you're naive." Zazou seemed about to launch into some kind of explanation, then laughed instead. It was a sharp sound without anything good in it. "Look," she said. "For what he does—what he *makes*—he doesn't need any kind of blood other than his own. Okay? Which means we don't have time to hunt down some junkie loser has-been who's already had his moment—"

"He seemed to be important to the hybrids," Ramsey said. He told her about the DVD he and Jess had found in the motel room.

Zazou listened, pressing her lips together. "You have no way of knowing the context—"

"I can get the DVD. I can show it to you. Maybe you can translate."

"Ramsey. I know this guy sold you out. I know this guy was with you in the desert and helped turn you into a blood-slave, but—"

"This is not about revenge!" Ramsey thought back to the desert, his most vivid memory of Lucas: looking up at his face, noticing the thin lines of what seemed like claw marks crossing his cheek. *Nice scars,* he had said, and Lucas's reaction had confirmed what he'd already suspected. "Asha left some kind of *mark* on him. You said that Bones left something of himself in Asha. So maybe she passed something on to Lucas. Maybe it's like a fucking virus. I don't know. Or maybe Asha sought him out in the first place because there was *already* something in him, his music, that connects . . . that connects . . ." He could feel his words, his thoughts, running out. He took a breath. "The darkness of angels," he abruptly heard himself say, and felt surprise. Where had that come from? "That connects him to the darkness of angels."

"That's a nice turn of phrase. Poetic."

"If I was a betting kind of guy," Ramsey said, "I would bet everything that this dude—this Bones dude—will seek him out the way Asha did. He serves some kind of purpose for them. Kill him, take away that purpose, and I bet we hurt Mr. Bones. Maybe even enough for it to matter."

How strange, to hear himself talk about actually killing somebody—somebody who was full-blooded human, not a hybrid. Somebody he had once looked up to, been a fan of, stored his music on his foster family's computer. Ramsey considered himself a moral kind of guy. So maybe he should be feeling at least a sliver of guilt and horror at what he was suggesting. But he didn't. And it didn't bother him that it didn't bother him. Maddox was a menace. Maybe he was human, but he was too contaminated.

And a threat to Jess.

Zazou stared at him, her lips thinned into a grim, bloodless line, and she gave a nod. "I want to see that DVD."

Then she picked up the long bundle of black velvet lying on the table. "Now," she said, "don't you want to open your package? Because I'm damn curious about it myself."

Chapter Twelve

Jess

The smell of fresh paint—acrylics—registered first. Then the voice. "Jessamy," it kept saying. "Time to begin."

She opened her eyes. She was curled up on the floor of the hotel suite's entrance hall. "Jessamy," that voice said again. It was the voice of a little girl, which made its note of maturity incongruous.

But before she could attend to the voice, she was noticing the swipes of paint on her hands and wrists. There was paint encrusted in her fingernails in a way it hadn't been since . . . how long had it actually been since she'd picked up a brush with serious intent?

She didn't understand what had happened, but she knew what she would find.

Bracing herself, she looked.

A jumble of images were dashed across the walls of the suite. Some of them she recognized—the Boom-Boom Man from her childhood nightmares, with his melted-off plastic face and his rocket-launcher arm—the tigers she drew obsessively after her uncle took her to her first circus when she was thirteen.

Others were more foreign. One wall was completely

taken up with a mural of a brown-haired man with his face turned away from her, walking through some kind of postapocalyptic landscape. On the road behind him, deformed belly-slithering creatures who seemed vaguely human—*posthuman,* Jess thought—pulled themselves through dirt and rubble, broken shards of mirror where their eyes should have been. The road was lined with telephone poles that on closer look turned out to be crucifixes, the bodies of the dying nailed in place with one arm extending in the same direction.

Pointing the way.

She could only guess at the nature of the destination.

"So they drugged you," said that little-girl voice, "and made you paint visions for them. Is that about the size of it?"

Jess's gaze went directly to the mirror hung within the little alcove. "You again," she said to the child inside the glass. "Who are you?"

"A little piece of your heart," the girl said.

"You don't look it."

"I'm a manifestation of yourself. Your shadow-mind. A way for you to help organize your thoughts." The girl grinned, and the grin did look familiar—something sad and reckless in it—the way the paintings on the walls looked familiar, even though she had no memory of creating them. "I am," the girl rattled on, "quite literally *you,* talking to *yourself.*"

"So why," Jess asked slowly, "are you wearing a shark's tooth?"

The girl paused, and her image rippled, as if a sudden wave coursed through it.

"For luck," she said.

The door chime sounded, the long high note startling Jess as if a gun had gone off.

"You should get that," the girl said.

The corridor outside her room had gone dark. It wasn't the same corridor from before; it wasn't the same suite. There was magic at work here. She could feel it

in the air: dense, layered, masterful spellcraft weaving
and extending all around her, catching her in the center,
spiderweb and fly. Faint sounds drifted down toward her:
winds, moaning, the rustling of leathery wings, what
might have been the roar of some animal. She could
heighten her senses to parse the sounds more clearly,
but she didn't feel prepared to know the what or the
why. Enough to focus on the item dropped off by her
door.

"So what is it?" asked the mirror-child.

Her. More spellcraft. Although the nature of this felt
different than what lay in wait for her beyond the
corridor. The Dreamline energy behind the mirror-child
felt as sinuous as a snake slipping through water. If its
nature was that distinct from such built-up, complicated
flow-forms as Daughtry's, then maybe the child was
some kind of projection on her part . . . ? A projection
that Daughtry had somehow triggered out of her?

It made sense.

The shark's tooth dangling from a black leather cord
bothered her a little. If she saw something of herself in
the child's eyes and brief reckless grin, she didn't
understand the tooth at all.

The child leaned forward in the mirror, her forehead
pressing against the other side of the glass. "Let me
see, see!"

Jess showed her.

It was a circlet fashioned from delicate strands of gold,
so airy looking that it seemed a wonder it held together
at all. But as Jess turned it over in her hands, examining
the seven bloodred stones set within the design, she
could sense just how deceptive that appearance of
fragility was.

The stones glowed, as if a miniature flame had been
placed inside each one, playing shadow and light along
the undersurface.

"So what is it?"

There was a blurring of air in front of the mirror; Jess

caught the faintest image of the child's arms, spilling out over the frame as she leaned over as far as she could to get a better view.

"I know what this is," Jess said. Her eyes went to where she'd painted it on the wall: a much cruder, thicker version, the toy she had actually played with. "It's from an imaginary quest I used to play out when I was a kid. I had to get this tiara to the palace on the other side of the forest—which was really a couple of sycamores in our backyard—before the lights in the seven stones went out. If I reached the palace in time, the king would choose me as his wife and I'd be queen." She turned the tiara over in her hands, marveling at this little piece of art wrought from childhood fantasy. "I got the idea from chess. The pawns, you know—get a pawn all the way to the other side and you can exchange it for a queen. It seemed like magic."

"And you were a little pawn who wanted to be queen," the child said. "And now it *is* magic. What would happen if you didn't get it to the king in time? Someone else would be queen? Someone undeserving?"

"The crown would explode," Jess said. "Like in an action movie."

"You played this game a lot?"

"Yes. It made me feel good."

"You played it all by yourself?" When Jess didn't answer, the mirror-child said, "The self-invented game of a lonely, friendless child?"

"I wasn't the type of kid who . . ."

"Who what?"

"Made other kids feel comfortable."

"Why not?"

"I'd lost my parents. I was angry. I was wild."

"And gifted," the child added. "Gifted kids so often fall out of step. They get isolated and lost. But nobody worries about them. They just let them fall through the cracks."

"Giftedness had nothing to do with why I fell through

the—" Why the hell was she even having this conversation? "This is self-indulgent bullshit," Jess snapped, "and has nothing to do with anything."

"Maybe it explains why you surrendered yourself to such a losing proposition."

This proved too difficult to ignore. "Come again?"

"That lonely child in you hungers for acceptance and belonging, right? And no wonder. You've been out on the edge for so long now. Here's your chance to be part of something. A group. A family. Your chance to feel enfolded."

Jess rolled her eyes.

The child went on, "But are you really blinded enough, stupid enough, to think you can win, Jess?"

"You see a reason why I can't?" Jess stared again at the child's image, then said, "Who are you really?"

"You've accepted their game, with their rules, on their terms. Do you see? You're not made like they are. You can't play the game the way they do. You have to discover your own rules."

"Really. So how do I do that?"

The child seemed to consider this. Then she said, "Maybe that's your real Trial."

Enough. This was idiocy. She had to get to work. "Nice chatting with you," Jess said, tightening her hand around the tiara. "I guess I'll see you when I see you."

"Soon," the child promised. Then: "You better hurry. You don't want to be late for your king."

Kai said, "Is she talking to someone?" At first it was just a muttered question to himself. Then he lifted his voice and said, "Jack, is there someone else in there?"

"No," Daughtry said. "She doesn't encounter a living presence until Zone Two."

Daughtry was a restless figure, pacing the room, examining the three-dimensional images even as they flickered all around him, or sometimes through him, so that it seemed he had his own role to play in Jess's Trials

other than the one of designer. He was raking his hands
through his hair, running the tips of his fingers around
his scalp, over and over again. He didn't seem aware of
the gesture, but Kai found it distracting and more than
a little odd. Maybe Daughtry's wig was simply
uncomfortable, or not properly attached—the
Summoner again skated his fingers along his scalp—but
then why didn't he just take the damn thing off?

Daughtry was at the far end of the room putting some
finishing touches on the final test, the one that involved
the animals. Daughtry had been as pleased as a kid at
a carnival when Jess revealed through her paintings that
he should do tigers. "Tigers are *awesome*," he said, in a
way that made Kai wonder just how much time he'd
been spending with the younger generations. "That will
be a fun scenario. For us, at least, if not so much for
Jess." His gaze flicked to Kai, then away.

Daughtry's magic had been coded to mirror and
replicate its own images within the conference room that
he had commandeered for this purpose. All around
them—the six Summoners who bore official witness, the
Designer himself, and Kai, whose role as witness was an
honorary one only, since it was assumed that he was
much too biased toward his *krikkia* to be objective—
the story of Jess's Trials would play itself out in three-
dimensional images the Summoners could manipulate
when they felt the need for closer study.

And already he was uneasy. He summoned the image
toward him and drew out the sound, but all he received
was an odd, high tone.

"Maybe she's talking to herself," the Summoner
named Romany said. "A lot of the new ones do that.
Talk to themselves as they cast."

Jess did sometimes speak the spellcasts out loud, but
Kai pointed out, "How could she be casting? She hasn't
even entered the arena yet. Jack, why can't I hear—"

Then the flickering simulation of Jess lifted her head
and her voice slipped through loud and clear: "See you."

The image turned and moved through the air and Kai directed it back into context. Jess opened the door of the hotel suite and stepped through.

Now she was in the arena: the spaces set aside for the spell-constructions to be layered upon them, woven through them. Jess had not been in her original suite, but another, identical one in a different part of the hotel. Daughtry had renovated much of the southeastern quarter specifically to hold his spellcrafts, and after the Trials would doubtless renovate them again. What Jess was moving through now was half reality, half illusion. Some of that reality could kill her—but so could some of the illusion.

I wouldn't let that happen.

Jess worked through the first trial zone, meant mostly as a warm-up: opening locks, sensing hidden doors and passageways, flexing the tension of the Dreamlines in order to levitate objects. She was nervous, Kai could tell: some of her work lacked finesse, the rocks and sculptures and odd bits and ends she was forced to clear from her path swinging through the air too sharply, landing clumsily. She came to an intersection of corridors and made the wrong turn, stepping into a painful crosshatch of Dreamline energy that went through her like lightning. Beside him, Kai heard Romany murmur sympathetically. Jess stayed crouched on the floor for a moment, then stood up with a new expression crossing her face—it looked, Kai thought, like anger. Clutched in her left hand, the crown glimmered. One of its seven stones went out.

"Pick up your pace, girl," Romany murmured. "You're falling behind."

She came to the first room. This was the room of fire. Circles of flame overlapped each other, the fire flaming up orange, yet a pale blue at the base, the blue of Dreamline energy. Kai felt himself relax a bit. Jess was good with fire; she could make up some time here. Sure enough, she manipulated the flames with ease, sending

them away from her to close again behind her as she
stepped through the room.

The next was the room of ice. The intention here was
for Jess to control her body temperature as she passed
through the subzero environment, the white walls and
floor caked with snow and ice. Jess closed her eyes, and
Kai could see her turning inward, deep through her own
body. He flashed back to when he had first started
teaching her this, how to think through the body, use it
as your line of resistance. Jess's eyes opened. Kai could
see her mouth twist in a way that meant, *Ah, screw it,*
and she raised her right hand, palm up. She sent a
scorching blast of Dreamline energy rocketing through
the room. It hit the base of the wall opposite and flared
up in a kind of blue-orange firebomb. Jess ran through
melting ice, head down, holding the crown, as the air
sizzled around her.

In the next hallway, the golems came after her; she
took them apart with ease. She made her way through
the room of blood and the room of siren music. Another
one of the stones went out. This seemed to rattle her a
bit. Which was maybe why she had some difficulty with
the banshee winds, failing to calm the forces that picked
her up and slammed her against a stone wall. She held
up her arms and inched forward. The winds whipped
around her, slipped past her. She had thrown up a
protective wall around herself, using the same spell he
had encoded in an amulet for Ramsey. Her approach
was effective, but by the time she reached the far door,
another stone had gone out.

Then she disappeared.

The air went dark. There was a faint hissing sound
and Kai breathed in damp air, tasted salt on his lips.
"Jack!" he yelled. "Jack, what is this?"

He heard Daughtry yell a reply, but his words were
picked up by a sudden wind that twisted them into a
moan.

Then the electricity came back on, light flooding the

room; another moment, and Daughtry's images appeared. But they were sketchy, flickering, and when Kai beckoned forth the sound, all they heard was that flattened moaning sound from before. "What?" Kai said, feeling that sound run through him, leaving him cold and shivering.

Daughtry dropped in the chair beside him, leaning across the table toward the ghostly images, saying grimly, "I don't know."

The shivering left him. Kai resisted the urge to strike the table with his fist, grab the lapels of Daughtry's silk shirt, and yell right into his face. "Where is she?"

"There," Romany said.

The faintest suggestion of Jess's form flickered up near the left corner. There were only hints and traces of whatever environment she was moving so cautiously through. Kai thought he saw the glint of a mirror behind her. "Where is that? What zone is that?"

"I don't know."

"What do you mean you don't know?"

"I mean"—there was a bite in Daughtry's voice now— "that isn't anything I designed."

"She's talking," Romany said. "Kai. You were right. She's talking to someone."

Kai looked squarely at Daughtry. "So who's in there with her?"

"Like I said. This isn't anything I designed."

"We need to get her out of there." Kai pushed back his chair and stood, just as Daughtry grabbed his arm.

"Wait," he said. "Wait. Look. She's in Zone Six."

That strange glint behind Jess was gone, replaced by another space resolving itself around her. She was outside now, in what was normally a back parking lot but had been sectioned off and redesigned by Daughtry as an urban street scene. This was a warcraft test, as both illusory and real hybrids—hybrids that Daughtry, with help, had collected and imprisoned for this very purpose—came at Jess from different directions.

"Something's wrong," Kai said. "We need to stop this—"

"We can't. She's come too far—"

"There's something wrong."

"You stop this now," Daughtry snapped, "you think she'll ever get a second chance? Given your relationship with her? Given that it was a *demon* who quickened her? It's one thing if she fails. It's another if the Trials are aborted due to some kind of *saja-ken.*"

Saja-ken. Corrupted magic. In this case, magic corrupted through the incestuous relationship between a mentor and his dream-child. The fact that Jess's latent talent had been kicked into life with the help of an imprisoned demon named Del only gave the Sajae another reason to be wary of her. Kai became conscious of the other Summoners seated in their chairs, looking at him. Romany touched his arm. Kai felt a flaring deep inside him, reaching up through his body, his blood, gathering behind his eyes. He passed a hand across them so the others would not see what color they were. If Jess was officially pronounced *saja-ken,* they would both be exiled, made outcasts, like Salik. If not for the rumors Kai had picked up from his observances of the hybrids, if not for the information Zazou had confirmed, if not for the possibility, even if remote, of what they were preparing for, Kai would not have cared. He had lived without his Pact before; he could do it again. But if the Traveler once again had this world in his sights, they needed the strength and power that could only come through Summoner unity.

"She's more than halfway through," Romany whispered. "Look at her. She's doing well. Let her finish. Whatever else happened in there, she will tell us herself."

Kai nodded. Feeling as if he'd suddenly put on another century of age, the kind that dragged on you like deadweight, he sat down beside Romany and folded his hands on the table in front of him. Jess was working her way through the onslaught of hybrids, picking out the illusions from the real ones, the illusions disappearing as soon as they passed through her body. It was an eerie effect, Kai thought, as if the illusory hybrids were entering through her clothes and skin to take possession of her.

But this was Jess Shepard in her element. Her talents were for both the blood- and dream-forms of warfare: the magic of a born warrior. They watched as she fell into the movements he had taught her, spinning and lunging, her palms flashing through a succession of angles to cast darts and pulses of deadly energy. They watched as the hybrids were ripped apart.

"Yolla's balls," Romany muttered. "Don't mess with *her*."

She flung herself through the door and slammed it shut, the last of the hybrids' cries still ringing in her ears. She was bruised, battered, and sore, but she shut her mind to the pain.

"No. Use the pain. Use everything."

She knew that voice. Pushing herself to her feet, limping just a little, she studied the space in front of her. Long, shadowed, and narrow.

Mirrors.

They hung on both sides of her, full-length mirrors in ornate gold frames. Her own reflection skated across the surface; beneath that surface, that reflection, was a dark rippling that reminded her of water. Then the rippling lightened, turned transparent, and through it she could see the distant image of something else: a naked man strung up in chains.

"What is this?" she whispered.

"An intermission."

The voice was coming from her own reflection. Except it was no longer her reflection—or rather, it moved as she moved, stared and blinked and lifted her hand as she did, but it was not her.

It was the little girl, her image stretched out like the

reflection in a funhouse mirror so that she equaled Jess's height of five feet, nine inches.

"You've been having some problems," the girl said.

Jess looked at the crown in her hand. Four of the seven stones had gone out. She didn't know how much time she had left; the stones seemed to go out randomly, as if they were measuring out their own kind of time that had nothing to do with hers.

"You must fight them," she said, "if you want to be one of them. You must fight them and love them, both. They didn't teach you how to do that, did they? How to combine love and war in the way of the true Summoner, the kind of Summoner they've forgotten how to be." She paused. "They're afraid of you."

"What is this?" Jess said. "This is part of the Trials? This is a dream? What?"

"Jess." The girl's tone was chiding. "You're not being disruptive enough. How can you discover the rules that work for you if you don't disrupt the rules that work for them? You can never be a Summoner if you try to be like the Summoners. Haven't you figured that out yet?"

"You say you're some kind of part of me," Jess said, "so how come I don't understand what the hell you're talking about?"

"You do. You do. Because you know what you're doing wrong, Jess. You're trying to command and control, when real power does neither."

"So then what does it do?"

"The real power is learning from what is inside you. Using that. You know this. But you shy away from it because you're afraid. You sidestep your true power. Don't be afraid, Jess. Be ready."

"Be ready for what?"

"Be ready to get hurt," the little girl said.

Her image disappeared into Jess's own, as if the latter had swallowed the former.

And Jess was staring through her reflection, through the faint rippling behind it, to the image of the man in chains. He lifted his head and for a moment she thought he was staring at her, through the glass, through all the distance that lay between them.

Her breath caught in her throat.

"Lucas," she said, and touched the mirror.

It cracked beneath her hand. The cracks raced off in all directions, running into the frame; then the glass fell apart, sliding to the ground in a brilliant smash of sound. One by one the other mirrors did the same, a staggered symphony of breaking glass. Jess felt a breeze sweep her face, tasted salt spray on her lips, felt energy race through her like fire. Then it was gone, and the floor was coming at her much too fast—

She thought she had lost consciousness, but suddenly she was entering yet another room. This one was small, shadowed, light pouring in from a small window high up, and the little girl from the mirror was assembling a sculpture out of bones. "Hello," she said, smiling over at Jess, as she fitted another bone into place.

Jess said, "Is this still my Trials?"

"Your Trials are over. Or they're just beginning. It depends on how you look at it."

"So then I'm just dreaming," Jess said.

The girl said, "You have interesting dreams."

Behind her, Lucas Maddox sat on a stool, strumming a guitar. He was naked, bleeding, chained, and shackled, but none of these things seemed to bother him. He strummed, sang something beneath his breath. "Hey, painter," he said.

Jess looked at the sculpture. It was of some kind of house. She wondered if the little girl meant to live in it.

"Hey, painter," Lucas said. "It's time to come together. You know the way, right?"

"No," Jess said. "I have no idea what you're talking about."

"Then let me show you," Lucas said. "Because this is where you'll need to find me."

And as the melody flowed from the strings, as Lucas moved his head to the rhythm, a different kind of song took shape inside Jess's head. A music that arranged itself into the image of a winding, glimmering road. She felt this new knowledge light up inside of her, and all she had to do was obey it.

II

Hell Came Down

. . . They can't tell us it didn't happen. They can't try to spin us with their "reasonable" theories. I was there in the desert when hell came down. I was not insane or crazy on drugs and neither were you. And if you don't think that that hell will come again then you're one of those folks makes me weep for humanity. There are devils and Others out there and they want our world. Believe it. So the question is do we just let them take it?

Is it theirs for the taking?

—comment by "Mr Brighteyes" on the blog
Notes from the Angelside, 9/9/07

. . . the abrupt disappearance of Jessamy Shepard from the New York art scene, which had pegged her as one of the new wave's most brooding, charismatic, enigmatic figures. Ms. Shepard would hardly be the first or last to reject "the dark seductive machinery"—her own words—of an art scene that can seem detrimental to the very art it is supposed to be about. By all accounts she was a rebellious, troubled teenager who grew into a hardworking if haunted young woman, but no true rebel can wear

*with ease any star the so-called Establishment sees
fit to pin upon her; would not be satisfied until she
came up with a dozen innovative conceptual ways
of throwing it back in their faces. Which, by walking
away from the kind of acclaim any "reasonable"
artist would kill for, is exactly what one might say
Ms. Shepard has done. The mystery of her unexplained absence is a piece of art in itself—quite possibly her last—as damning and apocalyptic as any
of the paintings for which she was swiftly becoming known.*

—Erin A. Wilson, "The Curious Art of Jess
Shepard," posted online in Artbloggers, 10/14/16

Chapter Thirteen

Del

Demons in the modern world.

Oh, how Del liked the sound of that!

He paced the length of his prison-sphere, clambered up the walls, hung from the ceiling, and dropped. Did it all again. Flicking his tail this way and that, getting a nice little rhythm going; darting his tongue along several rows of teeth tasting always of meat and blood. Nerves on fire. He felt *electric* with knowledge, *electrified,* and sweetly dangerous, like a killing fence that others might throw themselves upon. Where had he gotten that image, electric fence? An image from the modern world. From a book Mina, his Guardian, his Keeper, had read to him? From one of the memories Mina sometimes fed him, bringing people down down down, underground, to this little cavern, Del's home sweet home, his prison-sphere a glowing, radiant thing hovering above his ring of broken glass, stained glass, pretty pieces arranged in a pretty mosaic. He liked to look at all that glass, could lose himself in happy contemplation of the designs and colors, rearranging them all in his head, again and again and again, so that one design multiplied into a million.

Good way to kill time.

He had so much time.

Also his memory collection, to keep him busy. His collection was everything to him, and kept him reasonably sane and sedate, which is why Mina made sure through the years that he was well supplied. Drawing his awed human visitors closer to him, his cage, close enough so that he could reach out with one psychic hand and crack open their dainty skulls (not literally, of course, shame shame shame) and scoop out the meat inside. Quite an education. He hadn't been out in the world for, what now, hundreds of years? Thousands? Hundreds of thousands? There was no telling, not for Del. Still, he and the modern world were on a friendly basis. Del felt this. Knew this. Could recognize the modern world across a crowded room, put face to name. He could wave, say, *Hello, modern world, whazzzup?* Say, *How's it hangin'?* Say, *Rock on, my brother. Get your groove on. Catch ya later. I'll call you. Let's do lunch sometime. Have your people call my people.* Such words and phrases! Del liked to roll them around in his head, shooting them at each other like marbles. One of his favorite stolen scooped-out memories had to do with crouching in an alley and playing marbles with pretty little boy-meat friends, while the smell of frying food filled the air and images flickered across a television screen in a nearby window. Ah, television. What Del wouldn't give for a television of his own. He would try the words out in different combinations. *Whazzup rock on my people let's do lunch special today is spiced Cuban chicken.* When he got tired of this he moved over to a storehouse of favorite mental images: *mushroom cloud* was one. Blooming so bright. So pretty. *Rodney King riots* was another. And: *concentration camps.* And: *JFK assassination.* And: *today on Jerry Springer, child stars gone bad!*

Demons in the modern world.

They couldn't compare to him, of course. Not him or his little group, his brothers and sisters, scattered in very special prisons around this human world. Six of them in all. Used to be seven, seven special little demons, but then Asha escaped, raised hell. *Attagirl! You go, girl! Girl power!* Asha, however, was gone now—when he reached out for her in the Demonlines, he sensed echoes of her. Traces. Ghosts. Part of her lingered on, yes, had even found continuing life of sorts within her very special friend, but the hot, molten center of the entity known as Bakal Ashika, as Del had known and loved her—well, sort of loved—had left this realm for another, faraway one. He wished her the best. *Hasta la vista, baby. I'll be back.*

They, Del and Asha and the other five, had been human once. *More* than human: Sajae, descended from the angels themselves, angels fallen into this world-realm to mate with pretty human mortals. More than Sajae: they had been like Summoners, trained and bonded in the rituals of deep magic . . . only they had gone about it underground. Illicit magic, slave magic, bad magic. Very so delightfully bad.

This had been in the days of the Labyrinth, that fabled city deep in the African desert. Long gone now. Turned to sand. Asha and Del and the others had done this, taken revenge, *smashed the system, raged against the machine.* Anyway, Del had never lived in the Labyrinth proper: in those days when he was still Delkor Lokk, humble (and somewhat shady) artisan, he had lived above the smells and noise of the *akilla* markets, where Sajae dealt with the Outsiders who came to buy and sell—or came seeking other, more underground forms of business—before he took the plunge into the magic-toxic lands beyond the Westgate. When you Westgated, you had that mark on you. You started to look, talk different. People started to avoid you. But Del had risked the land's shifting, transient nature along with the other misfits and outcasts, the fugitives, the escaped slaves, the thrill seekers you found in such parts. Out on those edges—where the Labyrinth was breaking down, radiating strange energy that made the place unstable and dangerous—Del had been left alone to do as he would. And it was he who had discovered the place where the seven of them had performed the ceremony that opened holes and tunnels between the worlds, so that the demons could come down, come down . . . come down into them, as they turned themselves into living human vessels.

Demon soul in human flesh.

More than human.

Sajae flesh.

Summoner flesh.

Reign of fire, death, blood, and plague.

These new demons in the modern world, inside their merely human packaging, were cute, but so very sadly limited. They were dying because of it.

They could use a little help.

And from what Del could tell—as he sensed the entity pressing up against the membrane of this world, so keenly watching, and already casting such a long, dark shadow that Del shivered happily in awe—*help was on the way!*

For the Great One himself was moving once more among the Lines, having returned from a long time ago in a galaxy far, far away. The Great One, still nameless and faceless, stalking the spaces between and below the Dreamlines, those spaces and corridors where only hell-children could travel, casting out his message: *I am preparing the way for you all. Hold on. Keep faith. Soon I will open not one door, but many.*

So the last time Mina had come down to visit him, he had stared at her through the sphere, at the auburn-haired glory of her made rippled and distorted by the layers of spellcraft between them, which in Del's opinion only added to her beauty, added greatly, and he had hurled himself against the sphere-wall in the way he figured most impressive and dramatic, and he had flattened his hands against the wall, stretched out his long fingers, showing off his talons—again, the drama, so important to give them the drama—and hissed, "The prince. Bring me the prince. Bring me the princeling, the pretty, pretty princeling."

The prince—oh, now *he* was a creature of beauty, real beauty—had gone by many names during his time in the world. They all had, the Summoners, so long-lived that every now and again they had to husk off their old identities and create themselves anew. A fun game to play, Del always thought, and regretted that he never got to play it. Be at play in the modern world. This latest name the prince had chosen for himself: Kai Youngblood. Perhaps a touch cheesy? But Del liked the word *Kai*, sweet sharp syllable clacking in his mouth. Liked the word *blood*, for obvious reasons. And *Young*, well, was that the prince's attempt at irony? Perhaps Del would ask him. There were many things Del wanted to ask him.

And Del had some power now, imprisoned as he was. Del had cards to play . . . and such *big* cards they were! And you could tell, from the look in Mina's eyes, that she was aware of this. Which meant that the others—the prince—would be aware.

Things were about to get interesting.

Ah, they should *thank their lucky stars* they had him, Mina's little pet Del: the trickster, the wild card, the X factor! It wasn't that Del cared if they won or lost, saved this world or not; if humanity burned and turned to ash, or thrived and moved outward to populate other planets—and shouldn't they have done this by now? Perhaps the modern world was not so modern after all. Weren't there supposed to be flying cars and helpful robots all over the place by now? But no memory Del had ingested seemed to speak of such things, despite the dreams and expectations he had absorbed so many decades ago, along with those memories of episodes— ah! Television again!—of *The Jetsons*.

All Del wanted, simple creature that he was, was a *fun* war.

An *interesting* war.

Or, truly, what was the point?

Chapter Fourteen

Jess

She woke up alone in a strange room. Alone, except for the androgyne seated beside her, plucking shards of glass from her arm. Jess struggled to sit up, blinking rapidly to clear her vision, breathing in the scent of blood. Her blood. The androgyne's features swam into view. "Stop that," Jess said. "You can go. You don't have to do that." But the androgyne just shrugged, gave a half smile, and eased another sliver of broken mirror from Jess's arm. It dropped into the bowl with a clink. Jess saw a jagged heap of such bloodstained shards and slivers; the bowl could barely contain it. She had a memory of falling into a crouch, lifting her bare arms over her head as the mirrors exploded all around her. "You can go," she told the androgyne again. "I can take care of this—I can heal this myself." She didn't have a talent for that kind of spellcraft—for healing in general—but wounds like this were novice stuff, and it would be good practice.

She felt tired, though.

So tired.

There were images jostling through memory, her mind turning fully toward them. Wanting to address what had happened. Wanting to make sense of it. *No,* she thought, and slumped in the chair as another clink sounded in the bowl and the androgyne moved a warm, wet cloth across her lower arm. *Can't we just be done with this . . .*

"You can go," she snapped at the androgyne. "Go."

She jerked her arm away, but Daughtry's servant seemed unfazed. And Jess finally got it: the androgyne took orders from only one person, and that person wasn't Jess.

Words were spoken from the doorway; soft, sibilant, underscored by an odd kind of whistling. The androgyne hopped back, clutching the bowl to its chest, then swiveled to look at Kai. He leaned against the door frame, head ducked down and slightly to the side like when he was studying something. Jess wondered how long he had been studying them. Her.

She tried to speak but no words came.

The androgyne tipped its body toward Kai, ponytail spreading across its shoulders, then slipped into the hallway beyond. Kai smelled like soap and a light, clean cologne as he straddled the chair beside her cot, gestured for her to extend her arms. She thought maybe he'd play nursemaid, check the bandages, but instead he took her wrists lightly in both hands and massaged them, slowly, deeply, sending pulses of something that wasn't exactly pleasure, yet felt good nonetheless, rippling up through her arms, smoothing over the pain.

"So you'll tell me what happened in there," Kai said.

She drew her arms away and folded them across her chest. He stared at her with that cool, blank impassivity that only a high-blood Sajae could pull off. His eyes were a crystalline gray—his poker eyes, she called them, when he went so deep inside himself that not even his eye color could indicate emotion. It was the color of clouded ice. Of numbness. She didn't see it often. Maybe she should feel alarmed by it, except she was feeling pretty numbed herself.

"So, the Trials," she said. "So how'd I do?"

No response. No flicker in those poker eyes. "Kai," she said.

"Aborted." He lifted his head. "Your Trials were aborted midway through. You remember?"

"But I failed. Right?"

When he didn't answer, she said, "Right? Just say it. Say it, and make it real, and I can deal with it. But—"

"Trials only get aborted for one reason."

And then she realized.

"It's not like I failed. It just went wrong. It went wrong in there."

"Yes."

"So the magic went wrong, and now everybody . . . now you all think I'm wrong? Like, I'm crawling with radiation or something?" She looked around her, heightened her vision enough to see the sheen of magic on the walls. The kind of magic that would keep her in here. This wasn't a hotel room; this was a cell. "Am I in some kind of quarantine? Are you waiting to see if I turn into anything . . . strange?" She was thinking of the stories he'd told about the no-man's-land beyond the Westgates in the Labyrinth. Was this the same thing? Was that what incest magic was?

Incest magic.

"It's because we've been together," Jess said. "We've been sleeping together. So this is what happens, right? Bastard magic. So do I start growing a second head or something? Do the walls turn to cheese?"

The faintest flicker of amusement in his voice. "The walls turn to—"

"Does everything start to melt, like in a Dali painting? What does toxic magic do to a place, anyway?"

"Jess. You need to calm down."

"You could have prevented this," she said. "You were the older one, the wiser one, the one I was supposed to trust. Who was supposed to know about consequences. Because I didn't realize I had to make a choice, that it was either you or the magic. You made that choice for me. You—"

"I need you to calm— if we're going to talk about this—"

"—could have just said no, the night I crawled into bed with you. I wanted you," Jess said, "but I didn't know what it would cost me. You knew. And you just went ahead and let me pay—"

"We're both paying—"

"—when I didn't even know there was a price."

"You were not such an innocent," Kai snapped. "Okay, I'm mostly to blame, but let's not pretend that you were just some lamb wandering around in the daisies—"

"Why did you let this happen?" Jess said. "When you knew what might happen afterward?"

"Because I needed you."

She curled up in the chair. He seemed to catch himself, looking at his hands, examining the nails and palms. She felt that heat recede from her, saw that glow in his skin dim back to what passed as normal for him.

"You needed me," she said. "Okay. So that justifies everything."

"I thought we were going to die, Jessamy. I didn't think we'd be *around* for any *consequences.* Even if I had truly believed there would be any. Which I didn't. I thought it was—what's that phrase in English?—an old wives' tale, meant to keep mentors from seducing their students."

"You thought—" She stared at him, trying to incorporate this confession into her view of things. "You thought we were going to lose? You never told me that."

He stood up, and then, in a gesture that stunned her, he grabbed the chair and flung it across the room. It rebounded off the wall, smashing to the floor like a dead thing. "I don't know what I thought. Okay? And I was so close to just not giving a damn—you don't even know—" He was struggling for words, and it was such an unusual state to see him in that Jess couldn't disguise her own fascination. "This is not an easy world, Jess. Walk through it for nearly eight centuries and it gets to you. It gets to all of us."

"But you're still trying to save it," Jess said. "The world."

He shrugged. Looked weary. "You are the world and the world is you," Kai said. "And that's just the way it's been for me. I won't apologize for that. I see no need. I gave myself to Asha. I let her put me on that fucking rock. You know what happened next. Or do you want me to go into detail?"

"No details," she whispered.

"You cross the line once, you can't cross back. We are what we are. I'm not interested in regret. Because compared to what's coming—"

"Stop," she whispered.

"Look at me."

She didn't respond.

"Look at me."

She said, "It wasn't toxic magic. There was someone in there with me."

He stepped back and it felt as if some divide fell between them, soft and silent as gauze and yet the more divisive for that.

"Tell me," he said.

"Some kind of— A little girl."

Another beat of silence.

His voice calm, reasonable: "No."

"A little girl. She said she was me."

"And you believed this?"

"I don't know. No. But—"

"Why are you lying to me?"

"I'm not lying to you," she said. "There was this girl—"

"Lucas." He bit off the word. *"Maddox."*

Ramsey, she thought. The kid was loyal to her, but he wasn't blind or stupid. Fooling him was a whole different thing from fooling herself.

"Was he the one you were talking to? In the Trials? Was he somehow . . . present?"

"Echoes of him, maybe," Jess said. "Traces. He's—"

And she realized then that he was fighting the urge to slap her. She knew he wouldn't do it—he would never do it—but flinched away from him anyway. *I gave myself to Asha. I let her put me on that fucking rock. You know what happened next.* Lucas had been there. Lucas had watched. He had probably laughed, even though sadism wasn't his thing, not exactly.

"You've been communicating with him," Kai said.

"Dreams," Jess said. "Just—dreams—"

"You've been *communicating* with him. Tell me now, because you sure as hells never did before. *Tell me.*"

She stared at him. She tried to formulate a response in her head and transfer that response to her voice but it didn't seem to be happening, and then she just gave up. In the vivid, crackling power of his presence it was like she was folding in on herself, disappearing. She didn't want to lie to him. She didn't want to fight. She was tired of this slow, inward vanishing act, tired of this fear that there weren't other options. So she stared at him, and said nothing, and it wasn't because she wanted to hurt him any more than he already was or make him feel further betrayed. It was because she felt so far removed from who she was and everything that was between them. She lacked the strength and energy to cross all that distance.

But in her silence he read something different; she could see it in the flare of his eyes, and she knew he had the urge to throw the chair again. Throw anything. "Everything I've done for you," he said, "and you . . . and you . . . I mean, hells, Jessamy, we're talking Lucas fucking Maddox—"

"Everything you've done for me?" The words lashed out of nowhere. Or not nowhere: some deep little shadowspace inside her, acknowledged for the first time. "Was it for me? Really? You changed my life. And I liked my life. You took away everything I was, everything I worked for."

"But I gave you more," Kai said. "So much more."

"You brought me into this . . . this fold of people who . . . despise me. And you did this for me? Really? You believe in me. Is that for me or is that for you, so you can feel justified? You need to believe I'm so great—that I have all this potential—so you can rationalize every action you've ever taken since you broke into my loft . . ."

"Not your loft," Kai said quietly. This was true; she'd been house-sitting for an older, much more successful friend, but this didn't seem the time to quibble over technicalities. "And I hardly broke and entered." She had to stare at him, bemused at his reluctance to admit to this, the crudeness of it. It's not like she had slipped him a key.

"You have to hold me up as the great new hope," Jess went on, "in order to keep your ego intact. Because if I'm not . . . then you're the one who's wrong. And everybody knows it. And you were on thin ice before me, weren't you? None of the other Summoners trusted you. Were prepared to follow you. You were the rogue—the arrogant, dissident, spoiled little princeling—"

"Stop it, Jess."

"And this," Jess said, gesturing between the two of them, "this thing we have—it can't be just some fling, some affair, because then it's tawdry and not worth the price paid, the taboo broken. Right? So it has to be some great deep love. It has to be—"

"You don't know what you're saying."

"—but what if it's not? What if it's not really love, just some . . . decision you made, a bunch of rationalizations and justifications and . . . and spectacle. Daughtry plays to the crowd, puts on a good show. So what if this is your way of doing the same? Of—"

"Jess. You are Shemayan's heir. Did you forget this?"

"Fuck Shemayan. I am not Shemayan."

"No. You're not. Shem was precise. Controlled. Patient. He didn't grab at magic the way you do, always needing the next spell, the next thrill, no matter what it did to his body. How much do you weigh now, Jess? Do you even know? It's almost like you *want* to destroy yourself—"

"If that's true, then you're not exactly stopping me, are you? You were barely around. And I had a job to do, remember? It's not like I was turning toads into princes or frolicking in the fields with purple fucking unicorns—I was *killing,* Kai. I had monsters to kill. Because that's what I am now. I'm not a Summoner, I'm not a painter, I'm barely even a person. I have all this magic and I use it for death. That's what I am. That's what you've done for me."

"You think I don't know what it's like to hunt them? Kill them?"

But you're so good at it. I think you like it.

"I don't want this," Jess muttered.

He couldn't help rolling his eyes. "None of us *want* this. But not all of us are . . . *whining* about it."

"You don't choose my life for me! *I* choose my life."

"Magic chose us. War chose us. We don't get to do the choosing, Jess. We don't have that privilege."

"That's not true."

"You Americans always think you can be anything. Have anything. I just showed you the truth of your life. Your power. That's what I gave you."

"The truth," she said.

"Jess—"

"So I die young? Right? What about *that* truth?"

She waited for the denial, the expression of incredulity; she waited for him to call her a fool. But all she heard was the silence of his response; she saw his face smoothing over, his eyes turning gray. He was retreating deep inside himself, leaving her more alone than ever. When he still didn't say anything, she pressed, "Aren't you at least curious about how I found out?"

"Yes."

"Lucas told me."

"How the hells could *he* know?"

"So isn't this the part where you tell me . . . *It's only a dream, Jess, and dreams can't hurt you?*"

"Not if you're dreaming of him."

"What is this, Kai? Why does he know and you know and I—don't?"

"I don't know how he plays into this. But obviously he does."

"Play into what, Kai?"

"You." For a moment just that, just the syllable, as if that was all he could think of to say. "You reincarnate, Jess. Down through Shemayan's family line. I don't know why. It's unusual. It means that for whatever reason your soul is chained to this realm—to Shemayan's bloodline—until some action frees it, allows it to pass through the Dreamlines into the next phase of existence. Whatever that might be."

Her knees slipped away from her. If she wasn't already sitting she would have collapsed. "Oh," she said. She was streaming away from herself, off to that vanishing point, and when she reached it she wouldn't be Jess anymore; just some shell, some walking, talking, demon-killing shell of herself. "Okay." Another thought came to her and she looked at Kai, blinking rapidly. "And you. You've been tracking my family line for . . . how many generations now? You've been watching. So you've known me—you've known me for a very long time . . ." She laughed. A hollow sound.

"I know you," Kai said, the word twisting with irony. "I know Jessamy Shepard. You're not just a copy of a copy of a copy. It doesn't work like that. Too many things go into who you are for it to be the same each time. So I know you now, in this life. I didn't know you in the others. It wasn't my place to interfere."

"But you interfered with this one."

"I had to. This life is the one where everything culminates. This is the life all those others were leading up to. I believe that."

"Just because I slept with you?"

"Maybe."

"But if I was so different in those past lives, then how could you tell it was always—it was me?"

"I didn't, not at first. But I noticed things. Saw things."

"A pattern," she said.

"Yes."

"Because I die young."

He didn't say anything.

"Because I—"

"Yes. You die young."

"How do I die?"

"Different ways."

"What kind of ways?"

"I'm not doing this, Jess."

"How much longer do I have? In this life? As the one and only Jessamy Shepard?"

"I said I'm not—"

"Goddammit, Kai, just how old do I get to be? How old?"

"Thirty," he said. "You die at thirty."

She tried to swallow, but her throat was too dry. "I turn thirty next month," she said. "So whatever it is you need to get out of me—whatever it is I'm supposed to accomplish—you need to do it soon, right? So is that how you've been looking out for me? Because I didn't know we were on such a tight schedule."

"Jess. It's not—"

"Why didn't you tell me?"

"It's not preordained."

"Bullshit it's not preordained! Because it always happens. Didn't you think I should know? So maybe I could adjust some of my life goals accordingly? You know— my long-term life plan?" Not like she'd ever had one.

"It's not your plan," he said. "It's my plan."

"Oh. Your plan."

"I plan"—and his eyes were the darkest she'd ever seen them—"not to let you die. Not in this life. Not you."

"You have some spell-form that can guarantee that? 'Cause I'm not aware of that. And being brought back from the dead is hardly the same thing—"

"You don't die young in this life," Kai said flatly.

"—because I've seen that up close. When you're not alive, but not dead either, and it's no way to . . . to be. You wouldn't do that to me. Swear to whatever gods you people believe in that you wouldn't do that to me—"

"I won't have to."

"How can you say that?"

"Because this is when the pattern breaks. Whatever is supposed to play out, it plays out now. Whatever chains you to that early death, it gets broken. You live. And we go to war together." He nodded, as if it was just that simple. "That's the plan."

"Oh," Jess said. "I feel so much better now." Then: "So when do I get out of here?"

She could see him evading the answer. "Where do you think you'll go?"

"I don't know."

"To Lucas?"

She didn't answer.

He sighed. "You can't leave, Jess."

"Because I'm—contaminated."

"They need to discuss. The Summoners. There needs to be a council—a ruling—it's just how things are done. How they need to be done."

"You mean *you* need to discuss. You're one of them, after all."

"We need to figure out what's going on. And you're not safe."

"Not safe to play with others."

"I mean *you're* not safe."

"You can't keep me here like a prisoner," Jess said.

"You're not a prisoner. You're just . . . slightly detained."

"Let me go," she said softly. "Don't make me face them again. Daughtry. The others. Just let me—let's get away from here, start over. Figure out a new plan."

"We can't afford to alienate them, Jess. We need them."

"You need them."

"I need you," he said simply.

"You need me more? Then prove it."

Not taking her eyes off his face, she stood up and pulled off her leather jacket and tossed it to the floor. She unbuttoned her blouse, raising her chin just a little, and they held each other's gazes, waiting to see who would be the first to break. She shrugged the blouse off her shoulders, felt the whisper of silk down her skin. She stood by the bed, hands hooking in the back pockets of her jeans, shoulders thrown back, and she knew how she looked in that moment. She saw herself reflected in his face, the desire he didn't try to hide. She waited to see what he would do. He could leave. Maybe he would. The mood in the room was not exactly loving.

He stood by the door with his head slightly bowed and he shook his head and said her name and came toward her, ignored the bed and pushed her up against the wall, and his mouth was warm on her throat, a little too ticklish because her skin there was so damn sensitive. She moved her head and then they were kissing, the deep, warm, hungry kind of kissing when you fit into each other, each other's taste, each other's smell, and he was such a big man that she could climb all over him, her legs tangling round his waist as her hands played at the buttons of his shirt. She sucked and bit his throat and shoulder. She wanted to leave marks. He responded by pressing harder against her, pinning her to the wall, his hand moving up through her long hair and grasping her head, pushing it away from him. "Ow," he muttered,

and she laughed at him, and then he was kissing her
again and she bit down on his lower lip so hard she
tasted blood. He let her. He was flailing off his jacket;
his hands were warm on her body and all over and she
was dragging her nails—what nails she had—across his
chest, the back of his shoulders, and he took her wrists
and held them easily in one hand and pinned them to
the wall above her head as he adjusted himself and entered her, drove against her, both of them making auto-
matic, minute adjustments for the better angle, the
better fit, long practiced with each other, knowing how
to extract the most, the finest, the best of the pleasure
they wanted and needed. He pressed his head into the
hollow of her neck and shoulder, and she tightened her
legs around him, felt her wrists come free from his hold,
but all she could do now was wrap herself around him
and hold him close, closer, moving her mouth across his
skin, the cool smooth surface, feel the rise of heat from
deep inside, moving up through him, finally breaking
through his skin and rising up over her. Enfolding her.
The light of him, sweeping through her own banal
human body as he pushed sweat-streaked hair off her
face and flicked his tongue along her cheek. Drinking
her. The salt and musk of her. There was no comparison
between them, though, could be no comparison, because
as the deep shudders wracked through him and drove
her own trembling body deeper into the corner, as his
eyes hazed over with that smoky brightness she could
never look at directly, she pressed her mouth to his skin
and tasted the glow flowing from it. This was another
thing he had given her. The knowledge of the taste of
light.

When it was over he slumped against her, bracing
himself against the wall just enough not to crush her.
She braced herself for the tumble of foreign memory,
his memory, letting the images fall through her mind: a
dinner party in a room draped with damask and velvet,
snatches of dialogue in different languages, a dark-haired

woman setting a bowl of fruit on a table, a radio spitting
static in the background, a man speaking urgently in
Italian. Jess heard the name Hitler. She touched Kai's
chest, traced the lines and ridges of muscle, as if she
could take those bits of his soul and put them back in
him, where they belonged, where they'd have nothing to
do with her. But he shared them with her now: every
time she took him inside her, every time she lost herself
in those great shuddering waves of climax, more of his
memory braided itself into hers. Maybe one day she
wouldn't be able to tell them apart: a memory of upper-
class Europeans discussing Hitler in a dimly lit drawing
room would seem just as familiar as a memory of her
own friends arguing in some shabby café in the industrial
depths of Tribeca over which Britpop art stars would
still be respected in ten, twenty, fifty years.

Or maybe his memories would obliterate hers entirely.

He had so many, after all.

She gathered the silk cotton weave of his shirt in her
fists, grazing his shoulders with her knuckles. His head
was bowed, the last of the light still shimmering off him,
a warm mellow tone different from the ghostly energy
drawn from the Dreamlines. He was breathing hard.
They both were. He lifted his head and his eyes had
dimmed enough so that she didn't have to look away. It
was difficult to admit to herself that, even now, his eyes
could still frighten her.

"Let's get out of here," Jess whispered. "Let's just go
somewhere. Figure this out on our own."

He brushed her hair back from her eyes. Laid his fingers across her lips. Something inside her crumbled and
broke. She let her eyes roam his features: the once-
straight Roman nose broken so many times throughout
his long life, the soft lower lip, the cleft in his chin, the
fine dark eyebrows, the light-bronzed skin, darker when
he'd been in the sun, darkest of all when he was fresh
off the Dreamlines. She'd left bruises and bite marks
on his throat and shoulders, scratches on his chest and

back. Good. He would go to his council with his Summoners and they would see him; they would know. They could dismiss her as unworthy and lock her away but she would still be with them, written right there in his skin.

She stood there, naked from the waist down, her shirt hanging open. She knew she was too thin, even by contemporary American standards. She also knew the Summoner aesthetic prized long, sleek, angular lines, a kind of frailty that seemed to transcend itself. She doubted that even among the Sajae, many women managed to attain and maintain this kind of gaunt appeal. She wondered what it was supposed to symbolize, what made it desirable in the first place—because of how the magic ate away at you? Made you seem smaller and weaker even as you deepened in power? Hinted at recklessness, abandon, a willingness to go over the edge?

"I confess. I'm not sure about you, Jess. I don't know what happened to you in the Trials. And if . . . if you've been communicating with this . . . this person—"

"Lucas," Jess said coldly. "His name is Lucas." How odd, she thought, that neither man seemed willing or able to speak the name of the other. Jealousy here, at least of a sort, but neither man would ever admit to it. She wondered how or if something like love even entered into this. A man like Lucas wasn't capable of love, which was maybe why he could do so well writing songs about it: he offered his fans the kind of fantasy they wanted, demanded, which Lucas himself probably took for truth.

And Kai. Standing there in the doorway, in his rumpled shirtsleeves.

He loved her. She knew this.

She also knew he was a man who liked to own things. A wealthy man who took ownership for granted. He didn't feel threatened by Maddox because he saw him as some kind of rival; he would find the very idea of that absurd. Whatever jealousy was at work here had nothing to do with love: just ownership, possession. They both felt they had some kind of right to her. And anything that she had to say wouldn't matter: they would continue to feel it, believe it, see her as someone who only needed to be persuaded. Shown the truth of things.

Your real life. Your real power. That's what I gave you.

"I have to go," Kai said. "I have to process all this. We'll talk more when I—"

"*I said I don't want to stay here. Did you hear me, Kai? I'm telling you to let me out of this place. We can meet somewhere afterward if you want, but I don't want to be here anymore, which means you're holding me here against my will.*"

"You don't seem to understand just how serious this is. The other Summoners—"

"You're the one who put me in this situation. You're the reason I'm even here."

"Either you've gone toxic," Kai said, and the coldness in his voice froze her breath in her body, "or you're in some kind of psychic relationship with a man who does *not* have our best interests at heart. So what am I supposed to do, Jess? Which of those scenarios should I prefer?"

She was silent.

"Now," he said quietly, "I have to go persuade my colleagues that it's not in their best interests to imprison or exile you. Or worse. Do you understand?"

"Are you going to tell them about—"

"I don't know what the fuck I'm going to do."

The door closed quietly behind him.

She was alone.

She sent a mindcast through the room, probing the walls, the ceiling. She sensed layers on layers of magic, hastily thrown up and woven together but no less formidable for the haste. The room had been turned into a kind of bubble, sealing her off from the Dreamlines, which meant the only potential magic she had on hand was whatever energy still lingered inside her. Which,

after the Trials, was next to nothing. She pressed her
hands to her face for several moments. Forced herself
to breathe slowly and evenly. Got up and went to the
door, needing to feel it with her hands, explore the cold
steel physicality of it even as her mind touched again
the dense crafting of magic that kept it shut and locked
against her. She had to take a grudging moment to marvel at the quality of the spellcraft. It was different from
Daughtry's—not ordered and architectural, but dense,
intricate, tightly woven, shimmering within its different
folds, the Dreamline energy not simply shaped and
crafted but coiled within the very crafting, like a spring
pulled back, just waiting to be triggered.

She knew this magic, recognized its style, its signature.
She even recognized this feeling of being humbled, how
it reminded her all over again who was the student and
who was the master.

Kai.

Kai hadn't just left her in this prison . . . he had built
it. Of course he had. Who knew her own game better
than he did—the one who had taught it to her, who had
from the beginning analyzed her strengths and weak-
nesses, possessed a better knowledge of them than she
did?

*This is their house. They built it. Just because they're
letting you play with their tools, you think they'll let you
build one of your own?*

The little girl in the mirror had told her that. Jess
wasn't a fool. She knew they were manipulative words; the
girl in the mirror, whatever it was, whatever thing crouched
behind it, was trying to fit Jess into its own agenda, just
as Kai was, or Lucas, or the other Summoners . . . everyone, it seemed, except Ramsey, who only wanted to
make sure that she took care of herself, and didn't get
eaten alive by her own dreams and magic. But it didn't
change the fact that this room was indeed Kai's house.
She could try to dismantle it, try to escape, but all she
had were the tools he had given her, and he was so

much better with them. She could feel the last of the Dreamline energy turning rancid inside her. She needed to express it in her journals, but she didn't have them; she needed to get back on the Dreamlines to recharge, but Kai had cut off all access.

She put her clothes on. Her shirt was missing all its buttons—she remembered the sound of them hitting the floor, remembered thinking they were Kai's buttons. She tied the shirt at her waist and looked to the corner for her leather jacket, when her eyes fell on the suit jacket Kai had forgotten to take with him. She wanted him to come back so she could yell at him. So she could claw at him, throw things at him. The force of her emotion frightened her. She wanted him to say he was sorry. His love had become her second skin, and she could feel it ripped off her, leaving her exposed and cold. That alone was a reason to hate him. She pushed her arms through his jacket, felt it drag on her shoulders, sleeves slipping past her hands. It smelled of him. She curled up on the bed, her eyes dry as stone, hugging the jacket against her, marking off all the reasons why she'd be better off without him: no longer his little *krikkia*, his student, his duckling, his slave. Kai's scent was in the fabric she pressed to her face, the taste of his light in her mouth.

Chapter Fifteen

Jess

She was lost in the kind of sleep that went beyond exhaustion.

So she didn't know when the tall figure with the long black hair and the walking cane entered her room, using magic of his own to unweave a path through Kai's.

She didn't know when he held his fist over her body and loosened his fingers, a grainy, purple substance filling the air. Like fairy dust. Except—if she'd been awake to see—she would have known it was hardly that.

She would have known exactly what it was.

And then she was on a dirt road winding through a blasted landscape. Large birds with oily black feathers and humanlike faces passed overhead, sending shadows in front of her, before settling on the telephone wires strung along either side.

People had been crucified on the poles, blood running down their arms and legs, dripping to earth. For some reason they just wouldn't die. They had been nailed up in such a way that they were pointing to some place in the distance, some place the road was meant to take her to . . . except she knew they weren't pointing for her.

This road belonged to someone else, and she was only here by accident. Maybe that's why, when she saw the crucified people moving their mouths, she heard nothing but traces of old voices blown on the winds. Their language was not meant for her.

When she crested a hill she saw him, in the near distance, following the road. Beyond him, she saw the towering spires, the black billowing smoke, of some kind of city. She heard a distant booming, a thumping sound, a rattle of gunfire. City at war, she thought. Going up in smoke. "You," she called, and Lucas looked over his shoulder, then turned toward her in astonishment, walking backward even as he yelled out to her.

He said, "What the hell . . . ?"

He was deeply tanned, his face smudged with dirt, his shirt ripped at the shoulder, his jeans ragged with holes.

She said, "What world is this?"

He shielded his eyes with his hand. "I'm not sure." He laughed, but there was a bitterness in it. "I'm a stranger here myself."

"What are you doing here? Where are you going?"

"I'm not sure." Then: "To his house, I think. His real house."

"No," she said. The word escaped her before she knew she would say it.

He laughed again. "Don't you have problems of your own to be dealing with? They're trying to kill you, you know. So go wake up."

"You can't go where you're going," Jess said. "You need to turn back."

"You need to turn back," he said, and despite the space between them she saw his face turn hard. "You need to get away, stay far away from the place I'm going. That place is dangerous for you."

"That place is dangerous for everyone."

"Especially for you."

"Come with me," she said.

"You think I have a choice?"

"Yes."

He tipped his head and smiled. "Ah, painter," he said. "My sweet, reluctant killer. We don't get to choose, you and I. We're the chosen."

Something kicked her in the side. She felt the blow, more startling than painful, and looked down at herself, her body. Something kicked her again and this time she cried out, pressed her hands to her side, and Lucas said, "Wake up, honey. You've got people trying to kill you and people coming to steal you. You're busy."

"I can't seem to wake up," she said. She dropped to her knees. She held her hands in front of her face and saw the weird purple grit on her skin. "I'm trying, but I can't seem—"

"The drug," Lucas said, as if agreeing. "I got dosed with it too. It's a bitch."

"—time to rise and shine, you bitch."

A jarring, sliding sensation as something slammed the bed. She managed to open an eye. She felt the bed jolt again, took another blow to her rib cage, but no one was touching her, not even the man looking down at her. She felt another pulse of Dreamline energy hurled into her body, knocking her right off the mattress. She couldn't seem to find her breath. Her head was filled with purple cloud, pulling her back to the road of the crucified, because they were all getting down from their telephone poles, yanking nails from their wrists and ankles, then dropping low to the ground; they were coming for her now, because Lucas was right, this country was most dangerous for *her*—

"Come, come, Jessamy. It's hard, I know, but you have to fight it." A man's voice, with its lilting, old-fashioned cadences that could only be those of a Summoner, sounded familiar to Jess, but in a distant way, as if recognition had to come tunneling up through too many sediments of memory. She rolled over on her back and clenched her jaw and hands, and wrenched herself out of this heavy, hazy feeling, off the bloodstained road still twisting through her mind. For a moment she felt like she was in two places at once. Then she opened her eyes and looked up into the face of a tall, thin man with long black hair and a walking stick topped with a golden lion. He tapped the floor with it. "They're trying to kill you, you know," he said. "I'll help you, Jess. You only have to ask. But you *do* have to ask."

"Salik," she said.

He turned his head, and she saw the knots and welts of the scarred half of his face, the dark bronze patches of skin. So this was what fire did to a Summoner. She stared openly at this discolored face, the features remolded into a grotesque beauty, or a beautiful grotesqueness. She wanted to paint it.

There were many questions she could have asked him, but she started with, "Who's trying to kill me?" It hurt to breathe. She looked up at the faint purple shape suspended above her, saw it come apart and drift over her body, her arms. Before she could stop herself she had breathed in more of it, felt it working down through her lungs, forcing its way through her skin, her bloodstream, felt pricks and jabs as the blood pushed it through her heart, her brain.

"Who do you think?" Salik said. "I'm waiting."

"It's not—this is not—" The air was suddenly so much thinner. She was starting to feel light-headed. "I can't believe the Summoners would—"

"Not all of them. I believe—actually I *know*, because I'm the one who gave them this stuff—that there are a couple of rogues in the bunch who decided to forego the pleasures of decision by committee. Careless of the prince to let this happen, don't you think? He always did overestimate us. One reason why so many of us can't stand him. You could do so much better, Jess. In fact, I know a man who's eager to see you. He's in chains, of course, but perhaps you're the type who would find that attractive."

"This is—" Jess gestured at the air. "This is . . . jax? But it's—"

"Different. Poisonous. You've got ten minutes left, Jessie."

"Don't call me Jessie."

"Annoying," he brayed. "My price just went up. Now I want you to beg."

"This stuff doesn't seem to be affecting you."

"I've built up some immunity. You do realize you're dying, Jess? Maybe you should stop with the questions, be a bit more . . . proactive?"

She was sucking at air. She wanted to laugh. This whole situation was absurd. Salik was absurd. "So there's an antidote or something?"

"Well, yes, but I don't have it with me, and it's not like my clients were asking for it. They wanted to send you on a strictly one-way journey. Tick tock, Jess. Let's get to the begging, okay? I'll help you figure out what to say. So just take a groveling kind of position at my feet, and then maybe—"

She had managed to pull herself into a sitting position, and now she used the wall to brace herself as she stood. Standing was so exhausting. How absurd. She leaned against the wall and looked at Salik and saw, behind him, the unending road of the crucified, leading into the boiling black air of that city. A death city. And it wanted Lucas, meant to swallow up Lucas, but why? *We're the chosen.* Why that pronoun? What did she have to do with him, his fate, that road? "How do I know," she said to Salik, "that you're not just another delusion?"

He struck her across the face. Not quite a punch, but more than a slap. The taste of blood filled her mouth, and she laughed. "That's for Ramsey," Salik said. "I mean, that truly is for Ramsey, for everything he put me through, that audacious and conniving little shit. Since he's not here, you'll have to pass on the message. But I want to be fair, so this one's for you." This time she saw the blow coming, blocked it with the knife edge of her hand. He only said, "So does this seem real enough to you?"

"Why?"

"Why ask why? Beg me, Jessie. Go on. There's a good girl."

"Why should I believe it's not some trap?"

"You don't feel trapped enough already?"

"I know what you are," Jess said. "You're a traitor."

"I'm a realist."

"People always justify themselves by saying they're *realists*."

"No they don't," Salik said. "They justify themselves by saying whatever they think they'll get away with. This world is ending, Jess, and we'll soon be at war for the new one. Two of us knew this long before the others. The prince. And myself. Let's just say we chose different strategies."

"But you were wrong," Jess said. "The apocalypse didn't happen. The world didn't go to the demons. You chose the wrong side. You must be feeling pretty stupid."

"You think you *stopped* it? Hells, you people don't even need demons; you're ending yourselves so neatly on your own. Convenient for us. Leaves a whole world ripe for plucking, if we can get in there and take it before you people completely fuck it up."

"You talk a lot," Jess said. "And you don't even answer my questions."

"I was sent here," Salik said, "to collect you. And I'd prefer not to have my body rearranged, or stuck on the other side of those goddamn freaky mirrors of his. So if we could just—" He cut himself off. He was the kind who talked too much. That must have annoyed Kai back in the day, Jess thought; Kai couldn't stand people who never shut up, never knew when to offer silence, or accept it.

She laughed. "Sounds like you need me to help you."

"We both have something to gain. And I'm not the

one about to die. Two minutes, Jess. Let's go. Beg me—"

"You really made that thing," Jess said, "that thing, that monster, that killed Ramsey's girlfriend while you and your cronies watched and made some kind of game out of it. He told me all about it."

"His name was Bubba," Salik said. "I made him, yes, a very long time ago, when I could still make things like that. When I was still an artist. Like you. Like the Traveler." Salik smirked. "But I do what I can. I've brought something for you. Very special. So if you would please get to the begging part, I can go ahead and show—"

Jess laughed again. It was nice to laugh; her head felt very light and very clear, and Salik was hilarious. She had once watched him impale a woman just because she said the wrong thing at the wrong time. He had worked out a business relationship with a young sociopath, taking street kids in exchange for the drug called jax that he made in his little gallery in San Francisco. He took the kids away to be killed in a series of festive gambling games held with others of his kind: Sajae-born and Summoners gone corrupt or crazy, and the humans deemed rich or attractive or stylish or interesting enough to bother with. "I'm not going to beg you," Jess said with disgust, as if he'd just asked her to scrub out his toilet. "So you might as well go. I'll lie down on this bed and get comfortable and die." She heard herself saying these words, but they didn't seem to mean anything. Although a nap seemed like a good idea.

"You're bluffing," Salik said.

"I really don't think so."

"Of course you want to live. Everyone wants to live. Except the ones who kill themselves, of course, but that's not exactly—"

"I've had a really, really bad day. Okay? So fuck off."

Salik sighed. "Attitude," he muttered. "Some other time, then." He grinned, the scarred half of his face looking tortured by the gesture, and then whistled loud and high. Jess flinched and covered her ears. When she looked up again Salik was gone. Had she imagined him? She hunched up against the headboard and hugged her knees to her chest, and struggled to get her mind straight. It no longer hurt to breathe, which was something; or at least, those jabbing little pains were still there, but no longer seemed part of her, as though they'd been cut from her body and set adrift in the purple air. She heard sounds coming from beyond the room, way beyond: thudding, thumping sounds, footsteps running, shouting, panic. Something was going on out there. Or maybe that was a delusion too. Was she still breathing? Her chest felt like it was unhinging, her head so light she wondered why it wasn't rising off her neck. Maybe it was. The blood road, the death road, was coming back for her. It was snaking deep out of her mind. Not just her mind. The air in front of her was opening up like a window. She stared. Couldn't stop staring. She had never witnessed magic like this. She was staring right through into that other space, that bleached-out, writhing landscape, as the crucified helped themselves and each other off those poles, as the birds looked on and shouted *jak-yak-yak*, and the crucified lifted their heads and saw her, and started shuffling and limping toward her. They were changing, she saw. Their bodies were thickening, their faces melting, and some of them were falling down on all fours, and then onto their bellies.

"Lucas," she yelled, her voice booming down into that landscape, but there was no answer. Was he still in there? Did he care?

And then a body unfolded up in front of her, one of those twisted, crucified human-things whose face had gone beyond human. Jagged shards of mirror where its eyes had been. She looked into those eyes and saw her own dazed and bewildered expression as the thing's hand moved out through the window between the two realities, and she couldn't move, or breathe, or do anything except understand that this was what her death would be, as the thing clasped her wrist and raised her hand toward the lipless hole opening to show all its teeth.

The ceiling exploded.

Chunks of concrete and plaster dust rained over her, some large, dark, cannonball of a shape landing in front of her, the posthuman thing with mirror eyes disappearing, the air around it snapping shut as the death road vanished from the room and from her mind, snaking back to wherever it came from. What landed in front of her was almost, but not quite, a man. Naked except for a pair of frayed denim cutoffs, he had a lean-muscled torso and thick, powerful legs. His skin was a smooth, dark olive green, and the leathery wings that swept up from behind his shoulder blades were several shades darker than that. A piece of leather studded with silver circled his neck. His ears were pointed and lay flat against his head, and ivory-colored horns curled up from his temples. She had time to think, *Is that a gargoyle? Holy fuck, is that a gargoyle?* His long arms swooped round her, spidery hands grabbing her shoulders. She felt her mind go blank with confusion, not sure if she was awake or dreaming or even, quite possibly, dead.

The floor plunged away from her, tapered nails biting into her shoulders as this visitor held her close, the beating of his leathery wings stirring his smell all around her, the smell of earth and moss, and they were rocketing up through torn, jagged ceilings and blurs of rooms, and swinging out through a window that was already broken. Her feet dangled above an endless drop and she clutched at him, the stone-smooth body, wondering if she had enough energy left in her to save herself if she dropped. They kept rising.

The new Eden hotel was burning. Flames surged out from windows, the heat rising up to stroke her feet and legs, and something in the hotel groaned and crashed, and down through the acrid billows of smoke that teared her eyes she saw fire engines and paramedics and police racing up the drive, saw people running and screaming, and then those sights also fell away and she was looking at dark tar. She was dumped on a roof with no time to prepare for the fall, an ankle twisting beneath her. She pushed herself up, standing, ankle blazing but clearly not broken, and she was beyond caring, looking instead at the helicopter on the landing pad in front of her.

Two men emerged from behind it. One was Salik, dressed in a silk tunic, silk pants, and sandals, glossy black hair streaming to his waist. He held his walking stick in his left hand, his right hanging loosely at his side. Jess remembered what Ramsey had told her: one hand was a prosthesis, which Salik had used in his San Francisco days as a handy storage place for jax. She wondered if it still served that purpose. If that's where the purple dust unloosed in her cell had come from.

The man beside him was someone she'd never seen before. Tall, Nordic, white shirt, khaki shorts. She studied him carefully for any signs of demon, but he seemed human—some Sajae blood, probably, but human, studying her as she studied him. Salik leaned on his cane and smiled at her. None of them seemed in a rush to speak.

They're trying to kill you. Surely that couldn't be true. Just manipulation on Salik's part, so she would trust him more and the others less. Except her trust for the others was not exactly solid. And in any case, where had Kai been, the one she was supposed to trust most? *I won't let that happen to you. I won't let you die.* But he almost had, just hours after that particular conversation. Funny, that, but not in a ha-ha kind of way.

You always die young.

But she wasn't thirty yet.

One thing she knew for sure. She had shown her real self to Kai. He knew what she was, and what she wasn't. The false Jess, the imposter, had been exposed. Maybe she should feel relieved, but all she wanted to do was throw up.

The blond man and Salik still weren't saying anything. Maybe they were waiting for something—like for her to speak first. They could wait forever, for all she cared. Motion caught the edge of her eye. The gargoyle with his leather wings folding and unfolding behind him, perched on top of the helicopter. He cocked his head and gazed at her. She saw the smooth sheen of his skin, remembered how it had felt, like a kind of living stone. His toes, wrapping the edge of the helicopter roof, were the same spidery length as his fingers.

A gargoyle.

"I didn't know you could speak English," Salik was saying to him.

The gargoyle shrugged. "You were funny. Talking my language. I enjoyed." To Jess, he said, "My name. Kaos. You are the Jess."

Salik tossed something up in the air—small and silver—that Kaos plucked from the peak of its arc and put in his mouth. He untied the leather cord around his neck. Other silver items dangled from it, glinting against his dark skin.

"He's a gargoyle," Salik said, needlessly, to Jess.

Kaos looked up at the word. He was threading the cord through a hole in the silver disc, refastening the necklace around his wide throat. "Gargoyle," he agreed.

"Glad to hear it." Jess looked from Kaos to Salik to Kaos again. The gargoyle offered up a grin, his incisors long and curved. She had the sense that if he had a tail, he would wag it.

Kaos tossed back his head and gave a low, howling sound. He shot up into the air, wings unfurling. Then he was gone.

I can't believe I just met a gargoyle, Jess thought. *I can't believe that just happened.* It felt like a moment of grace, a gift of transcendence and wonder.

But the moment was over.

The helicopter sputtered into life, rotor lashing the air. Jess saw the pilot through the window, an anonymous figure in dark glasses, even though it was night. Something about him seemed odd, but she couldn't pinpoint what it was. Below her, something crashed, and fresh heat and smoke billowed over her. "Jessamy," said the blond man. He had to shout to make himself heard over the sirens, the fire, but seemed as calm and friendly as if they were meeting in a café. "We need to be going. We were hoping you'd come with us."

Jess laughed. Somewhere below her, a wall of windows shattered apart in a bright silver spray of noise. She imagined the fire uncoiling up through the building like a leviathan rising from the ocean depths, jaws unhinging, ready to swallow the sun and the moon if it could.

"You're asking," she said.

The blond man affected surprise. "This isn't a kidnapping, Jessamy. We saved you, remember." Salik turned his face aside, as if to hide a snigger. "My boss very much wants to meet you, and work with you, but he's made it clear that you must choose us of your own free will. He's not interested in hosting you if you'll only try to escape." The blond man tipped his head. Something happened in his face, then: a slight rippling of skin, a shifting of cheekbone, the shape of his eyes grew more rounded. Yet Jess couldn't sense any signs of demon. This was something else. Something odd. Despite herself, she was curious.

"Come with us." Said so simply. The man added, "You can change your mind later, if you want."

"Somehow I doubt that."

"You'd be surprised."

"I'd be *shocked*. Who's your boss?"

"I think you know," the blond man said, and she felt a cold hand reach inside her. "I think you know," he said again. When moments passed and she remained silent, he added, "He believes he can help you. He can teach you what the others failed."

"Which is?"

"How to live."

And the words shafted through her.

"Don't you want to live, Jessamy?"

A boom went off somewhere in the building, shuddering up through the roof, through her whole body. She stumbled and caught herself. The blond man was finally looking nervous. "I hate to rush you, Jessamy, but we're running out of time. Take your chances here, or with us, it's all the same to me. Less, even."

How to live. It was absurd, given the likely source, and yet the words opened up inside her, as if a whole new option was blooming into being. It didn't feel evil, or wrong.

It felt like hope.

And if it wasn't, if it was something malignant, as in the end she knew it must be, she didn't have to stay long. The blond man was lying when he said they'd let her leave. But they couldn't prevent her from killing herself . . . and maybe she wouldn't have to, her future measured out in such a short dose. But maybe there was still enough of it for her to turn herself into a spy. She could learn things, gather information, find a way to pass it on to Kai—

Kai. She mentally yelled his name through the space below and felt nothing. Only smoke and flame and noise and panic.

Only void.

Jess jerked her head at Salik. "He doesn't come with us," she yelled. "That's the condition."

Salik said, "What? When I was the one who—"

"Fine," the blond man snapped. "Then let's go. Now."

Then she was throwing herself into the back of the helicopter before she could think too much about what she was doing. As the blond man dropped into the seat right in front of her she saw another rippling across his back, something rising up to press against his white shirt, like a gun, or a pointing finger. Jess jerked her gaze away from it just in time to see a face surface through the back of the blond man's head: a woman's full lips, smooth skin, questing eyes. But then the face was gone, and his shirt lay smooth and flat. Jess slumped against the window, her eyes wide, her body trembling. They were rising into the air, veering sharply away from the burning building, dark smoke thinning out around them. Below them, Salik waved his cane in their direction, then stepped off the edge of the roof and fell from view.

Chapter Sixteen

Kai

Kai wasn't there to witness but learned from other sources, including the news. How three individuals, two men and one woman, came into the Eden, the two men dressed in long cashmere overcoats despite the heat outside, the woman in gym shorts and a tank top as if she'd been working out, a duffel bag slung across one shoulder. They came through the revolving doors one by one and then scattered: the woman to the left wing, one man to the right wing, the other man to the central reach of the hotel. Once there, they waited. Then, at fifteen minutes after eight, a skinny youth in denim shorts and bare feet, a bright yellow knapsack hanging off his bony shoulders, entered the lobby. His eyes were bloodshot and he reeked. People moved away from him, looking at him in disgust, even horror, and security guards were already moving in his direction when he paused in front of the bed of tropical flowers and yelled, "I save myself and you from the reign of the Lord of Bones!"

Elsewhere in the hotel, the woman and the two men yelled the same thing.

And then, with a shattering boom, they flew apart into

fire and smoke, bits of flesh and sprays of blood, sending destruction and panic throughout the hotel.

Kai was sealed off from it all, in the almost ridiculously grand *kkaji-jut* that Daughtry had included in each of the suites designed specifically for Summoners. Kai had almost laughed out loud at the . . . the staginess of it all: the layered rugs with the intricately patterned designs meant to evoke traditional Sajae textiles, the shelves on shelves of thick white candles. The *kkaji* forms were meant to be done in shadow and candlelight. The room smelled new, clean, untouched.

But it made him remember the *kkaji-jut* of his youth and the first stretch of his adulthood, before the destruction of everything he knew forced him and others out into the vast, strange reaches of Europe and Asia in the Middle Ages. The fake new smell of this stage set of a room made him remember what it was like to work in those other, vanished places, where the histories of practice by so many of his kind had been absorbed into the very air: layers of still-fading Summoner energy, the lingering, acrid scents of the light that was Summoner sweat. Thinking of that, remembering it, inspired him to work through the kind of *kkaji* he had not practiced in years: not the simpler forms he'd passed on to Jess and Ramsey—had planned for Ramsey to pass on to Zazou and her growing band of wannabe soldiers. Not those. But the advanced forms, precise and uncanny and complicated, demanding an absolute perfection of timing, meant to lift you through the barriers of yourself to enter into the life-fire of the Labyrinth. If those lower levels of form were meant as a warrior art, taught to cultivate focus, stamina, and intensity as well as the fighting skill sets, the highest forms became the ultimate expression of Sajae prayer.

And he had not prayed in several decades.

He was so rough that any thought of spiritual communion was ridiculous. The forms had taken him—the most gifted of students since Shemayan himself—fifteen years of intense daily training in the various *kkaji-juts* spread throughout the Labyrinth in order to master, and once mastery was achieved he'd been set the whole new challenge of maintaining it.

Still, these first bumbling attempts had been enough to make him contact Peter Worthington, the man who managed Kai's London estate, and have him overnight Kai the mate of the Sajae sword he'd spell-modified and given to Ramsey. Nice to have it in his hands again. As a rule Summoners disdained actual weapons. Weapons were crutches, meant only for those who couldn't make the magic do the killing work for them. But Kai had always liked swords, as a child and a youth and a Summoner, and then as an exile in the outside world. He had eventually replaced the collection he lost in the fires of the Labyrinth—all swords except for two—once his long-held fascination with Paris became mitigated by the pleasures of Japan, and the arts of the samurai that had partly contributed to his own Sajae heritage were no longer just an agonizing reminder of the world taken from him.

Already the sword felt like an extension of him, slanting along his body, slashing, and carving the air. As he turned and stepped and lunged, drew and retreated and advanced, he felt the warmth of the Dreamlines flow through him. His speed deepened. The edges of his vision blurred and went dark. It became impossible for him to pick himself apart from the sword and his dance with it.

And a window opened deep in the oldest part of his memory. Long before he called himself Kai Youngblood, or any of the other names he had put on and eventually cast off, when he had been a prince for real, he sought communion with the source, the soul, of the Labyrinth. The simple rituals of acknowledgment braided into everyday Sajae culture meant nothing to him. He wanted the kind of knowledge, the sense of life-fire, that the priests of the various Orders liked to claim. With no wish to become a priest himself—the thought made him shrink inside himself in horror—Kai tested one Order after another, genuflecting in their temples and performing their rites of art or blood or sex or pain.

He concluded that the Orders were frauds. Every one of them. Finally the only things left untried were the high forms of the *kkaji*, but only Summoners did them. *Could* do them, given the quality of magic required. When the call came down for him to enter the Academy, when the nature of Kai's true talent could no longer be denied or ignored—not even by him—it was his thoughts of the *kkaji*, his yearning curiosity, that gave him the will to cross the Academy threshold to life on the other side.

Now, as he spun and cut and plunged, he allowed himself to open up another memory. How he had gone to Asha, his enemy, and how she had chained him to a rock in the desert and tortured his body and soul through carnivorous magic; how he had turned that magic to his own purposes, using it as the ultimate blood-price that was required to hurl himself into the heart of the Dreamlines—deeper than he had ever gone before or would ever go again—and where he had experienced multiple versions of his own death. And a voice had poured like sunwarmed water into his soul's broken places: *You may rest now. You're not required to do anything more.*

He wanted that voice again. He could use its guidance.

He had witnessed so many times what love did to others. How it seemed to take the brain and rewire it, like a drug, or bad street-magic, until crazy things seemed logical and logic made no sense at all. They believed what love wanted them to believe.

He wanted Jess Shepard to be great.

She's much too young, born much too late, Mina had

told him, and Kai knew the other Summoners in his Pact agreed with her. *The days of true learning are over, Shemayan's descendant or no. The sooner you accept this, the sooner you can let her go, and we can deal with what's in front of us. She is not without her uses, Kai. She has abilities of a sort. Potential. But she is not this . . . this heroine figure you make her out to be.*

He whirled, and turned, and drew the blade high . . .

. . . and saw, through the blur of his vision, Makonnen standing in the doorway.

Kai brought himself to a full stop. The room, its edges and corners, came back into focus.

"Hello, Mak," he said.

Makonnen was part of a Summoner Pact—Kai's Pact—but for all his asocial and enigmatic nature he might as well have been *runaen*, rogue, one of the rare Sajae who crossed through his Trials and entered deep magic alone, bound to no one, but unable to benefit from the kind of shared power that characterized any Pact. Mak was guarded to the point of paranoia, often shielding his mind with a white static fuzz to ward off potential thought-reads. He didn't trust Sajae courtesy or even Summoner law to prevent a violation of Summoner mind, in particular his mind, a feat which in any case was always difficult to accomplish. Kai often wondered what had happened to him to turn him this way, but Mak's personal history was a secret one. Known as a gifted warrior who gravitated to regions of conflict and war, he sought out a level of experience that even Summoners considered extreme. He tended to disappear for long periods, cloaking his presence on the Dreamlines in a way that Kai hadn't known was even possible and, for a stretch of time just before Jess, had attempted to emulate. It was rumored that for more than one of those periods Mak had *sajar ifinti zazee*—gone crazy—the way some Summoners tended to, buckling beneath the weight of all the memory they carried. They usually recovered. Usually. Still, the *ifinti zazee* left a mark on them, a certain twist to their presence signature, a splinter in their eyes. Others would disagree, but Kai found no such mark on the elusive, sun-darkened Summoner. If there was a crack in Mak's gaze, it was of a kind that had always been there.

The other Summoner stepped down into the room, dark hair hanging down his back in an intricate network of braids. Candlelight flickered in the alcoves. Kai had never lost his love for candles, the smell of them, the shifting crosshatch of light and shadow. The houses, lofts, and apartments he'd lived in through the years had always been filled with them. "You realize," Mak said in the accent he had picked up in South Africa and chosen not to lose, "that we are the outcasts, you and I. They think I'm a little . . ." He held out his hand, wavered it side to side. Kai found it a very human gesture. ". . . loony," he finished. "And they have wondered about you for a while now."

"Because of Asha," Kai said.

"We both have connections to her. Unusually vivid connections."

Kai laid the sword on the table. He was breathing hard. He could feel the exertion rising off him, lighting up his eyes and skin. "She was my half sister."

Asha's blood-claim to him could not be taken lightly. And could never be dismissed. Not when the Sajae had evolved their power structure along an obsessive study of the bloodlines, dating back to the first fallen ones, the winged ones, who had given rise to the first of *them.* Bakal Ashika was a child of rape and incest, exiled with her mother—one of Kai's attractive young aunts—beyond the walls of the Labyrinth and brought back, years later, as part of the slave trade, her pale skin and fair hair passing her off as one of the barbarian tribes no matter how the girl insisted otherwise. Sold as a slave, but with the magic of the Dreamlines in her veins. It must have been obvious, Kai thought, to anyone who looked closely; but who looked at slaves? Even when she told him who she was, begging him, he had refused to look truly, or at all.

"You are, in your own way, just as much an outsider as Jess," Makonnen said. "And you read her books. Just as I did. We have that in common, you and I. Did you forget?"

Kai looked at him.

Mak said, "Or didn't it occur to you at all?"

Every Summoner kept a series of notebooks, spell-books, which chronicled their evolution through the magic as well as the specific, individual forms the magic took with them. The books also acted as a repository for excess energy, which would otherwise build up in their minds and bodies until it damaged both. After Asha was imprisoned, and after two hundred years of searching, her books were found and locked away. They were dangerous. They had a life of their own. When you read such a book, the book also read you.

"I had to read them," Kai said now. He still remembered the crawling sensation of Asha's mind entering his; still remembered that howling, bottomless hunger, and the conviction that the only road to peace went through annihilation. "I had to read them in order to get a sense of how her mind worked . . . what she was planning."

"Those books," Makonnen said. "They change you. The others all know that."

"I only had them for a short time." Kai eyed the other Summoner. "You had them for months. Or so I heard."

"I was fascinated by them," Mak admitted. He flashed a smile, very white against his sun-darkened skin. "You had a taste. I had the meal."

"Why bring this up with me now?"

"The one that made her," Mak said.

Kai sighed. "Yes."

"From what I read in her books, and from how they've lived on in me," Makonnen said, "I have developed a belief. I haven't told this to the others. They are wary of me as it is. But he's been closer to this world than we thought. And he wants another student. Another dream-child."

"Another Asha," Kai said, disbelieving.

"Not like Asha. Different. This has been a long time in coming . . . Asha was more or less a random choice, available to him and convenient. This one is . . . already marked and chosen."

"Ah. The chosen one." Kai had to scoff a little.

Makonnen grinned. "Like in all those human stories."

"The movies." Kai had always liked movies, even bad ones. When this world finished dying out, he hoped movies would be one of the things that survived into the next one.

"It's presented as a positive thing."

"I never understood that either. So much better to be the chooser," Kai said, "not the chosen." He could think of the ways in which he himself had been chosen, the sense of a destiny handed down to him when so many others could forge their own. Often they didn't even know what a privilege that was, so dazzled by false ideas of freedom that they were blinded to the true ones. When he was younger, Kai had tried to teach those ideas, playing to some half-baked fantasy of emerging as some kind of guru or even prophet, but either people were too closed off to what he had to say, or he had no clue how to reach them. Probably the latter. He was so much older now, with a deeper sense of his limitations as well as his strengths.

His mind flickered around Jess, also banging and kicking at the walls of the chosen, even as Makonnen said, point-blank, "So could it be her?"

Kai looked at him, the question barely registering, even though he had known it was coming. A day ago—hours ago—Kai would have angrily laughed in response, leaped again to Jess's defense, his knee-jerk response as her lover and champion. Now he said, slowly, speaking to himself just as much as to Mak, "I knew the Traveler

in his last incarnation. I was there when Shemayan and
his Pact did what they did to him. When they mutilated
him. I was a small child, but I remember.

"I've experienced this woman on so many levels. I've
seen her live and die so many times I stopped counting.
If she was . . . If he had somehow marked her out,
wouldn't I have sensed it at some point? Picked up even
the faintest glimmer of it?"

"You think you know her that well."

"I know who and what I am. I know what I can do.
I would have sensed it by now."

Makonnen hesitated, then said, "The others, and myself, and I know you must have, as well—we've all been
searching for clues to this. On the Dreamlines."

Kai picked up an ebony-handled dagger that had been
sitting on the table. Kai had always liked this dagger; he
thought of it as the kind of good-luck charm he didn't
believe in, but liked the idea.

"We've been searching for information, answers,"
Mak pressed. "About Jess. Those Trials. We're planning
to take it up at council later, but I wanted to speak to
you beforehand. Because on the Dreamlines—"

"There's nothing," Kai said. He was turning the dagger through his fingers. "There's nothing. No signs, no
visions, no clues, just static. Blank spaces. Gaps and
breakage in the Dreamlines."

"So then we need to move to the demon ones. The
demon lines will show us where he is, Kai. Where the
Traveler is hiding. Even he can't remove himself completely from the Dreaming."

"Easier said than done."

Mak said, "I'm speaking to you on my own now, my
friend. I won't bring this up with the others. They won't
support it. They already hold Del against you, and how
you used him to quicken Jess—"

"Yes."

"So you know what I'm asking?"

Kai didn't answer. He balanced the dagger on his palm.

When he had introduced Jess to her Sajae blood, her Summoner potential, the one thing that they did not have was time. Time for training and cultivating and coaxing out those talents buried so deeply inside her human self that other Summoners—Mina came to mind— thought it was pointless to attempt it at all. Instead of putting her through a traditional education, he fast-forwarded her development by taking her to one of Asha's six imprisoned demons, the one called Del, who prized novelty and stimulation to such an extent that he would happily cooperate with his captors as long as he thought he might find it interesting. He found Jess very interesting. He had used demon magic, demon manipulation, to get into her brain and rewire it, stirring to life Jess's considerable Sajae talents for Kai to shape and train. And all it had cost Jess were the memories that Del had plundered, to while away the time as he paced and revolved in his prison-sphere, and through which he could absorb a world that fascinated him even as it remained unknown to him.

"You know what I'm asking," Mak said again, taking the question out of his voice.

Demon spaces, demon lines.

He meant the shadow underworld of the Dreamlines, the dense, tangled fragments that the demons had long ago stolen for their own, in a war too ancient for anyone to know anything about, other than that it had happened. The demon lines were a corrupt, complicated, toxic mess of pathways that only a strong demon mind could pick its way through. There were stories and myths, down through the last two millennia, about Summoners who had attempted to walk them, seeking glory or knowledge or both. What they found instead—and what it had done to them—became a warning for the following generations . . . as well as an entire genre for Sajae novels and epic poetry and drama.

"Del could do it," Mak said. "Del would do it. For you."

"At a price."

"But he would do it. Think of it. We would have a demon pet, a spy, ranging those spaces none of us can touch, that most of the hybrids themselves can't even handle, and bringing back such a treasure trove of information . . ."

Kai had already thought this out: backward, forward, inside out, it all led to the same conclusion. "Del is no one's pet. Just when you think he's been domesticated, he'll turn around and bite your arm off."

"Is there an alternative?"

"There might be," Kai said. "There's a hybrid named Za—"

Which is when they heard the first explosion.

And the second. And the third. And the fourth.

He didn't wonder what had happened, or where; he could feel the vibrations of panic and pain, smell the brutal tang of fear that salted the air, cast off by so many. So many. He knew the hotel was burning—the smoke, the sirens, the screaming—knew the fire had not yet reached the lofts and quarters and corridors Daughtry had set aside for another brand of client altogether. He also knew, more than anyone, how trapped Jess was, a busted butterfly in a web of Kai's devising. The fire would not get through Kai's magic. But she would die of smoke inhalation.

Except something else had found its way into the room.

She was gone.

He found the bodies of the four people guarding her—two Sajae-born, two Summoners—sprawled in the hallway. The door to her room—her cell, he thought, there was no point in pretending otherwise—was open. The room itself was a shambles of dust and broken plaster, the bed buried beneath a chunk of ceiling. He looked up through the gaping hole, its edges ragged, up through similar holes in three more ceilings, as if a cannonball—

a very large one—had dropped through with supernatural force.

He didn't think it had been a cannonball.

He probed the remnants of the spellcraft—his own—that lined the walls. Felt the thinned-out layers and ripped-out patches. Someone had worked it over with magic of their own. Kai explored further, sending pulses of mindcast through the spellcraft, testing the weavings, noting how the interloper had gone immediately for the weaker places. Had known what to look for: the vulnerabilities, cracks, and fissures. Someone with an obsessive knowledge of Kai's game.

And someone who knew his magic, knew *him,* that deeply meant that the relationship between them touched on something more than old classmates or Pact-mates or rivals. Someone he'd trained with, grown into deep magic with. Someone he'd been close with, intimate with, someone who no longer loved him. There were only two possibilities. One was supposed to be secluded in foreign mountains, living in a demon's prison, doing the guarding she had made her life's work. The other was supposed to be dead.

Then he found an odd substance that had not completely dissipated; he drew it out of the air, enough to smear between thumb and forefinger, observe the faint violet glint of it, the burning sensation as it penetrated his skin. But he was a long-lived and experienced Summoner; this substance would only make him high, and the amount in the room wasn't enough to have much of an effect. But someone like Jess would suffer a whole different level of damage.

Someone in the doorway.

He absorbed the Summoner's presence, put a name to it, and knew.

He turned, looked at Daughtry face-to-face.

"What in the name of old Yolla's balls—" Daughtry said.

"She's gone."

"I see that." Daughtry was keeping his distance, his eyes flaring. "Did you— Were you—"

Kai smiled a little as he stepped toward the other man. Bits of plaster crunched beneath his shoes. "You think I had something to do with this? You watched me throw the spellcraft, you tested it yourself—" The talk was distraction. Before Daughtry could register his true intention, he had his lucky dagger at Daughtry's neck. The advantage of the Summoner prejudice against human-made weapons: Summoners never expected their own kind to use them.

"Any movement," Kai hissed, "any summoning of any kind, and I swear on the life-fire of the Labyrinth itself that I will take your head off."

"I'd be careful, Prince," Daughtry said. But he couldn't hide his shift in eye color, the white shine of fear. "Very careful."

"Take it off."

"What?"

"That thing on your head," Kai said, and then did it himself, grasping the flesh-colored fabric melded to the man's skull, simulating baldness. He ripped it off and Daughtry yelped.

Kai saw jax marks.

This was what Daughtry had been hiding: the wide, thick bands of jax permanently scored on his scalp, the drug used so often, for so long, that its points of entry were tattooed into his flesh. The tell had been Daughtry's habit of running his hands across his head, his addict's compulsion to trace the jax marks with his fingertips. Kai had expected it, yet was still so stunned by what he saw that he let down his guard just enough. Daughtry hit him in the chest with a fierce blast of Dreamline energy, and while stumbling off balance he felt another wave of magic catch him from beneath and hurl him back into the wall, pain spreading out along his back and shoulders, the back of his head. A half moment of darkness and he was on the ground, struggling for orientation.

He felt a ripple in the air as Daughtry loosened a chunk of ceiling, but in the moment before it came down Kai drew a scorching line of energy through his body, channeling it into his hands: streaks of blue lightning reached out for Daughtry, snaked over him, and took him down. Above him, the ceiling gave a final splintery moan and came tumbling down, Kai swinging up a quick wall of magic to knock aside the debris, hurling himself from beneath it.

Then he was on Daughtry, grabbing the lapels of the ridiculous velvet jacket and slamming him against the wall, yelling, "Salik! You knew he was alive all along. You made some kind of deal with him. To feed your addiction."

Daughtry turned his head to the side and coughed, the color draining from his eyes until they were nearly the same shade as the plaster at their feet. "Whatever gets you through the night, right?" He tried to grin, getting as far as a crooked grimace. "Just, sometimes that night never ends. You of all people should relate—"

"You hired him to poison Jess."

"The girl," Daughtry said, his voice now coming in gasps, "needed to die. Salik knew she was here. He offered to do it."

"That death would *never* be for you to decide. Under *any* circumstances."

"She's a menace. She's been toxic all this time. Maybe she's made you toxic, infected you, you ever think of that?"

And he saw, then, the way Daughtry's eyes narrowed, grew reptilian; saw the way his mouth twisted in distaste. Realized the extent of his fakery, his dramatics. He'd preached about accepting Jess as one of their own when all along he'd been the most prejudiced against her.

Kai brought his face close to Daughtry's and whispered, "You helldog jaxer fool. You Westgate trash. Sal-

ik's a traitor. He chose the other side. He's probably
working for them already. You think he wouldn't take
Jess straight to the Lord of Bones himself if he thought
she would fetch a nice price?"

"So long as she dies," Daughtry rasped. "So long—"

He sucked in air, then stopped in midbreath. His eyes
widened, his hands scrambling at his grotesquely bulging
throat. Blood dribbled between his lips, then he jerked
forward and opened his mouth, and sprayed blood across
Kai's shirt, more blood gushing out of his nostrils,
streaming from his eyes. Kai cried out, revulsed, bewildered, stepping back and pushing him away. Daughtry
fell back against the wall and gurgled an attempt at a
scream, clutching his rippling throat, his eyes growing
almost comically round, as the voice that came tunneling
up through him forced his mouth to open so wide that
Kai heard the sharp sound of his jaw breaking.

*The child is with me now. The child comes to me.
There comes a new Labyrinth, of blood and smoke and
ash and fire, and it is mine. There grows a new Labyrinth,
built off the smashed bones of the winged ones, and it is
mine. I will be the creator of the new age. The Sajae will
bleed and weep before me, and the Summoners will be
my slaves. So come to me on your knees,* sankkia. *Come
to me . . . and beg."*

Then Daughtry pitched forward as if pushed into Kai,
and as Kai instinctively pressed his hands against Daughtry's shoulders, fire blazed up from the dying Summoner's body and swarmed around Kai's hands. Kai shrieked
in pain, reeling back and staring at his hands, burning
like torches as he frantically summoned a cooling energy
that whistled out through his mouth, extinguishing the
flames and damping the pain. Refusing to look at the
blackened, ruined skin, Kai cradled his hands to his
chest, backstepping, nearly tripping over Daughtry. For
the space of nearly a minute he had completely forgotten
about Daughtry.

A black snake was poking its head out from Daughtry's

mouth. It slithered down his body to the floor, and evaporated. Daughtry curled into a fetal position, whispering, "Kill me. Kai. My friend. Kill me now."

Kai gazed down at the dying man, and listened to the screams and sirens echoing from other parts of the hotel. The smoke was eddying down the hallway now, extending its first tendrils into the room. He could be merciful. He could regard Daughtry as a victim in his own way, his judgment addled by drug use and filtered through a prejudice so deep and long-held it had scarred his soul just as permanently as the jax had his scalp. He could reach into the better part of his nature and feel a kind of pity for a man so foolish as to think he was the manipulator, when he had been the one manipulated. Nothing in Daughtry's continued suffering would undo the damage that Daughtry had done; it could not bring Jess back.

"Kill . . . please kill me . . ."

"So long, Jack," Kai said, and turned away.

Chapter Seventeen

Ramsey

She came to him as the sky slowly paled into dawn, knocking on the door of his little room. He was staying at the end of a second-floor hallway in what had once been a boarding house. Now, putting down the weapon he'd been practicing with, he came back to himself, heard the insects rustling inside the sun-bleached wood, took a lungful of air coming through the open window. It was dry, desert air, infused with the sharp tang of alkaline.

Ramsey opened the door and she was there, in cargo drawstring pants and a sweatshirt unzipped over a white tank top. The ghost light of dawn picked out the freckles across her snub nose and beneath her almond eyes. She held a satellite phone in her hand.

"I need you to do something for me," Zazou said.

"Sure," he said.

As if there was any other answer.

Down the stairs and out of the building, he followed her across the compound. They called this place Tumbledown. There was another camp not far from here, called Oasis, and Zazou had told him there were other camps scattered through the West, in barren, windswept, isolated places, where the nearest neighbor might be a rocket-testing site.

Tumbledown had been built around the remnants of a town called exactly that, that had once existed off a road that no one used anymore, which now ran past them into nothing. There were an antiquated gas pump, ramshackle houses, some beaten-up storefronts with the kind of faded signs that didn't bother with names but cut right to the heart of the matter: GROCERIES, BAR AND RESTAURANT, GENERAL STORE, HAIRCUTS HERE.

Trucks and SUVs were parked throughout. Campsites ranged to the west and north, the breeze rustling through canvas roofs. Not everyone was sleeping. Off to the south, beyond the stark looming rocks, Ramsey heard the rattle of gunfire, the first of the day's practice and training sessions rolling right along.

The two Summoners attached to the camp were conferring beneath a blue awning, rifles laid across the table in front of them. The younger, redheaded one—Cameron—exchanged friendly greetings with Ramsey, but the taller one couldn't be bothered. Some of them were like that, Ramsey had learned. Maybe social niceties got old after you'd lived through several centuries of them. They were taking inventory of the spell-modified rifles, flipping through the reports from the practice range, discussing results. The shooters had to respect the magic, its tics and quirks; they could never take anything for granted. Three days ago one of the pistols had backfired, neatly severing the left lower leg of the guy who'd been holding it. No blood, no pain; the guy simply watched part of his own body divide from the rest of him and fall to the sand. That night a Summoner who specialized in healing was trucked in from the Oasis camp to reattach the leg, but the guy would walk with a limp for the rest of his life. He was taking pride in it, though, showing the wraparound blue scar at the slightest provocation.

Ramsey spent a lot of time alongside Cameron, teaching the same fighting skills taught him, the same meditation exercises that helped open them up to the magic within the weapons. He spent just as much time alongside Zazou, lecturing about the nature of the hybrids, how they liked to attack, highlighting potential weak points. They were a good team. Ramsey brought the perspective the others could relate to, as well as his experience of what had and had not worked in the chomping teeth of battle. Often he just told stories, anecdotes, trying very hard not to embellish anything for the sake of dramatic effect.

And often he just listened to Zazou.

Zazou talked a lot about what it meant to be a hybrid—not fully one thing or the other. How it felt to bring your demon soul, your demon life, into this strange package of upright flesh and bone. The human body, she said, was easy enough; it was a bit like learning to drive a car. Since Zazou herself didn't drive, Ramsey wasn't sure how she could know this.

The human brain, Zazou went on, was a different beast altogether. It felt heavy in her head, a lumpy knot of useless gray matter that was tasty enough to eat— Zazou seemed oblivious to the revulsion that went cringing and wincing through her audience—but seemed to serve no actual purpose other than the headaches.

But then, as time passed, this started to change. Like the body that belonged to it, the brain became something they could learn to use more and more to advantage. The hybrids who were hardy and clever enough to survive this long—who hadn't gone insane, or suffered some accident in a world they did not understand and that could be just as dangerous as they were, or been picked off by one of the Summoners hunting them— were learning to access their human side and rifle through the resources of memory and knowledge they found there. "Don't let them do this," Zazou said. "Don't allow them the space and silence they need to do this. Part of fighting them is knowing how to over-whelm their senses. Flood them with stimuli—disorient them—and this keeps them anchored in their primitive selves. Which makes them easier to predict. To kill."

She talked about how they perceived the world. Even with human eyes, their vision was designed to track even the slightest movement; sometimes the only real way to elude a hybrid was to stay . . . absolutely . . . motionless, turn oneself into just another part of a landscape already so foreign to them. "And be very careful when you bleed," Zazou said. "Human blood has a particular blood-scent, a coppery-musky perfume that attracts them, pulls them in. It's a lust that overrides everything else. If they smell human blood, they will come for it. For you."

Often, she said, they didn't have to kill the hybrids; they could injure a hybrid and count on him to make it worse. "Remember, this is still a new body," Zazou said, "a new way of being. We're still not completely inte-grated. We still think of the body as alien from us, some-thing that can be taken . . . *off.* So when the body hurts, our instinct is to take that part, that wound, and try to . . ." She paused. "Try to cut it out," she said. "Cut it off. Get it away from us."

He and Zazou worked out a series of drills and move-ments teaching how to attack and defend against the hybrids. Zazou amazed him; she was like opening up a treasure chest of knowledge. The kinds of things it had taken so much trial and effort and danger to find out, she could lay flat for him in minutes. *See, if you do that, then it's our instinct to do this, to move this way. We'll mostly move counterclockwise.* What they learned from each other they brought to the classroom, discussing hand-to-hand combat as well as combat with different kinds of weapons, and with fire: *We still think fire is our friend*, Zazou told them. *We forget that, in these bodies, fire can destroy us.*

Later, alone in his room, Ramsey worked his way through a different set of exercises, first with his knives,

then with the sword Kai had given him. Feints and
strikes and slashes and parries; the way a blade flashed
through light still gave him pleasure. His weapons grew
warm in his hands as the movements triggered their
magic. They took on a rhythm of their own and it was
all he could do to keep up. He could feel the magic
moving down through his wrists and forearms, a tingling
that started out faint, then grew hotter, sharper. When
it became too painful to continue, he tossed the knives
in the corner, or replaced the sword in its sheath. He
barely had the energy to drag his sweat-slick body down
the hall to the room with the claw-foot tub.

The only other person in the camp who didn't sleep
in a tent or share a room with a roommate (or two,
or more) was Zazou. Neither of them wanted to be an
exception, but it soon became clear that no one would
endure their strange sleeping habits. Or in Ramsey's
case, lack of them. Ramsey was increasingly insomniac,
his work with Zazou and his weapons like a wave of
warmth and exhilaration that lifted him high and would
only bring him down for a few hours. Then the image
of a clean steel edge swinging and singing through the
air pulled him to his feet again, eager for another ses-
sion, even if it was three a.m.

It was different with Zazou. Rumors circulated
through the camp that sleep released a different Zazou,
not the clear-eyed, forceful, daytime leader, but someone
who babbled strange languages, and did worse things
than that, although no one would speculate just what;
her sole ex-roommate had refused to tell them details
before leaving the camp altogether. The rumors were
one of the things reminding Ramsey of Jess. Of the times
he had to go collect her when she was submerged in
some mysterious dreamworld that had lifted her body
from her bed and sent it out of the room, sometimes
out the door to the edge of a yard, a parking lot, or
a freeway.

He was having some weird dreams of his own.

He kept dreaming he was back in third grade, sitting in detention while other kids played outside, their shouts and laughter slipping through windows everywhere. The teacher lectured about magic. *You can't control it, not even the scraps they think to throw you,* she was saying. *You will never be a Summoner.* Then she unfolded great white wings and punched through the ceiling, spiraling into a comet-streaked sky, and he was left alone in the shadows and rubble.

Now she led him into the little house—not much more than a shack—with drifts of sand against the front steps, the hum of the nearby generator the only sound. It was dark inside; Zazou's vision worked fine in shadows. Her use of light was for guests. When alone, she rarely bothered with it.

So Ramsey was surprised to see all the burning candles. They formed a circle on the floor of the attic she had chosen for a bedroom. Candles of all shapes, all sizes, all white. For a moment he thought of the demon Del— he had never seen Del himself, but Jess had described the stone chamber, the collection of broken glass arranged in a circular mosaic beneath his prison-sphere, and then he thought of Kai. Any time they had stayed in one place longer than a few days, Ramsey had noticed how white unscented candles tended to accumulate, scattering across surfaces as if they were breeding behind Ramsey's back. Sometimes he even suspected that Kai, for all his appreciation of modern luxury, would have handled it just fine if electricity had never been discovered at all.

"I need you to watch over me," said Zazou as she stepped inside the circle of candles. She didn't drop so much as ripple down into a sitting position—it was an odd thing to see—and she sat with her legs bent beneath her and fanned out like cards. It didn't strike Ramsey as a comfortable position.

Her gaze was direct and forceful. "I need you to keep

all these things lit," she said with a wave at the candles.
"It's important. You need to keep them all burning. You
hear me?" She picked up an object and held it out to
him. It was one of those long lighters used in barbecues
or fireplaces; it felt a bit like a gun in Ramsey's hand,
although clearly without magic in it.

Ramsey said, "What is this about?"

"I'm going to travel the demon lines."

"The what?"

Zazou sighed. With a look of impatience—Zazou
never bothered to conceal her emotions, and Ramsey
wasn't sure if she didn't care to, didn't know how to, or
if it just never occurred to her—Zazou explained. Her
speech was rapid, her pitch spiking up in odd places, but
Ramsey got the gist of it. Some kind of ancient war over
the Dreamlines. Bad angels versus good angels. Scraps
and patches of Dreamline were somehow stolen and
claimed by the bad angels, which is when the demons got
involved—Ramsey wasn't quite sure if the bad angels and
the demons were in collusion with each other, or if the
bad angels actually *were* the demons, or somehow *became*
the demons, but this didn't seem the time to ask for clari-
fication and detail. The demons used these stolen 'lines for
information and communication, and also as odd vantage
points on the Dreamlines themselves—from their undersides and in-between places, or from corners high up, like
insects scurrying through a room's nooks and crannies of
which the room's denizens were barely aware. They also
allowed the demons to see into other worlds, which,
Zazou went on hurriedly, is what had pointed them to
humans in the first place. What had incited such hunger.

"Jess never talked about any of this stuff," Ramsey said.

Zazou snorted. Her face went flat. It was an ugly expression, and Ramsey thought again of the face that lay
beneath the human one.

"The Summoners don't even like to acknowledge their
existence," she said, "because they can't walk them
themselves. We made sure of that, over the eras. The

humanity in them won't allow them to. So they like to think the demon lines are smaller and less important than they are. That's the funny thing about Sajae." Zazou looked up at Ramsey with eyes gone demon-bright. "They kill us, but sometimes they need us, to do the things they can't."

"You kill them too," Ramsey said softly.

"You need to watch over me and keep the candles lit. Every single one of them."

Ramsey nodded. He didn't see how it could be too hard; the air was warm and dead. Maybe Zazou just wanted some company as she did this, some moral support, but couldn't admit to it. That was probably it.

When something she'd said finally registered with him: *the humanity in them won't allow them to.*

But you're part human too, he started to say, when Zazou's eyes jerked back in their sockets and flooded with silver light. Her face went pale and still, her body rigid: no signs of movement, of breath, of any life at all. She was a statue.

Across from her, Ramsey sat down cross-legged, lighter in hand.

He waited.

Minutes passed, and he was getting restless.

Zazou's body gave a sudden jerk. There was a sound like tearing paper, although Ramsey couldn't tell where it was coming from. He looked around the room, and then at Zazou. She stared back with those wide, blind, silver eyes, what looked like molten metal welling up along her eyelids, then streaming down her face. Her mouth dropped open and cold wind issued forth, frosting the air, swirling down around her body. Ramsey leaped forward with the lighter just as that sound came again— the sound of tearing—as veins leaped up against her skin and turned into silver lines racing across her face and throat and bare arms—

"Zazou!" Ramsey yelled. Three candles had gone out; he relit them all with a shaking hand. "Zazou!"

She lifted her face to the ceiling—and gave a huge gasp, as if sucking in life itself.

The raised silver veins faded back to skin.

She started to speak but her body gave out, crumpling sideways. He lunged for her before she could fall across the flames. He put out some of the candles by stepping on them before kicking them aside and half lifting, half dragging her—despite her slight, compact body she was surprisingly heavy—outside of the now-broken circle.

She stirred, touching his hand. "Thanks," she said. Her voice was hoarse; she spent a moment clearing it, testing it, then said, "That was intense."

"For both of us," Ramsey said.

"I need a couple minutes. Then I'm going to try again."

"You didn't get what you needed?"

She snorted. "Not even close."

"What you said about the Summoners not being able to—their humanity. You have some of that. I mean—humanity. Are you sure—"

"I know what the situation is." An edge came to her voice. "I have to keep trying. It's important. You have no idea how important—" Her eyes went flat, in that way he had never seen in anyone else. "Look, if you can't handle this, I can always get someone like Cameron—"

"I can handle it."

"Good."

"Why are you doing this?"

"Youngblood asked me too." She took a breath, then said, "Beyond that, I can't talk about it. Not yet."

"I don't mean why you're—why you're doing this stuff," he said, with a glance at the candles. "I mean why you're doing any of this at all."

"Any of this?"

"Why you're, you know. On our side."

"I remember you, you know."

"What?"

"From the desert."

"The desert," he said, as if drawing a blank. Which they both knew wasn't true.

She took a breath, then said, "You know—when your soul goes down into this other body, this vessel—do you know what it feels like? It feels good. Feels like fire streaming through you, even as you are that streaming fire. You feel . . . purged . . . and then so strong.

"But then the hunger starts. It's incredible, that hunger. It never stops. Never stops. You want to eat the world. Eat it all up, everything in it. That's what the first months are like—just dealing with the hunger, learning not to be so controlled by it. All you want to do is eat meat." There was a dreaminess in her voice. "Pounds of meat. Raw, bleeding, thick. So very lovely—"

A shudder worked through her. She rubbed her hands across her face. "I have a memory. Of drinking from you. In the desert.

"How it felt to drink from you.

"How eager I was to do it.

"I liked you from the moment I first saw you. And I had the feeling, as damaged as you were, as messed up as I was, that you liked me too. That didn't stop me from drinking from you . . . right here . . ."

She pulled down the collar of his shirt and touched the scar on his upper chest. "Right here," she whispered. She was about to say something more, then abruptly closed her mouth. He knew she had swallowed back a comment about how he had tasted, or how his blood had felt in her mouth.

She said instead, "Then I stepped back and looked at you again. You had such a gentleness in your eyes. And I felt afraid, ashamed. But I also had this feeling that you . . . forgave me. Or at least, you weren't holding it against me. Were you?"

"I don't know." He shifted uncomfortably. "I don't remember you at all. I don't remember much of that stuff at all."

"Maybe you will." She didn't look like she believed him.

"It's over with. It's in the past. What matters is the future."

"The future," she said, a bit dreamily. Then: "That moment, in the desert. I looked through your eyes and saw beauty. And that memory stays with me. Won't let me go."

"A memory of beauty," he said, and gave an awkward laugh. It was hard to link that word to himself in any way. It made him embarrassed.

"That's what I want," she said. "Beauty. That's what I strive for. The demonkind—the world they bring, if we let them—has nothing to do with beauty. But there's a chance for us—for some of us—to become something new. Different. In these bodies. These skins."

"Stolen bodies," Ramsey said. "Stolen skins."

"No. The bodies we steal, we can't stay in for very long. The brain comes apart, the body decays, and we're right back where we started. This body—" She raised and separated her hands a little, staring at her fingers as she flexed them, testing them. "This body chose me, just as much as I chose it."

"Are you sure about that?"

"The people who come here, to Tumbledown," Zazou said suddenly, sitting up. "Who do you think they are? Where do you think they've been? A lot of them—most of them—are desert survivors. They were there. They saw what was happening. And they ran. They got out. This girl—" Zazou touched her wrist, her throat, her head. "This girl, she didn't run. She waited for her demon. She wanted it. She drank your blood, she participated in the rites. I have that memory. She and I, we came together. We turned into each other. She made one choice. The people who came here—" She made a sweeping gesture with her arm, as if to indicate everything beyond the room, Tumbledown and the camps beyond that. "They made another."

"Are you so sure she knew?" Ramsey said, his voice turning very quiet. "They were persuasive, those people. Asha. Lucas. They used music. They used drugs—"

"Enough. This isn't going anywhere."

"Asha could be beautiful at times," Ramsey persisted. "Is that the kind of beauty you're after?"

"That was a false beauty. I want the real thing. The truth of it."

Zazou sprang into a crouch, her fingertips lightly grazing the floor, her eyes flashing at him. He jerked away from her. She laughed and stood up, and shook her head. "Do you know what drives you?" she demanded. "You people. So much flailing around inside some vague idea of who you are. I watched you people for a long time. A long time. You say one thing and then do the opposite. It's like that expression—how your right hand never knows what the left hand is doing. A disconnect between your words and your actions, so that sometimes it seems like your words don't mean anything. I used to think you were all liars. Now I realize you just don't know any better."

"That's not true. Not always true."

"So sure about that?"

"You're being harsh," Ramsey said.

Zazou laughed. "That's not harsh. That's not even close."

She went back to the circle of candles, rippled down into a sitting position, and looked at him expectantly.

The day passed. The shadows pulled themselves into stubs and then lengthened across the floorboards again. For hours at a time, Zazou remained lost inside the otherworldly shell of herself. Every now and then, a wind gusted from nowhere, the flames surging high, but then faded away again. Sometimes a candle went out, and Ramsey scrambled toward it with the lighter.

But mostly nothing happened.

Most of the time the only force Ramsey had to fight

was his own boredom. He wished he had his iPod. Music made even the worst of things a little better.

Then Zazou would come out of it, her body starting to loosen like a fist unclenching. She was too weak, in those moments, to get out of the circle without help. They would sit together on the floor—for some reason it never occurred to them to move to the chair or ratty sofa or boxspring mattress tossed beneath the window— and Ramsey would listen to the gasp of her breathing and feel the kick of her heart, as her skin went slick with sweat. Then, as her body calmed, as her mind calmed, they would talk for a bit.

When he was back on watch, he passed the time by looping through their dialogue, seeing a journal entry appear on the clean white page inside his head so he could remember to write it down later:

> I asked, "What is this thing with you—" I never know what to call her to her face: should I say, you—hybrids? Demons? Clearly she doesn't identify herself with them; she sees herself as someone, something apart. But she doesn't identify as human either, does she? Every time I look at her and am reminded in some sharp, startling way—something in her eyes, her movements, her way of speaking—that she is partly alien to me, and I mean really truly alien in a way that sure as hell is no metaphor, I'm conscious that I have the exact same impact on her. "What is this thing with you guys," I finally said, "and fire? Why is it so vital to have all these damn candles lit?"
>
> She shrugged. She was thinking of other things. I could tell this question, this whole topic, bored her intensely. "Fire points the way back," she said. "It is our guiding principle."
>
> "Fire is your friend," I said, remembering something she once said in class.
>
> "Not anymore."

"I don't think you should do this anymore," he said finally. "It's time to call it for what it is. Switch to plan B."

"Not yet," she said.

He sat on the floor with his legs splayed and she slumped against him, his arms a loose circle around her. Her skin looked too pale, and sometime in the last hour or so it had picked up a weird waxy sheen. He didn't like the way her eyes looked, with deep, dark smudges beneath them, not bags so much as bruises, or the hollowed-out stare that reminded him of someone at a rave, flying high for hours, not eating, not sleeping, and not coming down even as the sun came up, bringing another pill from his pocket.

He was getting a grotesque sinking feeling.

She turned into his arm and leaned her damp, waxy forehead against him. "One more try." Her voice a rasp. "One more."

"No more," Ramsey said.

"So leave if you want. I'll do it with or without you."

"Christ. Is it just your nature to be so fanatic?"

"My nature," she said, and he realized that she didn't understand the question.

Then she said, "He asked me to do this. He needs me to do this."

He almost groaned out loud. "That's right. I forgot. Kai asked you to do this. The magnificent Mr. Young-blood."

"So what if it was?" She seemed puzzled again. He had noticed by now that her sense of humor was under-developed, to say the least; she picked up on ironic or sarcastic tones enough to recognize a shift in expression, but didn't yet know how to interpret them or why any-one would even use them in the first place.

"Are you in love with him or something?"

"Love? You mean, like, in those television shows?"

He refrained from asking what television shows she might be referring to.

She shifted inside his arms and said, simply, "He's beautiful. He's—why are you laughing? Why would that be funny?"

"It's not funny, it's just . . ." He sighed. "He seems to have that effect, I guess. I shouldn't be so surprised."

And this time she missed the sarcasm completely, agreeing, "You really shouldn't be."

It always struck Ramsey as awkward, even comical, to apply that adjective, beautiful, to a man, but he supposed that Kai, in those moments when he could seem so still and silent and beyond human, fit it as much as any man could. He thought of the way Jess sometimes looked at him, how it went through love to a kind of awe and fascination mingled with a hint of dread. Would any woman ever look at Ramsey that way? Of course not. He wouldn't kid himself.

But then he thought, *No.* Beautiful wasn't the right word for Kai either. Zazou was just using language imprecisely, the way most people did. But he got what she meant: whatever ideal she expressed as beauty, she also saw in Kai.

He couldn't help it. He rolled his eyes.

The last time she tried the demon lines, something happened that wasn't like anything that had gone on before.

It started out like the previous times. He saw her go deep into herself, saw her body turn rigid and her eyes fill with light. The candles burned. The air was still.

Then the light in her eyes went dark.

"Zazou," he muttered. He didn't realize he had spoken her name aloud until her head turned slowly toward him. Except he knew she wasn't in her body. The dark sockets that were this Zazou-thing's eyes didn't look into any soul at all.

All the candles went out, as if they'd been snuffed out.

He sprang forward with the lighter, fumbling at the wicks. Smoke eddied in the air, then drifted toward Zazou's form as if drawn to it. As the smoke began to spiral round her, it thickened, and it seemed to him that the outlines of her body were blurring into the smoke, that she was turning into smoke too. "Zazou," he yelled, "Zazou," not knowing if yelling her name helped at all, but it seemed the least he could do, and if fire could be a guiding principle, guiding her back from whatever weird space she was in, why not her name, called over and over again in a familiar voice? Six candles left to light. Five candles. Her body seemed to be turning into smoke, composed completely of smoke, its edges dissolving, disappearing, as if a wind were eating away at it . . .

Two candles. One.

"Zazou!"

And then the huge, wrenching gasp—he had never heard a nicer sound in his life. Her body seemed solid again, an ink-blot darkness racing over her skin and then disappearing, giving way to the crosshatch of candlelight and shadow.

This time he didn't get to her before she collapsed, candles scattering from beneath her body. He dragged her away from them, checking to see if she was singed or burning. "Zazou," he said, "come on, wake up."

She groaned something at him, swatting his hands away from her face. She turned onto her side and curled into a fetal position, and he saw her tumble deep inside herself, only this time it was in sleep. Thank God.

The phone rang.

The satellite phone. He had forgotten that it was even there. He found it in the corner of the room—either he or Zazou must have kicked it over in one of those post-trance scrambling-from-the-circle moments—and pressed the TALK button. He held it to his ear and waited.

The man on the other end of the line said, "Zazou."

"Zazou is indisposed," Ramsey said.

"Ramsey?"

"How are you? 'Cause Zaz and I have been having a *bitch* of a day."

Kai was silent. Ramsey listened for any background noise that might give clues to where he was, but heard nothing. Kai said, "Any progress?"

"Some freaky stuff, but not what you're looking for. Whatever that is."

"She's about to try again." Supposed to be a question, Ramsey figured, but expressed like a statement of fact.

"She is not about to try again," Ramsey said. "Stick a fork in her, she's *done*."

"Ramsey. This is important."

"And it's important that you listen to me. She's done."

"Put her on the line, Ramsey."

"No," he said, surprised at his own defiance, but he had the feeling that if he put Zazou on the phone she would then put herself right back in that circle, and this time he wouldn't be able to relight the candles before she blew away. "Because what I'm saying is important too. She did her best, it didn't work, and now it's time for her to recover and for you to switch to plan B."

"There might not be a plan B."

"There is always a plan B. You just don't have it yet."

"If Zazou can't pull this off, then what I might have to do is rather drastic."

"And what you just put her through wasn't?"

No response on the other end. He was aware of Kai mulling things over. He wondered if there was some voodoo Kai could work over the phone to make him be a good boy and put Zazou on the line. Before Kai could speak again, Ramsey blurted, "Don't you get it? She nearly died. Okay? She risked her life ten times over and you want her to try it again, when she's so exhausted and depleted?"

"Yes. I want her to try it again."

"You're ruthless, aren't you?"

No answer to this. More silence, more mulling.

Ramsey said, "How's Jess?"

And when Kai still didn't answer him, Ramsey felt

that leap of insight, as if something in his head had unexpectedly vaulted from one groove to another. "Wait. This involves Jess, doesn't it? Whatever you need Zazou to do for you—"

"This involves all of us."

"But especially Jess. Right? What happened to her?"

No answer.

"Kai. *What did you people do to her?*"

A click.

The connection was gone. Kai had hung up on him.

Ramsey stared at the phone, as if expecting Kai's voice to spring out like a frog—*Just kidding, we're all fine, why don't you head on back to us and we'll all go out for a beer. And bring Zazou. I had a feeling you two would get along.*

But this didn't happen. Ramsey fought the urge to throw the phone across the room, then figured, *What the hell,* and gave in to it.

Chapter Eighteen

Kai

He arrived in the middle of the night.

Given his purpose for being here, Kai found that only fitting.

He could still hear Ramsey's words: *You're pretty ruthless, aren't you?* But what he kept remembering—and what he almost wanted to tell Ramsey, explain to Ramsey in a way that of course he would not do—was the vision he'd had on the Dreamlines, when he'd gone on them to call Jess's name, to hunt her down himself.

He found her, but not in the way he'd expected.

Her Dreamline ran into darkness, like a bridge that suddenly gave out with nothing but abyss beneath. And what it gave him was a vision: Jess on her knees, her hands behind her back, a blindfold over her eyes. Hovering over her was a dark figure, his torso impaled with shard after shard of colored glass, and in his hand was a crown made of razor blades. Jess's head tipped forward in a gesture of surrender as the figure lowered the crown toward her. And as Kai cried out, the figure moved over Jess and into her and engulfed her completely. She was lost.

If Zazou could not work the demon lines the way he

needed, he would go to the demon who had once been so powerful he had helped bring down the Labyrinth itself. He would go to Del, and get him to do what he wanted and needed, and whatever the price turned out to be, Kai would pay it.

The seventeenth-century chateau sat behind a semicircle of cliffs, deep in the Pyrenees, at the end of an ancient Roman road. The Summoners had long ago used magic to cloak that road from normal human view. The spell had been thinning out over the years, but held up well enough. If Kai heightened his senses, he could hear the rush of a distant waterfall and smell, through the pine and evergreen, the sulfur of a nearby hot spring.

But everything here came second to the silence.

It was a deep, reverent silence, as if nature itself were bowing down before the powers that met and mingled here. This place where the membrane between two realities had ruptured. Where impossible things became possible, dark and light things both.

In Sajae language, this place was called a *sorenikan*, a sacred place of pooling, free-flowing Dreamline energy that changed the nature of time itself, slowed it down, so that one year here could equate to six months or one month or two hours in the world. There was no telling, no pattern or rhythm to these things. He had brought Jess here to awaken her to her own abilities and show her how to use them. He had brought Ramsey here to train him as a hunter and fighter, dusting off his own warrior skills as he passed them on to the boy, hoping that spell-modified weapons could help make up for Ramsey's lack of any link to the Dreamlines. No hope of attaining one. Not a drop of Sajae blood in that boy's body; he was all Russian and Irish and English instead, although Ramsey himself didn't know anything about his heritage. Kai kept meaning to tell him these things about himself, the kind of history you found in the blood, always so intriguing and revealing in its own right, Sajae or no, Dreamlines or no—but it always seemed to slip his mind. As fond as he'd become of the boy—fonder than he'd realized, actually, the affection a thing sneaking up from behind—there were always higher priorities.

Mina was waiting for him, a tall, auburn-haired woman with a white fur-trimmed blanket wrapped round her, leaning in the doorway. "My prince." Every time she greeted him, he noticed a little less warmth in her eyes, more coldness in her smile.

He figured he could change that, if he wanted.

Instead of standing aside to let him in, Mina readjusted her hold on the blanket. "So you're here to see the demon?"

A beat, just enough time for Kai to think, *Am I really going through with this?*

"No," he said. "I'm here to see you."

Mina had an ever-shifting staff of servants and personal assistants, people in their twenties and early thirties who found this place through years of dogged, determined searching, fueled by rumors and half-formed personal connections that linked to more connections that sometimes—every once in a while—led them to a Summoner who brought them here, depositing them on Mina's doorstep like lost puppies. To them the place was a kind of Shangri-la, to find themselves or their spirit or their bliss or whatever term they used for it these days, and to do it without losing much time in the real world, still young enough to go to law school or have a baby or party in Ibiza while enjoying the perks and benefits of their newly matured and centered and spiritualized selves. Most of them couldn't hack the reality of what the place turned out to be—a prison built for a demon, who hummed and turned and dreamed in his sphere deep below, his presence casting up all through the house like a mist, or an odor—and left within a week. But a few of them stayed for a long time.

This one, a strapping young Nordic blond with biceps setting out spiced nuts and fruits and a kind of curried pudding that dated back to the days of the Labyrinth, looked familiar. He'd been around for a while, at least since Kai's last visit; maybe Mina was making use of him in bed as well. From the way the guy avoided Kai's eyes, the faint lines of a scowl around his eyes and mouth, Kai figured that she was. He also guessed that, since his last visit, Mina had filled him in on some of their own personal history. He had to grin, tugging at the man's sweater, forcing him to meet his gaze. "We'll need some glasses for this," he said, taking a bottle of *rajika* from his coat pocket and setting it on the table.

Mina noticed it at once. "Where the hells did you get that?"

"Daughtry."

He was about to take off his black leather gloves, but saw the edges of burned, discolored flesh that his heal-spells were still working on, and decided to leave them on.

They settled on the couch and he filled her in on what she hadn't already learned from the two Summoners—Eagan and Jacaranda—who had visited her in shade form. Their talk drifted to other things. Mina's time as Del's guardian had robbed her of any sense of urgency: time, to her, rolled endless and deep. He felt himself relaxing, saw the coldness in her dissolving. They had a history together. They knew each other so well it was like falling into a groove, everything so familiar, includ-ing the way she reached for him.

Afterward, in her bed, she moved away from him the way she always had when they were much younger. She was so quick to feel suffocated, confined. But he caught her long, cool body against him and whispered, "Stay with me like this for a little while. I need it."

"You odd thing," she said, and laughed.

He waited for his spellcasting, thin as gossamer, to escape her notice, to nudge her deeper and deeper into slumber. The feel and scent of her sent him back to those days in the Labyrinth when they had run wild together.

They were children of royalty who came of age during
the decadent—and doomed—Rule of the Five Bloodlines. She went slumming with him—she thought of it as
slumming—in the colorful hustling chaos of the outer-edge
neighborhoods, where he rented a room overlooking the
roranten markets. After they made love—sometimes with
friends of hers, or his, but more often without, since the
people they liked to play with were seldom willing to
venture so far out from the Labyrinth center—he would
look down through the window to where all that life was
happening. The stalls where you could find anything, get
anything, at the right place, including, it was rumored,
Summoner magic, brokered by those talented and crafty
enough to handle the wares and brave enough to risk
the death fines if caught.

He slipped from the bed, dressed, and left Mina's
suite.

The house itself opened into a network of rooms and
corridors so complicated that Kai could get lost if he
wasn't careful. He descended into the earth for what felt
like a very long time.

He brushed a hand across the stone, muttered the
spell's code words, and the door rumbled back against
the wall.

The demon was sleeping. His long, lanky body was
curled against the back wall of his prison-sphere, his tail
wrapped absently around one leg. The shadows of his
dreaming flickered across the walls. Kai could feel them
pulling at him, those dreams, could taste the ash and rot
of them.

A grin crept across Del's lower face, lips rolling back
from black gums and jagged teeth. "Ah," he said. He
opened one red eye. "You."

"Hello, Del."

"You're still put together so nicely. I'm glad that no
one's changed that." Del yawned, spreading fingers
across his mouth, peering at Kai above the dagger nails.
"I know what you've been doing, pretty thing. I smell

her on you. Playing backgammon, were you? Is she still a good backgammon player?"

"You know what I've come for," Kai said.

"Mr. Bones," Del said. "Mr. Bones has come back to play." Del blinked, the lids wrinkling down over his burning eyes. He scratched his chest.

"How do you know about Jess? Did Mina—"

"Mina doesn't tell me things. I tell her things. Let's not have any confusion over this. I was the one who quickened Jess! Went inside her head, unlocked her abilities, so you could help her become what she's becoming. Don't I get a reward? I can't help you again if I don't get a reward. I'm not built that way."

"What do you want, Del?"

"What do you think I want?"

"What makes you think I can give it to you?"

Del unfurled one long finger in his direction, slinking his long body along the curved wall. "I want cheeseburgers," he said. "I want MTV. I want to go to nightclubs in Tokyo."

"Del."

"Did you come here in a limo? I hope you haven't lost those crass materialist cravings of yours. It's one of the things I like about you." Del leaped to the ceiling of the sphere, turned himself around so that he was hanging upside down, the tips of his wiry hair brushing the floor; somehow he'd made the soles of his feet sticky—Kai didn't want to think how—for this purpose. "I want to ride in a plane. And a train. And an automobile." He swung himself, like a kid hanging from a jungle gym, until he'd gathered enough force to smash his face and upper body against the wall facing Kai. "I want the modern world, Prince. I want you to give it to me."

Del peeled himself off the wall, dropped from the ceiling, and said, "I want to see Frank Sinatra in concert!"

"He's dead."

"The Stones, then."

"What makes you think you're worth it?"

"The demon lines are a tricky business, Prince. You think some half-baked hybrid—some little thing who's been in this world barely five minutes, has barely figured out how to dress that human body—can walk them like I can? And you think any of my brethren, those poor, misunderstood, unlucky souls you and your people have locked up for so long—would be willing to help you? Oh no, no, no. You know this. Because they got lost in all that history. They hate you and everything you represent with the same howling fury as when we burned your city to the ground."

"Your city too," Kai said mildly.

Del shrugged.

Then he said, "But the point, my princeling—the point, the point, the point—is that they are stuck in the past. I, and I alone, have moved on. I know how to flow in the waters of time. They wash me up on new beaches and I am okay with that. I adapt. I move forward. Into the future. The others are just dangerous artifacts. Even Asha was an artifact. She flew at the world the same as before. Wanting it to burn, burn off, burn away. When if she had only looked . . ." Del paused, one red eye peering out behind spidery fingers. "I think she would have found that she liked this world, this modern world, the way it is already."

"But the world," Kai said, "would not have liked her."

"I am not Asha. She didn't know how to stop. I am different. I evolve." He whacked both hands against the sphere. "I don't want to burn the world, Prince. I just want to go to the movies. Give me that freedom—give me the chance to be in the modern world, not just drink it in secondhand—and I will give you anything you ask for. Anything. Including her. Jess. The one who dies young. Who always—"

Kai stepped forward, his gaze fixed on the demon. "Give me something. Right here and now. Convince me you're worth it, or I walk away. And this time I won't come back."

Del's ears pricked forward through his thick hair. His face twisted itself one way, then another, as he assessed the Summoner in front of him. "I give you this," he said. "The Traveler sent out a call. It went across the country."

"He did it on the demon lines?"

"He did it the regular way." Del grinned. "With his new hybrid mouth. His new hybrid voice. His words know how to travel. Hybrids can hear. And dogs."

"So the message?"

"To leave Jess Shepard intact. Unharmed."

"Because he has plans for Jess."

"He always has. He owns her."

Del's red gaze was open and frank. He'd known this since his last encounter with Jess, Kai realized; all this time, he'd been keeping it close, waiting for the moment to lay it on the table. Like now.

He said, "How is that possible?"

"He has part of her soul. A claim, a chain, or maybe he cut it out to keep in a jar on his desk . . . who knows? But it keeps her here. In this world. It keeps her coming back, life after life after life, unable to move on, through the Dreamlines . . . move on to the next level. As they say in the modern world. And when he calls her, she—" He blinked. Opened his eyes wide. "What the *hells* is a name like Kai Youngblood, anyway? What made you choose such a moniker? Don't you think it's . . . cheesy? I mean, seriously, *Youngblood*?"

"I got it off some movie," Kai muttered. "I liked the irony. Continue."

"*Youngblood?*"

"I'll make sure my next name meets your approval."

"You would do that?"

"No."

Del looked crestfallen.

"Del. 'When he calls her—' "

"She has to go to him. She has no choice in the matter. She might think she does, and he's the type who would let her believe that, lay out the reasons, the justifications, to convince her. He enjoys it. The game of it. But in the end he's just pulling in the chain. No matter how gently. She just doesn't know it. Why would she?"

His hands ached. Kai realized he was squeezing them into fists, over and over, silver nails raking his palms.

"Okay," he said quietly, "so that's how it is, that's what we're working with," and the demon shifted inside his cell, his body turning fluid, like water, pouring itself along the walls.

Del grinned. "He has part of her soul, my prince. He wants her with him. When the underground goes overground. But she'll die first."

"She'll fight him," Kai said.

"She sacrifices herself. It comes to nothing. She dies because she always dies young. She doesn't understand. It's not an army." Del grinned. "It's not an army. It's just a bunch of . . ."—Kai waited—"rough drafts."

"So if he's in this world, where is he?"

"Why would he tell us his location? He has enough material to work with. We'd only get in his way. But I can find out. I walk the demon lines in my sleep, Prince. It's easy for me. Second nature. Free me from this." He banged a fist against the wall. "Free me from this, give me what I ask for, and I will be your freak on a leash. I'll find out where he is. I might even know how to save her."

They watched each other a moment, and then Del said, carefully, "After all, isn't that why you came here? All the way here in the flesh?"

Kai said nothing. A Summoner could travel in shade form, but could only perform magic through his body. The body was like a lightning rod, calling the Dreamline energy down into it, grounding it, then releasing it as a physical manifestation. As a shade, he could have communicated with Mina, with Del, but he could not have even performed the simple code spells it took to access the demon's prison. He would have had to rely on Mina to do that for him.

"You slept with Mina," Del said quietly. "You tricked Mina, so she would be blameless. Isn't that right? So they won't blame her when they know that I am gone."

"What is Jessamy to you?"

The question seemed to intrigue Del, at least enough to shut him up for a moment. His eyebrows lifted, his mouth pursed, and he rocked back on his heels. "Well," he said, "a project of sorts, I suppose. I helped make her what she is. Did I not? You have to admit—"

"Yes. What else?"

"Maybe that's enough?"

"For what?"

"Your trust." Before Kai had the chance to laugh, Del lifted his hand and said, "I don't get to make things very often, not since my demon came down into me, all that time ago." Del's face shifted and changed, and for a moment Kai could glimpse through the layers of time to what Del had been in the beginning: a craftsman, a glassblower, before his interest in the forbidden forms of magic sent him to the nether-edges of the Labyrinth. "It's a nice feeling," Del went on. "Having made something again. I don't wish to see it—*her*—destroyed quite so soon. And then there would be the matter of you. Being in debt. To me."

And this time Kai did laugh, although he wasn't sure why.

"For that, my prince, I'd go to the end of the Dreamlines and back, and present her to you with a bow tied round her precious head. Which would still," he added generously, "be attached to her body."

"Thoughtful of you."

"My freedom for her life," Del said. "That's the deal. As you knew it would be."

"Come here."

Del crouched to his eye level. Kai said grimly, "You

fail me, betray me, I will not stop until I hunt you down. And I will make even the Traveler's sadism look like the play of a novice."

"Oh, Prince. The promises you make—"

"I can make your next imprisonment the kind of hell that not even *you*, my demon, would take any pleasure in."

"Interesting threat," Del said mildly, "coming from a man with no hands."

Kai glanced at his black-gloved hands. Del, he knew, would have smelled out the wounds.

"A technicality," he said.

Del's eyes narrowed. "You think you have my measure, my prince, but you misjudge me. The Traveler comes to claim what's his, and he brings war. You might find it handy, in the days ahead, to have a person such as myself on your side . . . or if not *on* your side, at least *near* it, hey hey?"

"Shut up. I'm tired."

Del pretended to run a zipper across his lips.

Kai stepped back. He mindreached, and gently explored the spellcraft of the prison. He was impressed all over again by what his Pact had performed that frozen, desperate night in 1499, some of them broken and many of them bleeding and all of them battered and exhausted. Del had writhed and screamed as the world—his world—clamped down small and tight.

For such a multilayered casting, undoing it was straightforward enough, if you knew the edges and angles. He murmured the code words, releasing the outer walls to light and wind. A stale, sour breeze swept his face. The sphere's interior was tinted pale blue. Del's whole body was jittering as he twisted the end of his tail and kept his gaze on Kai.

Kai worked his way through the layers of spellcraft. Every Summoner that night had thrown up a wall, and so it was a shock to encounter his own, the feel of his much younger self.

And then he burst through to the spell's throbbing, salty center, and the light surrounding the demon changed to the color of wine. Kai lifted his hands, braced himself, and called the energy to him. The wine-light flooded the cavern as the last of the sphere walls dissolved. Then, like a retreating tide, the light pulled back from the walls. It streamed around Kai. He began to chant the old, old words, holding out his palms and lifting his face, offering himself as passage back to the Dreamlines. Back home. And the light swept into his body, through his eyes and mouth and nostrils and the skin of his upturned palms. His vision churned, and the taste of blood and smoke flooded his mouth, his throat, threatened to gag him. He held himself still, enduring, and just when his body threatened to break—

—the last of the light faded through him.

It was over.

He ran his tongue across his teeth and spat blood onto the floor. That vile taste wouldn't leave his mouth. He suspected it would be with him for a while.

Del's body was still transitioning from the world-within-a-world of the prison-sphere. It was recalling the human form from long before. Except . . . Kai didn't remember his skin being this smooth and pale, his body so gangly.

This was not the Delkor Lokk from the days of the Labyrinth.

He'd been an eccentric glassmaker, then a sage of the dark arts, then a demon. He'd been imprisoned for over five hundred years. Did his release bring about another transformation?

What kind of creature had they made?

Del turned his face to Kai. His eyes had retained their demon-color, pits of fire blazing up through lanks of shaggy dark hair. Kai sighed. As if he wasn't conspicuous enough, with his height and skin sheen and odd eyes, now he'd be accompanied by this milk white, shambling, lava-eyed man-thing.

Del's eyes were wide.

"Ohhhh," he breathed, "you're a bad prince. A very bad prince. You're going to be in *trouble*—"

"Shut up."

Del tossed his head—his strangely human head—and laughed.

"Move," Kai said, pushing the little man ahead of him. Still figuring out the proper use of his new legs, Del wasn't walking so much as lurching around.

"Goooo-ing to the chapel—and we're—gooooonnnnna get maaaaarrrried—"

"Don't sing," Kai said darkly. "Just don't."

Chapter Nineteen

Del

In those moments—as the stale air of his sphere fled away on all sides and the modern world began to enfold him—Del surprised himself. He wasn't thinking or plotting for the future. He wasn't paying much attention to this bulky human package that encased him with such weight and gravity and *noise*, heart thundering, stomach snarling, bones moaning themselves into use. He was thinking of something Kai had said to him, the words looping through Del's reshaped head, so that Del ignored the prince's threatening looks and started up another happy hum.

My demon, Kai had called him.

My demon, my demon, my demon . . .

III

You're the One Who Kills Me

The Voice first came to me when I was but a Child. I was running through the New England hills of the family estate playing a game with my brother. The game involved shooting each other with toy guns and yelling "Boom! Boom!"—simple fun for young simple Souls. We called the game "the BoomBoom Man" and would ask each other, "Do you want to play the BoomBoom Man?" That morning it was my turn to be the Man and I was hurtling after my brother when the Headache came upon me in a blast of furious light. I hit the ground so hard, there was dirt and blood in my mouth.

And the Voice came into me and spoke with me.

Next thing I knew, worried grown-ups surrounded me. They said I had stopped breathing. They said my eyes were wide-open and still. They thought I had Died.

Perhaps for a moment I did. In Death, I found my Destiny.

You should be so lucky.

   —Stefan Holt, from his unpublished memoirs

Chapter Twenty

Jess

The helicopter chopped across the vast, rambling sprawl of Los Angeles, the valley giving way to hills giving way to the lush green outcroppings of the west side, the pools and roofs of the *über*wealthy tossing glints of light right back at her. It descended over a low, white stone villa: no pool here, but what seemed to be an elaborate statue garden instead.

"I made this place," Stefan said proudly. "I designed it."

They stood in front of an iron gate that rolled apart as if someone had said open sesame. Stefan pointed to the house visible beyond the sculpture garden, its clean, modern angles and whitewashed walls, the white marble steps leading up to the entrance. "All the energies that flow through here," Stefan said happily, "are possible because of me. Because of my calculations. Because of my hard work and devotion. Because of my gifts and intellect." There was an edge to his voice, a kind of accusation: *and don't you dare forget that.*

A woman giggled.

Jess started. She looked in the direction of the female voice and saw only Stefan, still lost in his absorption of the sleek, gleaming newness of his creation. Something was happening to the back of Stefan's head . . . odd bumps and angles rising up through his white-blond hair. Asha's hair was that color, she found herself thinking, as that cold sense of detachment and numbness swept over her again. The rounded lines and crevices were resolving themselves into a second face, now covering the back of the man's scalp more tightly and completely than a costume mask ever could. Blue eyes blinked, gazed at Jess with open curiosity; lips—twisted into what might have been meant as a smile.

"Jessamy! You're finally here! Brilliant!" A man came toward them with a long, loping stride, weaving neatly amid the statues without even glancing at them, as if his body simply knew where they were. His teeth were very white against the tan of his face. "Brilliant!" he said again, and Jess picked up an Australian accent. He wore a rumpled white suit and leather thong sandals. Shiny silver hair fell to his shoulders. Next thing she knew he had her hand in his, was shaking it enthusiastically. His grip was warm and strong.

"Now," he said, and clapped his hands together. "What should we do first? So much to talk about! Are you hungry? Thirsty? How was your trip? I hope it was comfortable. I apologize for how . . . unconventional . . . it was, but we do what we can with what we have to work with. Don't we, Stefan?" Before Stefan could answer—Jess wasn't inclined to say anything—the man said, "Stefan, why don't you go organize some refreshments? There's a good lad. Now—"

"Refreshments?" Stefan stood there and blinked at him. "But I thought—"

The man waved a hand. "Yes. Go. Fetch."

"But I thought—"

"We have a tiny problem, Stefan?" Just a hint of a shadow slipped through the man's cheerful tone, but Jess could still feel the chill.

"And our other guest. Please see if you can get him to eat something. I am growing mildly concerned."

Stefan tipped his head forward in what might have been a nod.

"And I forgot to introduce myself," the man beside her was saying. "That just shows you where my brain is! My name is Jaxon. Jaxon Twist. And once again, Jessamy, let me say how pleased I am to finally meet you. I think we'll work really well together. Jaxon and Jessamy. Jessamy and Jaxon. The names go together disturbingly well. Sounds like one of those—what do you call them?— one of those television comedy situations." He beamed. Then he said, "You must have so many questions."

But Jess's attention had fallen on the small object that hung below his collarbone. Jaxon lifted an eyebrow, a smile edging his mouth as she reached out and touched the shark's tooth dangling from the leather cord around his neck. She gave it a tug, let go. "So it was you."

"Me?"

Why did she feel so disappointed? Surely she had expected this? Known this?

"The child in the mirror," she said. "Who helped me."

He pivoted and walked to one of the statues, running his hand across the smooth flanks. "What do you think of this one?"

Her eyes skimmed over the thickset female body, the cold marble face, hands raised as if in self-defense or supplication, the mouth a round O of surprise. Or terror. "Did you do it?"

Jaxon grunted again. "This isn't my work. These are my materials." He gave the statue's head a friendly pat. The woman's blank eyes seemed fixed on Jess. She stepped aside, out of that dead line of vision. "My stuff, my real work, is stored elsewhere. In a very roomy place. Let's talk about your performance in the Trials."

"You lied to me."

"I wouldn't say I lied."

"You said you were an aspect of me. My way of talking to myself."

"I wanted to force you into a different kind of perspective," Jaxon said. He pulled a leaf off a eucalyptus tree, crushed it, and brought it to his nose. He sniffed deeply, like an addict with cocaine. "Truth is a multifaceted thing, after all. It's hard to see all of it at once. You have to turn it around in your hands. Hold it up in different slants of light. *Try* not to roll your eyes, Jessamy."

"Why did you interfere with my Trials?"

"Because you needed interference."

"Why?"

"Because you can be better, Jessamy." Crumpling the gray-green leaf in his hand, he tossed it, even as he ripped another from the same branch. Behind the scent of eucalyptus drifted other smells that didn't seem to have any place here. A smell of brine, like ocean air or even spilled semen. A smell of wet things rotting. "You have all the talent in the worlds, but you lack a lightness of touch." He *tsk-tsk*ed, wobbling his head from side to side. "It's painful to watch. I just couldn't take it anymore."

"A lightness of touch?"

"You need to be light, child. Strive for things, fight for things, sacrifice what needs to be sacrificed, yes yes yes. But once you have it in your possession, you need to let go. The trick to holding on is not to hold on at all." Again, the wobble of the head. He flicked the leaf at her. "You haven't learned that."

"You mean, not care?"

"You must care fiercely. But once you get what you want, treat it lightly. The things you own—own you, after all. They drag you down. And you need to keep your quickness about you. A freedom of movement."

"So maybe it's best not to own anything."

"Personally, I love to own things. It's in our very nature to own things. The trick is to own them lightly. This includes the magic as well. Lightly, lightly. Hold it, play with it, let it go." He turned and started walking along the garden path, white pebbles scattering beneath his feet. Jess followed, conscious of the statues they passed, the men and women and animals, the fixed, unseeing stares that still seemed to watch her. ". . . so fraught with searches for meaning and whatnot. He can't take what is and let it be . . . what it is. He has to hammer it into some kind of grand design. And who's the authority on that grand design? He is, of course. It's part of his sense of entitlement as a Summoner. They're all like that. All their history and tradition and rituals and ceremonies and whatnot. Sooner or later you can't help but implode under all that self-importance." Jaxon smiled at her over his shoulder. "I knew him when he was young. The one who made you."

"He didn't make me."

Through the windows Jess could see the blond man bustling about the dining table. He seemed to have too many hands.

"Of course not. You're very much a work in progress, aren't you? That's a good state to be in, child. Don't let yourself get finished too soon. Or at all."

Rose bushes reached out for her, thorns scratching her skin. She stepped around them, following him up the steps.

Stefan was carrying a tray of roast beef sandwiches with one pair of arms, pouring water into glasses with another.

"You have four arms," she said.

Stefan swung round. Just behind him Jess glimpsed a woman, her pale, slender arms setting down the pitcher of water. She began to realize what she was truly seeing, instead of what her mind had assumed it was seeing: the woman was not standing behind or beside or anywhere near Stefan. She was not standing at all. She was a torso extending from the side of Stefan's body. Peering around Stefan's head, she and Jess examined each other. The woman had the same coloring as Stefan, the pale watery eyes and white-blond hair. Her face was soft and rounded where his was angular, her eyebrows overplucked, her ears adorned with gold dots.

"Hello," Jess said. "I think I saw you before."

"It's no use talking to her," Stefan snapped. "She doesn't talk back."

The woman's body folded into Stefan's, like a fan snapping shut.

Jess said, one hand reaching out to brace herself against a wall, "I don't think I understand."

"Stefan's sister loves him very much, and thought they should be closer," Jaxon said, "and I felt a little sorry for her. So I gave her what she wanted."

"It's not what I wanted," Stefan said.

Jaxon ignored him, as if he were a small, whining dog. "I didn't mean for her to lose her voice. But sometimes these things happen. Stefan. This is when you leave, now."

Stefan's eyes lingered on Jess, turned hard. He stalked off.

Jaxon picked up a sandwich, spent a moment admiring its contents. "Eat," he said to Jess, not taking his gaze off the sandwich.

"What do you want from me?"

"Ultimately," he said, "I want you to work for me. With me. I brought you here in order to—how do people put it?—in order to groom you for the position. I know you came here under a bit of duress—"

"A bit, yeah."

"—but you stay of your free will. You can leave anytime. Run back to young Master Youngblood."

"What makes you think I won't?"

"Because you're an addict," he said, and she started at the word. "And like all addicts," he went on, pointing at her with one half of the sandwich, a sprig of lettuce hanging from the bread, "you're not exactly well rounded. You're a spiky personality. Obsessive. Extreme. My favorite kind. So you'll stay, because I can feed that addiction like no one else, and you know that. You know exactly what I'm talking about. And"—he raised a hand, cutting her off before she could speak—"I know your intentions toward me are not particularly honorable. I invite you into my home, you think you can spy on me, find a way to kill me. Save the world. But the world doesn't need saving, Jessamy. Not from me."

And now she decided to say nothing.

"You should really eat something. Want to share this with me?"

"No. I'm good."

He folded half the sandwich into his mouth and swallowed it, a large bulge rippling down his throat. Jess averted her gaze. "I want you to coax out my better self, Jessamy. I've been a destroyer for as long as I can remember. Trust me when I say that that's a long time. I am so bored." He shrugged, looking sheepish. "But I am preparing for a new role. As an artist. A creator. And I am working toward my masterwork."

"Which is . . . ?"

"A Labyrinth of my own."

"You're joking," she said flatly.

"Yes," he agreed, and went on so smoothly she wasn't sure if that exchange had even happened, "And I need you to help me. To inspire me. Be my muse, you might say." He raised a hand again, as if to cut her off, even though she still wasn't speaking. "You say: how can we work together if we don't trust one another? But I think as long as all our cards are on the table, our agendas made clear to one another, we can sidestep the whole pesky matter of trust. Because I don't want to hurt you. If anything, I'm hoping to charm you into becoming a more permanent . . . colleague of mine. And you aren't capable of hurting me. So." He opened his mouth wide—wider—his jaws actually seeming to unhinge, and shoved in the rest of the sandwich, his throat swelling as he swallowed it down. He hadn't even bothered to chew. He wiped his mouth with the back of his hand, winked at Jess. "So what do you say?" He raised his hand again. "I know. You say you're tired and over-whelmed. How about I give you some time to yourself? Mi casa es su casa. Wander around. Explore. Help your-self to anything. Or anyone. Come back to me in the morning and we'll make some real magic together. Okay?"

She didn't know what she would say until she said it. "You're a piece of work."

Jaxon craned his neck and laughed. "I am!" he crowed to the ceiling. "I am! A real piece of work!" He dropped his head forward, smiling at her. "You're de-lightful!"

Before she could react he took her face between his hands. She felt the pressure of his fingertips, imagined him popping her skull like an eyeball. She wondered why she didn't feel afraid; she felt, instead, like she was a million miles away, watching this whole scene unfold through the wrong end of a telescope. Whoever this woman was, enduring this bizarre encounter, it didn't feel to Jess quite like herself.

Then Jaxon's face was looming into hers and he kissed her on the mouth. A close-mouthed, avuncular kiss, not much more than a peck. His breath smelled of mustard. When he stepped away from her she felt herself reeling, and she had to grab the back of a chair for balance.

"Good night," he said. He walked out of the room, hands in his pockets, singing softly to himself: *"Come together . . . right now . . . over me!"*

She listening to the whistling, the footfalls, as they retreated inside the house. "Unbelievable," she whis-pered. She shook her head, pushing her hands through her hair, saying it again: "Unbelievable." She laughed. And somehow the laugh cut into a sob, and her knees went out from under her as if they'd been shot. The world went dark for a second and she found herself crouching in the corner, hugging her knees to her chest.

Someone was whispering, "I can't do this I can't do this I can't do this." Someone was saying, "I can't do this anymore." Her voice. Her words. Moisture on her face. She was crying.

She had to stop this. Pull herself together.

No way out but through.

But I'm going to die. The thought slipped into her mind like a blade between two ribs. *My death is somewhere in this house.*

She forced herself back to her feet. *You always have to make sure you're asking yourself the right questions,* Kai had told her once. *The right question directs your thinking. The mind wants to come up with an answer.*

So she asked herself now: *What's the silver lining here? What can I use to advantage?*

And the answer came so fast that she almost had to laugh:

I have nothing to lose. Which means I have nothing to fear.

She walked from the room into a grand entrance hall. White gleaming marble, threaded with veins of black: the walls, the floor, the ceiling, all the same. Elsewhere in the house she heard doors opening, other doors slamming shut. The murmurs and echoes of voices eddied through the air. A staircase spiraled up in front of her, a hallway opened off to the left, and the walls were hung with drapes of rich velvet that looked to be covering large paintings.

Or mirrors.

She gathered up a fistful of velvet. She meant to yank it off, see what hid behind, when a voice came sharply to her:

"You don't want to do that."

Stefan had appeared in the mouth of the hallway. He was holding another tray: it held more of the sandwiches, cans of soda, and bottles of beer.

Looking at him, Jess let the velvet fall from her hand. "Why not?"

"You just don't. Trust me."

"Not to state the obvious," Jess said, "but there's something extremely fucked up about this place."

"And this surprises you?"

"So what are all these?" She gestured at the row of cloth-draped frames.

"Mirrors."

"Jaxon doesn't like to see his reflection?"

"He loves his reflection." Stefan yawned. "Save it for tomorrow. Trust me, those things aren't going anywhere, and neither are you."

"The gracious host says I can leave anytime I want."

"Why don't you, then?"

She touched her fingertips to her mouth, recalling the sensation of Jaxon's lips brushing hers. The demon-king had kissed her good night. Her mouth felt stained. But a pleasant, floating sensation was stealing through her; she felt buoyant, optimistic. It was almost like someone had slipped her a Vicodin or two, even though she hadn't taken anything to eat or drink.

"Maybe you don't have anyplace to go," Stefan said.

She looked at him.

Kind of a buzzkill.

"Do yourself a favor," he said, "and get some sleep. Okay?"

"Who else is in this house?"

"There are lots of people in this house. This is a very big house."

"Where are they?"

Stefan shrugged. "They come and go."

He walked off down the hall.

Jess trailed behind him, summoning what little Dreamline magic she had in her to cloak the sound of her footsteps, curious to see where he was taking the tray . . . and not ready yet to be alone. Not here, in this weird fucked-up place filled with shadows that prowled the white marble. She felt kind of good, though. She felt like things might work out. She passed more of those velvet folds on the wall, concealing whatever they concealed. When she was alone, she would investigate. She would learn as much as there was to learn, and she would do it all in secret. No one would know.

For now, though, it was enough to follow Stefan, who was either oblivious to her presence or completely ignoring her.

Down some stairs, through more hallways—so many hallways in this place; were they people in a house or rats in a maze?—and then Stefan stopped. His shoulders heaved a sigh. He seemed to take a moment to brace himself.

He kicked open the door and took the tray inside.

Still walking on a thin layer of magic that swallowed all sound, Jess drifted toward the room . . . when a presence at the end of the hall thrust awareness at her, the sense of itself crossing her face like a slap.

Her whole body filled with a deep, rhythmic thrumming: this presence reaching out for her, somehow moving inside her. Like nothing she'd experienced before. It was swelling through her rib cage like a parasitic heart.

She let it draw her on, down the hall, until the floor gave way to hard-packed earth and a wind came whistling down to meet her, carrying notes of earth and smoke and high, sweet decay. The hall didn't seem to end so much as run out. She was standing at the mouth of a cave. She walked on dirt and rock, turning in a circle, her vision penetrating enough of the shadow to take in nooks and crevices and outcroppings of spiky rock. Some kind of chair was carved into one wall. And that steady sensation of *boom boom boom* continued to press in around her, like some kind of psychic heart that started small but was growing every minute; she could feel how it was growing, sense the history of that growth like rings in a tree, as the *boom boom boom* continued to build in her blood.

She closed her eyes and when she opened them she was sitting on the chair carved from rock, her head falling dreamily to one side. The heartbeat of the place, the bass line of the place, snatched a piece of her awareness and swept it on, down the twists and turns of tunnels extending like tentacles: growing, spreading out beneath the thin, unknowing surface of this world.

Acid flooded her mouth. Jess pushed herself off the chair and stumbled across the dirt floor. And still that *boom, boom, boom* came at her, came through her; it would sweep her up and back to that chair—that throne—if only she would let it. But now she could hear the song it was singing, how empty it was at the core. There was nothing here. There was worse than nothing. A hunger, rising up through the darkness, turning the air into a gaping maw that would consume everything it came across, until it left a world of nothing in its wake. If she didn't get out of here now, it would turn her into nothing too, no matter how many thrones it pretended to offer her.

And even as she stumbled back into the hallway she still felt it furling that deep, snaking bass line around her and through her, sending alien whispers into her mind:

Don't go.

Don't you dare go.

She kept her back to it, to that whistling, cavernous space that throbbed in the shadows behind her.

She ran.

Except she couldn't find her way back upstairs. Hallways led to more hallways, even when she slowed herself down and took careful note of where she was going, using her fingertips to make small scorch marks of magic to let herself know where she'd already been. White walls, white floor. Rat in a maze. She was so tired. And she hadn't eaten anything. That had to be why she felt so disoriented. Why it felt like the walls were watching her. Shifting themselves around her. As if they were guiding her to one place in particular. As if the house had a mind and an agenda all its own. She could choose left or right, it didn't matter—the choice had been made for her, long ago. Why was she thinking like this?

Magic chose us. War chose us. We don't get to do the choosing.

A door flung open in front of her and Stefan hurried out, ducking as something—a tray—came hurtling over his head. It hit the wall and broke in two. As the pieces landed and skidded, Stefan straightened, adjusted his shirt, and turned to face the doorway and whoever looked out from beyond it.

"That's childish," he said.

A plate flew at his head like a Frisbee. He stepped to the side and the plate smashed into the wall. "This," he said, as he stepped to the other side to avoid a flying fork, "isn't going to," and he ducked before a coffee mug could tunnel itself through his forehead, "help you very much."

Silence.

Broken dinnerware crunched beneath Stefan's shoes.

An empty beer bottle spun end over end through the doorway. Stefan raised an arm to his face, and the bottle struck his elbow and dropped to the floor.

"Are you done now?" he said wearily.

And a man's voice sounded beyond the doorway: "Why do I have to look at your ugly mug?"

A thinned-out voice, frayed at the edges, but still so familiar.

Jess felt a jump in her chest.

"People usually find me attractive," Stefan said.

"I want the other one. The better half. Can't you wave your hands and say presto, or something, and pull her out of yourself? So much *cooler* than a bunny."

"I hope you're amusing yourself. I don't know how you expect to improve your situation with this kind of behavior."

"I am amusing myself, thank you very much! So if sis wants to hide out down there by your pancreas, or wher-

ever the fuck she goes, then you can just fuck right off
right now. Go on now. Go on."

Stefan opened his mouth. Closed it again. Sighed. "It's
not like I wanted—like either she or I ever wanted—I
meant it when I told you—"

"So how's that whole master-slave thing working out for
you? Huh? The way to become some freaky dude's master,
is to first become his butt-boy, or something . . . ?"

Jess saw the stiffness take over Stefan's body, clamp-
ing his shoulders, the line of his jaw. A growling sound
came from his throat, morphing into the word "Soon."

And the other man started laughing.

Careful, Jess thought. *Be careful.*

"Soon?" she heard the other man say. "Soon? Soon
what?"

"Soon," Stefan said.

He looked down at his hands. Then he walked off.
Shadows closed around him. She walked toward the
room—toward its occupant—with a feigned kind of
casualness, slipping her hands in the pockets of Kai's
suit jacket. *Hey, no biggie. I was in the neighborhood.*
She stepped over the dropped fork. Her fingers touched
something round and smooth deep inside the pocket. A
stone. A red stone.

A stone from the crown in her Trials.

Then she was turning into the door frame, and she
saw him.

He was sitting on a ladder-back chair pulled out from
a small table. He wore frayed jeans and nothing else,
one bare foot planted on the chair, his knee drawn up
to his naked chest, tattoos inked along his biceps, the
front of his shoulder. He was too pale and too thin, his
ribs laddered against his skin. His eyes, when he looked
at her, were red-rimmed and burning. Not the burning
of a Summoner who held fresh magic within him; this
man was hollowed out.

They regarded each other.

"Hey," she said, because she figured one of them should really say something.

He was frowning at her, or maybe it was just a look of intense concentration. He gave his head a shake, blinked several times, and widened his eyes. A trick or a dream, she could see him thinking. A trick or a dream. "Hello painter," he said, and lifted his hands. She saw the chain, then, shackling his wrists and trailing on the floor. It was the same olive shade as his skin. The manacles were also skin-colored, and seemed like bony growths encircling both wrists. Lucas said, with what seemed part irony, part hope, "Have you come to rescue me? Am I your boy in distress?"

"How long have you been here?"

He had to think about this. "A year?" Chain sliding the edge of the chair, he lifted both hands so he could scratch his scalp. "A year and a half? Fucked if I know. What date is it?"

She told him.

"No," he said. "No. That's not possible. Because that would mean—that would mean—" His eyes were now very wide. He tucked his chin, hair brushing across his thin shoulders. "That would mean it's just been—days. How could it only be days?"

"Time can get weird in places like this," she told him. He didn't seem interested. "How did you find me?"

"I didn't. They brought me here."

"They know you're here?"

"I'm here as a"—Jess paused, then added—"guest."

Lucas plucked at the chain. He sniggered.

Then he said, "So am I."

Jess snorted. Then chuckled. Then she was laughing, his answer only deepening the hilarity. Lucas looked at her, his smirk fleshing out into a grin, and then he was cackling, his shoulders shaking with it, and she was laughing too, folding her arms across her chest only to laugh harder, curving forward with the force of it. Lucas doubled over in the chair. They went on like this for another minute. She couldn't remember the last time she'd laughed half this hard. Finally Lucas sat up again, shaking his head, tears streaming from his bloodshot eyes. "Oh god," he said, and dragged a hand across his face. "Jesus H. Christ. And I'm so rude. I didn't bring a gift for my lovely host. You?"

She shook her head.

"If only you'd thought to call me. I could have reinded you to pick up a little somethin'-somethin'. Flowers or shit."

"Wine," she suggested.

"Perhaps a potted houseplant."

"Or a scented candle."

"Scented candle," Lucas muttered, and then he was guffawing again, the chain clanking off the chair, slithering over his leg.

Jess let him work it out. She took in the rest of the space. It was set up like a studio apartment. King-sized platform bed in the corner heaped with pillows in velvet and silk. The concrete floor scattered with knotted silk and wool rugs. A door in the back opening into a tiny bathroom. Two of the walls were lined with books and CDs and DVDs, all of which looked brand-new, most of them still in their wrappings. There were a stereo system and a small television arranged to the side of a stone fireplace, a love seat angled in front of it.

Seating for two, Jess noted, just like the two chairs by this table.

"I should have offered you something," Lucas said suddenly. "Man, I really do have the manners of an animal. Do you want something to eat, or drink, or . . . ? I mean, there's not much, and a lot of it is on the floor in the hall, but there are some snacks and things in that little minibar—"

"You don't look like they're feeding you much."

"That's by personal choice. I'm kind of trying this starvation thing. Not to mention." He crooked a finger at her. "Kettle. Pot."

She ignored this. "They tortured you? You look—"

"Thing One and Thing Two—this was before they became Thing One *and* Two, and for the sake of convenience, I will now shorten that to Thing—took a whack at it. It really sucked, of course, but it was—for the most part I could still . . . But then—" She could see him hunting for words, for a language that could convey his experience instead of just breaking down. "The freaky dude," he said, and then stopped again. Then said, "It all changed when the freaky dude came. He can really get in your head. You know? Do you know this yet?"

"Tell me what happened to you."

"You really are too fucking thin. You should eat something."

"I will if you will."

"Kind of problematic for me. Eating would indicate a desire to stay alive."

"Eating usually does."

"They seem—he seems—to want me alive."

"Because he wants you to play music for him. Is that it?"

"It's so bad," Lucas said wryly, "to be so good. Everybody wants a piece of me."

"So you meant it when you said you wouldn't give them what they wanted."

"You doubted me?"

"Yeah."

"Wow. That might hurt my feelings. If I was the kind of man who had, like, feelings and shit."

"You wouldn't go with them voluntarily, so they kidnapped you. You still wouldn't play for them, so they tortured you. Is that the story?"

"Pretty much."

"So they're keeping you here—*he's* keeping you here—until you play what he wants you to play."

"Oh," he murmured, "I played. I did play."

"You what?"

He cleared his throat. "I played," he said again, a little louder this time. A look like a wound surfaced in his eyes and he shifted slightly away from her. "I played like he wanted. Everything he wanted. I couldn't stop playing. I played until my hands . . ."

His voice cut out. He closed his eyes. Jess felt the knock of her heart in her chest, the echoes of that other deep thrumming from where the house abruptly ended in the cave. That other heart. That center. Center of what? She remembered again the feel of the stone chair, how it fit itself so perfectly to her body. Center of a new world.

It was as if the tip of a blade touched her neck, sending a sharp, breathless shiver through her body. She realized she was rubbing a hand across her lips, and had been doing so for the last few minutes, trying to get something off them.

She looked at Lucas.

"Let me see your hands," she whispered.

He had slipped them between his knees. "Let me see," Jess said again, and he allowed her to grasp his wrists, draw them toward her. She gasped, but it wasn't because of his hands; this close, she saw why the cuffs that shackled him looked like part of him. Because they were now. She traced them with her fingers, felt how they had molded themselves to his wrists, how the bottom edges extended down through his flesh. "Does it hurt?" she asked him.

"Yes."

She turned his hands over, gently unfurled his fingers.

And for long moments she could do nothing but stare at the narrow, jagged wounds that crosshatched his palms, the undersides of his fingers. Some of them were long, narrow cuts, as if the guitar strings had turned to razor blades beneath his touch; others were blistered and blackened, with eruptions along the edges, giving off the odor of burnt flesh, as if something had come scorching out through them. The oldest ones had already closed over, laying ridged scars across his skin that were crossed with the most recent wounds, still swollen and thinly weeping. The blood looked black. At first Jess thought it was the light, until she angled the head of a floor lamp directly on them. The blood was so black she wondered if it was even blood at all. But it smelled like blood. It tasted like blood. She spat it out.

Lucas was watching her. He answered the question before she could even ask it. "Yeah," he said. "They hurt like hell."

"I'm so sorry."

He shrugged and took his hands away from her.

"I thought I'd be dead by now," he said. "I played until he didn't want me to play anymore, and now I can't play anymore, not with these fucking paws—" In the moment of silence that followed Jess knew they were thinking the same thing: if Jaxon Twist wanted Lucas to play, then Lucas would do so until the skin flayed from his hands and the strings bit through tendons and muscle to bone, and the music disappeared into the sound of his own screaming. Lucas said, "I'd say he's forgotten that I'm even here, except he keeps sending Thing down to feed me. Maybe he's keeping me around for some last task."

"So you're trying to starve to death?"

"It's not like I want to, you know, *die*," Lucas said, and flashed a sudden grin, which told her the old Lucas was not beaten from him completely, "I just want to piss him off a little. Kind of pathetic, I know, but it's what I got to work with. What about you, Jess? What's your story?"

For a moment she was too distracted to answer the question, feeling he'd said something odd. Then she realized what it was: her name. He had called her by name.

"I don't want to talk about it," she said.

"Yes you do. I tell you mine, you tell me yours—"

"Maybe later."

"So there will be a later?"

On impulse she got off her chair and straddled him on his. He took in a breath. His hands came up and over her head, and she leaned her body against him and rested her head on his shoulder. He patted her awkwardly on the back for a moment, his hands curled up to protect their raw-meat undersides. Then his arms tightened around her. "Stay with me," he whispered. "For a while."

It felt as though she were dreaming, and she kept having to remind herself that she was not. Time turned surreal, stretched out, like toffee; soon she didn't know if she'd been here for two days or two months. And on some level it seemed like she had always been here, drifting through white marble hallways, her fingers absently touching the place on her lips where Jaxon had kissed her, like a prince in a fairy tale. Except instead of waking her up, he'd put part of her to sleep.

She knew this, and yet somehow she couldn't find it in herself to mind. The part that should have been concerned—wildly concerned—was sleeping too deeply.

Jaxon liked to talk. Sometimes she felt that was the true reason he wanted her there: so he could have someone to talk to, or talk at, and perhaps she filled this purpose in a way someone like Stefan could not, although she wasn't sure why.

He spent most of his days in his studio. The studio door was always locked, and the hall just beyond it was always lined with hybrids, and even the occasional full-blooded human. They sat cross-legged on the floor or leaned against the wall or milled around aimlessly, like actors at an audition.

"What are they waiting for?" Jess asked Stefan one morning. Or what might have been a morning; maybe it was afternoon.

He was escorting her the way he always did through what Jess had come to think of as Jaxon's receiving hall.

She was conscious of the gazes examining her, crawling all over her, as the hybrids shifted and murmured to one another. But despite the hostility and distrust in their faces, they left her alone. They always left her alone.

"What do you think?" Stefan asked, opening the door and practically shoving her inside.

A sunlit rectangle of a room with off-white walls, a dark wood floor. A long table lining one wall was scattered with objects that Jess felt something in her head turning her away from, a mental hand gently guiding her attention to the man at the end of the room. He was hovering over his latest project, another life-size sculpture. He pressed his hands against the sculpture's shoulder, and the body bowed inward; he lifted his hand into the air, and a limb sprouted from the sculpture's torso, as if following Jaxon's gesture. The limb hung there like a windblown branch until Jaxon stepped back and wrinkled his face in disgust, and the limb dropped with a clunk to the floor.

He saw her, and his face lit up.

"Jess!" He waved her over. "Come closer!"

"I'm fine here," she said.

"But you're so far away!"

"I don't mind."

He laughed.

The sight of him put her at ease. Despite that, or maybe because of it, she felt no urge to get close enough to see details. Of his face, his teeth. Of the thing he was working on. She thought of how she avoided looking at the objects on the table, when in any other studio they would be the first things she was drawn to: objects of inspiration, things to work with, transform. She remembered how she'd promised herself that as soon as she was alone, she would take off those velvet cloths and see what hung beneath them. Yet she hadn't.

She touched her lips, felt again the stain, the invisible brand on her skin.

"You're a very talented girl, Jessamy. But what you

don't have," Jaxon said, with the serenity of someone unshakable in his convictions, "is—"

"A lightness of touch. You said this already."

His lip skinned back from his teeth. He eyed her for a moment, then said, *"Style."*

He ran his hand along the head of his sculpture. A series of horns rose up beneath his touch. He played with them, his fluttering hand gestures making some higher and more arched, while driving others back into the skull.

"Style is very serious, Jess," Jaxon said. "And don't confuse it with good taste, or having a good eye. You have an excellent eye. But although that's a requisite for style—or at least for hiring someone to have style for you—that, in itself, is not style.

"Take your Kai Youngblood, for example. Say what you like about that one—and I can say a lot of things about that one—" A chuckle, low and deep in Jaxon's throat. He made a tweaking motion with his hand and a curly tail rose from the sculpture's muscled buttocks. "But the man has excellent style. He just doesn't know enough to teach you about it. So take a moment to contrast and compare. What does he have that you don't?"

"Over six centuries' worth of experience."

"Don't use that as an excuse."

"Why compare us? It's useless. Apples and oranges."

"But you're trying to be like him, yes?"

"That's not true."

"Kai and his peers, they never felt they had to earn anything. That their natural gifts were their birthright as high-blood Sajae. Because the low-blooded ones, those who fell on the mostly human side of that great line—bloodline—of division, their fate was to serve, to cater, to support, yes? The best they could hope for was to be plucked from their fate by some random benefactor. To be chosen."

Jaxon ripped the head off the sculpture and hurled it at the wall, like a ballplayer going for an outside shot.

He looked at the work before him and wrinkled his face. "Stefan," he hollered. "*Stefan!*"

The door opened and Stefan looked hopeful. "Yes?"

Jaxon kicked the sculpture over. It crashed to the ground with unnatural force, scattering across the floorboards in chunks and pieces. "Clean that up," he snapped. "Bring me someone new to work with."

"Of course," Stefan said.

"Someone interesting," Jaxon said. "Someone inspiring. I know they all *think* they are—that's why they come here—but most of them are *mistaken.*"

"Of course."

"Do your damn job, Stefan."

"Always," Stefan said, and closed the door.

Jaxon stepped over a piece of lower torso and came toward Jess. When she instinctively backed away, he paused. Smiled.

Behind her, the door opened and shut, and Jess heard the sounds of footsteps and sweeping, as the mess of busted art was attended to.

"I've watched you and your mentor for a long time, and the problem is not that Youngblood has style. He takes style itself for granted."

Jess took breath to speak, saw Jaxon's eyes go dark, and changed her mind.

She realized she was rubbing the back of her hand across her lips.

"Kai's emphasis with you has always been on controlling the magic. But this makes magic your slave. Or else you're the vessel that channels the magic, in which case you're the slave. But to liberate the true potential, the relationship between you and the magic, you have to recognize that it is *not* about who is the master and who is the slave. It is a partnership. It is a creative collaboration. It is an ongoing conversation. And you, well, you have to hold up your end of the dialogue. You have to have something to say.

"You have to know yourself.

"That is the true power: working from the center of yourself, knowing what you stand for, knowing what your story is, so that every thing you say, every gesture you make, stands in for that story. You turn yourself into a concentrated force. Nothing is wasted.

"You, Jessamy, grab at magic blindly, you hoard it, you throw it around helter-skelter. You get by on the sheer brutality of your talent, but it is a crude process, and filled with mistakes. You have no strategy, no overall design. You're like a woman with an overstuffed closet but only one or two decent outfits. Don't look at me like that. If you were a man, which of course you are not, I would use the exact same analogy.

"For you don't just channel the magic through your body. An animal could do that. Sort of. You filter it through your self. Your sense of self. And that," Jaxon said triumphantly, "is style! You see?"

Another time, he said: "You need to be open. You need to expose yourself. You need to tell the truth and share the truth. Information you keep to yourself only puts blades in your soul."

The image of Kai flickered through her mind, but Jess forced her thoughts away from him.

"That is the ultimate way of putting the enemy off balance. You use the truth as a weapon. You give it to them freely—all they are is confused by it. So let's try an experiment," Jaxon said. "I want you to tell me something you don't want to tell anyone. That you don't think anyone should know. That you're not sure you even want to know yourself."

She thought for a moment, then said: "Okay. I'll tell you this: I like you. I know at some point I'll have to try and kill you . . . but I like you."

"That's very sweet. I like you too."

"Now you," Jess said. "Now it's your turn. Tell me something true."

He tossed his silver head and laughed. "My child. I wouldn't even know where to start."

"That seems a kind of cop-out."

"Then why don't you ask me a question? I'll answer it true. I'm not afraid of truth. I value truth." He shrugged. "I just like to lie."

"What do you fear in me?" Jess asked.

"Who says I fear anything?"

"But if you did," she pressed. "In theory. In a totally hypothetical situation. What could someone like you find to fear in someone like me?"

She could tell he was intrigued by the question, that it was a pleasure for him to search inside himself for an answer. "I suppose," he said slowly, "in this hypothetical situation, I would fear the elements in you that remind me of me. Yes." He beamed at her. "I would fear the me in you."

"Is that really true?"

"Well. I am a liar. But I have no reason to lie to you."

And that, Jess figured, was definitely a lie.

I tell you mine. You tell me yours.
So there will be a later?

That night, with Lucas, she told him about the window into another world that had opened up right in front of her: the tortured landscape, the man on the road who looked like him.

She heard his intake of breath, felt his muscles tense against her. "You were there, weren't you?" she said in a rush. She untangled herself from the loop of his arms, sitting up so that she could look him in the face. "That was you. You've been to the same—the same place."

"That would mean it is a real place," Lucas said softly. "I'm not so prepared to believe that."

"It was just another dream shared between us?"

"Something like that."

"It feels so different from the others—"

"So you think it's—it's what? Another dimension? And that special blend of jax takes us to it?"

Jess was silent. Then: "Maybe."

"Or maybe it's what they call a *drug-induced hallucination.*"

She was silent, playing with the cuff of the shirt that Jaxon had forced Stefan to loan her.

Lucas sighed and rubbed his hands across his face. "I still go there," he admitted. "In my dreams. But those are just dreams." He shot her a look, as if challenging her to disagree. "Bad ones."

"What happens to you in those—in those dreams?"

He hitched in breath to answer, but couldn't seem to, frown lines appearing in his forehead. His eyes were a melted-chocolate brown, and they stayed the same color all the time. She wanted to touch him. She moved her hand across the side of his face, then rested her fingers, lightly, on the base of his neck.

She said, "Tell me."

"I'm just walking. All I do is walk. Except I can't stop. Can't change direction. And the people nailed up on the telephone poles—they're dying or dead, except the dead ones aren't really dead because they keep whispering things—" He had to pause, readjusting the position of his shackled wrists. "They whisper to me to keep going. Until I get to the house of bones."

"You think it's his house?"

Lucas shrugged. "I don't think anything."

"What do you think will happen when you get there?"

"Beats the fuck out of me."

"And if they're something more than dreams—"

"They are not."

"And if they're something more than dreams, do you think that's why Jaxon's keeping you alive, chained down here, like some kind of neglected pet? He's waiting for you to reach the bone house?"

She could tell from the sudden darkening in his expression that he had never considered this. Never allowed himself to consider this. "They're just dreams," he said again, and how often had she told herself the same thing? "And I know this—I know this—because I want

to get there. I want to get there because I know that I
belong there, even though . . ." His forehead drew tight,
his eyes narrowing a little. "Even though what I really
want . . . who I want—" She wanted to say something
that would comfort him, comfort both of them, but
couldn't think of anything. There was nothing to say.

She took his face between her hands and kissed him.

At first he was too surprised to react. Then he swung
his arms over her head and down her shoulders and
pressed her to him, the chain catching in her hair. His
kissing was hungry, open and deep, his stubble an unfamiliar rasp against her skin. She had only intended to
kiss him once, on impulse, didn't mean for this—making
out like horny teenagers with a clock ticking, a curfew
hovering, trying to get the most out of what little they
had—but every time she meant to draw away, it was as
if he could read her mind and didn't let her, and in truth
she didn't want to.

Until she found herself light-headed. She went up for
oxygen, pushing him away. He flung himself back against
the pillows, the loop of chain pulling her on top of him.
She lay there for a moment, enjoying the hard, lean feel
of his body, then slithered out beneath the chain and
scrambled off the bed.

"You didn't have to stop," he drawled.

She went into the adjoining bathroom and shut the
door. She fell back against it and sank to the floor, buried her face in her arms. *What am I doing,* she thought.
I can't do this I can't do this I can't do this anymore.
She could still feel Lucas's body, the hunger it touched
off inside her own.

But what he had done to Ramsey. To Kai.

Ramsey and Kai. *They* were her men. But they might
as well be on a whole other planet now, spinning farther
and farther away from her.

Why am I even here?

It made no sense. Jaxon's lectures were engaging
enough, but it was not exactly hard-won wisdom. They

felt beside the point, like he was just killing time. He
wanted her artistic input, or inspiration, or so he claimed,
and still conducted most of his work in secret and had
yet to show her anything finished.

A voice, familiar in its annoyance, sounded from the
other room.

"You're such a good boy, you get a midnight snack
of milk and cookies," Stefan was saying. "You've got a
big day tomorrow."

A muttered response from Lucas.

"I don't think it involves my mother in quite that
way," Stefan remarked.

Jess returned to the room just in time to see Stefan
retreating. The sister's face had pushed out through the
back of his head and the sister's eyes connected with
Jess, and Jess noticed a hard light behind them, and an
ugly little smile. Something was in it, and not until Stefan
had closed the door behind him did Jess realize what it
was. Triumph.

She went on instinct, whirling toward Lucas, who was
already gulping down the milk. "Stop," Jess shouted,
lunging for him, knocking the glass from his hand just
as Lucas jerked away from her, eyes widening, hands
coming up to his throat. The chain tangled his legs and
he fell sideways, landing hard even as his body started
to convulse. His brown eyes locked on hers. She was
kneeling in front of him, moving her hands across his
chest, sending pulses of energy through his body to
cleanse the poison from his system, pushing it up
through his pores as she tried to draw it out with her
palms. His throat was closing in on him. She didn't have
enough finesse to force it open without the risk of ripping it apart. Instead she touched her finger to a spot
on his neck and summoned a line of energy that scorched
through her body and lasered a hole in his throat. His
body arched with the pain but then he was breathing
again, his hand grabbing hers. What looked like dirty

ash was still rising through his skin. It drifted across his chest. She swept it away with her hands.

She had little talent for healing. That form of spell always bored her; she was thankful now that Kai had forced her to master the little that she did know. "You'll live," she whispered to Lucas, who rolled onto his side and curled up on the floor. He was silent, which unnerved her more than any groaning could have. His body relaxed as the poison left his system, the hole in his throat slowly closing. Soon it would just be a faint scar. His eyes were wide and staring. Jess tangled her hand in his hair, lowered a kiss to his forehead.

"The freaky dude tried to kill me," he wheezed, but Jess knew he was wrong.

If Jaxon wanted him dead, he'd be dead.

This was something else.

"I'll be back," she told him.

Outside the room, she stilled herself and sent a mindcast through the halls. She could feel that dark rhythmic beat from the place where the house ended, calling to her, distracting her. Use everything, she thought, and moved her mind into that beat, into the pocket of it, and thought, *Lead me to Stefan.*

And she felt a response. It came rushing at her, sweeping through her; she heard a sigh, a groan, as the walls realigned themselves, whatever magic that ruled this place guiding her through the passageways, a stairway and another hallway, and then—a kitchen.

Stefan was standing with his back to her, beside a granite-topped counter, gulping down an energy shake. A jar of protein powder sat beside a block of knives. She came silently up behind him, until she could see the beads of sweat slipping down the back of his neck, see how he was trembling. He set the glass down with a thunk and covered his face with his hands.

"Stefan," she whispered.

He turned.

She hit him with a right uppercut to the jaw.

He staggered back against the counter, his pale face turning paler. He looked at her with the blank shock of someone who had never been struck in the face before. "You," he said, and he seemed too bewildered to be angry. He turned his head and spit blood into the sink.

"You're an idiot," Jess snapped. "You should have made sure he was alone. You know, before you tried to poison him."

He didn't try to deny it. He lifted his eyebrows a little and said, "I thought—"

"Don't worry," Jess said, and kicked his knees out from under him. "He'll be fine." And as he fell to the floor she kicked him again in the ribs.

She wanted to hit him again—she wanted to keep hitting him—but she forced herself to hold back. Her own rage unnerved her; she wasn't sure where it was all coming from. He was staring at the floor, hair hanging across his eyes, saying something over and over again: "Please don't tell him please don't tell him please don't tell—"

"I never liked you," Jess said.

He laughed. It was a skittering, unsteady sound. "I never liked you either. And to think, you two are supposed to be the—"

He stopped. His gaze had moved up beyond her.

Long, thin fingers draped her shoulder. "Step back, sweetheart," Jaxon murmured in her ear. "This is mine to take care of."

And then he was slipping past her in a breeze all his own, brine-scented, and crouching before the shaking blond man. "Stefan," he whispered, and Stefan braced himself against the counter, pulling himself up to his feet. "What did I tell you to do?"

"It shouldn't have been him," Stefan whimpered. "So unfair. So unfair."

"Did I tell you to feed and water him?"

"It should have been me."

"Did I tell you to feed and water him?"

Stefan nodded vigorously. "Wait," he said, the tremors rocking his body against the counter, his hands gripping the granite edge. "Wait. It should have been me. It's simple. I should have been the one—"

"But you're not, you see." Jaxon's voice turned gentle. "Stefan. Did I tell you to kill him?"

"It was supposed to be my destiny. Mine."

"Stefan. You did what I needed you to do. You built this house. You did a good job! You should have been satisfied with that, you should not have been so . . . grasping. It's unattractive. It's very annoying. *Now answer the goddamn question!*"

"His death was going to be my gift. My gift to you. He was never worthy—"

"Buzzzz! Wrong! The correct answer is: No, Mr. Twist, you certainly never told me to kill him! And why do you think I didn't want you to kill him? Because they are mine they are mine and I want them the way I want them and how some pathetic little worm like you could take it on himself to—"

Stefan pitched into him, and Jaxon staggered back. He flung the other man off him and looked down at his belly. "For crying out loud," he said. Stefan had managed to sneak a steak knife from the wooden block on the counter behind him and plunge it into Jaxon's belly. A black stain was spreading out around the hilt, darkening the pinstriped cotton. Jaxon sighed noisily and pulled the knife from his body. He tossed it in the sink.

He looked back to Stefan, who was cowering on the floor.

"Forgive me," Stefan said. "Forgive me."

"I don't really do that. Forgiveness." He pulled off his shirt and used it as a cotton rag, mopping the blood off his body. "Jess," Jaxon said. His voice was hoarse. Jess was still looking at his blood. The color of it. Angling his face away from her, Jaxon said, "this is when you leave now."

Chapter Twenty-one

Lucas

He was dreaming his way through a house made of skeletons. The images came to him in stuttering fragments: the looming curves of bone, the dark space beyond, and the heat, the pulse, that drew him ever inward. That was where he was supposed to go—to be—and it would be so much easier if he let himself surrender.

But he wouldn't, he struggled against it, and then in a seamless transition only possible in dreams he was onstage again, like he'd been a million times before, playing for the audience, their greed and their hunger. He knew what he wanted to play for them. He called the song out of him—or maybe the song was calling him—and sent it into the audience, bonding them to him, all of them caught in the grip of the music. And this time, when the music filled them and drove them to the stage, as they came surging at him with their claws and their teeth, as if through devouring him they could devour the music itself, he smiled and put down the guitar. He held his arms out to them.

He woke up with that song—that strange, sweet song

of his own gruesome death—tingling in his fingers. Ready to play.

He thought he might know how to play it now.

If he ever wanted or needed it.

The song had been living with him for a while now; he had taken it out of a dream with him and then mulled it over in his head, as a way to pass the time, unraveling the knots and working out the progression until he could hear it in his head, endlessly, in all its strange, shattering melody. He didn't know if it could do in real life what it could do in his dreams, but he knew it was a song of death and annihilation. His own. But there was a kind of sublime ecstasy in it too, and a power he could marvel over, and the song no longer scared him. More and more, he yearned to hear it played for real, and to hell with the consequences.

He was curled on the floor, where Jess had done some of her voodoo to extract the poison from him. Fucker had tried to kill him. Jess had slipped a pillow beneath his head, tossed a blanket over him. Moving gingerly, Lucas peeled himself off the floor and went for water. The chain dragged along with him.

What bothered him most about the chain was how much he'd gotten used to it. He remembered a friend who'd been busted in Miami with two hundred hits of ecstasy. When Lucas had visited him in jail, the dude looked at him with shopworn eyes that had aged about a hundred years since the last time he and Lucas had been tearing it up at Nikki's Beach. It ain't so bad, the guy said. You know how it goes. You put an animal in a cage and he rattles the bars and screams for a while and gets all depressed, but eventually he adapts. You get used to it. You adapt.

Lucas knew, without thinking about it, how far he could go in any one direction before the chain brought him up short. He knew how to walk, move his hands, twist his body without getting entangled. He knew how

to hold Jess as easily as if the chain were a part of him.
She still tried several times a day to break it, to crack
the magical code or whatever that bound the chain to
Lucas and Lucas to the chain.

He didn't remember much about those days immediately following his first encounter with Jaxon Twist. He
had flickering, sensory impressions of heat and blood
and desperation as Jaxon made the music tear its way
out of him. And pain, of course. There had been a fair
amount of pain. The ache in his bones where the shackles went into him seemed like a tickle in comparison.
He remembered wanting to die. He had begged Jaxon
to kill him. And when Jaxon withheld that favor—when
Lucas woke up to find his burned and wounded body in
this room, this chain, and when he realized it still wasn't
going to end anytime soon, he concluded that Jaxon was
keeping him alive as another form of torture.

He could have tried a bit of suicide.

Except he wasn't the type. Something in him blanched
at the notion. To die at someone's hand was acceptable,
sort of—it sucked, but some battles you just *lost* and
that was the way of it. But to die at your own hand
meant you'd been defeated twice over, by life in general
and yourself in particular. He had watched the love of
his life, way back in the day when that life was still
normal—a rock-star kind of normal, but whatever—walk
away from him, down a path to a secluded spot on the
beach, where she pressed the gun to her heart and pulled
the trigger. But she had been dying from a vicious kind
of bone cancer; she went to the doctor with an ache in
her hip that bothered her when she was running and
came home with two months to live. She decided to meet
death on her own terms. That seemed, to Lucas, the
only acceptable form of suicide, when the option was to
let something like cancer beat you to a pulp.

He, on the other hand, was healthy enough. He had
the kind of jailers who liked to bring him energy shakes.

At least until Stefan got tired of the glop dripping down his face and clothes.

And then—and then—and then there was Jess. Appearing in the doorway the way she had. He had spent that entire first conversation thinking he was hallucinating. *I'm a guest,* she had said, and he had laughed hard, although for the life of him now he had no idea why. It's not like it was actually funny.

But it still cracked him up.

Now, as he sat in his cell of a room and waited for whatever happened next, hoping for Jess to return and fearing, as he always did, that something had swallowed her whole, he found himself thinking of the kid. The Bloodangel. But his name—the kid's name, not the angel he'd carried inside him, or the sacrificial thing they had turned him into—was Ramsey. He and Jess had not talked about the events in the desert. They seemed long ago and far away, like they had happened to two other people. Except that wasn't true. Lucas could distance himself from it all he wanted but he knew what he had done. He had been the one who took the boy from Salik and delivered him to Asha, and they had rendered him helpless with jax and kept him in the back of a van with holes punched in the roof and sides for ventilation. Then they had offered him up to their audience.

It was, Lucas reflected now, a shitty thing to do to a kid.

So he could say that this little experience at the hands of Jaxon Twist was kind of what he deserved. If he was the kind of man who would ever say things like that.

Then Jess was in the doorway again, as if she'd been magically summoned herself. Pushing her hands up through her hair, knotting it at the back of her neck, then releasing it and letting it fall again: a gesture, Lucas had learned, that wasn't about preening so much as general agitation. "Let me tell you what I saw—"

"Come here," he said.

She did.

She straddled him on the love seat, took his face between her hands. He pushed hair off her face and smiled at her, but she wasn't smiling back.

"Let me tell you what I saw," she said again, quietly, "and what I have to do."

She told him about what happened to Stefan. She told him about how, afterward, all she had wanted was to get away from the screaming.

How she had come again to those rows on rows of mirrors draped with velvet. How she had finally done what she kept telling herself she would do: yanked off the velvet, one by one, to see the things concealed beneath.

The things that lived on the other sides of those mirrors.

"I think it's an army," she said breathlessly. "He's making some kind of army. And he's storing them inside the mirrors. In some kind of otherworld that's on the other side. . . ."

He listened, averting his gaze from the intensity of her eyes and staring at a spot on the floor. At some point his hand found hers, loosely clasped her long fingers. After she described the things that lived deep in the glass, Lucas nodded, touched a finger to her mouth, traced her lower lip. "Yeah, the mirrors," he said. "He came from one himself. I saw it. It's like Alice, *Through the Looking-Glass*—you read that when you were a kid? I thought it was a fucking weird story myself—I really liked it—this is like Alice, except—"

"Except really, really not."

"Alice was cuter."

"I think I can stop it," Jess said. "I can stop him. The Lord of Bones."

There was a calm resignation in her eyes, her tone of voice, that made Lucas sit up sharply. It jostled her a little, and she gave him a smile—the small, sad kind that continued to not make him feel better—and told him what she intended to do.

He said stupidly, "But you'll die."

She got off his lap. She seemed filled with a restless, pacing energy, even though she stood perfectly still. Looking at him like that, pushing her hands in the pockets of her jeans—looking very thin, very frail, very young—she couldn't seem to believe it herself: that she would die, or that she was willing to.

"You were the one who told me I die young," she said.

He was silent. Then: "I'm not sure I necessarily *meant* it."

Another smile flickered at her mouth, was gone. She looked at him with those steel blue eyes. "How did you know?"

"What?" Still preoccupied with the things she had told him, the thing she meant to do.

"What you told me in the dreams. How did you know them?"

"The music," he muttered. It seemed an inadequate answer, but it was all he could come up with. "After the music, it's like I just know things—"

He stopped.

Stefan's words came at him: *His voice doesn't come to me in words. His voice is like a bright light that flares up inside me—some new piece of knowledge is placed inside me. That's what guided me here . . .*

"Then you know," she said, and that pacing energy was in her eyes now, and Lucas sensed a kind of electricity charging the space around her, as if she were generating it from her own body. She probably was. At what cost? He again noted the jutting ridge of her collarbone. *Gives a whole new meaning to the phrase, "her work consumes her."* He didn't find any humor in that thought.

"Then you know. That hell-world, that world of the crucified—that's *our* world, isn't it? Some alternate version, parallel universe, whatever, but it's our world, it's us—and what if it's the future? It's the *here*, it's just not the *now* . . ." She was facing the wall, her back to him, but he knew what she was truly looking at, what vision was in her mind. "What if it's our future? Jax shortcuts you into the Dreamlines, remember, and time flows all ways there, the present is the past is the future—"

"It's a dream." The words snapped out of him.

"It's not a dream!" She whirled on him, hair swinging over her shoulders, her eyes as fierce as he'd ever seen them. But something in his expression—he didn't know what it was, didn't want to know—caused her to soften her eyes, the line of her shoulders. "Even if you do dream about it," she said softly.

He had no response.

"Humanity lost," she said. "Enslaved. Nailed up on the poles like that. Lining every highway in the country. Transformed like that. Turned into his things, his creatures." She gathered a coil of his chain in her hands. "Tricky magic," she muttered. "Very tricky magic—" And he saw something move through her face, an expression he hadn't seen before. It wasn't a look of concentration so much as surrender, like she was relaxing into something. She opened one hand, palm up. Then her fingers snapped closed as if she'd caught something fast and small. She brought her hand to the chain—and it came apart, the bottom half clanking to the floor.

Just like that.

He stared at his hands. The manacles still encircled his wrists, but already they were changing—dying—thin white lines splintering all through them; at some point they would simply drop off.

"Baby picked up some new skills," Lucas said.

"Go. Get out of here."

"You think they'll just let me leave?"

He got off the chair. Without the chain to drag him down or limit the way he could touch her, he had acquired all the freedom he needed. He walked toward her, and she backed away from him, smiling a little, shaking her head, and when he reached the spot where the chain would have pulled him up short, he lifted his foot and stepped past it.

"You have to try, at least," she said. "You have to do everything you can to get out of here. I told you what's going to happen."

She backed up against the wall. He put an arm out to steady himself, and lowered his head to breathe in the scent of her hair. He nuzzled her neck. He said, "I tried already. It didn't go so well."

"Lucas. It's your only chance."

"You're my chance," he said. He kissed her lips. She was still undecided, so he let her work it out, keeping his mouth close to hers, drinking her in. Making her part of him. "You're my chance," he said again. "I stay with you. I die with you. You're the one who kills me."

Beneath his hands, beneath his mouth, he felt the tension in her body turn liquid. "Okay," she murmured, "okay," and she moved herself against him.

Later, when he opened his eyes, she was watching him again, her naked body pale in the shadows.

"Come here," he said.

"The blood on your hands."

"What?"

"The blood. On your hands. The color."

He looked at his palms. The network of scars. The most recent wounds had finally closed over, but faint traces of black blood clung to his skin, no matter how hard he tried to wash them clean. He knew the color of the blood was unusual, but it was also pretty low on the list of things currently bothering him.

Jess said, slowly and with obvious difficulty, "Jaxon's blood is black."

She didn't have to explain any further. A kind of understanding—not as words or anything he could artic-ulate, but a feeling—swept through him.

You have in you the music of angels. Dark angels.

Staring at his hands, Lucas heard himself start to speak, and his voice sounded as if it were traveling from a place as ancient and distant as the music itself. "No one in my family is musical," he was saying. "No one. All lawyers and judges on my father's side, you know, verbal and analytical, and practical methodical types on my mother's, plugging away at whatever needs doing.

"No creatives. No artists. Nothing musical.

"So I was the freak. 'Cause I came out of the womb practically wrapped in music—it always came to me so easy—it was the first language I ever learned and the only one I needed." He had been a silent, solitary child, the kind who rarely made eye contact. He didn't speak at all until he was three and a half, when he looked quizzically up at his mother—or so she liked to tell it— and asked her, in a clear, little-man voice, *How come we don't have a piano? Don't you think we should have a piano?*

"And my mama always wondered all the time where I got it. The woman couldn't carry a tune if you held a gun to her head. None of them could."

His voice faded into silence, into shadow.

Jess was sitting cross-legged on the mattress, her head bowed as she took this in, mulled it over.

"So it's a mystery," she said finally. "It defines you, defines your life, but it's a mystery. This gift of yours. Nobody knows."

Something in his memory turned over, exposed a pale underbelly. *It wasn't meant for you.* Who had said that to him, that night in the parking lot by one of those anonymous roadhouses he had played in his Max the Minstrel days? Stefan? The sister, whatever her name was or had been? *Meant for a prince. Paid a high price. Black market magic. The story of you.* They had promised to tell it to him. If he was a good boy. But he had not been good.

And he had assumed that it was all bullshit, like their

stupid haircuts and their stupid accents and even the stupid bullshit way Stefan held a glass of wine.

"Jess," he whispered, and she lifted her head and looked at him.

He said, "Thing knows."

"He does?"

"Yeah. Somehow, yeah. Is he still alive?"

" 'Alive' is kind of a *strong* word." She pressed her lips together, then said, with evident distaste, "But I could still have a conversation with him."

"Do you know where he's being kept?"

He saw the grim settling-in of her game face as she braced for the task ahead.

She said, "Jaxon put him on display."

Chapter Twenty-two

Jess

Stefan—the thing that Stefan had become—was hung up in the center of the entrance hall. His body had been somehow flayed and opened up and glossed over, the strips of him stiffened and shellacked. She couldn't look at him directly. Or understand how anyone could.

It had to be some form of necromancy, but Kai had never taught her anything like this, never hinted that such things were possible. Because Stefan's face peered from the center of the intricate, multicolored spiderweb of himself. And he was chuckling.

"So what do you think?" His voice, too, had changed; high and thin, it came whistling through him. "I am the master now. I look down on all of you. All of you." His mouth stretched apart in what might have been a smile. "So what do you think he'll do to *you*? What do you think he'll turn *you* into?"

"I don't know."

"Let your imagination run wild! And your boyfriend?"

She realized with a start that he wasn't referring to Kai.

"I don't know," she said again. Thinking: *He's not my—* Thinking: *He won't get the chance to do anything to either of us.*

"So, was he nice to taste? Was he worth it?"

"Is that why Jaxon brought me here? To put me with Lucas?"

"You thought you happened on the guy by accident?"

"Why would he want that? Or care?"

"I'll be damned if I know."

"But you do know a few things," Jess said.

His eyes widened a little. "A few things."

"And Lucas isn't worthy of what he has," Jess said.

Nostrils flaring, Stefan stared openly for a moment, as if forced to see her anew. She realized that he didn't remember saying this same thing to Jaxon, or that she had overheard it.

"It should have been you," Jess pressed.

"I should have been the one who carried the gift. Who carried that piece of him. I feel like I already do, you see. And he never saw it. Never realized. He has some issues, you see."

"You were so devoted to him."

"And yet I'm starting to think I can't trust him."

"Lucas carries his . . . gift," Jess said, trying to infuse her voice with the authority of someone who knew exactly what she was talking about. "His music," she said. "The music of angels."

Stefan snorted. *"Angels."*

"Dark angels."

"The darkest," Stefan agreed.

"Jaxon," she breathed.

"It was ripped from him. Stolen from him. A very long time ago." Stefan sucked in breath, then announced, "Shemayan did it. He was your ancestor, correct?"

Shemayan, Jess thought. Of course. And she felt again the burden of him, her seemingly all-powerful ancestor: Shemayan, the great and terrible, so pure, so perfect, so

austere, she didn't understand how he ever could have
lived at all. Who could rip music from the angels themselves.

"So he brought me here for some kind of revenge,"
Jess said. "Against Shemayan, Kai, the Summoners
themselves—"

"Well, yes. But I don't think that's all of it."

Stefan was watching her with wide eyes, his face ducking low in that web of himself, that web spun from his
own reconfigured body, and if she looked too closely at
the strands and fibers and veins, the gradations of red
and orange, she would double over and maybe not be
able to stand straight again. Acid rose in her throat and
she forced it back, covering her mouth with her hand as
if yawning. She felt dangerously light-headed. *I refuse to
faint. I'm not the kind of person who faints.*

"Shemayan stole the gift from Jaxon's blood, and
somehow it ended up with Lucas," Stefan said. "It
wasn't intended that way. It was meant for someone else,
who paid a very high price for it—"

"Black market Summoner magic," Jess said. "So
someone took it from Shem—and tried to sell it—"

"—to some figure of decadent nobility, yeah. Whatever. The deal went bad. And Lucas just happened to
be in the wrong place at the right time."

"So if this happened many centuries ago, then either
Lucas is very long-lived or else he . . ." Just say it, she
told herself. It was just a word. "It means that Lucas
reincarnates. Like me. He reincarnates just like I do."

She stepped back, turned her face away from the
Stefan-thing, and closed her eyes. She let herself fall into
memory, into that place where her memory gave way to
Kai's, the fragments of him that were now a part of her.
She went through it all, trying to find something, anything that would match up with what Stefan had just
told her . . .

*He is a teenager prince, trying to be the man he isn't
quite yet, keeping his eyes fixed on the scene before him*

despite the twisted, knotting feeling in his stomach. It is important that he is here. It is important that he witnesses this. The room is small, hidden deep within a labyrinth of corridors, so that only a few can gain access. Above him, the walls curve and veer at strange angles, designed to channel the energy that flows through here in the most effective way possible.

In front of him, a man is screaming.

His body lies flat, his arms bound to his sides. He is suspended in the air and he is screaming. Cloaked and hooded figures work over him, muttering incantations, moving their hands along his body.

And then they drive the shards into him, through him, one after the other after the other, shards of clear glass that, as the crown prince watches, slowly fill with black blood.

The man is no longer screaming. The figures remove the shards and arrange them very carefully within layers of ceremonial cloth. And as the man turns his face toward the crown prince, it triggers another memory, himself as a small boy walking hand in hand with this man through dusky courtyards, the night-blooming flowers just beginning to scent the air, and what he feels for this man is affection so great that it borders on love . . .

The memory ended there. She came back to herself with a gasp. The child prince that Kai had been had not merely known the Lord of Bones in his previous incarnation—he had felt for him what a son might feel for a father, what the young prince would have wanted to feel for his own father, but could not.

Life after life after life.

"Like I do," Jess said.

"Not like you," Stefan said, as if offended at the very notion. "Not like anyone."

They watched each other.

Jess struck a note of nonchalance she did not feel in any way. "Oh, come on. Reincarnation is reincarnation, right? Not such a tricky concept."

"When people die—" Stefan's voice went hoarse, choked off for a moment; he spent a moment collecting it again, tongue darting out to moisten his lips. "When most people die, whatever's left over flies up to the place—that thing—that place in between where the magic comes from—"

"The Dreamlines," Jess said.

"Whatever. Yeah. But you. It's different with you. You've got a soul a bit like a basketball that doesn't go through the net, right, just rebounds off the backboard and right back into this world. And it changes a little bit with each journey. Each journey there and back. But that one." He wheezed, then coughed, droplets of blood splattering his lips. "That one. Maddox. His soul never gets to the Dreamlines at all. It goes directly from the old body into the new. You want to know exactly how it goes?"

"Tell me."

"He gets a woman pregnant. When the baby becomes ensouled, Lucas—"

"Dies," Jess said.

"His soul goes out of the old and into the new. He dies. And is reborn. And I'm not talking spiritual metaphor. And that's how Lucas inherits his special talent down through the generations of himself. Which—" Stefan was interrupted by another flurry of coughs. Jess saw the spray of blood and stepped back; it hit the floor where her shoes had just been.

Stefan licked his lips, which were beginning to look like dried, cracked wax again. Jess felt her hand going up to her own lips. She had said to Jaxon Twist, she had said to him: *I like you.*

Jess said, "What would happen if Lucas never had a child at all? What if he just . . . died?"

"Not possible."

"How do you know?"

" 'Cause it hasn't happened. Has it? And it won't." He glared at her, as if daring her to find the audacity to contradict him. "What I went through. I kept asking myself if it couldn't be me, why did it have to be him, why not Bowie, or even Adam Levine, or—but him—" And at this he went off into hysterics, his laughter yelping down the hall, the whole web trembling and swaying. "Someone maybe not so—not so—" His laughter faded. The web calmed. His eyes were alight. He's insane, Jess thought, and of course he was, how could he not be? "Stupid sexy singer," the man-web said affectionately.

"But you tried to kill him," Jess said.

"I did."

"You knew he embodied some part of Jaxon, that Jaxon himself is going to great lengths to preserve, and you tried to kill him."

Stefan coughed, then said, "He was dying a little too slowly for me," and coughed and laughed, and said, "Plus he kept throwing food at me. Ruining my shirts. Those were expensive shirts. I couldn't let him die without killing him first." The coughing morphed into cackling, and Jess realized that he had been insane before he died, probably long before he died, and that this reanimation and re-fashioning of him had only given that insanity new color, new voice.

"But I was going to take the song from his blood," Stefan said eagerly, "because I figured out how to do it. I figured out how. I was going to take the music right out from his blood and give it to him, to Jaxon, return it, restore it to him, and then I will be his favored one, I will be the one to sit the throne beside—" His eyes went bright again. "Besides, I figured he'd already knocked you up. Maybe it was a risk, but it was a calculated one. I only believe in taking calculated risks. Hasn't he?"

"What?" She was barely listening, too busy running mental fingers through what he had already said.

Stefan said pleasantly, "Put you in the family way."

Jess lifted her head. "No."

"You sure about that?"

The thought of pregnancy was ludicrous to her. She checked inside herself and sensed only the spaces and corridors of her own flesh-and-blood body, all barren, prepared to carry nothing but the next coursing of Dreamline energy. She was a vessel for magic, not a baby. The magic took everything. Kai had told her that, and he was proving right so far.

Whatever Stefan saw in her face, it suddenly triggered him to say, "What is he to you?"

Again the pronoun "he" unbalanced her. But Stefan meant Lucas; he always meant Lucas.

Instead of attempting an answer, she said, "But I've seen what Jaxon Twist, or whoever or whatever he really is, can do. He doesn't need Lucas to get what he wants."

"Oh, really? What do you think he wants?"

"The world." It seemed an obvious answer.

"You think that's *it*? That's *all*? Hell, the world is already his—it just doesn't realize it yet. You think he doesn't already have a collection of them? Think about it." The man-web's eyes fluttered closed. "You can go away now," he said. "I am tired."

"But how—"

"I said I'm tired."

And Jess sensed something in him that went beyond fatigue; an ebbing of whatever energy kept him in whatever kind of life you could call this. She had gotten all she could out of him.

As she stepped away, she noticed a figure just behind him, standing still, her white clothes and pale coloring blending in so well with the marble surround that she could have been there for the entire length of the conversation and Jess wasn't sure she would have noticed.

"Ingrid," said Stefan's sister.

Jess said, "I'm sorry?"

The woman was staring at her with flat, hard eyes. "My name. He should at least have told you my name."

Ingrid faded down the hall, perfectly silent, as if she'd never existed at all.

Chapter Twenty-three

After she told him, Lucas sat in silence for a full three minutes. He stared at the floor, the wall, his hands, and at her. He said, "So it seems I need to die. Don't you think? And after the trouble you took to save my life."

"I was glad to do it," she said.

"I was glad you did it, too."

She opened her hand, showed him the red stone that waited in the center of her palm. "From my Trials."

"I guess that's kind of fitting."

"I guess so." She looked at him and said, "Walk with me."

"I'd be honored."

She thought the house itself might try to stop her, wall her off from her intended destination, but she threaded her way through the halls to the end of it. Which wasn't an end at all but a center. This whole house, she was beginning to realize, was a center, of some new, vast thing slouching itself into life.

"Jess," Lucas said, but she shook her head at him and stepped off the hallway floor onto the grit of earth and rock. She couldn't let herself be distracted by him now.

As her eyes adjusted to the darkness she picked out new shapes in the cave walls: the looming mouths of tunnels, made jagged by stalactites, exhaling their acrid-scented winds across her face.

"Come to me," she whispered, and she felt the pulse of the place reach up through the rock and down through the tunnels and into her body. She felt herself grow huge with it. She closed her eyes, closed out the image of Lucas watching from where he stood just inside the hallway, with that pale, stricken look on his face. *Use everything,* she thought, and she felt the pulsing energy of the cave move through her blood and mingle with the energy of the Dreamlines it found there. *Use everything,* and she let her fear and her anger and her loneliness move up through her as well, instead of trying to deny or suppress any of it, like she'd spent a lifetime doing. *Use everything,* and she reached into her memory for Kai, for Ramsey, for the love she felt for them, and now, somehow, Lucas was in there too, in her mind and her soul and her heart.

The ground began to vibrate beneath her feet.

The vibrations gathered into a tremor, rolling like waves across the cave floor, rippling into the hall, where Lucas braced himself against the walls and called out to her. His voice reached her as a kind of abstract shape that she absorbed with everything else, including the ripening earthquake now sending shudders along the cave walls. Her fear turned over inside her and became something else: white, vivid, electric. She felt herself rising up through her own skin even as she hunkered deep into her own mind and flung open all the doors there, bringing forth the magic, the spell-images it had presented to her when she was still in training with Kai: she called them out now, all those images, those spells she needed now. She gave them names. They were all words that meant the same thing. Annihilation. And they merged into a sphere of white fire hovering behind her eyes. Then the sphere expanded as if someone were crouching inside it and blowing it up. But that someone was also, somehow, her.

She would become her own exploding star.

She lifted the red stone in her hand. The heat rising up through her skin triggered the magic coded inside it. It jumped into life, the bloodred light inside streaming out over her hands, her arms. She tilted her head back. The air was turning hot, then hotter; the light swirled round her and raced over the outline of her body and broke into deep, brilliant waves, shimmering through her, until the heat and the light became her, and she became the heat and the light.

And as her vision flared—

and began to dim—

and as the last edges of her consciousness registered the earth and rock tumbling around her, the ground buckling beneath her feet—*use everything*, and she used this too, the energy of death and destruction—she saw a patch of shadow inside one of the tunnels pulling itself away from the rest of the darkness, moving rapidly toward her, and as it emerged from the tunnel mouth and stepped into the cave it resolved itself into a man, a smooth-skinned, alien man with glints for eyes lifting spidery hands toward her, a man who looked strange yet familiar. So deeply familiar. "Hello, pretty Jessamy," he said. "I've been sent here to tell you that you don't get off so easy."

And somehow he was on her, like a blanket of darkness thrown over her, smothering the fire she was so carefully cultivating. Not all of it, though. Even as she felt herself enfolded in some weird, dark magic that could only be a demon's, as the cave came apart, dirt and earth and rock raining down, she could see the whirlwind swirl of energies she had set loose, could smell it in the air, like gas.

She only had to toss the match.

That part was easy.

And in the microsecond before the air exploded, Jess realized it was the day of her thirtieth birthday.

Chapter Twenty-four

"Ramsey. Time to go."

He started awake. Zazou hovered over him, a grimness in her voice but something else in her face that lit up her eyes and electrified her body so that Ramsey could practically feel the excitement crackling off her.

"It's started," she said.

He went through the next couple of hours in a kind of trance, still processing what Zazou had laid down for them during the impromptu meeting at the center of the camp. "We know where he is," she told them. "The Lord of Bones. We're going to go after him." Her eyes moved over the crowd, making contact with each person in it. The Summoner Kai Youngblood had discovered his location, Zazou said, and although she would not, or could not, say how he'd come by this information, she had no doubt it was valid. Ramsey believed in it also, and he remembered Kai's words through the satellite phone: *What I might have to do is rather drastic.*

Kai and a band of Summoners would close in around the location, flush out Bones and destroy him. It was their job to hold a perimeter, to keep people from entering the area . . . and to prevent anything from leaving the area.

"The Lord of Bones," she said, and paused, and Ramsey could see how she was wondering just how to put this, "likes to make things."

"Things," a man echoed.

"Nasty things. Killing things. Monsters," Zazou said. "He thinks of them as his . . . artwork. He stores them in his private dimension—a hell-dimension—and then sets them loose in whatever world he's come to claim. Now he's come to claim this one."

"An army," Ramsey said.

Zazou lifted one shoulder, but the gesture seemed neither a confirmation nor a denial. Army didn't seem a satisfying word to her, but she seemed to have no alternative—or at least not one that she was willing to share.

She gave them the address. It was a prestigious Los Angeles hillside neighborhood, a residential area above Sunset Plaza. A stretch of Sunset would form the bottom line of their perimeter. "Youngblood and his Summoners are there right now," she said, "using their magic to create a massive group hallucination that should have the area evacuated by the time we arrive."

The same woman who'd spoken earlier called out, "What kind of hallucination?"

"Fire," Zazou said. "The people within that perimeter and immediately surrounding it will think there's a fire nearby, and that it's headed straight for them." She gave them a moment to absorb this, then said, "And one more thing. If the Lord of Bones is able to do what he appears to be doing, then the house—and maybe it was specially designed to be in this particular spot in a particular way—must be a kind of *sorenikan*. And it's probably bleeding into the surrounding area as well. Which means that you're going to step into a reality that will no longer be reality as you know it. Things are likely to get trippy. Things are likely to get very weird. All right," she said, shutting down further conversation, "it's time. Let's go play."

Ramsey sat in the back of the van along with six others, all of them shut down inside themselves as the reality of the situation settled over them like ash. At one point the van stopped, the back doors opened and the Summoner Cameron clambered up inside, unusually awkward for his kind. The road twisted out behind him, the clouds sliding shadows across the barren landscape. As they got moving again, Cameron spent a few minutes crouching beside each of them, massaging their temples, his pale eyes examining their faces until he saw whatever it was that told him his job was done and he could move on to the next one. It was like he put some kind of switch inside each mind and turned it on. Ramsey felt sharp and alert, his senses heightened, a sudden surge of confidence bracing him for what lay ahead. "Good," Cameron murmured, watching his face; then, touching his shoulder, "Good luck." The van stopped again, and Cameron opened the doors and jumped out, moving on to the next vehicle in the convoy.

Game on, Ramsey thought.

Then they were in LA.

The van stopped for the final time. Zazou, from where she sat in the front passenger seat, yelled back to them, "This is it. This is as far as we can go."

And still, despite everything he'd been through and everything he already knew, Ramsey wasn't quite prepared for the sight that met his eyes when he jumped out from the van into the dry, mild air of a perfect afternoon.

The road leading up to Sunset was a mess of cars, the light skating off a mosaic of metallic roofs so that Ramsey had to squint against the glare. A helicopter chopped high overhead, and in the near distance came the sound of a siren. People were milling along the sidewalks, get-

ting out of cars—or getting back into them—or weaving
through the spaces between them. Some people were
even clambering up onto the car roofs to get a better
look at what was going on near the top of the road.

On foot, they started making their way uphill, jostling
through the throng. Ramsey touched the leather band
that ran across his chest, felt the gentle weight of the
sword strapped across his back. He wore a light cotton
trenchcoat to disguise it. The others carried knapsacks,
duffel bags, or in the case of a guy in the van right
behind them, a Prada messenger bag. No one would be
able to guess the contents. They looked like a normal
group, heading up to Sunset to check out what was going
on just like everyone else.

They passed the low-roofed storefronts, the palm
trees. Ramsey saw a news truck, its satellite dish raised
high in the air, a female reporter speaking at the camera-
man as someone else held a boom over her head. He
heard the word "evacuation" and veered closer, strain-
ing to catch what she was saying before a group of loudly
chattering teenage girls fell in between them.

As he passed news truck after news truck, their satel-
lites raised high in the air, the voices of the reporters
overlapped one another.

". . . a strange gaseous substance that appears to be
rising out of the very ground. While there is no concrete
word yet on whether this substance is toxic, there seems
to be evidence that, at the very least, the gas induces
strange hallucinations, and people are being told not to
go back to their homes until more information . . ."

". . . unusual events began unfolding early this morning when residents fled the area, believing that a forest
fire was on the verge of burning their homes to the
ground. Obviously . . . as you can see around me . . .
no such fire actually exists, but that strange event was
followed by something even stranger, when . . ."

". . . a series of minor earth tremors starting at six
forty-five a.m. The kind of things your average Califor-

nian wouldn't think anything of, except that immediately afterward a blue-tinged, odd-smelling gas started rising from cracks and holes in the ground. This happened right on the heels of what appears to be a mass hallucination involving a deadly forest fire . . ."

Up ahead he saw police cars. Through shifts in the still-gathering crowd he caught glimpses of yellow tape and uniformed officers holding back the crowd, while men who weren't in uniform but still had an official look to them stood around and conferred.

And then, cutting toward them through the crowd, was Kai.

He appeared so suddenly—rising over everyone around him, thinner than Ramsey had ever seen him, his face more shadowed and hollowed—that for a moment Ramsey thought he was a hallucination, like that reporter had said. Ramsey yelled his name anyway. Kai's gaze jerked toward him and he nodded, but it was a brisk, absentminded gesture and then Kai was crooking a finger at Zazou, who was instantly there beside him. Something bit down in Ramsey's chest, something he refused to believe was hurt, and he focused instead on what was happening beyond the yellow tape.

It was deserted. No cars, no people. The restaurant shaped like a train, the Starbucks, the stucco-walled strip of boutiques, the hipster hotels, the newsstand, the billboard in artistic black and white showing four nearly naked people on a big white bed while a bottle of perfume rose behind them, the houses climbing the hillside above all the way up to Mulholland: it all seemed normal.

Except for the smog.

But smog was such an innate part of Los Angeles— or at least of Ramsey's idea of it—that at first it didn't even register. It was the smell that first struck Ramsey as alarming: a bit like the ocean, except darker and more corrupt, like an ocean filled with the dead and dying. As if on cue Ramsey registered a sudden chill in the air, so unlike the warmth of the rest of the day that it was like one weather pattern slamming up against another. And should smog really . . . move like that? Through the general vapor he saw eddies and swirls of the stuff that seemed independent of each other, moving to no logic of air currents that Ramsey could discern. His gaze followed one tendril of mist unfurling itself across the billboard: in the ad, the model with the long dark hair raised her head off her partner's chest and turned her gaze to Ramsey.

It happened so smoothly, so quickly, that Ramsey wasn't sure it had happened at all. Had the ad been like that all along, the dark-haired model's body arranged like that, even if it seemed to throw off the composition of the photograph, her gaze angled so directly at him, just a coincidence of where he was standing?

"Sir! You can't go up there! Sir!"

Kai was strolling up Sunset, a sudden eddy of mist swirling past him, obscuring him from view. Behind him were other figures, tall like he was, Summoners. Ramsey counted half a dozen of them effortlessly breaking their way through the crowd and striding past the officers as if they didn't exist. "You!" The officer who had yelled before was still targeting Kai, as if recognizing him as the head that must be cut off in order to regain control.

The officer jumped the tape and started after Kai.

Kai turned. Maybe he made the slightest of gestures—hard to tell through the smog—and the officer was tilted back at an impossible angle and dragged backward, the heels of his boots scraping pavement, until he was tossed into the crowd. And maybe Kai made the slightest of gestures again—hard to tell—because the nearest parked police cars, with a groan and thud of metal, flipped up on their sides, screeching over the roadway, until . . .

A *boom* shook the ground, seemed to shake the air itself. Once, when Jess and Ramsey had been hunting demons through Florida, a space shuttle had reentered

the atmosphere there and the sonic boom had made
Ramsey think that a bomb had gone off outside their
hotel.

This was similar, but Ramsey doubted that a space
shuttle had anything to do with it.

Somebody was pounding on the ceiling below him.
Ramsey pulled his attention away from the mist and the
boom, and realized that there was no ceiling; what he
was registering was a knocking inside the earth itself, a
steadily growing vibration.

Silence fell on the crowd, people attuned to the shaking beneath their feet, waiting to see how it developed.
It grew more intense until Ramsey dropped into a
crouch, afraid it would knock him off balance.

And then the ground erupted.

He heard the rough grumbling sounds of the ground
coming apart, concrete chunks falling, dirt crumbling.
Someone was screaming. People were screaming. Ramsey hurled himself to the side just as the ground beneath
him dissolved, earth and gravel raining down into a pit
that opened itself up out of nowhere. "Zazou!" Ramsey
shouted. "Cameron!" Something was breaking up through
the ground right behind him—some kind of wall, as if
the road were reconfiguring itself, except the road hadn't
been made out of this dark, shiny, glimmering stone that
seemed to be oozing something, but Ramsey didn't have
a chance to look at it again as the mist came reaching
down over him, over everyone, and with it that *smell*.
That rotting-ocean smell, as if the very womb of the
planet was diseased. Was dying.

People were screaming, stumbling, stampeding. Ramsey struggled to stay upright in the jostling crush of bodies. He tried to find Cameron, Zazou, or any of the
others who had come here with, but between the mass
panic and the shifting earth and the thickening mist it
was hard enough just to see what was happening right
in front of him. "Get back," he found enough presence

to tell people around him, touching shoulders, guiding them away from Sunset. "Get away from here. Get back." He wished he could do magic, like that thing Cameron did to him in the van, to make people calm and alert and focused.

And then someone familiar was beside him, a freckled twentysomething dude named Ryan but whom everyone called Mustard for some reason that remained unknown to Ramsey. "What do we do?" Mustard was yelling at him, stepping aside with a yelp as the ground bubbled and cracked right beneath him. "What do we do?" and Ramsey was yelling back, "We stay here and hold the line, like we're supposed to," and Mustard yelled back, "What line? What goddamn line?"

He had a point. The mist ebbed and eddied and thickened and thinned and Ramsey saw new formations of earth and concrete and stone—that dark, glistening, alien stone—shuddering themselves into being all around him. The earth jolted again, reeling him back, slamming him into the edge of a tall obelisk-shaped stone that had not been there ten minutes before.

At least the screaming had faded.

Through the shifting mist he saw that the crowd had thinned out to the point of disappearing. "Zazou," he yelled.

"Over here!" she shouted.

His shoulders went loose with relief. Something snagged at his knee; he looked down, stepped out of a coil of yellow tape, and kicked aside the pylons. Where was he, exactly? He looked around, trying to get his bearings; he looked up, and saw the perfume billboard through a drifting veil of smog.

The lanky bodies on the bed were . . . writhing.

They moved in a herky-jerky, stuttering motion. The dark-haired model was kissing the chest of the man beneath her . . . and then biting into it, as his hands tangled in her hair. The blond female model slithered over both of them and slammed her hands against the undersurface of the billboard, her mouth stretching wide. Blood dripped from her teeth . . .

. . . down across the billboard . . .

. . . down the side of the building . . .

. . . and rained to the ground.

"Do you see that?" Ramsey wasn't sure who he was asking, maybe Mustard, who was a vague shape somewhere to the right of him. "Do you see that?"

"Over there," Mustard said.

On the billboard on the side of the hotel, a well-known thirtysomething actress brandished a luxury watch. Except she was striking her own face with it, driving the metal edges into her skin, again and again, smiling seductively out at her audience as welts and cuts and bruises disfigured her.

"So you see that?" Mustard was saying, his voice rising, thinning. "You see that, right? That's not just me?"

"It's not just you."

The woman struck herself on her cheekbone, leaving a gash so deep Ramsey glimpsed bone.

"Group hallucinations?" Mustard sounded very close to babbling; Ramsey wished he would shut up. "Like the fire? There's, like, LSD in the mist, or something?"

"No," Ramsey said. "I don't think so. Listen."

Mustard started to speak again, but Ramsey cut him off. Someone was laughing.

The sound was coming from somewhere above them; the models in the perfume ad all looked in that direction, then began to whisper in each other's ears. The laughter came floating down toward them, and spread out all around them, as if it mingled with the smog itself.

"It's so cold," Mustard said. "It's gotten so cold."

"Ramsey!" Zazou's voice, from an unseen depth of mist. Her voice seemed to shiver apart, echoing through the air in weird ways, so that Ramsey couldn't tell where it was coming from, where she was. "Ramsey, watch out! There's something in here!"

Someone was lumbering toward them. Ramsey touched Mustard's shoulder and pointed. "Hello," he called out. No answer. As the figure came closer, Ramsey heard the snuffling, dragging sound of it, and then the mist rolled back and they saw what it was.

It had once been human. Ramsey knew this, because it was made mostly of human parts, in among the other materials: steel rods, razor blades, a severed dog head, iron spikes, and shards of mirror. It came directly at them, even though its eyes were sewn shut; it had its face lifted, the animal nostrils flared and sniffed the air. Ramsey took out his 9mm and aimed, willing his hand not to shake, and shot it.

It was an easy enough kill, though not a fast one; he shot it five times before it went down.

"Others," Mustard said as gunshots sounded elsewhere in the mist. From somewhere else came a snarl, a shout, then a scream turning liquid with pain. Mustard had his sawed-off rifle in hand, taking aim at the multilegged thing dragging toward them from the right. He took it down, and Ramsey fired at the bulked-up thing behind it, its face pushed out and distorted. The ground lurched beneath him and he jumped to the side, whirled, shot down the bear-thing lunging toward him. Something small on the ground, quick and darting, with tentacles; one whipped out and caught his ankle, burning, and Ramsey shrieked more in revulsion than pain as the thing jerked him to the ground and he saw a blind, puckered mouth filled with teeth coming at his face. He raised his gun just in time and shot the thing through what appeared to be its head, its blistered flesh ripping apart in an explosion of pulpy gray matter. It was dead, but the tentacle was still wrapped round his leg, all the way up to his thigh. Ramsey couldn't shake it off; he threw down the gun and reached behind him, pulled the sword from its scabbard, and brought the blade down on the piece of tentacle by his foot. Grimacing, he used his free hand to uncoil the thing from his leg—it had a dry, pebbled skin, with a hard rope of muscle beneath—and cast it aside.

He heard something whistling through the air right above his head. He dove to the side just as the blade of an axe buried itself in the broken pavement beside him. There was shrieking, chittering: he knew those sounds. This monster, at least, was familiar. A beat, and then a black-haired man, what had once been a man, was zig-zagging toward him, very fast, his skin turning yellow and thick with his Altering as Ramsey forced himself to wait, find his moment, and then he brought his sword up and sliced the hybrid's head off. It went flying. The body didn't seem to notice; it went running right past Ramsey, into the mist, before Ramsey heard a wet smack as it made impact with some kind of stone.

The air was filled with sound now: chitters and grunts and gunshots, people yelling out at each other, calling or giving warning. But the space immediately around Ramsey seemed devoid of noise or movement. "Mustard," he called out softly. His foot came up against something: his dropped gun. Carefully, his gaze darting all around him, he stooped and picked it up. The sword in one hand, the gun in the other, Ramsey stood there and wondered what the hell he was supposed to do now.

The smog drifted.

That briny, rotting-corpse smell thickened.

He would have covered his nose with the top of his T-shirt except that would involve letting go of a weapon.

Footsteps behind him, light and quick.

Ramsey whirled, lifting the sword, and the mist discharged Zazou.

His relief was so strong that he suddenly found himself doubling over. Then a tight, cramped feeling overcame him, and he thought he might retch; images of the past twenty minutes swarmed through his head, shuddered through his whole body. He felt too hot and too cold at the same time. He was dripping sweat.

Zazou didn't look much better; her shirt was soaked

with blood, her face was smudged with dirt and blood. "Not my blood," she said briskly, then angled her head to her right. "We need you over there," she said. "We're calling them to us."

Ramsey looked in the direction she was indicating; he saw what looked like small streaks of red lightning flickering the air. Cameron's work. Fireplay. "There's a lot of blood over there," Zazou said. "A lot of blood. They'll be coming. We need to be waiting. The way those walls came out of the ground—we can corral them."

"We need to find Mustard."

"No."

"He's around here somewhere."

"No. I mean, he's dead. Back there. And you don't want to see him."

"Dead." Somehow the word didn't register. Mustard had been right at his side minutes ago, complaining about the cold. He wasn't much older than Ramsey. People shouldn't die at that age. It was unnatural. "No," Ramsey said. "Maybe he's just injured. We should—"

"Ramsey. They tore him apart."

When he didn't answer, she touched his arm. When he didn't move, she reached for his hand. "Ramsey. You're doing fine. You are. And we need to go now."

"Right," he said. He took a breath. He remembered the way he'd felt in the van, after Cameron had done whatever he'd done to his brain. The hyperalertness, the confidence. He wanted that back. He reached for that state of mind. Kept reaching. "Right," he said again, and followed Zazou through the mist.

Then, in the near distance, came the rattle of gunfire, more shouting.

"We have to get there," whispered Zazou, but Ramsey's gaze was fixed on the figure ahead of them. Tall, waving several pairs of unevenly matched arms, the bottom hands both carrying what looked like severed heads, this beast seemed to regard them with interest. Then the

air to the left went bright with another series of the
lightning-fire that Cameron was throwing up. The creature dropped the heads—they hit the ground with wet,
muffled thuds—and sidled off in that direction.

Ramsey lifted his gun and shot it neatly in the back
of its head.

He shot it again in the same place for good measure.

A man yelled out, "Hey! You! Are we alive? Are
we dead?"

Ramsey spun toward the voice, but like every other
sound there was no clear sense of where it was coming
from.

"Why the hell am I still alive? Are we on another
fucking planet or what?" The voice, the man it belonged
to, was somewhere to his right. Of that, Ramsey was
sure. "Ah, fuck it," Ramsey heard him mutter, and that
was the end of it. He thought he heard footsteps, but a
fresh wave of mist surged around him and erased those
sounds as well.

Ramsey turned to Zazou. "I can't go with you."

"Sorry?"

"I have to find him. That guy we just heard. Lucas
Maddox." As Zazou continued to look at him blankly,
Ramsey said, "*Maddox*. He can't be allowed to—I have
to find him."

"Ramsey." Zazou's voice was tight. "You don't know
what you're doing."

"I never have. It's just my way."

What he did next surprised him. He reached out for
Zazou and meant to kiss her forehead, but somehow
found her lips instead. When he stepped back from her,
she was watching him, wide-eyed, and something else,
Ramsey thought. Regretful. Like she might miss him if
he never found his way back.

"I could go with you," Zazou said.

"They need you over there. Plus, Maddox is a singer,
not a fighter. He lets other people do the bloody stuff."
When she looked unconvinced, he added, "You heard

the dude. He doesn't sound dangerous. He sounds lost and confused."

"Just come back to us."

"Stay alive," Ramsey told her, "and I will."

She nodded again, looking down at the ground; then, before either of them could say anything more, she turned away from him, picking her way across the broken, uneven road toward Cameron and the others.

Ramsey felt a kind of solitude he hadn't felt since Vegas. It wasn't unpleasant. He was alone in a mist filled with otherworldly or unnatural things that wanted to kill him and eat him, not necessarily in that order, and yet he felt his spirits lift a little. He had purpose now. A clearly defined and necessary purpose. Let the others grapple with this *holding the line* bullshit; he would find that contamination passing itself off as a man and eradicate it, before Lucas Maddox could help kill the world.

Chapter Twenty-five

Lucas

"Walk with me," she had said.

But when they came to the end of the house and the strange, shifting world it contained, she would not let him follow. There was a gesture she made and a look in her eyes, and he found himself bound to where he stood. And so he could only watch as she slipped away from him into the shadowed, vaulted space of rock and moss and earth.

She transfigured herself, and he was her witness.

Light surged out of her, spilling over her skin. She was a woman on fire, except instead of consuming her the flames were carried on her, riding her, racing along the outline of her body. She didn't seem to be touching the ground anymore, seemed through the flame to be turning transparent, as though a reflection in a dark window: trapped in the space between, the threshold. He felt hollowed of all breath, on the verge of blacking out or leaving his body.

So intent was he on the woman in front of him, he barely even noticed the earthquake.

Not like any earthquake he'd been in before, though, and as a long-time LA resident he'd been in a few of them. The ground rocked and jolted to a weird, irregular rhythm, and the ceiling above him popped and snapped as cracks zigzagged their way across, then spread down along the walls like a plague.

Which is when, through the dazzle, the press of heat, he saw a figure come darting from a tunnel behind her.

A man, he thought, if moving in a way no man ever could, with fleeting zigzagging strides, not across the ground but slightly over it.

He yelled her name in warning.

And just before the figure—a demon, Lucas realized, how could it be anything else but a demon, unlike any of the hybrids he'd encountered, who in fact showed them up as the hatchlings they were—tossed darkness on her light, her eyes snapped to his. And the force in them struck him in the chest, like a giant hand shoving him backward. Backward, and down, as the walls and ceiling and floor splintered apart all around him, breaking and shattering, sending him tumbling, down and down into dark.

So, am I dead? he thought.

He could hear a lot of screaming.

Dead, and in hell?

A lot of screaming: voices crashing together in the worst kind of pileup.

This would seem to fit the general description.

He opened his eyes.

He felt like shit. As a dead person he was hoping he'd be in better shape than this. But the body was working enough to stand upright, to feel with its hands the jagged rock of ceiling, the deeply pitted walls. He was in a tunnel, and he could see some kind of glow in the distance.

Well, fuck me blind. There's a light at the end of the tunnel.

He arranged his banged-up limbs and sent them shuffling forward. He wasn't quite sure if he was going to the light or if the light was coming at him, but suddenly it was all around him, a blazing full-body halo that spat him out into desert.

The desert? But I was in LA, so how . . . ?

Hell is a desert?

He felt a vague disappointment.

Then the sunspots that dazzled his vision began to fade, and he looked onto the landscape and saw where he was. And wasn't.

He stood on a ledge of rock that shoved itself out from a mountain of dark stone. The stone had a sheen to it, as if it streamed water, even though it was perfectly dry. The mountain curved away to his right, and he saw how it was pitted and bubbled like dried lava, and he saw the rows on rows of tunnels that went burrowing into it, and the rough-hewn stairs crisscrossing its surface all the way to the top.

But none of that had his attention for long.

He was looking out into the source of the screaming.

The ground below him was littered with the burning, writhing bodies of—he didn't know what to call them. They didn't seem like creatures so much as creations, constructions built from machine parts, body parts, animal parts, rearranged, reinvented, reshaped, revised. Among them he saw very odd things, odd because they were so familiar: a billboard advertising perfume, half sunk in the sand; an overturned Volvo; a partially submerged Western-style bar. He wondered how they had gotten there—fallen there—but not for long, his eyes going again to the things that were dying all around him, burning in the same flames he'd seen racing over Jess.

They were the things Jess had described to him, the things she had glimpsed in the mirrors.

The grotesques.

He's making an army.

But what the hell kind of army was *this*?

They seemed built to give hurt, that much was true. To stalk and hunt and maim and cause terror. He could imagine them unleashed all through California, or the whole country, or even the world. But for all the ferocity he saw, there were a lot of things he didn't see: purpose, for one. Organization, for another. Technology, for yet another. Beyond the ability to scare with their appearance alone, beyond their teeth and claws and spikes and nails and blades and bayonets and axe heads—beyond the fear they inspired and the animal violence they were no doubt capable of—what advantages did they have against a real army: organized military might that could blow them up without even getting anywhere close to them, just by pushing a button? They would surprise the world, sure, they would shock the crap out of it, they would cause all kinds of terror and destruction and death, and once that advantage was gone, when the enemy had regrouped and accepted what it was seeing, they would be obliterated through superior firepower. Where was *their* technology, the dark magic that had gone into their making in the first place? What the hell was Jaxon doing? Was he really so stupid as to think that by putting a human torso on the hindquarters of a goat and topping it all off with antlers made of antlers, he could enslave or eliminate humanity? So much better, and smarter, to teach the hybrids how to steal a nuclear bomb.

This didn't seem like an army.

This seemed like a . . . *body of work.*

And the themes were pain and sadism and death and destruction and chaos and confusion. Lucas was older than Jess, had been a musician for much longer than she'd been a painter, and he looked down at what he saw over the edge of his own experience and saw the living, breathing artist's obsessions, the questions Jaxon was asking of himself and then answering over and over again in his work.

I've been a destroyer for as long as I remember. I am so bored. I want to create.

But what was the vision that drove him, that Jaxon had come into their world to fulfill? What was the agenda behind it? *What the hell was going on?*

He thought back to Jess's description of her final conversation with Stefan:

You think he just wants the world? He has a whole collection . . . This world is already his, it just doesn't know it yet.

Not all of the grotesques were burning, dying, or injured. The ones still whole and functioning were weaving through the bodies, toward the black-rock mountain. Some of them slithered or pulled themselves up the walls; others shambled or loped or picked their way up the steps. They disappeared into the caves.

The tunnels.

Were they, then, some kind of passageway between the worlds? If he turned and went back into the tunnel, was that the way home?

But what was there to get back to—the house that Jaxon built (or had Stefan build), whatever was left of it crawling with these things he'd made, those who'd survived Jess's assault? He thought again of the figure fleeing toward her, throwing himself over her, darkness on her light, stealing away so much of its ferocity. Her interrupted assault, he corrected himself. Was this what she had wreaked, then, hurling destruction through the tunnels, through whatever thinning membrane separated one reality from another, to catch the grotesques where Jaxon had been storing them?

She saved me? She drove me down into one particular tunnel and saved me?

It stood to reason, he thought—hoped—that different tunnels opened into different places: if he wanted to avoid Jaxon's house, he just had to choose a cave a good distance away from the cave that had ejected him here. Assuming every tunnel led back to the same world, his world; assuming he wouldn't find himself on the moon or in a world of talking apes or even hell itself. One of the hells.

Fuck it, Lucas thought.

He had expected to be dead by now.

So either he was on borrowed time that was already running out, or he really *was* dead and this was some version of an afterlife served up just for him. It didn't seem like he had anything to lose. After everything he'd been through, death seemed like a quiet, comfortable room he would enter with relief. He wasn't afraid of pain, which was temporary, and which—compared to the vast, ancient reaches he'd sensed in Jaxon's voice and eyes—would be brief indeed. There was black blood in his body and his music had summoned a demon-king. Maybe all he'd been in his life—in what he thought in some way was his "real" life, the one before he ever knew that a demon wasn't just a thing in some Clive Barker movie—was a musician with an inability to carry his own success and talent, but he had lived the way he wanted. More or less.

And it was enough.

He should have died with Jess.

But, he had no intention of going anywhere near those monstrosities that littered and yowled and moaned beneath him. Although the rock wall opposite him was crawling with the things, his side seemed left alone. It occurred to him that even though he was standing in plain sight on the ledge, looking down into the twisting, shifting sea of monsters, none of the monsters were looking up at him or taking any notice of him. If anything, their gazes were angling in every other direction but his.

He sidled along the ledge, the stone marble-smooth beneath him, the glossy surface refracting such a dazzle of light that he wished for sunglasses. If you were dead and in some kind of afterworld, would you do something so banal as wish for sunglasses? The darkness in the caves seemed more and more inviting. The inside of his mouth was beginning to feel like beaten leather.

When he heard a light, trickling echo from the cave he was approaching, he immediately assumed it couldn't,

wouldn't be water. No way the powers that be would
cut him that kind of break. Still, he curled his hands
around the top edge of the cave, felt the cracked and
flaky bubbles erupting through the smoothness of stone,
and ducked his head to peer inside.

And there it was: water, trickling along the back wall,
slipping down into a small pool.

He picked his way over the sloping, uneven ground,
careful not to lose his footing, thinking how much it
would suck to fall and break a leg here with no one to
call 911. There was a sharp, acrid scent in the cave, and the
stalagmites were furred with an ashy-gray substance that
might have been some kind of moss. Hellmoss, he
thought, and clapped a hand across his mouth to stop
himself from laughing. You had to watch out for that,
the kind of laughter that might knock loose what remained of your sanity.

And if the water was toxic, he didn't care. When death
was like a bird that rode on your shoulder and spoke in
your ear, when it became a familiar, even comforting
presence, you could pretty much do what you wanted.
And he wanted to get rid of this fucking thirst.

There was something odd about the surface, although
he didn't realize what it was until he was crouching on
the rock and reached out his cupped hands. He could
not see himself reflected on the surface. There was no
reflection at all. What he saw, instead, was a person, a
woman, standing deep inside the center of the pool.

The woman lifted her head, turning her face up to
Lucas.

His breath shoved out of him. He grabbed at the rock
for balance.

It was Jess, her long, dark hair rippling around her
like snakes.

He might have said her name. He wasn't sure. His
chest was a frozen, heavy thing and it was painful.

She reached both arms toward him.

And he felt invisible hands come surging from the

water and clamp his shoulders and pull him off the rock. He smashed down into the pool and it didn't sound like water at all. It cracked and splintered, even through the onrush of cold and dark and wet. Lucas had never been a swimmer, never liked the water, never been a kid who wanted to jump in the pool or go on a boat, and that childhood panic returned to him and sent him flailing, thrashing, breath burning up his lungs.

Then a voice in his ear said, *Calm.*

And he went calm, as if the word was more than a command, as if the word worked a magic all its own. He realized the pressure of those hands was still on him, gentle now, drawing him deeper through the darkness and shivering cold. Then they were lifting him up, the dark thinning out to gray shot through with threads of light. The surface came at him hard and fast—

And then he was bursting up through it, and this time the water sounded like water should. He gasped at the air, eating the air, sucking it in, whacking the surface with his arms as if beating it into submission.

He was in a swimming pool.

A goddamn swimming pool.

Mist drifted over him, but through its furling and unfurling tendrils he saw grass, a child's swingset, the back wall of a faux Italian villa.

He managed to thrash his way to the side of the pool, and clambered over the edge. He spent a moment just sitting there, dripping and shivering, saying stuff under his breath. Nonsensical stuff. Babbling. *I don't believe this I can't believe this holy shit I just can't do this anymore Jess Jess oh painter oh Jess.* Then he told himself, *Stop being such a fucking toddler,* and managed to shut the hell up. He closed his eyes, and again thought of death as being like a little black bird perched on his shoulder, and somehow that made it better. *Calm,* he thought.

He cut through the yard to the house, cold grass squelching beneath his bare feet.

Dead bodies on the porch. He saw them enough to register their ripped-up, clawed-apart appearance, and the fact that they didn't have heads, before jerking his gaze away. In the near distance, he heard gunfire, shouting, and someone screaming. And beyond that he heard sirens, but the sirens sounded so far away, filtered so thinly through the mist, that they might have been in another world altogether.

They probably were.

Shit's going down, he thought, and opened the sliding glass doors and stepped into the living room.

He wanted shoes. Dry clothes. He had been living half-naked in the same pair of jeans for longer than he cared to know. He found the kitchen first, one of those kitchens that seemed lifted from a magazine but never actually used. He went to the fridge and found bottled water. He drank. He found a rotisserie chicken still in its paper bag, pulled it out, and chomped into the side. The chicken dangling from his mouth, he rummaged through the front hall closet and found a trench coat that looked his size and an Armani leather jacket that looked too big. He went for the leather jacket, wiping his hands on his jeans so he wouldn't get grease on the leather, pulling it on with a sigh. Scattered on the closet floor were loafers, sneakers, a pair of high-heeled patent leather boots. And flip-flops. They would do.

He turned away from the closet and saw a telephone on a little side table, the message light flashing red. On impulse he reached out and pressed the button.

" . . . *hope to God that you both have come to your senses. Jeremy got here around noon and told me about the fire and that you guys just didn't believe it, said he was nuts, said everybody's just seeing things, and that you were staying put and all that. Mom, Dad, I know you're both stubborn as hell but please please please just get out of there, come see me and the kids, the kids would love to see you, please if just for the peace of mind of your own son and daughter—*"

Lucas opened the front door.

A nightmare filled the doorway.

About seven feet tall, thin, with a head that had once been human and was now covered with spikes. There were broken shards of mirror jammed where the eyes should have been. It had six arms taken from six different bodies, and its bottom pair of mismatched hands dangled a severed human head from each.

The thing looked at Lucas and Lucas looked at the thing.

He could see bits of his own distorted reflection in the mirror eyes. Could hear the thing breathing: long, whistling exhalations, sudden lurching inhales. Could smell it: body odor, seaweed, and blood. It lifted its upper hands, and Lucas saw the long steel blades it had instead of fingers. Clicking them together, it reached for Lucas's neck.

"Oh, fuck right off," Lucas said irritably, and in one darting movement swiped his palm along a steel edge. "See that?" he said, holding up his palm, the black blood drizzling down his hand. The cut was deeper than he'd intended and hurt like a bitch; he probably should have rethought that, but whatever.

The nightmare paused. Lucas could hear an insectlike clicking coming from deep inside it. It appeared to be thinking. Lucas took a step toward it and the thing actually took a step back. "You know what I am," Lucas said softly. "You know who I am."

Again, the clicking.

Then a voice issued from the ruin of a mouth, shockingly human and achingly young: "I know what you am. You know what you am?"

Chuckling to itself, the thing pushed past Lucas's shoulder, the mirror-eyes flashing at him, and went down the hall.

He was in Los Angeles, except this wasn't part of any Los Angeles that he had ever known.

Walking through the cold, mist-filled gray, Lucas felt like the last man on earth.

He knew this wasn't true. He kept hearing bursts and spikes of gunfire, shouts, and screams. Sounds of warfare. There were also times he felt eyes on him—things lurking or crouching in the mist, or looking down at him through windows, doorways, the top edges of the glistening black stone walls that looked as if they'd broken off from the mountain shot through with caves and tunnels, that alien mountain in that alien world, and shoved themselves up into this one. The streetscape had changed, perhaps drastically, but with this weird smog everywhere it was impossible to know just how much. And at that, he felt a touch of sadness, or maybe it was nostalgia. Already missing what had been.

The death-bird in his mind shifted its weight, rustled its wings.

The things in the mist, the grotesques, the nightmares, the monstrosities: they all left him alone. He and they understood each other. The blood dripped steadily off his hand and he let it lay down a trail behind him.

Mist and flickering, random lights and shadows passed near him, footfalls echoing, voices rising and falling and fading. Someone was singing. Streetlamps stammered, then went dark, then flared with new violence of life. A figure in a cloak huddled against a wall and held out a cup. "Please." He grunted the word, his hooded face lifting toward Lucas, and Lucas saw that he didn't have a face at all, just a stretch of pink skin pulled smooth, tiny bits of mirror for eyes.

Something sleek and furry rubbed against his leg.

Dark shapes fluttered and cawed along the telephone wires.

The road had thrown up hills of dirt and rocks and chunks of concrete. Cars were overturned in the street, crashed up on sidewalks, folded around streetlamps. Beyond them, music thumped out from a Western-style bar, but it sounded strangely atonal. And the building itself seemed to be thumping with life all its own, sending snakelike undulations along the road. He took note of what he saw, not trying to understand any of it, just filing it away in his mind.

Somewhere high above, a window shattered, somebody screamed, and a body came pinwheeling down. An ugly thump. Someone laughed.

To his right was a little restaurant with the awning half caved in. Figures dressed in black and white were righting the tables, the chairs. He could smell cooking meat.

He was seeing and not-seeing the man and woman with long, twisted faces sitting at one of the tables. The woman picked up a menu and said something to the man. Her voice was low and chittering. The man turned his head and hawked and spat. A gob thwacked onto the sidewalk near Lucas, where it hissed and sizzled.

So was this what LA was turning into? The whole world? Had it already happened or would the change just spread out like oil from a spilled tanker, strangling whatever life-forms it came across, leaving weird new ones in its wake? He felt an odd, hollowed-out sensation in his chest. The world ends not with a bang, he thought, but a demon-king shoving one reality right through another, like two cars smashing head-on in an intersection.

He kept walking. Then his gaze fell on a familiar figure moving off to the right of him: the tall thing with the arms. The cut on his hand throbbed in memory.

The air ripped apart with the crack of a single gunshot, and the thing with the arms faltered.

A second shot, and it went down.

The mist swirled and eddied, and thinned out enough for Lucas to glimpse two figures standing together, one of them holding a—was that a *sword*?—and they didn't look injured or dead or mutilated, they looked normal, they looked like actual . . .

People, he thought. Oh, god, human voices, human warmth. "Hey!" he yelled, and kept calling out as a fresh

surge of mist thickened the air, obscured the figures,
until he realized he was on the verge of losing it. "Ah,
fuck it," he muttered, and walked on.

The traffic light ahead of him went from red to green
to red again. He crossed the street, swerving to avoid a
spiky outcropping of black, bloodstained rock, crunching
some scuttling thing beneath a flip-flop. He knew where
he was. He knew this plaza set beyond the sidewalk:
tanning salon, boutiques, Mexican fast-food place, falafel
sandwich stand, cut-rate plastic surgery clinic.

And the guitar shop.

It sold used and vintage guitars. There was a beauty
in the window: a mahogany-bodied, double-necked guitar that made his hands twitch. He rattled the door.
Locked. He looked again at the front window, then cast
around for something to smash it with. A broken-off
chunk of concrete had possibility: he moved to pick it
up just as something whistled coldly past his neck, taking
some flesh along with it. His hand slapped to the wound,
and he was thirteen years old again, in the fields outside
his uncle's farmhouse, stumbling into a wasps' nest. Then
the memory faded and the thing that had stung him
wasn't a wasp at all, it was a wood-handled throwing
knife. He picked it up, stared at it dumbly, then heard
a light footstep behind him and spun to his left as a
second knife slammed the store window where his head
had just been.

"Maddox," said a voice.

A young man's voice.

A voice that triggered an avalanche of memory: a
burning house and the weight of a boy gone limp in his
arms and sand that got everywhere, in your eyes and
everywhere, and the smell of desert alkaline, and Asha
and jax, and the music, such music, music the like of
which you never heard before and would never hear
again, and a black-haired Summoner prince chained
across a rock in his own personal hell and, again, that

kid in his arms, a pathetic, helpless, paralyzed figure with
his skin scrawled over in jax marks, eyes opening to look
up at Lucas, saying suddenly, unexpectedly, *Nice scars.*
Those claw marks on his face from Asha, his precious,
remarkable, feral, and gorgeously insane Asha, and
Lucas heard everything that went on beneath those
words, the scorn, the real message: *You're just Asha's
bitch, Asha's slave, you have no power over me except
what she chooses to give you.*

"Ramsey," he said, turning around, bracing himself
for any more sharp-edged little missiles. "How you doing,
kid?"

Maybe not such a kid any longer.

Ramsey said nothing. There was a coldness in his face,
a set to his jaw that undercut the fine, pretty-boy features. He still had that shaggy, street-waif look to him,
but the vulnerability that had marked those brown eyes
was nowhere in evidence now. He came forward, moving
easily, loosely, ready to fight and confident he'd win, and
Lucas saw that now he had scars of his own.

"You know," Lucas said amiably, "I was thinking
about you the other day—" but Ramsey just kept coming forward. He reached behind his back and drew out
a sword—a fucking honest-to-god sword—and brought
it down in front of him, holding it lightly, casually, and
Lucas felt the first cold pricking along the back of his
neck. But no. He refused to believe that he could ever
fear *this* kid, this fucking *kid*, even as said kid suddenly—
and for the life of him Lucas wasn't sure how it happened, only that he'd better get out of his head and start
paying closer attention—had him up against the front
window of the guitar shop, the edge of the blade at his
throat. And Lucas thought of the double-necked guitar
waiting on its stand right behind him. Thought of it itch-
ing for him, the same way he itched for it, needed it,
needed it *now.*

He forced his attention to Ramsey.

The kid's eyes were filled with a hard, fierce light, a

killer's light, but then it ebbed a bit. He was studying Lucas's face as if trying to decode it, to square the reality of the man in front of him with whatever he had going on inside his head.

And Lucas felt the urge for another wisecrack, that tone of false, mocking joviality he slipped into whenever the situation felt beyond him. But no. Ramsey deserved something else from him, something better.

"You want revenge," Lucas said quietly, "and I could never blame you for that."

And in the way Ramsey's expression shifted, and then shifted again, Lucas became convinced that any other response, including silence, would have ended with the sword through his neck. But that was just one moment; now they were into the next moment, and the sword was still poised to kill him.

"I'd be careful," Lucas said. "I'd be very careful."

"This isn't about revenge," Ramsey said.

"Then you're a better man than I am. I would want to take me apart, given what we did to you."

"I *am* a better man than you."

This rankled a bit.

"I swore I would kill you," Ramsey went on. "I need to kill you. It would be the great good deed of my whole goddamn life."

"I know you're a killer now. Hunting down the hybrids and all that. But killing a man is a whole different thing, right? Jess told me—"

Ramsey came at him again, slamming his body up against the glass, the blade a fraction closer to his windpipe. Lucas felt his breath catch. Because how and when he died—it mattered, after all. It mattered. And he couldn't die like this.

He had to play a song first.

Ramsey looked caught in some inner conflict, as if there were questions he was struggling to ask and not-ask, afraid to give away some advantage. Lucas studied his face, the rawness in it, saw the kid he still was and the man he was becoming.

"You want to know about Jess," Lucas said. Of course he did. He saw, quite clearly, that Ramsey loved Jess, was maybe even *in* love with her, in the way of someone who knew he'd never have her, so he pretended it was strictly a brother-sister thing. Maybe.

The kid said, "What did you do to her?"

"I didn't do anything to her."

"Why are you in her dreams?"

"I don't know. Why is *she* in *my* dreams?"

"You should have just left her alone."

"If I could have," Lucas said wearily, "I would have. Believe me."

"What is she to you?"

Good question. We never quite figured that out.

"I'm not her enemy," Lucas said at length. "I'm not your enemy either."

"But what you did—" He was struggling for words, and getting careless with the blade. Lucas kept himself very still, willing it not to slip, or himself to slip against it. "Kept me in that van," Ramsey spat out, "like a *dog*, except only a monster would treat a *dog* that way. You bought me from Salik like some—rough trade."

"You were never that," Lucas said gently. "Give us that much." And technically Salik hadn't sold him, either, but gifted him to Asha with Lucas as the middle-man. Salik had been sucking up to a powerful demoness, angling to get on her good side. Someone else had sold Ramsey to Salik, but it didn't feel like a good time to point that out.

"You want me to say I'm sorry?" Lucas said. "I'm sorry. And you don't have to hold me at knifepoint. Swordpoint. I'd still say it. And mean it."

"This . . ." Ramsey swallowed. The blade was trembling in his hand. "This isn't about revenge. This is about—This is about—"

And then he tilted his head to the side.

He seemed, for a moment, to be listening to something. Someone.

Someone unseen. Speaking right in his ear.

And for a moment Lucas could hear it, or imagine he heard it: a whispering, familiar voice, a female voice, and in his mind came the image of her, the way she'd moved and rocked beneath him, and his body strung out along the ache of it.

Distracted, Ramsey relaxed the blade. Lucas saw his chance and went for it, bringing both hands up against the flat of the blade, shoving it back even as he brought his foot up against Ramsey's leg and pushed out, putting his whole body into it.

Ramsey went stumbling back, then tripped on the curb. As he fought not to fall, Lucas stepped inside his reach and grabbed his wrist and twisted. Ramsey yelped, and Lucas twisted harder, then remembered he was supposed to push down as well. Ramsey's grip broke, and the sword went clattering. Lucas kicked it away, before thinking he should have picked it up, used it himself. Too late for that. The sword slid across concrete and fell into a gap that had opened up in the pavement.

"That was *mine*!"

Lucas felt a force slamming into his back, hurtling him to the concrete. Skin scraped off his hands and arms, the side of his face. He rolled round and kicked out, but Ramsey evaded him, then was on him, landing blow after blow after blow. Lucas shielded his face with his arms, felt the blows move down his torso. Ramsey got careless, gave away some balance, and Lucas managed to flip over, hooking Ramsey with his legs. Lucas descended into the haze of fighting, his focus so intense that his vision went dark at the edges. They grappled and thrashed. Lucas had the advantage of size, the kind of advantage that would win out in the end—all he had to do was get there. Ramsey was fast and agile, eel-slippery. There was a precision to him, the way he knew to choose the moment, the angle, fist flying at Lucas's jaw, temple, eye, even though he wasn't wearing gloves, even though at one point Lucas heard the snap of small bones. It made no difference. Whatever physical pain the kid had to be in, he wasn't feeling any of it.

So Lucas took the blows.

He took a lot of blows.

He didn't want to hurt the kid in return. He only wanted to make him *stop*. But every time he caught the kid in a clench, both of them breathing hard, exhausted, Ramsey somehow slipped and squirmed away, then came at him again, with that same determination to beat the living shit out of him.

Except every now and then, he'd pause.

His head would tilt to the side, his eyes searching the space around him, around them both. And again, Lucas could hear it, sense it, that voice whispering words that were not meant for him.

The final time it happened, Lucas took advantage of Ramsey's distraction to work his way free of him. He spat out the blood that filled his mouth, massaged a loosened tooth from its socket and spat that out as well.

"I know what she's telling you," Lucas said. He grinned, and used the sleeve of his leather jacket to wipe the blood from his lips. "She's telling you to quit trying to kill me. Right?"

Ramsey shook his head. Kept shaking it.

"Telling you not to kill me. You know why? She cares for me. She loves me." He wasn't entirely sure this was true, but why the hell not? It felt good to say. And he was pissed off at the kid for hurting him like this, wanted to drive it in. "She loves me," he said again. "You know her, right? You trust her? Can I be such a monster if she loves me? What do you think, ki—Ramsey?"

"I think she's out of her fucking mind," Ramsey said slowly, but Lucas saw the doubt working his face, the uncertainty. Ramsey tilted his head again, as if catching more whispers, then closed his eyes and did more head-shaking. "I think maybe she's unbalanced. Somehow you unbalanced her. You're the one responsible for this. All of this. It all started with *you*, right? It ends with *you*."

"Oh, kid," Lucas said, and there was nothing false or mocking about the sadness in his voice. "Ramsey. You give me way too much credit—"

Ramsey charged, and Lucas was too tired to evade him, or offer much resistance as he went stumbling back, as he saw the dirty glint of the knife wrapped in Ramsey's fingers, the throwing knife he must have retrieved from the ground. Lucas moved his body enough so that when the knife went into him, it took him in the side: a cold, sleek, sliding pressure, followed by a fire-trail of pain.

"Okay," Lucas said. "Okay."

And instead of the slice and slash of follow-through, Ramsey stepped back.

The knife was in his hand. And Lucas wondered, how could his blood be so black like that? When he was a kid, a youth, a younger man, he had bled the same as anyone else. So what the fuck had happened to him? What had there been, deep inside him all this time, waiting to be turned on, to transform him?

He thought of that long-ago night with Asha, the family she had slaughtered, *they* had slaughtered, because of course he'd done nothing to stop any of it. What she had done to him afterward. The snake. The taste inside him afterward: cold ash. *I gave you a little piece of my heart,* she had said. *I think you'll like what it does for you.*

"Okay," Lucas said again. "Is it enough?"

Ramsey's face was leeched of all color, his eyes wide, red-rimmed, and bloodshot. Blood on his face, his shirt, his hands: some of it his own. Some of it.

"I don't know," he said.

Lucas looked down at himself, pressed a hand against the wound. He felt the slick of blood, the gush of it down his stomach. Felt it soaking the top of his jeans.

"I'll tell you something," he said, surprising himself. "Although if you ever tell anyone, I'll deny it, then hunt you down and kill you." He smiled a little, to let Ramsey know he was kidding. Sort of. Mostly kidding. "I'll tell you this, because I think I want to tell someone, and it might as well be you. Hell, maybe it shouldn't be anyone else. Just you."

Ramsey said nothing. He didn't do a lot of talking, this kid. Before, all through that time in the desert, Lucas had attributed Ramsey's silence to being traumatized and just generally fucked up. Which no doubt had been true, but now he saw it was also Ramsey's nature.

"I love her," Lucas said. "Isn't that wild? And weird? I actually love her."

"You can't love." Ramsey's voice was flat and hard. "You're not the type."

"See. That's what I would have said."

Lucas examined his hand. The glisten of fresh blood, the old scars and welts. Touching Jess. The heat and taste of her. She wouldn't be the one who killed him after all. Although in some ways she already had, and a metaphoric death was still a death, at least of sorts. He looked up at Ramsey, who was watching him now with a kind of open fascination, wondering what he could possibly say next. Lucas said, "You know the myth of Orpheus?"

"The guy who played music. And—" Ramsey paused, scratched his nose with a bloody finger, then admitted, "That's all I know. Not so much into myths—Wait. He's the guy who went into the underworld, to rescue his girlfriend. Only he looked back. And he wasn't supposed to. And he lost her. Because you're not supposed to look back."

"Sure, whatever. You know how he died?"

"He—" Ramsey paused. "No."

"He got torn to pieces. The music he played was just too amazing, made everybody want him too much. Like they needed to eat him up, or something. Or maybe he just pissed them off." He shrugged. He discovered it hurt to shrug.

The kid didn't look like he was going to rush him again. Lucas figured he must look pulverized enough, finally, to give Ramsey some satisfaction. *This is not about revenge.* What bullshit.

He limped over to the window display of the guitar shop. He braced himself, then slammed his elbow into the glass. Slammed it again. The leather jacket offered some padding and protection from the glass, but it was still another bit of pain he could have done without. He stepped up inside the window, lifted the double-necked guitar off its stand. He didn't sit so much as collapse into the chair arranged beside it. As he strummed a few chords, tested and tightened the strings, he felt a kind of bliss move through him, displacing aches both old and new. This was it, this was home. This had always been home to him.

He looked up at Ramsey. His witness. His audience.

He said, "Do you know what I am?"

"You're Lucas Maddox."

"I'm a vessel. Just like you were." Then he amended, "Maybe not quite like you were."

Ramsey absorbed this in silence. Then said, a bit too self-righteously for Lucas's tastes, "I had an angel inside me. What do *you* carry?"

Lucas didn't bother to answer. He was reveling in the firm love-bite of the strings, the call and response of player and instrument, and now he was liking what he heard. Jimmy Page had played this same model of guitar in "Stairway to Heaven" and "The Rain Song." There were worse ways to go. He paused for a moment, closing his eyes, gathering himself. He would probably pray now, if he were the kind of man who did things like that.

He opened his eyes and looked at Ramsey.

He said, "Brace yourself. Things are about to get interesting."

Chapter Twenty-six

Kai

"I'm enjoying this," Del had said.

The demon-man was taking his first bath. He had buried himself in bubbles, lounging and lolling in the white marble basin. He had ordered generously from room service, taking his favorite bits of cheese and fruit and meat to arrange along the edge of the tub, not to eat, it seemed, but just to look at. He was a constant collector of small things, odd things: the inside pockets of the overcoat Kai had bought him filled with rocks and dead flies and cigarette stubs and broken glass and other things he insisted on picking up off the sidewalks, "flotsam and detritus," he had said happily, "so interesting, interesting." He was particularly proud of the delicate mouse skeleton he had plucked from behind a Dumpster. But he didn't restrict himself to garbage; he couldn't stroll through a store without palming things off the shelves, sometimes not even bothering to palm them at all but mind-slipping them into his pockets: candies and pencils and paperbacks and figurines and mood rings.

Not that Kai took him into stores. Kai's goal had been to keep Del as suppressed as possible, whisking him in and out of planes and cars and hotel rooms. But Del had a way of escaping him, despite the binding spell Kai had cast. He couldn't go far, of course; the binding wouldn't allow it, although Kai nurtured the uneasy suspicion that the spellcast hadn't worked as effectively as it seemed to, and that Del was to some extent pretending.

But Del didn't want to go far. He wanted to check out alleys and back lots and bus terminals and convenience stores. He wanted to follow the woman walking the Yorkie terrier to tell her that the terrier didn't like her three-year-old and would take a chunk from her ankle if she whacked him with her doll one more time. He wanted to climb telephone poles and sneak into movie theaters and chat up the kid at the hot dog stand, telling him to tell his father to get out of denial and go to the doctor before the cancer could spread any further. He wanted to eat hot dogs and hamburgers and steaks and quesadillas and chocolate doughnuts and muffins the size of cabbages. He wanted to drink cappuccinos. He wanted a cell phone and a laptop and an iPod. He wanted a plane ticket to Phoenix, even if he didn't know or care where it was, because he had always had a soft spot for phoenixes and wanted to visit this city that had been built in honor of them. He wanted to sit cross-legged on the floor in the middle of a Best Buy and watch the national figure skating championships on high-definition television. He wanted to learn guitar. He wanted to watch *The Empire Strikes Back* five times in a row.

"I'm enjoying all of this," Del said, "so very much, so very sweetling much, yes, I say yes always yes yes," and slipped his face beneath the bubbles, beneath the water, so that for a moment Kai hoped he might drown.

"Enjoying himself" was not a phrase that Kai himself would have used. He was not particularly enjoying the doubt that kept creeping through him, or this new habit of constantly second-guessing himself. Not enjoying this sense of being trapped in some kind of dog-and-pony show, some hideous odd-couple kind of warped-living sitcom. Every time he looked at Del, the demon he had freed under the thinnest of pretexts that he could keep him controlled, he felt himself wading deeper into quagmire, felt himself groping more and more blindly through this blasted situation, finding his footing only to lose it again.

When Del's upper body exploded up through the bath, water sloshed over the sides and splattered Kai's pants. Kai turned, feeling oddly in slow motion, to see Del's eyes expanding and swirling with dark. His hands lifted, his fingers plucking air, and Kai realized that he'd gone onto the demon lines. Just like that, without pomp or ceremony or preparation of any kind. Del was on the demon lines.

Del sighed and laughed, his body twisting toward Kai, his head taking a long moment to follow. Then language spilled out of him, gushing like blood, and in the chattering, clacking syllables Kai recognized one of the demon languages, but his knowledge of it stopped there. Del talked, his voice pitching high and dropping low and then pitching high again, his fingers raking the air, cutting at it, slashing.

Then he paused, and the darkness in his eyes lightened to blue.

A cool, steady, intelligent steel blue.

"Kai," said Jess. Except it wasn't Jess at all, only her voice; her voice, speaking through a demon-man's mouth. "I'm not your angel, Kai. Are you the one? Are you the one who kills me?"

Kai stared. Angled his head as if about to shake it. "No. Never."

The blue streaked from Del's eyes, down his face, rivulets of blue trickling down his body and disappearing in the bubbles.

"Jaxon Twist," Del said. "Jaxon Twist." He rolled his eyes toward Kai. "I know where they are."

"Can you get to her in time?"

"Maybe."

Before Kai could respond to this, Del spoke again, his voice dropping deep, a shadow turning through it: "But you have to understand. You can't hide from him. Maybe some of the others, yes. He cares not for the others. But you're one of his, you see. You always have been."

"What . . . ? Del, what the *hells* are you—"

"One of his *interests*," Del said loudly. "He pays *attention* to you, Kai. He's been following your career, such as it is. You should take it as a *compliment*." Del's long, thin fingers twitched the air again. The bubbles had nearly evaporated, and Kai could see his pale belly through the water. "But what it means, my Kai, is that he will see you coming." Del nodded, as if in satisfaction, as if he felt no one could sum it up any better. "You"—as his lips curled back from his teeth—"he will always see coming."

He had gone to Makonnen. The one Summoner who so often seemed the least trustworthy was, in this case, the only one he could trust. Mak had looked at him with a grim set to his face but there was something else in there too, flickering deep in eyes gone gray-blue, and Kai thought it might have been delight. Makonnen said, "And Mina?"

"Asleep for several days."

Mak nodded. "Then in the meantime we will say that I am the one who came across this information. That I somehow retrieved it from a memory of reading the spellbooks of Bakal Ashika, found it in some kind of prophecy or something. Just like in a movie." He grinned. "Isn't there supposed to be a prophecy?"

And so they put together their small band of Summoners, drawn from Kai's Pact as well as a couple others, then widened their circle to include a white-haired rogue named Ysandra. Their plan was simple. If Kai truly could not hide from the Lord of Bones, then he would walk right up to his front door. As for the others,

they knew from Mak's instructions—Del's instructions—
where to go. They would be waiting.

Even though Kai had been expecting it, even though
it was part of the plan, he was startled and even unnerved at how quickly Jaxon Twist and all the names
carried inside that one—the Lord of Bones, the Traveler,
the Stranger, and other names that went winding and
echoing back through the corridors of time, to whatever
origin had spawned him—found him, there in the swirling murk.

It seemed like only minutes after he'd separated himself from the others when the voice came slinking around
him, sneaking up to him like a cat:

Youngblood. My youngblooded princeling.

Have you finally come to play?

The mist thickened and closed in around him, sealing
him off from everything he knew must be going on
around him: the transformations, the violence. The mist
moved over his skin, breathed itself into his nostrils, covered the ground until he felt like he was floating. He
didn't fight it: he let it carry him forward, guide him,
walls of mist forming and dissolving and reforming to
either side of him, drawing him down its winding, makeshift corridors.

Have you finally come to me?

Everyone comes to me, little prince. Sooner or later,
they come to me.

They know.

They know what I am.

They know that I am everything.

I offer them everything. I offer you everything.

You only have to beg.

"But I don't want everything," Kai said. The sound
of his own spoken voice seemed too loud, unnatural,
refracting through the mist like light on shattered water:
it didn't seem to roll forward so much as loop round

him. If he wasn't careful, he might find himself caught inside a noose of his own making. "I've already had it. Frankly, I found it overrated."

That's only because of what you suffer from.

"Which is?"

A limited imagination. You always did, you know. A pause. Kai could sense the Traveler's voice coiling in on itself, preparing for a strike. *As did your father.*

"My father," Kai scoffed. "Old news, don't you think?"

We were friends, you and I. When you were small. Do you remember?

"I remember you screaming. That's what I remember."

You were so curious. As a child, as a youth, as a young man. Look at all those places you let your curiosity take you. Those things you did. The people you loved, if never quite enough, and never in the way you let them love you. The shame and dishonor you brought upon your noble family.

All because you were curious.

I liked that about you.

"Hard to bring dishonor on a father like mine."

True. But beside the point.

"Why did you come back?"

Unfinished business.

"Revenge," Kai said.

It has nothing to do with revenge.

"So why Jess Shepard? Why take Jessamy, of all people?"

Every Lord of the Underground needs his bride, don't you think? His queen, the mother of his children, his favorite slave and plaything? Why can't she be mine? What do you think Shemayan would have thought of that? His blood will run through my children, Kai. My children who will populate the new world. The new Labyrinth. The one that I am creating even now.

"Come out," Kai whispered. He scanned the mist, but the ghosts and figures he saw moving through it were only tricks, he knew. Mind games. "Come out. Show yourself."

A pause. A chuckle.

Not yet. I'm enjoying this.

And Kai did something he had not done in several lifetimes.

He stopped, there in the mist, and dropped his head and offered a prayer to the life-fire of the Labyrinth. He recalled the warmth of that all-enfolding presence, and he found himself speaking to it now, down through centuries of time and his own vaults of memory. He didn't know what he would say until he heard himself say it. He thought he would ask for help and guidance, but what came out was something else entirely:

I found you too late and lost you too soon. It rained blood and fire and ash and we were forced into a world lost in a dark age, and our war with the demons only made it darker. I was cut off from you. It was like I'd been blinded. But did I give up on you too soon, for the wrong reasons; convinced I'd been right all along, that you can't keep that sense of tenderness, it will only catch fire and burn you alive?

I was stunned, I know. I was dazed. Lost in plague and carnage and war and the most bloody, violent, gruesome magic, the kinds of castings I never wanted to know were even possible . . . The magic changed me and made me open to you, and then shut me down all over again. Maybe that had to be the way of it. Maybe that's the only way I could have focused and endured and survived.

Or maybe those are only excuses.

So now that I'm hundreds of years removed from you, the heart and soul of you, how do I begin to find my way back?

How can I serve you now?

Assuming I truly want to?

*   *   *

"Show yourself," Kai said. "Show me. Show me."

Silence.

And then a dark, sleek, shape poured upward through the mist.

The air sighed. It waved and rippled, then the grayness began to dissipate. In the flat, cool light that remained, Kai followed the Traveler as he rose in the air, his hands held out to his sides, palms up, as if proving he had nothing to hide.

But this, Kai knew, was a lie.

The Traveler moved up over the edge of a nearby roof, then came to rest on its peak. A wind kicked up around Kai, pulling at his coat, and through the wind he felt the pressure of unseen hands surging across his body, probing, pressing, hammering him down.

"The child is with me now." The Traveler was speaking and not speaking; the words came out of the air like rain. "The child comes to me. There comes a new Labyrinth, of blood and smoke and ash and fire, and it is mine. There grows a new Labyrinth, built on the smashed bones of the winged ones, and it is mine."

Along his shoulders, behind his knees, the pressure of those invisible hands grew, and gathered, and beat at him. "So come to me on your knees, *sankkia*." The weight on his shoulders almost unbearable now, his knees beginning to buckle. "Come to me . . . and beg."

And Kai went deep inside his mind, called up the feeling of performing the *kkaji*, the smooth lunge and spin rising up on each movement before it, until he was lifted high enough to draw back the veil, reach into the life-fire, life-force, of the magic that had once been his home—

And it fired up through his body, found release through his extended hands, fresh pain ripping through the still-healing flesh. He shrieked—couldn't help it—and cradled his hands against his chest. The bolt of energy took no color, no visible shape, but ripped apart the mist and drove through the body of the Lord of Bones.

Jaxon fell.

Kai strode forward, summoning wave after wave of that same ferocity, bracing himself against the fire in his hands, riding off the pain, driving everything he had, the force, the energy, into the body of the man on the ground. His vision went dark around the edges, the heat of the magic rising up through him, until he began to feel light-headed, hollowed out. Burning.

Figures appeared in the mist, a ring of shadows closing in, taking on form and detail as the mist rolled back from them and the other Summoners gathered in a circle around the fallen Traveler.

And as they began the spellcraft of imprisonment, the first layer of sphere carving itself through the air and sinking down around Jaxon, a single thought shafted through Kai: *This is much too easy.*

Jaxon lifted his head toward Kai . . . and grinned.

His body jerked once, as if convulsing . . . and then was gone.

Silence.

Mist drifted.

The white-haired Summoner, Ysandra, was the first to speak. She had time enough to say, "I think—" before a steel arm erupted through her chest.

Her body slumped, as from behind her Jaxon lifted his foot and pushed her body off the steel-bladed thing that had been his arm. It happened in less than a heartbeat. Then the arm was an arm again as Jaxon stepped up to the Summoner nearest him and plunged dagger-fingers through his throat.

And then it was chaos.

Kai was striding forward with no idea what he was going to do, only that he had to wing it, stop it, when Jaxon met his eyes and blew him a kiss. A kiss of ash, dark, burning ash that swarmed him like bees, invading his mouth and nostrils and throat. He dropped on his knees, choking, fighting for vision, when a blow landed across his face, reeling him back, and then a blow landed squarely in the center of his chest, toppling him backward. As he fought to find the magic that would clear the ash from his eyes, allow him to breathe again, the force hammered him again and again, his ribs and side and stomach and thighs.

He felt the inner electric snap of Dreamline energy and the black ash was gone. He was on his hands and knees and he saw a boot swinging toward his face and he wrapped both arms around it, jerking its owner off balance.

Ramsey.

It was Ramsey.

It was Ramsey leering at him, laughing at his surprise, as he scrambled back up to his feet. His features began dripping like wax, his whole face melting, reforming, his light brown hair turning long and sleek and dark—

And it was Jess coming at him now, coming at him with her boot in his face. And he was too frozen to react, because even as he knew, of course he knew, that these were just masks worn by Jaxon, the shock of their faces wrenched with such hatred was enough to cut him down. Because beyond Jaxon he could see what had happened to the other Summoners, the thing that Jaxon had made of them, including the corpses, the weeping, screaming ring of braided, woven human flesh, studded with eyes, flaked and scaled with broken mirror, dragging itself over ground.

And he screamed.

He rose against Jaxon, clutching his arm that no longer worked right, and now it was Shemayan delivering the blows, which Kai ducked and evaded as best he could, until a series of hammer strikes on his head and shoulders had him on the ground again. A large hand clamped the top of his skull and lifted.

Kai looked up into the face of his father.

It was like a lightning bolt of memory, ripping through him, searching for ground that just wasn't there, dissolving beneath him until he dangled over an abyss, the only

thing that prevented him from falling his father's grip
on his hair. The sensation was so strong, so vivid, that
Kai had to look frantically beneath him to make sure it
was a hallucination, that he wasn't about to be dropped
into some void past imagining. *And that is not my father,*
he thought, *that is not my crazy hellbeast of a father,*
even as he stared into the same long, almond eyes he
had inherited, the face like a broader, rawer variation of
Kai's own, the body hard and thick and roped with muscle in a way unusual for a high-blood Sajae. His coarse
dark hair was braided back from his forehead, fell in a
warrior's rope to his waist, as if his father wasn't nobility
at all but a member of his own guard: and Kai remembered that too, his father's growing disdain for the softness and decadence of noble life, burning the heirloom
silk cloaks, wearing leathers instead.

"I want you to know," his father said. "I want you
to die knowing what you and your wretched kind have
released. Me. I will have this world as my raw material.
I will have the child of Shemayan as my slave and my
bride, and she shall bear my legion of children, as Shemayan's bloodline disappears into my own. I will smash
the Summoners and rule the Sajae. I will turn this world
into the new Labyrinth and take my place as the center
and the source. Creation shall begin and end with me. I
will take the Dreamlines. I will rule the Dreamlines. And
I might have tossed a crumb to you. If only you'd
begged, you stupid idiot blinded fool of a child."

Kai slipped his better hand beneath his coat, across
his shoulder, touched the edge of the sheath. His fingers
blazed with the contact.

And it was then that he felt a veil draw aside, a force
of golden light flood through him, as an ancient voice
seized his body to use his mouth for its own. He looked
up into the face of the thing that wore the father-mask
and let the language rise: *"You forget what you are, Lu-
kanfir, old nemesis. You can't make such a thing when
you don't have any talent. When all you are is an old bag*

of bones. Return to the Dreaming, old one, and leave this world for those who know how to nurture it."

The pain in his hands was suddenly gone. Kai had the sword out. He slashed it round.

Through his father's legs.

The air filled with music.

The air filled with it, trembled, spilled over, and everything came crashing down.

He didn't hear the sharp, shattering chords so much as feel crushed by them as they tore through his gut and sent his mind reeling. Kai heard a hoarse, visceral screaming, and for a half moment thought he was the one making it. Then, as he adjusted to the music both inside and outside him, like a man stumbling from a tunnel into dazzling light, he saw that the father-thing, the Traveler, was thrashing and flailing on the ground. He was attempting to grow new legs from the black, bloody stumps of the old, but the emerging flesh looked ragged, the bone too thin.

A new series of notes, shafting and probing the air, then swinging high, holding, coming unhinged in a shrieking tumbledown of sound. Just as it seemed to be resolving into a melody—mournful, searching—the harmony broke up again into jagged spears of music, and Kai felt every one of them shafting through him, dissolving inside him. He sensed the call inside one, the deep and ancient command, but in him it was like an echo that only trailed to nothing.

The music wasn't meant for him.

And as the Traveler tossed back his head and continued to scream, carving out the veins and hollows of his throat, the mist grew thick with drifting, shuffling figures. They came from behind Kai, all around him, but paid him no attention, breaking around him like a river against rock.

The dead.

The grotesques, the hybrids, the humans, the Summoners: all the freshly killed. Their wounds looked waxen, their skin took on a high, unearthly sheen, and their faces filled with yearning.

Jaxon pushed himself to what remained of his knees. "You morons," he yelled. "That music is me. Don't you hear it? That music is me, of me, so what—"

He kept yelling as they fell in around him.

No one was listening.

And as more bodies jostled around him, the air thick with the smells of rot and blood, Kai limped backward, cradling his wounded arm, until he found the ruin of a lamppost to lean against. He could hear the tearing, rending flesh as they ripped Jaxon apart, could hear the wet grinding sound of his body in their jaws; he dampened all his senses and turned away, but this only made him more aware of the dark song that strung out the air, calling them, calling all of them, calling them back to their center, their source, the artist of their own end.

The mist eddied and flowed.

He didn't see Zazou or Cameron or the others who had come with them, either living or dead. He shut out all sound except the music.

He put himself in the line of the song.

It coursed over him and away, and he walked into it, against it, and through it, his footfalls echoing over the broken ground as figures shifted and writhed on the billboards above him. Dark, glistening stone jutted out at odd angles, disrupting the street into something that no longer resembled a street . . . but more like, perhaps, the beginning of some kind of maze. Drops of moisture fell on his face. It was starting to rain.

He walked into the song, stepping over rubble, up a small incline, into the ruin of a plaza. A man was seated just inside the frame of a front window, broken glass scattered all around him. He was bare-chested, a leather jacket crumpled next to him. He was hunched over an elaborate guitar, brown hair hanging in his face.

And Lucas Maddox lifted his head, and saw him.

If Kai knew he looked bad—and he did—he figured Maddox looked worse.

Covered in grime, blood, and sweat, hair hanging matted around a carved-out face, his eyes reflecting the manic light of someone who'd used up his reserves some time ago and was running beyond empty, Lucas rolled his head on his shoulders and pushed the guitar off his lap. He jumped down from the window, crunching broken glass, and stumbled; he braced against the window frame for a moment.

He looked at Kai.

"Death song," he wheezed out. "I dreamed it. But not . . ."

"Not your death," Kai said quietly.

"Not my song. His. All this time. His."

Mist drifted like ghosts between them.

And in the size and shape of everything that went unsaid between them, Kai felt them enter into an odd state of grace. He felt the presence of Jess Shepard, poised like a rifle between them. He saw in the other man's eyes both a ruin and a wasteland that reminded him, briefly, of himself. Price paid, he thought. You never knew what it would cost until it was done.

Lucas gave a small, ironic smile, took a step forward, then swayed.

Still looking at Kai, he collapsed to his knees.

He was fighting to hold on to the last shreds of consciousness. Footsteps from behind him: Ramsey emerged from a murk of shadow and called out Kai's name. Kai looked to him and for a moment saw through him to the other Ramsey, the one that had towered over him, smashing and stomping, hatred deforming his face. And now it was his turn to falter, fighting to clear the images from his head, to focus on the real. Ramsey was alive, unhurt. This boy hardly wanted to hurt him, kill him; this child was part of his family.

Kai said to him, "Come here."

And as Ramsey edged round Lucas, a bloodstained hand darted out, clamped down on Ramsey's arm.

Lucas yanked him close. Jerked him down. Ramsey tried to pull away, but Lucas had him by the hair, now, forcing him close. Whispering in his ear.

And Kai noticed, then, the expression on Lucas's face, the new note of terror in his eyes. "Promise," he snarled to Ramsey.

The boy jerked away in distaste and this time the musician let go.

His eyes closed. His body swayed again, like a snake being charmed, and then slumped to the side.

"Kai!" The name broke from Ramsey. The toughness fell away and he was a kid again, running to Kai, crashing into him in a way that sent fresh pain bolting through him. Kai laughed, looping his better arm around the boy and pulling him close. "Is it over?" Ramsey was saying. "Is it over, god please, is it over?"

Kai thought of Jaxon's sprawled body, disappearing beneath the onslaught. Thought of the grotesques and the dead, driven to answer the call of Jaxon's own dark force turned against him. He looked to where the musician lay collapsed and unmoving. He noticed the tattoos on his biceps and chest. Jess had seen those tattoos, he knew, had touched them, traced them, kissed them, and not just in dreams.

But Ramsey was staring at him, waiting for an answer to his question. Struggling to remember just what the question was, Kai suddenly picked up on a new sound, a light and curious clatter-roll of glass, and turned his head toward the sound.

A small object was traveling down the concrete toward him, tossing off glints of amber. It was a glass bottle, barreling along the smashed-up pavement, swerving round pit holes and tree roots and bouncing over cracks and gaps, as if set on an unerring course toward him.

From the sudden tension in the boy's body, Kai knew he saw the bottle as well.

Ramsey said, "Where is—"

"What did Maddox say to you?"

Ramsey looked at him. He pressed his lips together and looked away. "He wanted me to get a message to Jess."

"What was it?"

"It's nothing. It's stupid."

"Tell me."

"He was just trying to—"

"Tell me."

Ramsey looked at him again.

He said, quietly, "He told her to look for him in the bonehouse."

When Kai didn't respond, Ramsey said, "It's stupid, right? He was just delirious, right?"

The glass bottle came clinking to a stop against his foot.

There was something inside.

He fumbled with the bottle, and smashed it on the ground. A small square of cardboard lay in a nest of broken glass. Ramsey was on it before he was, scanning it, then handing it to Kai. Kai avoided the boy's face, not wanting to see the anxiety, or the demand for explanations he didn't have the strength to give right now. Answers, explanations. They weren't his strong suit to begin with.

Have your girl. What a mess.
Took her to good healing place. Back soon.
Get ready.
Hugs,
Del

Epilogue

In the days that followed, there was rain.

There was nothing but rain.

When Zazou left for Tumbledown, she asked Ramsey to go with her. When he refused, there was no surprise or disappointment in her eyes. It was the answer she had expected. Ramsey suspected that if she didn't have her sense of duty to attend to, she would make the same decision for the same reason.

Kai had rented a suite at the Hotel Bel Air. He went into the bedroom, shut the door, and didn't emerge for three days. He hadn't exactly invited Ramsey to stay, but Ramsey figured he hadn't told him to leave, either, so Ramsey set up camp in the Tuscan-inspired living room, napping on the beige couch, eating and reading in front of the wood-burning fireplace, and pretending not to watch that closed bedroom door. From inside came the sounds of voices, music, sometimes gunshots and explosions. Kai was watching movies, one after the other after the other. When Ramsey rapped on the door, Kai didn't answer except to say, "No." No housekeeping. No room service. No entry.

The only time he answered differently was when a

uniformed bellboy showed up at the door with a fresh
stack of DVDs in his hand. Ramsey took them to the
bedroom, knocked, and called Kai's name, and this time
Kai didn't bother to answer at all. Either that meant yes,
Ramsey thought, or that Kai was unconscious or dead.

He opened the door.

The windows were shut and curtained, the air stale.
The images flickered on the television screen provided
the main source of light. Kai was on the unmade bed,
slumped against the headboard, a slender bottle of
rajika—the drink that Daughtry had salvaged from the
Labyrinth—beside him. Ramsey didn't have to be a
Summoner, or even Sajae-blood, to know that gulping
rajika without the preparation rituals of cube and match
and flame was nothing short of barbaric. Kai barely
glanced in his direction, the light from the television
screen picking out the still-healing wounds on his face
and body.

Ramsey left the DVDs on the dresser and tried to
think of something to say. He couldn't think of anything.
Not that it mattered. Kai clearly wasn't in a listening
mood.

That night Ramsey lay on the couch with his hands
laced behind his head and watched the shadows slowly
move across the ceiling. He had to figure out how to
handle this. As soon as morning came, he would storm
into that bedroom and stage a one-man intervention of
sorts. But what to say? *You're not the only one who
misses her.* Not enough. *There are others who still need
you.* Too obvious. *You can't live just for her.* That
seemed a little better, he thought. The way to get to Kai
would be through his highborn Sajae pride, his alpha-
male Summoner ego. Lying there, unmoving, Ramsey
worked through several versions before settling on the
speech he would use, and then mentally rehearsed it
until he did the one thing he hadn't expected. He fell
asleep.

In the morning, Kai was gone.

The bedroom doors were wide open, the curtains pulled back, sunlight pooling along the rumpled bed. Ramsey studied the room, then ordered coffee and a very large breakfast. And waited.

The Summoner was back by midafternoon. Ramsey was halfway through *The Matrix*—one of the DVDs he'd taken from the bedroom—and when he noticed Kai standing quietly in the open doorway, he stabbed the remote at the screen to turn it off. He practically leaped off the couch.

"Get your stuff," Kai said. His dark hair was brushed back from his face, his skin the fairest that Ramsey had ever seen it. He hadn't known that Kai could even get pale. "We're moving."

"Moving?" Another city, Ramsey thought. Another hotel. Still, this was better, this was definitely better, than what—Shrugging it off as if the news were so obvious that he shouldn't have to bother with it at all, Kai said, "I bought a house."

It had rained nonstop for almost one month: heavy sheets of water flung across the city, dumped from the sky in an endless cascade. Streets flooded, cars crashed into one another, the earth was churned to mud, sometimes moving a house down a hill; people marveled in awe and dismay and shook their heads and stayed indoors, talking about El Niño, global warming, anything that might explain a rainfall like this when it hardly ever rained in LA.

More puzzling than the weather, however, were some of the things that people reported seeing through the dark-gray wash of rain: strange winged men, except they weren't men exactly, with their crouching muscled bodies and the raw angularity of their profiles, their horns, and most of all their way of springing into the air, riding the winds, disappearing into the watery air. The sightings first appeared in the tabloids, then began to permeate the mainstream media. Theories were put forward link-

ing the sightings of the creatures to the hysteria over
a fire that had never actually happened, yet compelled
hundreds of people to flee their Westside homes. Something in the air, maybe. Something toxic. Causing visions,
hallucinations, which people reinforced in each other,
because the sightings kept being reported, by groups of
people as well as individuals, and often these winged
creatures were glimpsed carrying things in their hands,
sometimes even gripped in their feet. Things that looked
like . . . body parts.

"Gargoyles," Makonnen told Ramsey.

Mak had been dropping by a lot lately. Mak seemed
amiable enough, a laid-back dude in the beaded cotton
caftans he favored, or, when the nights got colder, a
leather aviator jacket so old and beat-up it could have
been something from Ramsey's own closet. But Ramsey
never felt completely comfortable around him. Maybe it
was the grin, or the faint red tint so often in his eyes,
or the scent of the oils he used in his hair. Hell, maybe
it was just that feeling of Summoner . . . *foreignness.*
After all, there were times when even Kai could make
him uneasy, and Kai was practically like a father to him,
if in a weird, demented, supernatural kind of way. Still,
it was cool, those times when Mak and Kai and Zazou
and Ramsey would hang out for a little bit, listening to
the rain drum off the canvas awning, the smell of Mak's
cigar smoke hanging in the air, just taking some comfort
in being together. Being alive. It was during one of those
times when they talked about the gargoyles, their scattered, enigmatic, tribal existence in this world long ago,
their disappearance, the rumors that they had somehow
managed physical travel through the Dreamlines to some
other, better place.

Now, it appeared, they were returning.

"That has to be them," Mak said, clipping the end off
a fresh cigar. "They're cleaning up the dead, the way
they do."

Trying to get ahold of this—because weren't gargoyles

those stone things that perched up high on buildings?—
Ramsey said, "You mean they're scavengers? Vultures
or something?"

"They're honoring their war gods," said Mak. "Purify-
ing the scene of the battle. Even if the battle wasn't
theirs."

Kai shifted in his chair. He was looking out into the
rain, his brow furrowed. He was . . . not *unkempt*, exactly, Kai wasn't quite capable of letting himself slide
that far, but more mussed and rumpled than Ramsey
had ever seen him.

He was thinking about Jess, Ramsey knew.

But the subject of gargoyles got his attention. "What
do you think it means," he asked Mak, "that they're
coming back, after all this time?"

"Your guess is as good as mine. Maybe that other
realm just isn't so comfortable for them anymore."

"Or maybe this one is changing," Kai mused, "in a
way that makes it more comfortable for them. Something new in the air, maybe, that appeals to their odd
little gargoyle sensitivities."

"Are they dangerous?" Ramsey said.

"They can be."

"But not if you leave them alone." Mak exhaled
smoke through his nostrils. Took another puff on the
cigar. "The trick is to leave them alone."

After a while, Mak and Kai would go inside. Ramsey
would hear them talk in low voices. He was excluded,
but that was okay with him. He just wanted a break
from it all. That wasn't so much to ask, was it?

He missed Jess.

He and Kai never spoke about her. Her absent presence moved constantly among them, and their shared
sense of it was so palpable that they felt no need to
acknowledge it. Words hurt, after all, and things hurt
enough as they were.

It was Makonnen who ended up translating the DVD
that Ramsey and Jess had found in the motel room way

back when, and that Ramsey had almost forgotten about.
Almost.

Kai had finally allowed Mak to work on his hands; the
heal-magic that Mak had been wanting to try was, as
Kai put it, "experimental," and Kai was neither enthusi-
astic about the process nor optimistic about the outcome.
As Ramsey scrambled eggs in the kitchen, he heard Mak
muttering things, followed by a span of silence. Then the
Summoners were talking about healing magic in general
and demon wounds and demons, which then segued into
an argument over demon languages. Mak seemed to
demonstrate a point, speaking in a way that was both
intensely alien and oddly familiar, the sounds spiking the
air. "That's not a language. That's a dialect," Kai said,
rather crossly, Ramsey thought, "albeit a very—"

"When you learn to speak any of them, then we'll have
this conversation," Mak said. "Until then, you're just
forced to acknowledge my superiority in this matter."

"I don't agree."

"Regardless. I remain superior."

Ramsey had stuffed the DVD deep in one of his knapsacks after Zazou had watched it and failed to understand any of it. But he thought that the language Mak
had just spoken resembled the language on the disc.
Afraid that it might be wishful thinking, he tried to tamp
down his excitement.

Mak took the DVD away with him.

He rang the buzzer early the next morning. When
Ramsey shuffled down the hallway, yawning hugely,
Mak was sitting at the kitchen table drinking coffee and
flipping through the newspaper he'd brought in from the
driveway. He tossed the paper aside and said, "So,
where's His Highness?"

Hello to you too, Ramsey thought. "Wherever he goes.
He'll be back."

"Where's Lucas Maddox?"

"What?"

"Is he still at Cedars?"

"Comatose." Maddox wasn't expected to live. The doctors said vague things about a brain embolism, puzzled expressions on their faces. Ramsey mostly tried to ignore the situation since thinking about Maddox gave him a strange knotted feeling in his stomach. Ramsey said, "You know that Kai and some of the others are monitoring the situation pretty closely. So—"

Mak's expression was grim. "We need to address this. Now."

He had not been able to understand all of it; the hybrid spoke quickly and used unfamiliar expressions. But he was confident about the gist. "It's a suicide group," he said as the day's first wave of rain swept against the windows. "They call themselves"—here Mak faltered for a moment—"Sun-death Rising. Something like that, anyway. The speaker is preaching about a 'third alternative.' Not this world stalked by murderous Summoners, noisy and confusing. Not the coming world held in the sway of the Lord of Bones. But a way forward, through what he calls fresh death, into a higher, better realm. Where you will be rewarded. Especially if you bring a Summoner along with you."

Kai nodded. "The suicide bombers at Daughtry's hotel."

"Even if they didn't know we were there," Mak said, "and I'm not convinced they did. They still would have known it was Daughtry's hotel, what Daughtry is. Was," he amended, and Kai looked away.

Ramsey said, "And that thing about Maddox?"

"The speaker calls him the son of the apocalypse. Says that he is all and he is nothing, the end and the beginning. That his—and I assume the speaker is referring to death here, Lucas's death—will . . . something about 'swallowing the first morning's star.' I'm not sure what that means." Mak's eyes darkened. The rain-splintered light shifted across his face. "But I have an idea."

"It means he will rise again," a familiar voice said from the entrance hall.

Zazou. Ramsey felt a happy kick in his chest, even as he thought, *Doesn't anybody wait at the door anymore?* Zazou hadn't even made the pretense of buzzing. Her eyes skipped past Ramsey to Kai. "I heard about the new place," she said. "I wanted to check it out." Her gaze rested on Makonnen, and Ramsey understood. Mak had summoned her here, and whatever he'd conveyed to her had been powerful enough to get her attention.

He was out of his chair without even realizing. He wanted to hug Zazou, but she wasn't the type to be hugged, and as he began to hold out his arms she eyed them warily. He settled for pulling out her chair.

Makonnen said, "Morning's star is a reference to the Traveler, is it not?"

"The Lord of Bones," Zazou said. "Yes."

"And swallowing—"

"In that context, it means taking in someone's soul. It's like he's being prepared as a vessel, except on a much higher, grander scale. The ultimate vessel. It's kind of—it's kind of our version of holy." She paused. Her eyes assumed that hard, flat look that made Ramsey uneasy. "It means he'll be reborn. Not just changed. He'll be reborn as the Lord of Bones. That that's been his purpose all along." Zazou coughed into her fist. "Remember, this is just some random dude, some crazy cult group. It doesn't mean it's true."

"No," Kai said. His voice was barely audible, and his eyes had turned glossy, opaque, the way they did when he pulled inward. "It's true. I'm not sure how, but it's true. We should have seen it."

"I find it ironic," Zazou said, slamming a bottle on the table in front of Ramsey, "that you're old enough to help save the world, but not old enough to have a drink."

"I don't like that stuff anyway," Ramsey said, eyeing the sake. She had gotten it from Kai's little collection.

Kai had a taste for the stuff, and now, it appeared, so did Zazou.

They were out on the terrace of the house that Kai had just leased in the hills above Beverly Hills. The house was a sleek white bachelor pad that opened out to an infinity pool and spectacular view: now that the rains had finally stopped and the air had cleared, he could look out over the hills and down into the grid of the city. The first time Ramsey saw it, he was shocked at how familiar it seemed. He was sure he had been here before. The sense of déjà vu was so strong that he had braced himself for some new, weird revelation when Kai told him that the house had been used in a famous movie that Ramsey had seen seven times.

Zazou poured sake into one of the little clayware cups, then tossed it into her mouth. "I think you're probably supposed to savor that stuff," Ramsey said, eyeing the faded Japanese label, "not shoot it." She shrugged, wiping her mouth with the back of her hand. Ramsey asked, "Did we really save the world?" He was thinking of one of the first things Zazou had ever told him, that night in Las Vegas: *You didn't stop it. You only slowed it down.*

Zazou said, "It depends what you mean by 'world.' "

"What do you mean what do I mean . . .?" He thought for a moment. "The world as I know it."

"No. That's over."

Her voice sounded so calm, so even.

"I mean," she amended, waving a hand—she had started to experiment with hand gestures—"it's not over yet, but it's ending. Winding down."

"How can you know?"

She shrugged. "Rising sea levels. Nuclear proliferation. Disease. The usual. Plus . . ." She drank off another sake and slammed down the cup. "*I'm* here. And others. And others yet to come." At Ramsey's expression, she laughed. "Everyone knows, Ramsey. Except your kind,

I mean. But we've been watching you for eons. And anyone can predict the future by looking into the past. You don't need the Dreamlines or the Summoners for that." Reaching for the bottle, she added, "Why do you think all this shit is coming down? There's a cool new world up for grabs. That's not the kind of thing that goes unnoticed."

"Then what . . ." He kicked at the leg of the table, pushing his chair back. "What was all that for, what we did, if it doesn't matter in the end? What was it all for, if—"

"For more time," Zazou said. "For those who aim to be the carriers of civilization, from the ruins of the old world into the birth of the new. And for the Dreamlines themselves. There was a war over them once, remember. There could be again. If the Lord of Bones has his way."

"But he's gone."

"Yes."

"Isn't he?"

She set a cup in front of him and poured. "Hey, cheer up. The sky is finally clearing. Tomorrow will be beautiful."

Kai sensed her as soon as he came into the house.

He gave no sign. He was afraid it was only wishful thinking. He pretended to go about his usual business, tossing the car keys in the dish, heightening his senses for signs of Ramsey, Zazou, before remembering they were out looking at apartments.

His reflection gliding through the mirror, he stepped into the sunken living room. Sun shone through the glass to lie in bright rectangles across the rosewood floor.

Beyond them, in a pocket of shadow, she was waiting.

She was slouched across the club chair, dressed in jeans and a crisp white shirt.

"I got here as soon as I could," she said.

He could feel the force of her presence like sun on his skin.

She was up and crossing the room and he was reaching out for her. Then he had her face in his hands, looking for changes, signs of trauma, damage. Her skin, normally so pale, was the darkest he'd ever seen it, her long hair streaked with white. The blue of her eyes had both deepened and brightened: the blue of the Dreamlines. He could feel the Dreamlines inside her, all that coursing energy; her presence smoldered with it.

"You're okay?" he said.

She nodded.

"Where's Del?"

"Not far."

"Where did he take you? Where were you?"

"I don't remember much. Different places. Nooks and crannies of the Dreamlines that I never knew existed. And he showed me things. Visions."

"What kind of visions?"

"Like I said. I don't remember much."

"It'll all come back to you," Kai said. "And when it does, we'll deal with it."

She nodded. She didn't seem particularly concerned. "And you?" Her gaze went to his hands, the gloves. "Are you okay?" She had one of his hands between hers, was peeling away the thin leather. Her breath caught just a little when she saw the scars. Thanks to the heal-spells his hands were functioning fully and free of pain, but it would be a long time before the scars began to fade, and this bothered his vanity more than he wanted to admit. He'd rather wear the gloves.

She lifted his fingers to her mouth, touched her lips to the damaged skin.

Looking down at her, he felt himself detach, disengage. "You know Lucas is comatose," he said.

She tilted her head. And he sensed a new, cool smoothness to her, as if something inside her had closed to him: he could feel boundaries, edges and barriers, where before there had been places for him to fill with himself.

"Ever since I found him with Ramsey," Kai said.

She only nodded.

And he was thinking of how odd it was, after so many centuries of sexual play—that ruthless drive for variety, novelty, adventure—that his hunger could hone itself so completely against the edge of this one woman. She seemed new to him all over again. Unmapped, unconquered. He felt himself at risk with her. It was a strange feeling, and he didn't much like it.

"*Deeply* comatose," Kai couldn't help adding. "Whatever he did to the Lord of Bones, that song, it also did a number on him."

"Oh."

"Oh?" He touched her hair with one gloved hand. "So, tell me. If Lucas Maddox weren't quite so vegetative, would you still be here?" When she didn't answer he said, a little louder, "Would you still have chosen to come to me?"

"You mean, would I have chosen you?"

"It's not a complicated question. A yes or no kind of question."

"But it was never a question," Jess said. "The choice has always been you."

"Good." He gave a nod. "Because I need more you." He pulled her into him again—"I need more you."—and, mindful of whatever healing process she might still be undergoing, held her as lightly as he could.

The house was theirs now.

It was the house that Jaxon had built, calculated to be in the heart of a new *sorenikan*, where realities mingled and time took on a different meaning. Where many things were made possible—dark and light things both.

Jess stood just inside the gate, taking in what the property had become. The statue garden had been torn down, the earth ripped up where grass had been. Parts of the house had been reduced to rubble, the sun glinting off heaps of broken, dirty marble. The back of the property had been turned into a construction site, the walls torn down and replaced with scaffolding, the ground turned to mud, crossed with the tread marks of trucks and cranes. Today, and for the next few days, the property was silent. The Summoners were performing some renovations of their own.

No one seemed to be around, but she could feel their awareness of her, the vibrations of their silent communications to each other, as she picked her way up the driveway, around broken concrete, over a fallen palm tree. Someone would be waiting for her at the door, and she knew, but she wasn't prepared for who it turned out to be.

Mina.

"Jessamy," Mina said. "Welcome back." The greeting was sincere enough, and Jess could see the effort it cost her.

Jess said, "I need to see him."

"He's not particularly interesting."

Mina led her through hallways that, in the bright light of day spilling through the broken places, no longer seemed familiar. The air seemed hollowed out somehow, and Jess realized it was because of the silence. The archway where the man-web had hung was now just an archway.

And now they were descending stairs, and the stairs were giving way to earth, the air turning cool and dank. Jess felt the deep thrum of new magic all around her, fortifying the walls and claiming the tunnels. New magic, but familiar; modern variations on an ancient code. Multiple spells of entrapment and containment, thickly layered, richly woven, still with a raw, unfinished feel. A work still in progress.

A prison built to hold a demon.

The tunnel widened into the first of a series of chambers. In the shadowed alcoves along the walls, figures sat in stillness, silence; the walls were lined with guards. Summoners taking shifts of duty as well as people with no magic except the spell-modified rifles slung across their chests.

In the second chamber, a fountain made of glossy black stone filled the middle of the floor, its swooping, curving lines reminding Jess of her time at the Eden. Blue flame traced arabesques in the air and filled the basin with a soft glow. Mina knelt and touched her fingers to the wick of one of the candles near the fountain. The candle came to life, its flame the blue fire of Dreamline energy. After a moment, Jess did the same. She gave her respects to the Summoners who had died in their confrontation with Jaxon Twist, and sent warm pulses of healing toward the hospital rooms deep in another part of the house, where the wounded and the altered were being tended to by those Summoners who had made heal-magic their life's work, traveling here from different points across the globe.

The Summoners were coming together, Jess thought. Slowly but surely, a new community was being formed, a culture rediscovered in fragments.

What a shame that this was what it had taken. This was the cost of it.

The third chamber was also a guard chamber, or would be once it was finished and the alcoves assigned. Here Mina paused, and turned to face Jess directly. "Go through the door behind me," she said, "and he's there."

Jess nodded. Neither of them moved or looked away from each other. There was still something else to be said.

Mina hitched a breath, seemed to deliberate a moment. Then: "You were in contact with Del."

"Yes."

"And he told you . . . Did he tell you . . . how he came to be free?"

"No."

Mina's eyes flared yellow-green, searching Jess's expression. Jess felt herself gauged and measured. Whatever Mina found didn't seem to satisfy her, but neither did it put her on edge. At length she said, "Del's escape remains a mystery. But tell Kai I would like to speak with him. I would like to speak with him soon."

"You could tell him yourself. It's not like he's avoiding you."

Mina arched a delicate eyebrow, but said nothing. Jess took this as her cue to leave, turning toward the final chamber, toward Lucas, but then Mina's voice caught her: "It seems great risks are taken for you. Maybe a world put at stake."

"The world was already at stake. You know that, Mina."

But in her mind, she could hear again what Kai had told her: *What I would do for you. I think it makes me dangerous.*

Oh, Kai, she thought now. *What you did. What I know you did.*

They had not talked about it; she knew they would not until they were forced to. Now, staring at Mina, she could feel their shared knowledge of Kai between them. It was a sad and heavy weight. Kai would pay, she knew. For reasons of her own, maybe simply because she, too, had loved him, and maybe still did, in her way, Mina was holding off the inevitable, carving out a state of grace for him: her gift, or her power over him, or both. But it would end—a state of grace always did—and Kai would be held accountable. And meanwhile Del was out there, roaming, exploring, busy with his own agenda.

"Great risks," Mina said again. "Make yourself worthy of them. Or I will destroy you myself. And take pleasure in it."

Before Jess could react, could even register the words, Mina turned on her heel and left, the back of her long auburn hair fading through the shadow. Jess would find her own way out.

She had expected, beyond the closed stone door,

something blatantly paranormal, another hovering sphere
like the one that held Del. What she stepped into, instead, was the complete re-creation of a hospital room.

The room was filled with flowers.

For some reason this surprised her, until she was surprised by her own surprise. A quick glance through the
little cards attached to the bouquets or propped by the
vases told the story: Lucas Maddox, who had risen to
fame in the early nineteen hundreds with his band Slippage, then gone solo for a brief period before dropping
out entirely, only to resurface and reinvent himself alongside a singer who could howl her way to the abyss and
back, still had a lot of fans. Especially now that he was
another of the mysterious victims, another strange conse-
quence, of the Sunset Strip earthquake. Lucas would have
been feeling the love, if not lost in his unexplained coma.

Jess looked down on him for a long time.

Laid out like this, the monitors beeping behind and
above him, he wasn't the Maddox that Jess remembered,
either in her dreams or in real life. His face too delicate,
the hollows beneath the ridges of cheekbone and the
way his lashes lay across his lower lids. The holes in his
earlobes where the studs and hoops had been. "Where
are you?" she whispered, smoothing brown hair back
from his forehead. "Are you gone?" She leaned in and
kissed his mouth. "Maybe you should stay gone."

She turned to go.

And as she walked to the door—

*She hears the rustling of sheets as he sweeps them aside.
The cot groans beneath his shifting weight. The soft, cat-
like sound as his bare feet touch floor. She is at the door
when he comes up right behind her, his arm darting out
across her shoulder to slam it shut, and then the warm
bulk of his body pressing her up against the door, cold
hands slipping under her T-shirt, drifting up to grasp her
breasts, and he's kissing her neck, she feels his breath, his
warm tongue, feels her body loosen against him, can't*

*stop herself from doing it, doesn't want to, wants him
inside her, his voice in her ear saying be my queen my
slave be my queen my slave be my queen—*

She gasped, her eyes jerking open.

She spun round, then backed up against the door,
even though there was nothing and no one to threaten
her here. Just a comatose man lying on a bed, trailing
tubes, the machines tracking and recording the rhythms
of him as his chest rose and fell. Beneath his closed
eyelids, his eyes made no movement. He wasn't dreaming at all.

Be my queen my slave

"Stay gone," Jess said fiercely, and slammed the door
hard on her way out.

The dog was waiting for her by her car.

A medium-sized black dog with short, shiny fur and
peaked, fringed ears. He was sitting and gazing at her
with a friendly expression, his head cocked to one side.

"Hi, boy," she said cautiously, car key in hand. Something about the dog was familiar. And then, as he
jumped to his feet and wagged his tail, memory clicked:
this was the dog at Lucas's house the night she'd
dropped in on him unexpectedly, the dog she had sent
a mindcast to, warm images of chicken and cheese and
affection, if only he would not bark, not alert Lucas to
her presence until she wanted him to know she was
there.

"You're a good dog, aren't you?" she said, and he
wagged his tail. *Good dog, yes. He was good, and in
need.* He wagged his tail again. Lucas's dog. She sighed.
"Well, I guess you're with me now," she said, and she
opened the door for him. He leaped into the car, clambered over the gearshift and into the passenger seat. He
sat neatly on his haunches and looked at her.

She got in and shut the door. Already the car smelled
like dog, but she guessed she didn't really mind. She

turned on the radio and turned it up, and then she simply sat there a minute, feeling herself still and quiet,
one hand on the steering wheel. Maybe she wouldn't go
straight home. Maybe she'd swing by an art supply store,
treat herself to fresh new tubes of paint, a whole new
collection of brushes. Just imagining the smell of them
made her a little bit giddy. It was time to start painting
again—really painting. There were dark clouds just starting to line the horizon. But for now, the rain was behind
them. The sky was clear and sunlit; the air felt brand-
new. This was gorgeous Los Angeles weather, and she
was determined to enjoy it. Beside her, the dog gave a
small yip of what might have been glee as she pulled
away from the curb and got moving.